THE COMPLETE CASES
OF THE RAMBLER, VOLUME 1

OTHER BOOKS IN THE DIME DETECTIVE UNIFORM EDITION LIBRARY:

The Complete Cases of Cass Blue, Volume 1 by John Lawrence

The Complete Cases of Inspector Allhoff, Volume 1 by D.L. Champion

The Complete Cases of Keyhole Kerry by Frederick C. Davis

The Complete Cases of The Marquis of Broadway, Volume 1 by John Lawrence

The Complete Cases of Max Latin by Norbert Davis

The Complete Cases of Mr. Maddox, Volume 1 by T.T. Flynn

The Complete Cases of Vee Brown, Volume 1 by Carroll John Daly

FRED MacISAAC

THE COMPLETE CASES OF THE RAMBLER

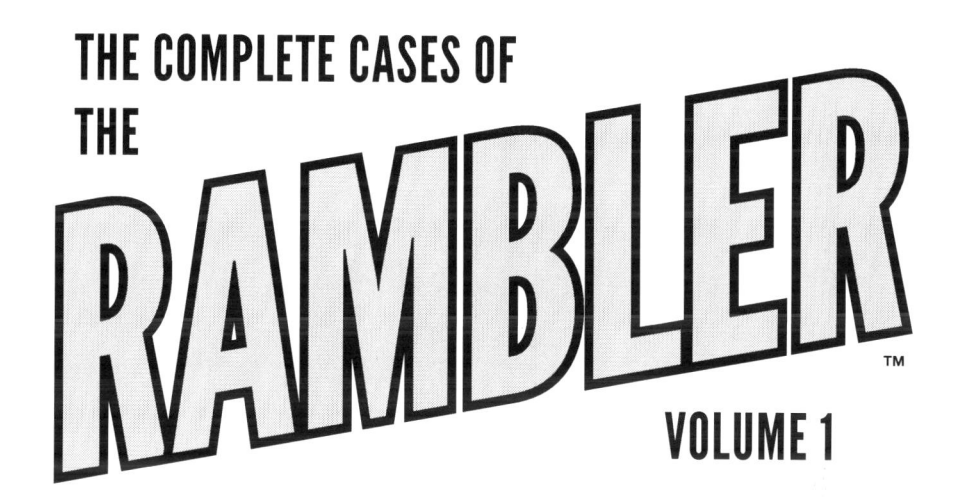

VOLUME 1

FRED MacISAAC

INTRODUCTION BY
ED HULSE

ILLUSTRATIONS BY
JOHN FLEMING GOULD

ALTUS PRESS

BOSTON • 2014

© 2014 Altus Press • First Edition—2014

EDITED AND DESIGNED BY
Matthew Moring

PUBLISHING HISTORY
"Ramblin' 'Round Hollywood: Fred MacIsaac and the Movies" appears here for the first time. Copyright © 2014 Ed Hulse. All Rights Reserved.

"The Affair at Camp Laurel" originally appeared in the October 8, 1932 issue of *Argosy* magazine.
"Alias Mr. Smith" originally appeared in the April 1, 1933 issue of *Dime Detective* magazine.
"Ghost City Set-Up" originally appeared in the September 1, 1933 issue of *Dime Detective* magazine.
"Go-Between" originally appeared in the June 1, 1934 issue of *Dime Detective* magazine.
"Murder Reel" originally appeared in the August 15, 1934 issue of *Dime Detective* magazine.
"Heir-Cooled" originally appeared in the June 15, 1935 issue of *Dime Detective* magazine.
"Meet Mr. MacIsaac" originally appeared in the February 15, 1930 issue of *Argosy* magazine.

Copyright © 2014 by Argosy Communications, Inc. All Rights Reserved.

THE RAMBLER is a trademark owned by Argosy Communications, Inc.
Published by arrangement with Argosy Communications, Inc.

THANKS TO
Joel Frieman, Ed Hulse, Everard P. Digges LaTouche, John Locke, Rob Preston, Christopher Roden & Ray Skirsky

ALL RIGHTS RESERVED
No part of this book may be reproduced or utilized in any form or by any means, electronic or mechanical, without permission in writing from the publisher.
This edition has been marked via subtle changes, so anyone who reprints from this collection is committing a violation of copyright.
Visit altuspress.com for more books like this.
Printed in the United States of America.

TABLE OF CONTENTS

RAMBLIN' 'ROUND HOLLYWOOD:
FRED MacISAAC AND THE MOVIES 1
THE AFFAIR AT CAMP LAUREL 1
ALIAS MR. SMITH 41
GHOST CITY SET-UP 89
GO-BETWEEN 137
MURDER REEL 185
HEIR-COOLED 229
MEET MR. MacISAAC 275

RAMBLIN' 'ROUND HOLLYWOOD: FRED MacISAAC AND THE MOVIES
ED HULSE

FREDERICK JOHN MacISAAC was born on March 22, 1886 in Cambridge, Massachusetts. A tall, burly redhead, he matriculated at Harvard and toiled for many years on Boston newspapers, initially covering the waterfront but later becoming a police reporter and, finally, a drama critic.

MacIssac seems to have taken up fiction writing full time in 1920, when he placed a series of sports and animal stories in Street & Smith's venerable *Top-Notch Magazine*, a long-running pulp that began life as a nickel weekly aimed at boys. His career picked up steam a few years later when he cracked Munsey's *Argosy All-Story Weekly*, in which magazine he became a fixture and chugged along for years as one of its most prolific and reliable contributors. Beginning in 1926 he also sold frequently to Charles Agnew MacLean, whose once-powerful sheet, *The Popular Magazine*, was just beginning its period of decline. MacIssac's best tales for that Street & Smith pulp, especially the memorable war novel "Tin Hats" (June 20–August 7, 1926), briefly slowed the magazine's inexorable downward slide.

The former journalist experimented with several genres, specializing in yarns with criminous elements but showing surprising facility for fantastic fiction, most of it published in the Munsey magazines and some of it quite memorable. "The Vanishing Professor" (*Argosy All-Story Weekly*, January 9–30, 1926) dealt with a disgruntled scientist who invented an invisibility machine and briefly embarked on a life of crime before reforming. "The Great Commander" (*Argosy All-Story Weekly*, July 3–24, 1926) chronicled the exploits of omnipotent, egomaniacal industrialist King Nelson, who actually plotted war against Japan to justify extra-constitutional powers bestowed upon him by a malleable President and Congress. MacIssac anticipated the atomic bomb's development in "World Brigands" (*Argosy*

All-Story Weekly, June 30–August 4, 1928), set in 1940 amidst a proposed conflict orchestrated by unscrupulous magnates from economically ravaged Europe. "The Man of Gold" (*Argosy,* July 26–August 30, 1930), a lost-race adventure, posited the existence of a treasure-rich hidden valley in the Columbian Andes. "The Last Atlantide" (*The Popular Magazine,* December 17, 1927–January 21, 1928) revolved around the discovery in Yucatan of a document purporting to explain the decline and fall of Atlantis. Perhaps MacIssac's most famous piece of fantastic fiction, however, was "The Hothouse World" (*Argosy,* February 21–March 28, 1931), which followed the adventures of George Putnam, a college student placed in suspended animation by his eccentric professor. Awakening in the year 2051, Putnam found himself in a mile-square, domed-glass city erected in anticipation of a comet strike that annihilated most of Earth's population and rendered much of the planet uninhabitable.

Remarkably productive during the Depression years, MacIssac never really became a highly regarded pulpster on the order of Max Brand, H. Bedford-Jones, Erle Stanley Gardner, or Edgar Rice Burroughs. Like them, he belonged to the prestigious million-words-a-year club, but his yarns—while conventionally entertaining and certainly popular with readers—lacked the indefinable something extra found in those penned by the above-named fictioneers.

MacIssac's first successful series character was Hollywood press agent Bill Peepe, who debuted in a novelette titled "The British Blonde" (*Argosy,* December 13, 1930). Like most of his brethren depicted in fiction and on film, Peepe was a cynical, wisecracking opportunist. Like his creator, Peepe lived on Lookout Mountain in the Hollywood Hills, but he knew every inch of Tinseltown and was familiar with its denizens. He occasionally mingled with members of the underworld—was on a first-name basis with some—and wasn't above participating in shady schemes, especially those calculated to advance his career or his financial interests. Peepe liked his liquor, too. And unlike most pulp-fiction protagonists he was *married,* having tied the knot with a glamorous actress introduced in "The British Blonde." Later installments in the series referenced the press agent's desire to live off his wife's money, but more than once MacIssac intimated that Peepe possessed a roving eye and was likely to stray while his spouse was far away, shooting a picture on location.

Although he prided himself on his ability to think and talk his way out of trouble, Bill Peepe wasn't above using fists or guns to extricate himself from tough situations. On one memorable occasion he became a two-gun man to rescue his wife from gangsters.

Peepe was a predecessor of the Rambler to the extent that, like the *Dime Detective* hero, his background at least partially mirrored that of his originator. MacIssac's experience as a journalist and drama critic brought him into regular contact with press agents, and as a long-time resident of Hollywood he was amply familiar with the behind-the-scenes goings-on of a corrupt town built and sustained on artifice.

While still contributing regularly to the Munsey pulps *Argosy* and *Detective Fiction Weekly* (sometimes credited in the latter as Donald Ross), Fred MacIssac cracked *Dime Detective* with a non-series yarn, "The Phantom Nugget," published in the June 1932 issue. Editor Rogers Terrill, at that time running hard-boiled fiction of the *Black Mask* type alongside outlandish murder mysteries with horror-story trappings, was a proponent of using recurring characters as a way of building circulation and maintaining a loyal readership.

A tall, rangy redhead like his creator, the Rambler behaved like a tramp, wandering from city to city, often arriving on a railroad boxcar, never taking root. Renowned for his reporting skills and deductive abilities, Murphy never had any difficulty landing a job with the local newspaper; wherever he wound up his reputation preceded him. And he had a knack for getting into trouble, as each series installment demonstrated. Every search for a front-page scoop put the Rambler in jeopardy sooner or later; he ran afoul of violent gangsters, wealthy businessmen, corrupt politicians, crooked cops, and the occasional double-crossing dame.

Like Bill Peepe before him, this roving reporter wasn't averse to slugging or shooting his way out of trouble. But pulpdom's most effective tough guys were judged not only by how much physical punishment they dished out, but also by how much they could take. "Frank" Murphy, as you will see, took more than his share.

Most of MacIssac's Rambler stories ended the same way: with the newshound leaving town just as he started getting comfortable. His legendary wanderlust prevented him from settling down with any number of beautiful women, at least one of whom was prepared to marry him on the spot. More than one city editor warned Murphy that he was likely to end his days in a flophouse, alone and unloved. But the Rambler couldn't be dissuaded. Another train always whistled, another town always beckoned.

The seventh series entry, "Murder on the Mississippi" (December

1935), attracted the attention of a story editor at Universal Pictures Corporation, which negotiated with MacIssac for screen rights in the summer of 1936. Control of Universal had just been wrested from the company's founder, Carl Laemmle, following an ill-advised attempt to compete with larger studios like Paramount and Metro-Goldwyn-Mayer in the production of million-dollar epics. The new regime, committed to manufacturing the "B"-grade product on which Laemmle's firm had built its reputation back in the silent-movie era, was in the process of licensing a slew of pulp yarns that could be brought to the screen inexpensively.

Screenwriters John Grey and Jefferson Parker were hired to adapt "Murder on the Mississippi," which went into production under that title on October 5, 1936. The 22-day schedule reportedly encompassed two weeks of shooting in and around New Orleans, where the story took place, although you'd never know that from a screening of the finished film. Associate producer Val Paul and director Arthur Lubin, having pre-planned the location jaunt to the nth degree, completed the potboiler without undue difficulty. Even though early publicity photos bore the *Murder on the Mississippi* title, the 56-minute melodrama was released nationally on December 27th as *Mysterious Crossing*.

Starring as Addison Francis Murphy was "professional Irishman" James Dunn, making his second Universal film appearance in fulfillment of a three-picture deal. A former stockbroker, vaudeville performer, and stock-company player who rocketed to movie stardom following his well-received turn in the 1931 Fox film *Bad Girl*, Dunn was already losing favor in Hollywood as a result of his heavy drinking and erratic behavior. His ebullient screen persona was somewhat at odds with MacIssac's characterization of Murphy as a hard-boiled cynic, but Grey and Parker tailored the role to suit their star. They also made popular Universal contract player Andy Devine a sidekick to Dunn.

Mysterious Crossing begins with Murphy (who is never called "the Rambler" on screen) crossing the Mississippi on the ferry to New Orleans. He borrows money from singing hillbilly "Carolina" (Andy Devine), loses it in a crap game, and goes outside to reflect on his bad luck. While on deck he sees two men shaking hands, turns away, hears a splash of water, and looks back to discover that both men have disappeared.

Upon arriving in New Orleans, Murphy picks up unclaimed luggage belonging to Raoul Fontaine, assuming him to be one of the men who disappeared. He checks into a hotel with Carolina in tow and discovers in Fontaine's luggage a report on something called "The Arcadian and Southern Louisiana Swamp Reclamation Project," a fraudulent venture against which Fontaine—a bank owner, it turns out—has been advised to loan money. Sensing a scoop in the making, Murphy brings the suitcase to the Fontaine mansion, where the banker's daughter Yvonne (Jean Rogers) wonders why her father hasn't returned.

Murphy ingratiates himself with Fontaine's former partner, newspaper editor N.J. Stebbins (Hobart Cavanaugh), who hires him to investigate and report on the disappearance. Shortly thereafter Murphy and Carolina are interrogated by the district attorney but released when Fontaine's body is found in the river.

The Rambler makes an appointment with Yvonne to discuss her father's death and then files a story in which he claims there was an eyewitness to the banker's supposedly accidental fall from the ferry. Meanwhile, promoter Paul Briand, a Fontaine family friend, secures approval from the dead man's bank for a three-million-dollar loan financing his reclamation project.

Murphy misses his appointment with Yvonne when he and Carolina are knocked out, roughed up, and then imprisoned in the cellar of a saloon. Escaping through an old sewer duct, they arrive at the Fontaine mansion in a sorry state of disrepair. After talking to Yvonne, the reporter tumbles to the fact that Briand was the only person who knew he was coming to see her. Believing the promoter implicated in what he believes to be Fontaine's murder, Murphy shows Briand's photograph to employees of the ferry and train station, but no one recognizes him.

Learning that Briand is a champion swimmer, the Rambler realizes that his chief suspect could have swum to and from the ferry. Murphy and Carolina follow a clue to a nearby boathouse, where they find the thugs who attacked and imprisoned them earlier. In the ensuing struggle they capture a caretaker who admits to being involved in Briand's scheme. The promoter is arrested and Murphy explains to Yvonne that he must have pulled her father overboard, and then swam to safety. After inviting the girl to accompany him to Bermuda, Murphy leaves jauntily—with Carolina close behind, still waiting to be repaid for his loan.

Mysterious Crossing elicited marginally favorable if unenthusiastic reviews. *Variety* offered one distinguished by its distinctive "slanguage":

> Formula newspaper plot, but amusing enough perhaps for the palates of the duplex horde. [In other words, patrons of double features.] Worthy of the lower end of the uppers and lowers. [In other words, suitable for the bottom half of a double bill.] James Dunn is a tramp reporter who slides into a sensational murder case accidentally, on a train ferry across the Mississippi. Perhaps that's how the picture gets it name. The rest of the action for the most part is on terra firma... Devine shoulders the comedy end nobly. Dunn is too good for the role given him. The dialog doesn't help the lads much....

The Rambler film came and went without arousing much interest in moviegoers. As *Variety* had predicted, it was best suited for double bills and lent modest support to whichever "A" movie it was paired with. But MacIssac's series continued to flourish in *Dime Detective,* which by this time was being edited by Kenneth S. White, who had purged the magazine of quasi-horror yarns and was giving the legendary *Black Mask* a run for its money. All told, 18 Rambler stories saw print in *Dime Detective* throughout the Thirties. The last, "Object—Murder," appeared in the January 1940 issue. No doubt Ken White would like to have published others. But MacIssac wasn't writing them anymore.

After two decades in the fiction game, having sold hundreds of stories totaling more than ten million words, the once-prolific pulpster found himself written out. He had been afflicted with Writer's Block for a couple years, and rumor had it that later MacIssac submissions often required significant editorial intervention to make them printable. In desperation, the author attempted to master the less demanding craft of screenwriting. But he received only one assignment, joining experienced serial scripters George Plympton, Basil Dickey, and Sherman L. Lowe on a 1940 Universal chapter play, *The Green Hornet Strikes Again.* His part of the job was completed in April 1940. Very likely it earned him the last paycheck he would ever receive. Still residing in Los Angeles, the creator of Addison Francis Murphy took his own life on May 5, 1940.

In his 1967 memoir *The Pulp Jungle,* fecund fictioneer Frank Gruber recalled a poignant meeting with MacIssac in New York during the latter's lean years. As a young fan of pulp fiction Gruber had practically worshipped the veteran storyteller. He visited MacIssac one Friday afternoon after having seen several publishers and picked up several checks totaling over eight hundred dollars. As Gruber explained:

> I went down to the Hotel Chelsea on Twenty-Third Street, where MacIssac was staying. We chatted for a while and he asked how I was doing. I could not resist trying to impress MacIssac, one of the real giants of the business, so I pulled out the checks and showed them to him.
>
> "This week's," I said with restrained modesty. He looked at the checks and commented: "I wouldn't mind having a couple of these myself." I thought he was being indulgent with me and thought no more of it... but [some time] later MacIssac shot himself through the head and the story came out. He had not sold a story in more than six months and had not saved any of the huge sums he had earned through the years.
>
> That same afternoon with MacIssac he took me up the street to a café where the great Thomas Wolfe did most of his writing. He, too, was living at the Chelsea Hotel and MacIssac knew him well. He introduced me to Wolfe and we sat at the table and listened to a three-hour monologue by Wolfe. The subject was how great a writer he was.
>
> I did not like Thomas Wolfe and I still think fondly of Fred MacIssac, who had a million readers for every thousand who preferred Wolfe.

Frank Gruber had a pretty healthy ego himself, and *The Pulp Jungle* is littered with factual errors and erroneous suppositions. But it's obvious that Gruber had great affection for Fred MacIssac, who entertained more people than Thomas Wolfe or any five of his kind could ever have hoped to reach. I have little doubt that you'll share Gruber's fondness for his fellow pulpster after reading this collection.

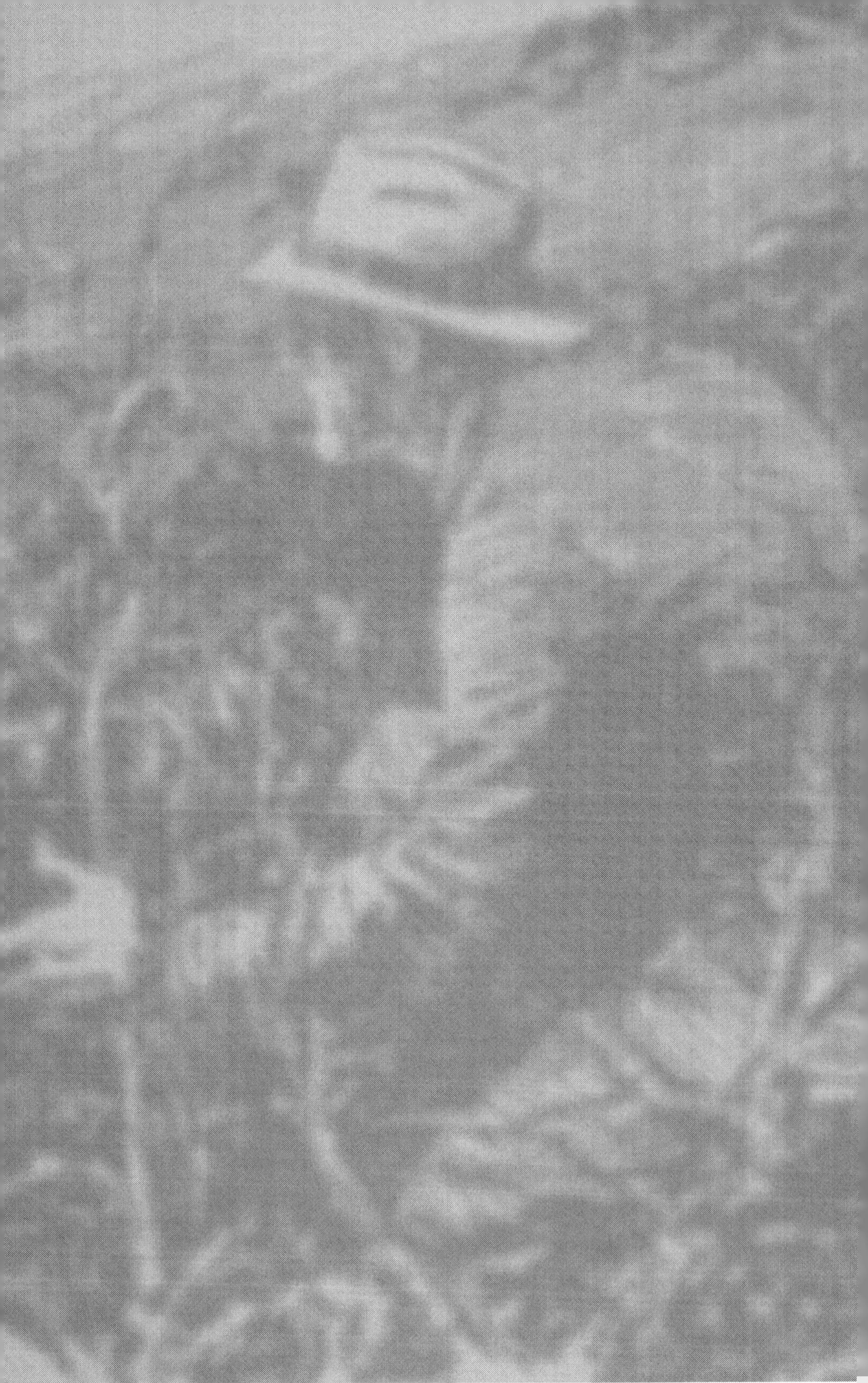

THE AFFAIR AT CAMP LAUREL

ADDISON DEXTER MURPHY, STAR REPORTER, HAD STUMBLED INTO A MYSTERY STORY THAT WAS EVEN BETTER THAN THE ONE HE'D BEEN SENT TO COVER—IF HE COULD LIVE TO WRITE IT.

CHAPTER ONE

THE LOAN OF A JACK

WEED, CITY editor of the New York *Sphere,* came out of the office of the managing editor and gazed discontentedly round the city room. It was a big room which bore much more resemblance to a banking office than a headquarters for desk men and reporters; and the well-dressed young men who sat behind rows of mahogany typewriter desks looked more like clerks than newspaper writers.

Weed was an old-timer. When he died or was pensioned, a journalist of the modern type would take his place. What he wanted just now was an old-fashioned reporter, and he didn't have one on the staff.

"Mr. Weed," said a voice at his elbow.

He turned and scowled at the man who had approached him on rubber heels.

"Two years ago," he said heatedly, "I told you to get out of this office and never bust in here again."

The young man grinned at him impudently. "But that was two years ago," he observed. "I thought you might have missed me."

Weed ran his right hand through his bushy gray hair and sized the young man up with a glance of his cold, blue eyes.

"You're on your uppers," he charged. "Well, your kind of reporter is as extinct as the dodo. We go in for snappy young men who go out on a story—"

"—and come back without it," finished the stranger.

Weed was unable to restrain a grin. "Where the heck have you been?" he demanded.

"Just landed from a fruit boat from Central America. Steerage passenger," the young man informed him. "I could use a job."

Two men carried a heavy burden.

"We're cutting the staff; firing, not hiring." He laughed and threw an arm over the visitor's shoulder. "Aw, hell," he ejaculated, "come in with me and meet the managing editor."

"New one?"

"Yes, lucky for you."

He led the way back into the private office, and a solemn-visaged man of thirty-five, with thick-lensed spectacles, looked up from the business of blue pencilling some typewritten pages.

"Mr. Palmer," said Weed, "this is Addison Dexter Murphy. I think he can do the job."

Mr. Palmer looked the Murphy person over with disfavor. The latter was a tall, loose-jointed man of twenty-eight or thirty, with a long, narrow face, a nose that was slightly aquiline, a large mouth, a square chin, gray eyes set far apart and surrounded by laugh wrinkles. There were lines on either side of the mouth, and dark circles under the eyes. It was not a handsome face and there was an unhealthy pallor upon it. His clothes were impressed.

"Not on the staff, are you?" asked Palmer, sharply.

Murphy grinned. "Not yet, sir."

Palmer looked at Weed. "What's the matter with a staff man?" he demanded.

Weed shrugged his shoulders. "Lot of messenger boys. This is a job."

"And why should we entrust it to a tramp? How do we know he won't sell us out? Who is he, anyway?"

"Shut up, Ad," commanded the city editor, seeing that Mr. Murphy was about to protest. "You look like a tramp, anyway." He turned to his chief. "Mr. Palmer, this fellow is a newspaperman, if you know what I mean. I had to fire him two years ago for flagrant violation of office rules. Smoking in the office and never getting to work on time and a few other little things that we won't go into. But I never knew him to fall down on a story, and he's honest and a fighting fool."

"Sit down, Mr. Murphy," said Palmer, smiling. "If Weed guarantees you, it's good enough for me. How much salary do you want?"

"Hundred and a quarter," replied Murphy as he seated himself.

"You value yourself highly. Well, you'll get that much if you bring in this story. If you fail, you're fired."

Murphy nodded. "Sure. Why not?"

"Do you know Herbert Laurel?"

"The millionaire sportsman? Never met him."

"You know he recently returned from abroad?"

Murphy shook his head. "Just came from South America myself.—Steerage. Had malaria down there. All right now."

"Oh, that's it. I thought you were just over a spree."

"No, sir. Broke. No free booze in South America."

PALMER unbent and laughed goodnaturedly. It was hard to be formal with Mr. Addison Dexter Murphy.

"Laurel landed from the Berengaria two weeks ago, and went at once to his camp in the Adirondacks. He's up there with his sister and his daughter. They were in California when he came home unexpectedly, and they joined him there."

"Yes, sir."

"Well, I've just had a letter from a friend of mine in Natal. He mentions casually that Herbert Laurel was abandoned by his safari somewhere in the Victoria Nyanza country, and either died of starvation or was killed by savages. But it appears that my friend was mistaken."

"Yes, sir."

"Laurel, however, on his return, avoided the ship newsmen. He did not visit any of his accustomed haunts, never went near his office, and drove at once to the Adirondacks. And he has been operating in the market in a big way since his return, by private wire from his camp."

"And you think?"

"His actions are causing his firm a lot of concern. Laurel entered Africa by way of Mombasa and Nairobi. About the time my friend wrote me that he had been lost, Laurel turned up at a port called Kismara with a tale of making his way alone over two hundred miles of bad country. He identified himself all right, and took a trading steamer north, instead of returning to Mombasa, where he was very well known. Nobody in Kismara knew him personally."

"He was probably sick of Africa."

"Well, I've another hunch. Supposing he died and some adventurer found his body and carried off his credentials? Laurel did not notify either his family or his firm of the steamer upon which he was landing in New York, and none of his friends here have set eyes on him since he arrived. Isn't that suspicious?"

"Pardon me, sir," asked Murphy with an impudent grin, "where did you learn the newspaper game?"

"In Chicago. Why?"

The reporter chuckled. "Thought so. Pleasure to meet you, Mr. Palmer. The chances are a thousand to one that Herbert Laurel is at his lodge in the Adirondacks, but if the person there is an impostor—what a story!"

A gleam came into the managing editor's eyes. "Of course, it's a wild hunch," he admitted, "but I'm paying the freight."

"Well, what could be the game?"

"Whoever is up there is liquidating the Laurel estate and taking enormous losses in the market to get cash. I understand a member of the firm went up to make a protest, and Laurel wouldn't admit him to the estate. Sent word he was head of the firm and would do what he damned pleased."

"But they must be sure of his identity or they wouldn't take his orders."

"True, but there is a faint possibility that they are deceived."

"That's all, isn't it?" Murphy asked.

Palmer smiled and nodded.

"I'm broke. I'd like a few hundred expense money," said Murphy.

"Weed vouches for you. If you trim us, I'll take the cash out of his pay."

"I'll stand for that," stated the city editor. "I'll undoubtedly have to fire this guy sooner or later, but he'll get the story if there is one."

"Take five hundred with you," said Palmer. "Best of luck, Murphy!"

"You're a couple of white guys," said Addison Dexter Murphy with a slight show of emotion. "It had begun to look as though I'd have to sleep in the park to-night."

"You sleep on the train," commanded the managing editor.

AT PLATTSBURG, Murphy hired a small roadster and headed for the mountains. He had learned that the Laurel camp was located about sixty miles to the northwest, not far from the Canadian border, and in the wildest and most remote part of a section of New York State which is somewhat less frequented than the New York Public Library. He had an automatic pistol in his hip pocket, relic of an ill-starred revolution in Honduras in which he had learned that Spigs can shoot straight, and have so little to live for that they don't hesitate to die.

He had weighed the probabilities, and had decided that Palmer was balmy, and that Herbert Laurel, in person, was inhabiting his camp. All he would have to do would be to drive up to the camp, present his card, interview Mr. Laurel, go back to New York and get fired. As his prospects of permanent employment depended upon the presence of a villainous impostor in the Laurel cabin, he discarded the probabilities. He would assume that a criminal was in his fastness, and he would creep upon him as a cat creeps upon a bird. He would abandon his car at a safe distance from the estate, work through the woods and see what he would see.

He was singing softly to himself as he drove through the green hills, stimulated by the piney tang in the air and the sight of roadside flowers and the possibility of excitement. Addison Dexter Murphy thrived on excitement. Having entered the newspaper business at a period when reporters of rival papers battled for the news, he had lived to see the disappearance of the competitive spirit as syndication, comics and perfunctory news services crippled individual effort. Every now and then Murphy would become bored with the game, and would commit some flagrant violation of rules, get discharged, go a-wandering, and eventually drift back to New York and take on again the only profession he knew.

Palmer was a man after his own heart, a managing editor who used his imagination and who spent the paper's money freely in following his hunches. Murphy had seen scores of wild surmises by an editor turn into tremendous exclusive stories; but such geniuses went wrong much more often than they went right, and cold-blooded publishers replaced them with prosaic men with a strong strain of common sense and economy in their natures.

What made Palmer's hunch appear unreasonable was the fact that the sister and daughter of Herbert Laurel were with their relative in his Adirondack camp. They certainly would know the millionaire when they saw him, and they would be quick to detect an impostor.

Ah, well, it wouldn't be long now before he had the facts!

MURPHY had driven thirty miles into the mountains when he came upon a stalled motor car, and as he approached it, a man stepped into the road and lifted an appealing arm. Addison stopped his car.

"Hey, feller," said the man in the road, "I got a blowout. Have you got a jack?"

Murphy nodded, descended, went around to the compartment at the back and pulled out the tool kit.

"There you are."

"Thanks. Say, I never changed a tire before. Can you tell me how to go about it?"

Murphy laughed. "I'll help you do it," he declared. "The sooner we get it changed, the sooner I get my jack back and go on my way."

"I'm damned glad I met you!" remarked the stalled motorist.

With a quizzical glance at him, Murphy, who was a bundle of nerves and quite incapable of standing by and watching somebody else work, placed the jack under the rear axle and began to lift the car. He was wondering what this fellow was doing in a rural district. The man had Tenth Avenue, New York, written all over him; and there was something vaguely familiar about him. The reporter engaged him in conversation as they worked, studying him covertly and trying to place him.

The car upon which they labored was a heavy coupé of an expensive make, and it didn't seem to fit with its driver.

"What are you, a chauffeur?"

"No," said the man laconically.

"Going far?"

"Down to the village, about ten miles below."

"Live round these parts?"

"Yes."

"What's your name?"

"Say," said the fellow truculently, "you ask too damn many questions!"

Murphy rose and dropped his tire tool.

"Change your own tire," he snapped. "For no reason, I hop on a job that you don't know how to do, and you won't even be sociable."

The stranger became conciliatory. "Aw, I didn't mean no harm," he said. "You're a good guy. My name's Coogan, if you want to know. What's yours?"

Murphy picked up the tire tool. "Dexter, that's my name. How are you, Coogan?"

"Fine," said Coogan with a grin. "What you doing in this Godforsaken place?"

COOGAN pushed his hair back from his perspiring brow and revealed a white line, where hair and forehead met, which was about three inches long. It was the unconscious gesture that identified him for Murphy. The last time Murphy had seen the alleged Coogan had been six or seven years before, when he was covering police headquarters, and this fellow was brought in on suspicion of having killed a policeman named Delehanty. He had been released through the influence of a West Side precinct captain, when the police admitted that they had no real evidence against him.

"I'm lining it for Canada," said Murphy with assumed candor. "Never mind why."

Coogan grinned. "It ain't, any of my business," he said cordially. "Know the way?"

"I was told to follow this road and watch the signboards."

"That's right. If you're in a hurry, there's a short cut. It's a bad road, but it saves ten miles. You keep on this one for thirty miles till you come to a side road on the left, with a sign that says 'To Laurel Camp.' Don't take that, or you'll get in trouble. It's closed. About five miles beyond there's another dirt road on the right. Turn there."

"Much obliged, old man. There's your job done. I'll take my jack and be on my way. How do you happen to know the country so well? Work here?"

"Sure. I'm working for a guy named Laurel."

Murphy pulled out his jack. "So long," he said. "You better buy a jack when you get to a town. You can charge it to your boss, can't you?"

"Yep. This is his car."

They shook hands and parted. Murphy was confident that recognition had not been mutual. A man who is being given the works for murder is not apt to pay much attention to one of a herd of police headquarters reporters. But he had not been mistaken about Coogan. He couldn't remember the fellow's real name, but he recalled the scar perfectly.

As he drove along, now, he was singing at the top of his lungs. Palmer's hunch had been right. There was something very funny going on at Herbert Laurel's Adirondack camp. If a New York gunman was employed in any capacity at the millionaire's lodge, it meant that trouble had already occurred there, or was going to occur.

Murphy had learned in Plattsburg that Laurel owned two or three square miles of wild country which included the best fishing and shooting in the mountains, and that the estate was fenced in with barbed wire, and that several armed gamekeepers were employed to keep out poachers and stragglers.

The isolation of the millionaire in such a place was complete; which was all right, if he were surrounded by people whom he could trust. He would be in a bad spot if his people were not loyal to him. And an impostor would be as safe in such a camp as a king in his castle.

Coogan, by no stretch of the imagination, could be a gamekeeper.

He was a pavement type who didn't know a partridge from an old black crow, and he would be even more incongruous as a servant. Laurel would have engaged his servants through a reputable agency, and there was no possibility that this tough person could secure its recommendation.

Smart fellow, Palmer. It was almost a cinch that Laurel had never returned from Africa. Some adventurer in the wilds had found his body, stolen his credentials and identifications, got in touch with ingenious criminals who had concocted a plot, and was now installed in the camp and engaged in the loot of the Laurel fortune.

How about the daughter and sister of the millionaire? Prisoners. They had come directly from California and joined the supposed Herbert Laurel at the camp. Their presence was convincing evidence to his business associates in New York that all was well; and if his market instructions seemed to his business partners queer, they had to obey orders.

CHAPTER TWO

PRIVATE SECRETARY

MURPHY WHIZZED over the paved road at forty miles an hour, and presently came to a dirt road on the right, marked by a signboard which said Camp Laurel. Murphy swung his car into this road, and moved slowly down it for a couple of hundred yards. It twisted and turned, and very shortly revealed a rustic gate ahead. At the left of the gate was a log hut from the exit of which a man came forth.

"Hey!" he shouted. "You can't come in here."

"Why can't I?" demanded the reporter.

The fellow came close and scowled up at him. "Because it's private property, see?"

"Well, what's the harm in letting me through?" whined Murphy. "I'm in a hurry, I am."

"Oh, yeah?" said the man with an evil grin. "Well, you back out of here or I'll shoot your tires full of holes."

"Whose place is this?" demanded Murphy. The gateman seemed as foreign to the Adirondacks as Murphy himself, or the fellow whose tire he had changed thirty miles back.

"It belongs to Herbert Laurel," said the man. "On your way, now!"

"Don't it go through to Canada?"

"It don't go nowhere."

"I'm in a hurry," beefed Murphy. "I been told I could get to Canada this way. Let a guy through, will yer?"

The man grinned understanding. "That's it, eh? Well, you go back to the main road, turn to the right, and four or five miles up you'll see another dirt road. That goes through the hills to Canada."

"Have I got to back all the way out of here?"

"That's what you got to do. Let's see you start."

The reporter threw his gears into reverse and slowly backed away. The gateman watched him until he had disappeared around a bend in the road, and went slowly back to his hut.

Having found out what he wanted to know, Murphy continued in reverse until he struck the pavement, and then drove contentedly on to the Canadian road, which he entered. About a mile down the road he came upon an open field, at the right; across this he drove until he entered thick woods, which blocked progress at the end of forty or fifty yards.

Looking back, he saw that the car was effectually screened from view of persons using the Canadian road, and he prepared to abandon it. He went around to the luggage compartment, took from it a trowel, and a box containing food and a couple of bottles of mineral water, locked the car, and struck off through the woods in the direction in which he supposed the Laurel estate lay.

BY THIS time, it was about two o'clock in the afternoon. He was going up a gentle hillside. Insects buzzed around his head and annoyed him until he remembered the kind of mosquitoes they had in Central America. He moved steadily upward through thickening pines for an hour, and came at last to a tight ten-foot fence of barbed wire. It was of the stout cyclone variety, barbed at the top. Murphy sat down at the foot of a tree, ate a sandwich, drank half a bottle of mineral water, removed his coat, rolled up his sleeves and picked up his trowel.

With this instrument he began to dig a hole at the base of the barbed wire, throwing the dirt on the other side of the wire. In half an hour it was deep enough to permit him to wriggle under the fence. He came up inside Laurel's estate, reached back through the hole and drew brush and leaves over its outer end. Very deliberately, then, he replaced the dirt in the excavation, until the ground was again level with the base of the fence. Some distance away, he dug up a couple of square feet of sod, and with it effectually concealed the fact that a human mole had been at work.

After hiding his trowel under a bush, he donned his coat and moved slowly and cautiously in the direction he surmised the road to Camp Laurel to be, and in half an hour he came upon the house.

By this time, Mr. Murphy was very tired, so he lay down in a well-screened thicket and slept for a considerable period. When he woke, it was dark.

With a grunt of satisfaction, the newspaper man rose, and began to move along the road in the direction of the camp. He kept to the edge, ready to dart into the thicket, for he suspected that the place was well patrolled.

The fellow he had met at the gate was of the same stripe as the man with the blowout; criminals, both of them. The camp was prepared to resist siege. He did not doubt that there were a dozen armed men guarding the occupant of the de luxe cabin which belonged to, but he was sure was not occupied by, Herbert Laurel. These fellows would shoot to kill, and in this wild spot they would have no difficulty in disposing of a body.

If, as Palmer surmised, the game was to liquidate the Laurel estate, there would be millions to divide among the criminals. It was an audacious scheme, and the inventor of it would carry on in a big way. Murphy had marched with a certain Army of Liberation in Central America without getting half the thrill which he was already experiencing from this present position. He was one of those abnormal people who revel in danger. Had he dared do so, he would have sung aloud with joy, and as he moved, he hummed under his breath a popular ditty called "Take a Little Walk."

By and by he saw a pin-point of light far off and high up. For some time he had been climbing, but so far he had heard nothing from the watchmen whom he expected to find on patrol.

Redoubling his caution, he moved along. Presently the woods thinned out, and he was crossing open pastures, and now he could see a dozen lights ahead, shining, no doubt, from windows of the camp buildings.

He left the road, and bending double, crept across the fields. The moon was rising, dissipating the friendly darkness. On and on. He could make out the dark bulk now of several buildings, long, low and silhouetted against the moon, which was low in the sky beyond. Back of the camp, water shimmered in the moonlight. As with most lodges such as this, a lake was near by.

FROM behind him came the rumble of a motor car, and he dropped flat, just in time to escape being revealed by the headlights as the car swung round a curve. It continued on, and came to a stop in front of one of the smaller buildings. He surmised that it belonged to the fellow he had met on the road, who had returned from his trip to town.

Murphy rose again, and bending low, moved more rapidly toward the camp. The motor car's lights went out, but lights from the windows of several of the buildings gave a faint radiance, and unconsciously his eyes were fixed upon them. And that was how it happened that he did not see the man lying in the grass until he fell over him. Instantly, the fellow was upon his back and doing his best to choke Addison Dexter Murphy into insensibility.

While Murphy was tall and thin, and somewhat weakened by malaria, there was a lot of fight left in him; and during his variegated career he had mingled in many brawls in which his opponent had the initial advantage. First, he braced himself with his hands on the ground, suffered the inconvenience of choking for a second while he drew himself upon his knees, with the assailant still on his back; and then he turned a somersault, enemy and all, and the other fellow was lying on his back with Murphy on top and the throat grip broken.

The reporter rolled off, felt for the fellow's face, and drove in a heavy right. He heard the man grunt, and then he felt the fellow's boot jam into his thigh. The thing to do was to choke him before he could call for help, and Murphy went in for that with right good will. It was his turn to acquire a faceful of fists, which he assimilated like a veteran. But suddenly the man had his hands locked at the small of Addison's back and was industriously endeavoring to break him in two.

The answer to that was a stiff knee to the fellow's groin, and it worked. The hold loosened, an involuntary groan escaped the man; and Murphy, having the advantage of being on top, smashed his right against the point of the man's chin, which evidently sent him halfway to Glory.

Murphy hit him two or three times more before he realized that his enemy was unconscious, and then he rolled him over and tapped his pockets for a gun. The man was unarmed.

This was very curious. It was too dark to see the fellow's face; and it had not occurred to Murphy, up to this moment, that it might be that he was not dealing with a member of the Laurel garrison. It was essential to Murphy to battle in dead silence, but the other man had also not uttered a sound. Was it possible—had he fallen over another reporter? He sat on the ground and gazed at his victim. Ha! Something gleamed very faintly in the grass beside him. He picked it up and inspected it. A gold cigarette case. Positively, the man was not a reporter, then. Murphy was reassured by the discovery.

The victim beside him stirred and attempted to sit up. Murphy grasped him by the throat, and thrust him back on the turf.

"A sound out of you," he threatened, "and I'll murder you!"

"Who are you?" whispered the unknown.

"You first, mister."

"Are you one of the men on the place?" the man asked.

"I'm not connected with the establishment," replied the reporter. "I crawled under the fence."

"A tramp?"

"I've been one, in my time. Suppose you answer a few questions. Who in hell are you?"

"I'm Mr. Laurel's secretary."

"Yeah? And why are you hiding in the grass?"

"Sssh! Somebody's coming."

A MAN carrying a flash light was walking along the road, a hundred feet distant, coming from the direction of the gate and approaching the camp. Murphy promptly lay down beside his late enemy and maintained strict silence until the fellow had passed. They watched him as he passed between them and the moon, and made out a bulky figure with a shotgun on his shoulder. They saw him go into one of the smaller buildings, and heard the door slam behind him.

"Answer my question," commanded Addison.

"Not till you tell me who you are," replied the other stoutly

"I'm a detective," lied Murphy. "Certain well known criminal characters from New York are employed here. That's my business."

"By Jove, I'm glad to meet you, Mr. Detective!"

The secretary thrust out his hand, and Murphy accepted it.

"Let's get further away from the house and the road," the reporter proposed. "Maybe we can do business together."

They crept away a distance of a hundred yards, and sat down side by side on the thick grass.

"Now come through," ordered Murphy.

"I've been Mr. Laurel's secretary for years," said the man, "but when he returned from Africa he said he wouldn't need me up here, so I remained in the office of the company in New York."

"Go on."

"Well, Mr. Laurel has been issuing instructions which the firm believes injudicious. He has ignored letters of protest and has refused to permit us to send some one up to remonstrate with him. A couple of days ago he ordered us to sell out his interest in the Derwent Company, which means that he takes a terrific loss, at present market prices, and loses control of a magnificent property.

"I was sent up to see him. I arrived to-day, and was refused admittance at the gate. The gateman phoned to the house, and was told to order me back to New York. So, I waited until it was dark, climbed a tree close to the wire fence, and dropped into the grounds. I was creeping up to the house when you fell over me; and being afraid that you were one of the people on the place, and that you would eject me before I reached Mr. Laurel, I tried to dispose of you."

"I wish I could see what you look like," said Murphy. "You seem to be quite a fellow for a secretary. You know Mr. Laurel when you see him?"

"Naturally."

"Fine. I've studied some photographs of him, but it isn't the same thing. Let's join forces."

"Delighted! What did you mean by saying that there were criminals about the place?"

"Listen," said the reporter. "What you told me convinces me of the truth of a crack-brained theory my boss had. He doesn't believe that Laurel is here at all. He thinks he died in Africa, and that somebody is taking his place. I took no stock in that until I discovered that two New York gunmen are working here. Now you tell me that Laurel is ruining himself by market transactions. There is no doubt that there is an impostor on the job."

"**IMPOSSIBLE.** Mr. Laurel definitely landed in New York. He communicated with his partners."

"Did they actually *see* him?"

"No, he phoned them."

"Why didn't they meet the boat?"

"His return was unexpected. They were not notified."

"Isn't it suspicious that he didn't go to his office?"

"No-o. He rarely went to the office. He gave his orders by telephone."

"You didn't see him either?"

"No, but I talked with him on the telephone."

"Are you sure it was he?"

"Positive. I know his voice."

"His voice could be imitated."

"I was his private secretary for years. I'm certain it was he."

"Well," said Murphy, "the thing for you and me to do, now that we're here, is to call on him."

"That was my intention. I was going to try to obtain admission to the house."

Murphy reflected. "You didn't have a notion that things were really wrong when you came up here, did you?"

"No, except that we thought he was acting without due consideration."

"And when your boss ordered you away from the gate, you took a chance and scaled the wall? You knew he'd fire you for that, didn't you?"

"Well," said the young man slowly, "I'll be frank. Miss Laurel phoned me yesterday. She said, 'Is that you, Frank?' and her voice sounded strained. I said, 'Yes.' She said, 'I want you—' and then she laughed and exclaimed, 'It doesn't matter!' and hung up on me. I called back and was told she didn't care to speak to me. That was queer."

"Why was it queer?"

"Well, I know her very well. I—er—er—"

"You're in love with her? Engaged?"

"No. She is Herbert Laurel's daughter. I wouldn't dream—"

"If I wanted a girl, I wouldn't care whose daughter she was," declared Murphy. "Only, I never wanted one. If, as I suspect, some criminal is posing as Laurel, try to visualize her position. Most likely, they caught her at the phone and forced her to cut you off."

The secretary groaned.

"Where's your gun?" demanded Murphy.

"I never fired a revolver in my life."

"You're going to be a great help!" sighed Murphy. "Well, let's sneak-up to the house and try to get in."

"All right," said the secretary quietly.

CHAPTER THREE

DRAGOMAN

THE FELLOW had plenty of nerve, thought Murphy, and it was a great break to have stumbled over him. Stevens could positively identify Laurel, and that was what Murphy needed. The faker probably looked something like the real Mr. Laurel, a sufficient resemblance to deceive a man who had nothing but a photograph to go on, and the reporter had to be absolutely positive of that fact before he dared shoot his story to the *Sphere*. A mistake would cost the paper millions in libel, and would run Addison Dexter Murphy out of the newspaper game for good.

No casual resemblance could deceive the man who had taken dictation from Herbert Laurel for years. Frank Stevens had been especially supplied by Providence, to establish Mr. Murphy in his job!

The pair stole cautiously across the open field, and drew near to the camp. If they escaped attention from the armed men on the place, Murphy hoped to obtain entrance into the millionaire's cabin by means of an unlocked window. After that, they would have to trust to luck.

"Ever been up here?" he whispered.

"Yes. Four years ago."

"Good. You know the layout inside?"

"We had better work around the house, and approach it from the rear," said Stevens.

"Right."

They made a wide detour, and Murphy observed that the huge Adirondack cabin had an "L" at the back, probably the kitchens. The main building was two stories high. Lights were gleaming from the uncurtained windows of the lower floor.

"If I can climb on your back, I can look through one of those windows," said Murphy.

"I can hold you."

They crept up under a big window. Stevens stooped, and Murphy climbed on his back and brought his eyes above the level of the window sill. He looked into a very large living room, furnished in camp style. The floor was of rough boards, upon which were strewn very fine skins. There was a flight of stairs leading to a balcony which went round three sides of the room. Most of the fourth side was occupied by a huge stone fireplace.

There was a fire in the fireplace, and three chairs were drawn up before it. The high back of one of the chairs was turned to the spy, who could not see whether it had an occupant or not. A powerful reading lamp revealed the occupant of the chair at the left, as stage lights reveal an actor. Though he was sitting forty feet from the window through which the reporter was peering, he was vividly visible to Murphy.

This man had a brown skin and a huge head, the top of which was either bald or shaven. He had a great, beetling brow, and a big nose shaped like the prow of a boat—curved, broad, monstrous. He had a large mouth with thick, Negroid lips, and a protruding chin.

AS THOUGH he had become aware that there was a spy at the window, he turned his head toward it; and Murphy saw a pair of very large black eyes set in deep caverns beneath the high, broad forehead. He was wearing what the reporter at first thought was a bathrobe, but it happened that he rose a second later and moved toward a bookcase. Then Murphy realized that the creature had on a dress, the skirt of which came to within two or three inches of the ground. It was of orange satin.

Murphy emitted an ejaculation of astonishment. The fellow was an Egyptian! In one of his enforced absences from the newspaper profession, Addison Dexter had worked as a steward upon a cruise steamer which touched at Alexandria, and had gone up to Cairo. He remembered hundreds of dragomen dressed like this person, and if the man had been wearing the red fez which Egyptians use to top off their gorgeous Mother Hubbards costumes, he would have placed him instantly. But who would expect to find an Egyptian dragoman in the interior of an American business man's Adirondack camp?

"You're getting heavy," protested the man upon whose back Murphy was standing.

The amazing and repulsive personality of the Egyptian had absorbed all his attention, but at the warning he glanced toward the occupant of the third chair.

This contained a rather handsome man of fifty, with iron-gray hair and regular features, who sat with crossed legs, an open book on his knee. Murphy gazed at him with growing perturbation.

"Okay," he said, after a few seconds, and leaped to the ground. "Get on my back and tell me, who is the fellow sitting on the right side of the fireplace."

He stooped, and Stevens clambered upon his back, balancing himself easily by grasping at the log wall of the cabin. It was the secretary's turn to peer through the window, and a few seconds satisfied him. He leaped down upon the soft ground again, highly elated.

"It's all right," he said cheerfully. "You had me terribly worried. That's Mr. Laurel in there."

"Are you sure? They might have got hold of somebody who looks just like him."

"Positive," declared Stevens. "There's a strong light on his face, and just as I was peering at him, he made a gesture which is very characteristic of him. He caught hold of his left ear lobe with his left hand. I've seen him make that gesture a thousand times."

"I thought he looked like the photographs," said the reporter dismally, "but I needed positive identification. So that's that!"

"Well," said Stevens, "I don't suppose he'll be glad to see me, considering the way I was received at the gate; but I'm going around to the front door and call on him."

"If you're smart, you'll go back to New York with me. Since that's Laurel himself, it's a cinch he knows what he's about, and he'll fire you as quick as he looks at you."

"I've got to do what I was instructed to do."

"What did you make of the other man?"

"Was there another man? I only saw Mr. Laurel."

"I'll go in with you."

"No. That might make him angry."

"Well, I'll pick you up on the road, about where we met, and you can tell me what happened."

"All right," said Stevens. He walked briskly, and without further precaution, around the cabin toward the front entrance.

MURPHY dropped upon the ground where he stood. He became aware that he was horribly tired and wickedly let down.

Palmer had a diseased imagination. He was a crack-brained Chicago faker, unfit to be managing editor of a big New York newspaper! It was obviously impossible for a man as prominent as Laurel to be the victim of a successful impersonation. No faker could have traveled halfway round the world under his name without being shown up. His firm was certainly not taking orders from its chief without being certain that he was their chief.

Supposing he had been selling his securities at a loss? He was a shrewd fellow who expected the market to go much lower, and he figured upon buying back what he had sold later at a big profit.

Murphy had started out upon this story with small hopes, but from the moment of his encounter with Coogan, the gunman, he had gone after it like a hound after a fox. The encounter with Stevens had convinced him that he was about to turn up one of the most sensational yarns in years, and he had had no more expectation of finding Herbert Laurel placidly reading a book at his own fireside than he had of peeking through that cabin window and gazing upon King George.

But this story was a complete dud. He had spent two hundred dollars, got the facts, and they wouldn't be worth a line; and with a man like Palmer, there would be no credit in returning with useless information. If an editor sends a man out on a big story and nicks the business office for big expense money, he has to fire the reporter who comes back empty-handed, in order to save his own face.

It was curious that rough characters from New York should be employed upon this millionaire's estate, that an Egyptian in an orange gown should be making himself at home in Laurel's company; but that wasn't a newspaper story.

Laurel wasn't dead in Africa, nor was an impostor sitting in his chair in that comfortable room. Laurel was on the job, and it didn't make the slightest difference how eccentric he might be, since he was Herbert Laurel.

With a sigh, Murphy clambered to his feet and began cautiously to work his way around the house in the opposite direction from that taken by Stevens. While Stevens could explain his presence, it might mean rough treatment for a newspaper man who was discovered prowling around the cabin of a millionaire who had demonstrated that he was exceedingly averse to having his privacy intruded upon. Addison would lie in wait for Stevens on the edge of the road, about a hundred yards from the house, then find out how the young man had fared.

He kept well in the shadow, and began to skirt the "L" of the house, keeping close to the wall. He had proceeded about twenty feet when he heard a slight noise on the roof above. He stopped in his tracks, bending forward, ears alert, and then a heavy weight descended upon, the back of his head, and he was driven to the ground, his face buried in the thick grass and consciousness knocked out of him.

COLD water, stinging him in the face, brought him back to a realization of things. He was lying upon his back, about where he had fallen. Peering anxiously into his countenance was a young woman in a black dress, who was upon her knees and bending over him. In the faint light he was able to discern that she was a very pretty young woman.

"Oh, you're not dead, are you?" she asked in a low, tense voice.

"I don't think so," he replied with a slow grin. "What happened to me?"

"I dropped off the roof and fell on top of you," she confessed. "I thought I had killed you. I'm so glad."

"I'm tough, miss. Who the deuce are you?"

"First, what are you doing here? Are you working for my father?"

"My name's Murphy. You're Miss Laurel?—Say, were you trying to get away?"

"Yes. I could have got away, too. I could have left you here, only I didn't want to. Are you going to take me into the house?"

There was so much fear and anxiety in her voice that the news hound reared his shrewd head. Maybe there was a story in this remote spot after all.

"I'm going to help you get away," he said. "Listen, Miss Laurel. I'm a newspaper reporter. I came up to find out why your father has shut himself in like this. You tell me why you're skipping out and I'll get you out."

"Hush!" she said. "The servants may hear us. Can you move now?"

"I'm all right."

"Well, we've got to be careful. There are men patrolling the grounds. There are some trees down by the lake."

"Yes."

"We'll creep down there, where we can't be heard."

Taking the girl's hand he conducted her swiftly toward a small grove of trees, a couple of hundred feet at the left of the house and upon the lake's edge.

"Now," he said. "Sit down on the moss and tell me what the trouble is."

"But I don't want you to put it in the paper," she said.

"Most likely it won't be worth printing. If you want me to help you, you'll have to show me reasons why I should."

"All right," she said. Her voice was low-pitched, mellow and pleasant. He had an idea that she was a very beautiful girl, and he wished he dared strike a match to see exactly what she looked like.

"I'm running away," she said, "because I don't want to be married in the morning to Mr. Horton."

"Who is Mr. Horton, Miss Laurel?"

"He's a lawyer. William Welles Horton is his full name."

"Ah!" exclaimed Murphy. "He's about fifty years old, isn't he?"

"Isn't that awful?—Besides, I don't like him. Let's hurry. We shouldn't stay here talking."

"IT'S ONLY about nine-thirty, and we have seven or eight hours of darkness before us. The later we make our break, the better our chances. So your father wants you to marry Horton?"

"He is forcing me to marry him. The minister is coming at nine in the morning," she said with great agitation.

"We'll fool 'em!" declared Murphy. He was getting excited. He knew William Welles Horton of old. Six or eight years back, the man had been a fairly successful criminal lawyer and divorce specialist. When the French law was amended to make divorce easy in Paris, Horton had abandoned his New York practice and opened offices in the French capital. Recently, Paris had been made less attractive for American divorces by the six-weeks residence law in Nevada, and Mr. Horton's business must have suffered. The fellow was a shyster anyway, and had risen out of the gutter. It was a very curious thing that an aristocrat like Laurel should be so anxious to have him for a son-in-law that he was forcing his lovely daughter to marry the brute.

"Take it easy!" Murphy said. "I'm with you with both feet. The luckiest thing you ever did was to knock me out. Don't you know you couldn't have got off the estate? The gates are guarded, and you couldn't have got through or over the barbed wire."

"I have a pair of scissors in my handbag," she declared. "I was desperate. I had to get away."

Murphy chuckled. "You can't cut barbed wire with a lady's scissors. We'll get out all right, and I have a car hidden outside which will land you in Plattsburg by daylight. Why does your father want you to marry?—Lie down flat! Somebody's coming."

His sharp ears had heard the padded footfalls of several persons on the moss, and as he listened, he heard a twig crackle. The moon peeped out uncertainly from me clouds, making a faint light.

They passed a few rods distant, unseen because of the trees, but they moved to the lake's edge and were visible in the moonlight. There were two men, and they were carrying a heavy burden.

"There's a deep hole right here," said a heavy voice. "Chuck him in. We can move the body to-morrow night."

"Oh!" murmured Miss Laurel. She was about to rise.

Murphy grasped her and thrust her down, pressing the palm of his hand against her mouth. His eyes were glued to the scene on the shore. The two men had begun to swing the inert body of the man they had been carrying. They swung him two or three times, and tossed him into the lake, a half a dozen feet from shore.

There was a big splash. They heard a brutal laugh, and the pair turned and moved rapidly away.

"Quiet!" hissed Murphy, "I'll get him. You lie still."

He kicked off his shoes, swung put of his coat, and bending double, ran the twenty feet to the water's edge, which he entered without sound, disappearing beneath the surface.

Heedless of his admonition, the girl was at his heels, and paused on the brink, peering fearfully into the black water.

The reporter swam down into the depths. He had marked the location at which the body had sunk, and he expected to meet it rising; but he touched bottom ten feet below, sank his hand to the wrist in the mud, and began to grope around. He could see nothing.

WHEN it seemed that he could hold his breath no longer, he touched a human ankle, grasped it, pulled until he had a grip upon the thighs, and kicked himself violently upward.

To his dismay, the body seemed to weigh tons and they rose almost reluctantly. Strong swimmer that he was, Murphy almost drowned before his head broke the surface; and then, though he was barely a dozen feet from shore, it did not seem as if he could make it with his burden.

Though he might have dropped the man and saved himself, there was too much of the bulldog in the newspaper man to dream of such a thing. He fought desperately. He saw the girl on her knees at the water's edge, leaning forward, and he pushed the body toward her. Her hands failed to reach it. Filling his lungs with air, Murphy sank again, came up under the body, and drove his head against the man's back, thus shooting it shoreward a foot.

The young woman's fingers closed upon the man's coat, and dragged him against the bank. Relieved of the heavy weight, Murphy came to the surface, thrust his shoulder under the man's neck, and almost broke it against something heavy and metallic. Miss Laurel had a good grip now, and held on. Murphy pulled himself ashore, and then dragged the body up on the bank.

"Oh, the fiends!" gasped the girl. "It's Frank Stevens!"

"Fiends are what they are," said Murphy grimly. "Look!"

Fastened around the young man's neck was a pair of ten-pound dumbbells, which explained the difficulty of getting the body to the surface. And Stevens was bound hand and foot.

"He's dead," moaned the girl. "Oh!"

"Shut up, you fool," said Murphy harshly. "Want to bring them back? Maybe he isn't dead. Look, he has a wound on the head."

He pulled out a penknife; cut the bonds, and removed the dumbbells, which had been tied so tightly around the secretary's neck that he would have choked to death if he hadn't drowned.

Turning Stevens upon his face, Murphy lifted him by the hips; and a quantity of water ran out of his mouth. Turning him over upon his back, the reporter then began the work of artificial respiration. While Miss Laurel wrung her hands and wept softly, the reporter kept grimly on; and in a few minutes he was rewarded by evidences of returning life. Presently Stevens became violently ill, and Addison contentedly ceased from his labor.

"He'll be all right in a minute," he said. "Lucky we happened to be around, eh?"

"Frank, speak to me!" she implored the injured man.

His right hand moved, caught her left hand, and drew it slowly to his lips. She permitted the caress.

"So that's how things are!" said Murphy under his breath. He rose and prowled about the grove, to satisfy himself that the killers were not in the vicinity and returned.

CHAPTER FOUR

THE MOB

WHEN MURPHY came back, Stevens was sitting up, supported by the girl's arm. His head rested upon her breast.

The reporter knelt down on the other side. "How are you feeling?" he demanded.

"I'll be all right," Stevens said, weakly. "Ruth tells me they sunk me to the bottom of the lake and that you pulled me out."

"Forget that.—What happened to you?"

The young man placed his hand wearily upon his forehead. "I've got a frightful headache," he muttered. "Oh, yes. I went to the front door and rang. A villainous looking servant opened. 'Who are you and what do you want?' he asked. 'I'm Frank Stevens, Mr. Laurel's secretary,' I said. 'I must see him on important business.' 'You wait here,' he said.

"The front door is on the right of the living room, and opens into a long-narrow hall which runs back to the servants' quarters. There is a door at the left, opening into the living room, which was closed. He opened it, and I caught a glimpse of Mr. Laurel in his chair, also a hideous yellow man in a bathrobe, and a third man whom I didn't know. I should have gone right in and spoken to Mr. Laurel, but I realized that too late. The servant spoke to the third man."

"That would be Horton," said Murphy to Ruth Laurel.

"I don't know," replied Stevens. "This stranger came out into the hall and closed the door behind him. 'Why do you wish to see Mr. Laurel? He sent word to you at the gate this afternoon to return to town,' he said. I replied, 'The firm wishes me to see him personally and discuss a business matter with him.'

"As I spoke, I heard a step behind me; and then I was hit with something. The next thing I knew I found myself here with Miss Laurel… I feel very ill."

"That's right. Take his head on your lap," said the reporter to the girl. "Close your eyes and sleep, Stevens. You're not going to be a bit of use to us."

"Why should they try to murder Frank?" demanded the girl. "Why didn't they want him to see father? Oh, I can't understand anything which has been happening."

"We're going to find out," Murphy said grimly. "Miss Laurel, has your father seemed to be normal since you came here?"

"Why, yes, except that he demands that I marry Horton. On every other matter he is kind and reasonable."

"There is no question in your mind that he is Herbert Laurel, your father?"

"Why how could there be?—Of course he is!"

"Who's this Egyptian?"

"He was Dad's dragoman, in Egypt. Father took a fancy to him and brought him to America."

"How long has he known Horton?"

"I believe they met in Egypt six weeks ago, after father came out of the interior of Africa. They came home together. He seems to have great influence with father."

MURPHY was silent. This girl and boy were a problem. It was going to be impossible for him to keep his word to escort her off the estate, and Stevens was too weak to move. He would be helpless for several hours perhaps. Yet they were in dire danger here, so close to the house. The treatment that had been awarded Stevens proved how blood-thirsty were the people surrounding Laurel.

Addison Dexter Murphy thought he was beginning to perceive the plot, and it would be an even better story than that which Palmer had sent him after—if he lived to write it.

Horton, doubtless on his uppers in Cairo, had encountered Laurel, weakened from his ordeal in Central Africa, and had ingratiated himself with him. While all divorce lawyers are not scoundrels, there are certainly a lot of scoundrels who are divorce lawyers. Upon the return to the States, Horton had persuaded Laurel to go directly to the lodge in the Adirondacks to complete his recuperation, and Horton had undertaken to put the place in readiness.

Probably he had engaged a crew of criminals and sent them up to the estate, and when Laurel arrived there, he was served by murderers and yeggmen. His sister and his daughter had entered, unsuspectingly, this nest of vipers. With Laurel at his mercy, Horton had doubtless put on the screws. He had forced the millionaire to sell vast quantities of securities for cash, which Horton, by clever forgery, would be able to draw out and secrete.

Of course, it would never do to permit Laurel to live, for he might attempt to prosecute Horton for his villainy, and so he was probably doomed the very day he entered his luxurious cabin. And the astute Horton had most likely decided to marry the millionaire's daughter so that when Herbert Laurel died, by "accident," of course, Horton would inherit what was left of the estate and so eternally thwart investigation.

The plot was as ingenious as it was audacious; and it might have succeeded, except for the disordered imagination of the managing editor of the *Sphere*. Ruth Laurel had escaped through her chamber window to the roof of the kitchen, and had dropped to the ground; but she could not have gotten out of the enclosure, and she would be rounded up and dragged back as soon as it was daylight.

The thugs from the house had dropped Stevens into the lake close to the shore. They intended to fish out the body in the morning, remove bonds and weights, and most likely transport it to some distant lake or pond, where it might not be recovered for a long period. Stevens's death would be judged accidental. If he had come in a motor car, it would be found and driven many miles away before it was abandoned.

The headlines of this stupendous story danced before the reporter's eyes, as he developed the situation in his mind; but he knew that it was a story which no paper would dare to print while Laurel lived, and while Horton retained his control over him.

Murphy ardently desired to smoke a cigarette. He couldn't think clearly without smoking, and he couldn't type a story unless a fag was hanging from his lip. He turned troubled eyes upon the helpless young people.

"I SUPPOSE you left your window open?" he said to Ruth.

"Yes."

"Your door locked with the key on the inside?—They didn't imprison you in your room?"

"Oh, no. I always locked my door on the inside."

"Your room opens on that balcony?"

"Yes."

"Where is your father's room?"

"Next to mine, on the left."

"And your aunt's?"

"On the other side of my room."

"What is your aunt's attitude regarding this marriage?"

"At first she was violently opposed to it, but she has changed. She doesn't seem to care."

"Where does Horton sleep?"

"Next to father."

"And the Egyptian?"

"Hussein? He lives in one of the guest cabins."

"You are familiar with the estate. Frankly, Miss Laurel, it will be several hours before this poor chap will be ready to march; and we are too close to the house for safety. Do you know of a better place to hide?"

"About a quarter of a mile down the lake there is a very muddy spot, beyond which is a dry spot that runs out into the lake. I don't think they would be apt to go there."

"You'll have to help me carry Stevens. I'm lighter than he is, and not as strong as I used to be. Malaria."

Stevens opened his eyes. "I think I can walk, if you'll support me," he said. "And I'll be all right pretty soon."

"We'll wait until the moon goes behind a cloud again."

In ten minutes they started. Stevens gained strength rapidly. By the time they reached a shallow swamp where the waters of the lake occasionally seeped across a low narrow isthmus, he no longer required a helping hand. The little peninsula had a scrub growth sufficient to conceal the fugitives.

"You're okay here," Murphy declared. "Miss Laurel, it's my opinion that your father is in the hands of criminals who are looting his estate and who will kill him eventually. I'm going to try to get him out of the house."

She clasped her hands in distress.

"If you only can!" she exclaimed.

"But they'll kill you, and then what will become of us?"

"If I'm not back with your father in an hour, you and Stevens make for the wire fence. Get sharp stones and excavate under it. You'll find my car hidden in the woods on the Canada dirt road, not far from the main highway. Use it."

"Look here," said Stevens. "There seems to be a mob of these men. The thing for us to do is to escape together and return with the police."

"And what will the police do when Mr. Laurel confronts them and orders them off his grounds? He won't be able to force this girl to marry Horton, but he will remain in their hands. And getting out of this place is no cinch. We might be captured, and you've already had a sample of their methods."

"I'll remain here alone. Frank wild go with you," said Ruth Laurel quietly.

"He's unarmed, and of no use to me. I have a gun."

"What's your plan?" demanded Stevens.

"To take advantage of opportunities," said Murphy, curtly. "Miss Laurel, do you know where I can get a ladder?"

"I suppose there is one in the garage," she said doubtfully. "I don't know."

"If I'm not back in an hour," he said, "make a dash for it. Don't try to help me. You couldn't do a thing."

The girl grasped both his hands. "If you only can!" she said with emotion. "If you can save father, I'll—I'll—"

"That's all right," he muttered, embarrassed.

"I feel like a dog," said Stevens.

"You take care of this kid. See you later, folks."

THE MOON was out again, and the reporter flitted like a ghost from tree to tree until he was out of the woody growth; then he wriggled like a snake upon the grass as he approached the rear of the house. He observed with satisfaction a birch tree growing a dozen feet from one of the kitchen windows, and he attained it, apparently without being observed. He calculated that there might be one or two men on guard at the entrance to the estate, a couple on patrol, and two more, perhaps, asleep in one of the guest cabins.

In the house would be Horton and the Egyptian and Laurel, and possibly one or two men servants. His plan was very sketchy. Laurel, of course, must surely be eager for escape from the trap in which he found himself. He was a remarkable man to take his situation as serenely as he appeared to be doing, when Murphy had looked through the window at him.

It was unlikely that he would be locked in his room, since his escape from the grounds seemed impossible in any case. If Murphy could reach him and persuade him to take the route out of the house which Ruth had taken, he thought the quartet could win to safety. Their advantage lay in the fact that the gang in charge of the place was still ignorant of the presence among them of a determined man with an automatic and plenty of cartridges.

As the moon again dipped behind a cloud, Murphy removed his shoes and went up the birch tree like a monkey. He clung to the trunk on the side nearer the "L," and as he mounted, the slender tree bent in that direction. Now he was five feet distant, now three, and then he landed upon the roof with a slight thump, while the tree flew back to position.

There was no question regarding Miss Laurel's window, for it was the only one opening above the roof. Screen and sash were up, and in a moment the reporter was inside the dark room. He saw by a thread of light beneath the door that the lights in the living room were still on, and noiselessly he opened the door a crack. To his satisfaction, he found that the balcony was so wide that those below would not be apt to observe an open door above. He slipped out of the room, and soundlessly closed the door behind him. Then he crawled to the edge of the balcony and peered through the rails.

Laurel was still sitting in the big chair at the right of the fireplace, and the scoundrel Horton stood with his back to the chimney, facing Addison, but as yet unaware of him.

However, the reporter had no eyes for Horton at the moment. The Egyptian was standing in front of Laurel, and was bending toward him and crooning something in low, weird, mysterious tones. And the millionaire was gazing up at him like a fascinated child.

CHAPTER FIVE

HYPNOSIS

THE MAN in the robe began to move backwards, and Laurel rose and moved after him, his face only a foot from the hideous countenance of the Oriental. They traveled twenty feet in this fashion, and presently Hussein paused beside a desk. Laurel seated himself, picked up a pen, and began to scratch his signature to one of a pile of documents. As fast as he signed one, Hussein removed it and passed it to Horton, who had come up behind him.

Murphy cursed under his breath. The thing was now clear to him. The Egyptian was a creature working with Horton, and he was a hypnotist. Horton had found him in Cairo, and had planted him with Herbert Laurel. The millionaire had returned home under the influence of the fakir, who took his orders from the shyster.

That was why Laurel was forcing his daughter to marry a villain. Hussein had also been able to persuade the girl's aunt to withdraw her objections. She had come under his influence. Alone in this remote spot, surrounded by Horton's weird creatures, and cut off from the world, Laurel was as helpless as an infant and as pliable as an imbecile. There was no chance in the world, Murphy knew, of persuading a man under hypnotic influence to run away from his master.

"Well done," he heard Hussein say in harsh, staccato English. "Now go to your chamber and sleep.—Sleep!— Sleep!"

Laurel rose like an automaton, crossed the room, and began to ascend the stairs. On Horton's face was a cynical smile. The great, terrible eyes of the Egyptian were fastened upon the back of his victim. Steadily, Laurel went up the stairs, his hand on the rail. He would pass the spy upon the balcony; though, if he were in a trance he might not see him. To return to Ruth's room was impossible, since the watchers below now stood in a position where they would see the door open. Murphy rolled over and flattened himself against the wall, holding his breath.

The miserable victim of the hypnotist approached. He was passing; he looked neither up nor down, right nor left. He continued on to his chamber, entered, and closed the door behind him. With a sigh of relief, Murphy crept back to his post of observation.

Horton was placing the documents signed by Laurel in a briefcase. Hussein, the Egyptian, was still gazing at the balcony.

Then Murphy got a terrible start.

"You, man on the balcony, come down!" Hussein said sharply.

Horton dropped his briefcase, pulled a revolver from his pocket and pointed it upward.

"Where is he?" he demanded.

The Egyptian's finger pointed to the spot where Murphy was crouching, deluding himself that he was invisible.

"Come down!" called Horton sharply. "Quick, or I'll fire."

He had the drop on the newspaper man; the game was up. Murphy rose dejectedly, moved toward the stairs, and slowly descended. In a few minutes, he realized sourly, he would probably land in the lake, with heavy weights round his neck. Nor would there be any one to rescue him.

HE REACHED the bottom of the stairs and walked sullenly toward the conspirators.

"Who in hell are you?" snarled Horton. "How did you get in this house?—What do you want?"

"That's for you to find out," replied Murphy with bravado.

Horton bore down on him, gun ready for action. "Don't you talk? Ah, I know you now. You're a reporter."

"Right!" said Addison Dexter Murphy. "Your little scheme has been busted wide open, Mr. Horton. You've squeezed your last dollar out of Laurel."

The lawyer's eyes burned with a vicious light, "Indeed?" he said evenly. "And how did you find that out?"

"Oh, it was the managing editor of the *Sphere* who got on to you," said the newspaper man. "He smelled a rat when he found out that Laurel had come up here with you and this female impersonator." He indicated the yellow-robed Egyptian. "We've got a dozen men round this place, so take that into consideration before you shoot off that gun."

"You're in this alone," declared Horton. "That's nothing but a bluff. Now you tell the truth or I'll—" He lifted the weapon.

"Master," said the Egyptian, "if you would like the truth, I'll get it for you. Tell him to sit in Monsieur Laurel's chair."

For the first time in his life, Murphy knew stark fear. He would have been willing to face death a hundred times before submitting to the influence of this Oriental magician. His imagination worked swiftly. He didn't know much about hypnotism, but for that very reason he was the more terrified. A few passes of the hypnotist's hands and he would babble all the facts; then, when they'd learned all they cared to, they would knock him on the head.

"Get over into that chair," commanded Horton. Death looked out of the muzzle of his revolver.

Murphy wanted to tell the man to shoot, but he weakened. Slowly, he moved to the chair. Perhaps he could not be hypnotized, after all.

He had heard that only certain types could be influenced. Of course! Ruth Laurel had been immune or she would not have objected to marrying Horton. Still, he was enfeebled by malaria.—Pshaw! His mind, at least, was as good as ever.

He seated himself in the chair. It had high arms and a high, winged back. He dropped his hands beside him. He heard the Egyptian approaching softly behind him. Suddenly he felt a sharp jab on the back of his upper right arm. Instantly he guessed what had happened. The Egyptian had used a hypodermic needle on him—probably some strange Arab drug that would weaken his will, his resistance to hypnosis.

"Look at me!" commanded the Egyptian, coming around in front of him.

Murphy shut his eyes. God, he couldn't keep them closed! Already the drug was taking effect. It seemed almost as though he was compelled to open his eyes, and slowly he did so. The terrible face of the Oriental was very close to his. His eyes seemed to be growing bigger; they were as big as saucers. Murphy was getting dizzy. He was going to cave in.

He slumped in his chair, and his right hand crept behind him. Horton was standing ten feet away, at the right, a grin on his face. It had to be done immediately or not at all. Murphy's fingers touched the little weapon in his hip pocket, drew it forth, slipped the catch.— He was almost gone! The eyes of the man before him were like two great, rapidly revolving wheels in multi-color.

Crack! A bullet struck the hypnotist full in the chest.

Crack! A second shot felled Horton before he could even lift his revolver. The two men dropped to the floor almost simultaneously; and instantly, with the collapse of the Egyptian, the fog in Murphy's brain cleared. A few seconds more and he would have been unable to act. The last desperate spasm of a powerful will had enabled him to save his soul, as well as his body.

He was out of his chair, leaping over the huge body of the hypnotist, and bending over Horton. The man was bleeding from a wound just above the heart, and he wouldn't last long. He mumbled a curse and lost consciousness as Murphy touched him. The reporter picked up the other's revolver and thrust it into his pocket.

A WOMAN'S shrill scream was heard from one of the rooms on the balcony. There came the bang of a door thrust open behind Murphy, and as he whirled, a bullet whined past his head. He fired a fraction of a second later; and a man in livery, standing in the doorway, went down with a bullet between the eyes. Murphy thanked his stars he'd learned to shoot straight in that Central American rebel army.

He leaped to the telephone. "Emergency!" he called when the operator answered. "Mr. Laurel's camp is being attacked by a band of criminals.—Send help!" Then he sped across the room, touched the switch at the bottom of the stairs, which plunged the big living room into darkness, sped up the stairs and stationed himself upon the balcony. Evidently Laurel's sister was having hysterics in a room close by. There was no sound from Laurel. Doubtless he was fast in a hypnotic sleep.

Voices could be heard outside the house.—But Murphy knew that it would be at least an hour before he could expect help from outside, perhaps two hours. Could he hold the fort? That depended upon how many gunmen remained, and what they would do without their leader.

Five minutes ticked slowly past. He heard the heavy front door open, and footsteps in the hall. Suddenly the lights flashed on, and three men stood in the entrance to the living room. Two of them had shot guns, the third had a revolver in his hand.

Murphy lay flat upon the floor of the balcony at the head of the stairs, watching them through the railing. He saw them stiffen at the sight of the body on the floor, and then one of them stepped over it into the room.

"They're dead!" the man exclaimed. "Somebody's killed Horton and the Turk!"

"I see him!" cried one of the men with shot guns, and he made to lift his weapon to his shoulder.

Spat-spat-spat! went Murphy's automatic. The man with the gun dropped without a sound; the second gunman clapped his hand to his right shoulder, and dropped his weapon; and the man who had stepped into the room leaped over two bodies and vanished, followed by the one who was wounded.

Murphy waited like a crouching panther. Four dead men, and he didn't have a scratch! He felt his luck was too good. How much longer would it last? How many more men were there, and what would be their next move?

A couple of minutes later he heard the starter of a motor car, and then the roar of a departing machine. Had they gone to get help at the gate, or had they taken flight? Or was it some trick to bring him down into the lighted room, so that they could pot him through the window?

All was still in the house. The woman with hysterics now made no sound. She had probably fainted. Time passed.

A second motor car started and departed. Half an hour went by; three-quarters of an hour. It certainly looked as though the whole crew had taken to flight. That would have been the natural thing to do, with their leader dead, with the supposed murder of Stevens on their shoulders, and with at least one straight-shooting opponent (who had already killed four men) to face.

Nevertheless, the reporter remained on his stomach at the top of the stairs, and when he heard an automobile drive noisily up he held his reloaded automatic ready.

The front door opened. There was heavy tramping in the hall, and then half a dozen armed men surged into the room. Murphy took aim, but dropped his weapon when he saw the silver star upon the breast of the leader.—This was a sheriff and his posse.

"Nothing for you boys to do now," he called. "We cleaned them all up by ourselves."

"Come down and give an account of yourselves," commanded the sheriff.

Murphy descended the stairs. It came upon him that he was going to be in a serious situation if Mr. Laurel, upon awakening, could not be made to realize what had been happening to him. Two murdered guests, two dead servants, and a killer who had no witnesses to justify his violence. Ah—Ruth Laurel and Frank Stevens!

"Mr. Laurel has been imprisoned here by this, shyster lawyer, whose name is Horton. That brute over there in the yellow gown is a hypnotist and had Mr. Laurel under his control; and a gang of New York gunmen were posing as servants," he said rapidly. "Miss Laurel and her father's secretary were hiding outside, near the lake, while I made an attempt to rescue her father.—I killed these men in self-defense."

"You did, did you!" said the sheriff grimly. "You hear that, men?" He turned to his whiskered crew. "Watch this fellow.—Where is Mr. Laurel?" he demanded, turning back to Murphy.

"Upstairs in his room, in a hypnotic sleep. You'll endanger his life if you wake him before morning. Miss Laurel will satisfy you about everything, and I'll take you right to her."

"Who are you, anyway?—Mean to say you took on this gang single-handed?"

"'All alone, sheriff."

"Fishy!" said the sheriff. "Handcuff this fellow, just for safety, and take away his gun. Don't wake up Mr. Laurel, but grab anybody else you find round here. Now, Mister Murphy, show us where Miss Laurel is supposed to be hiding."

HALF an hour later, Addison Dexter Murphy, free from handcuffs and suspicion, picked up the telephone in the living room of the big cabin, from which four dead men had just been removed, and called long distance.

"Give me the managing editor of the New York *Sphere*," he remarked. He glanced at his watch. It was eleven forty-five.

He waited five minutes impatiently.

"That you, Mr. Palmer?—Murphy talking. Clear off your front page. This isn't the story you sent me after, but it's ten times as good. Listen."

"**WHAT** can I do for you, Mr. Murphy?" asked Herbert Laurel, several days later.

"Not a thing, sir," replied the reporter. "I've a steady job, and I don't need a thing in the world."

"You saved my life and my fortune, my boy. You saved my daughter from an abominable marriage—"

"Is she going to marry Frank Stevens?"

"My secretary?—I should say not."

"Then that's what you can do for me; let her marry him. Stevens is a good guy, with plenty of nerve, and they love each other. If I've saved you a few millions, that's the way you can repay me," said Murphy earnestly.

The millionaire stared at him, astonished. "You're a remarkable man!" he exclaimed. "If Ruth wants Stevens, I won't oppose the match, though I had other ideas for her."

"Horton?" replied Murphy with a grin.

"You win," stated Laurel. "But I want to do something for you.—Money. A lot of money!"

"That wouldn't be doing anything for me," said Murphy. "I'm a vagabond, sir; a tramp newspaper man. I'd go crazy if I had money."

"I'll fix an annuity upon you."

"No, sir. I'd never do another stitch of work for the rest of my life."

"Well, what can I do for you?"

Murphy grinned. "When I'm fired from the *Sphere,* as I'll surely be, sooner or later, you can loan me a few hundred dollars until I get another job.—But you'll have to let me pay you back. That would be the best thing you could do for me."

"You can draw on me for any amount at any time!" said Laurel.

"Well," said Murphy, rising, "you might tell Ruth that she'll have to propose to that guy; and tell her I won't be able to attend her wedding, because as a small boy I promised my mother I'd never wear a high hat."

Laurel smiled. "Young man, I suppose you know that you're a damn fool!"

"Gosh!" said Murphy in shocked surprise. "I thought that was my secret."

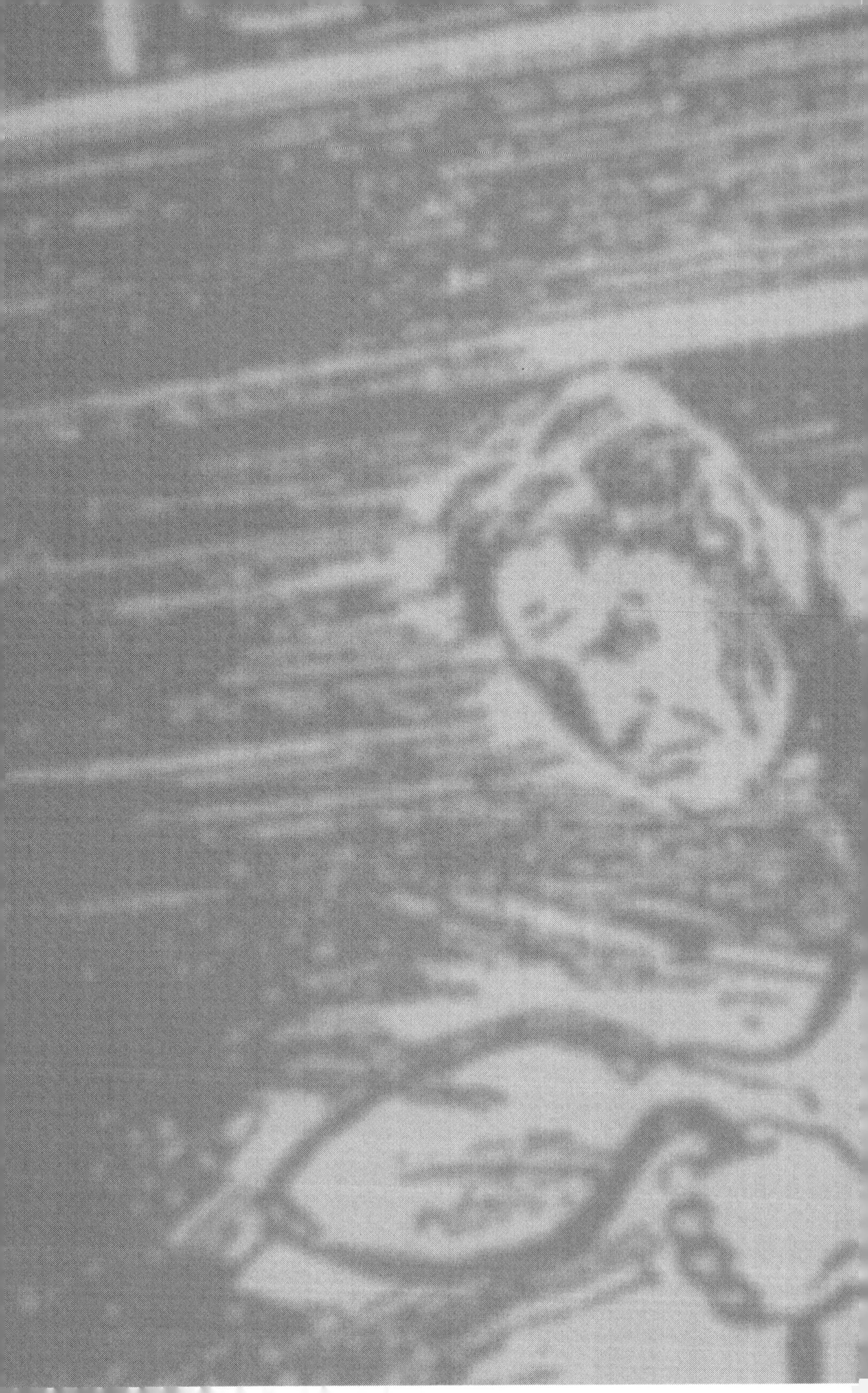

ALIAS MR. SMITH

THE RAMBLER'S BOSS SAID THERE'D BEEN NO HOT NEWS IN TOWN FOR MONTHS. SO WITH A SLAB OF WOOD FROM HONOLULU AND THE HELP OF A MAN NAMED SMITH, THAT ROAMING NEWSHOUND COOKED UP MYSTERY ON HIS OWN—PROVED THAT EVEN MURDER CAN BE PLUCKED OUT OF THE AIR.

CHAPTER ONE

MURDER FROM THE FILES

IT WAS big Tom Gorman—for a quarter of a century city editor of The Boston *Sphere*—who was speaking. "Rambler," he said, "you're obsolete."

"But not extinct," qualified Addison Francis Murphy.

"Practically. Newspapers can't be bothered with tramp reporters."

"No? How's your circulation?"

"Rotten," confessed the city editor. "I'm sorry for you, Rambler. You worked for me years ago. I know you're a live wire but you burn out. I'm firing—not hiring. There's no news in this town anyway."

"You're burned out, yourself," replied the vagabond journalist. "A good murder mystery would put fifty thousand on your circulation and pep up your advertisers. I'll get you one."

There was a flicker of interest in the blue eyes of the editor but he laughed contemptuously. "Out of the air, eh? We haven't had a big murder story for six months."

"I bet you've had ten and were too dumb to recognize them. Give me fifty dollars advance and a seventy-five dollar tab, if I make good, and I'll build up your circulation."

"I'm afraid you'd go out and commit the murder yourself," replied Gorman gravely. "You look desperate."

"I am but I'll find the murder story in your files. How about it?"

The big fellow laughed. "You bring back the good old days," he said." How old are you, Murphy?"

"Thirty-two."

"Well, you're a specimen of an almost extinct species. I'll take a chance on you." He reached for his order book.

"I want a shave, a new suit of clothes, new underwear, a square meal and a night's sleep. Tomorrow, I'll dig up the story."

"Down and out, eh? Well, I'll charge it up to charity."

Murphy was not offended. "Charge it to what you like," he retorted. "Give me an order on the cashier."

AT TEN next morning, Addison Francis Murphy entered the city room, nodded to the city editor and passed on into the "morgue" where the files were kept. Two hours later he came out, pulled a chair up to Gorman's desk and laid a sheet of yellow copy paper covered with notes in front of his benefactor.

"The mystery," he said curtly.

Gorman scowled at the almost illegible script. "Wasted my money," he ejaculated in disgust. "You're a swindler and you'd better beat it before you get the boot. The woman named her murderer with her dying breath. He's in jail awaiting trial and will be convicted without the jury leaving the courtroom."

"She didn't know she

He went over the stern—up to his waist in water.

was dying," declared Murphy. "The wound was not thought to be fatal. The doctors were surprised when she croaked. Probably the boy had jilted her and she accused him for revenge."

"Bah! The doorman and the elevator man saw him enter. He left after the shot was heard. She ought to know who shot her. How the heck can you make a mystery out of that?"

Murphy grinned. His grin was a bit twisted but it was attractive. "Got to. It was the only possibility in the files for six months back. I'm going out on the story."

"You can go to the devil," suggested Tom Gorman. "I'll be called on the carpet for giving fifty dollars to a rambling wreck."

"I may need a few days to get it started. And don't forget I'm on salary at seventy-five per. See you later, boss."

Addison Francis Murphy was a tall, loose-jointed man with a long narrow face, a square chin, and gray eyes, set far apart, surrounded by laugh wrinkles. There were deep lines on either side of the mouth. But the ready-to-wear suit he had purchased that morning fitted him very well. He was wearing a clean shirt for the first time in a week and he had eaten heartily at dinner and breakfast, and slept soundly. While he was homely and his black hair was unshorn, he didn't look as much like a bum as he had the night before, when he had dropped in upon The Journal city editor directly after a long journey in a boxcar. He was appropriately nicknamed "Rambler."

Standing in Newspaper Row he consulted his notes and walked briskly up to Tremont Street. There he entered the Tremont Building and presented himself at the office of John Bryce who was counsel for Quentin Robbins, indicted and awaiting trial for the murder of Dolores Vanini.

MR. BRYCE was a young lawyer who realized the advantage of getting his name in the newspapers so he admitted the representative of The Boston Journal immediately.

"I don't remember meeting you before, Mr. Murphy," he said with what the reporter recognized as a Harvard accent.

"I've just joined the staff, Mr. Bryce. Our city editor thinks there is more in the Vanini murder case than has come out; that, despite the dying girl's accusation, Robbins may be innocent."

Mr. Bryce crossed his knees. His trousers were newly pressed and he wore black spats. He drew a gold cigarette case from his pocket, offered Murphy a weed which was gratefully accepted and lighted one himself. He had a prominent nose, small blue eyes and a struggling blond mustache.

"I have to believe my client is innocent," he said thoughtfully, "but he admits having called on the woman about the time of the shooting and there is her dying statement. Frankly, I don't think I can save him."

"Who is he, anyway? I'm a stranger in town, you know."

"Robbins is a painter. He had a studio in the Fenway Arms. No money to speak of. His paintings seem to be worthless. He is about twenty-seven years old and came to Boston after two years in Paris."

"I understand he had an affair with Miss Vanini."

"He says he didn't. They were engaged to be married but she broke it off."

"Well, who was she?"

"An Italian girl. Artists' model. It was in the papers at the time. Lots of pictures."

"I've been over the files. Could I have a chat with Robbins?"

"No. He won't see anybody."

"How about the other woman?"

"What makes you think—"

"There's always another woman."

Murphy was gazing shrewdly at the lawyer and realized that his guess was correct, but Bryce removed his cigarette, gazed at it fixedly and said, after slight hesitation: "So far as is known, no other woman is involved."

"Were you appointed to defend him by the court?"

"Well—no."

"Thought you said he had no money."

Bryce smiled. "None to speak of. Naturally he wished to engage a lawyer and I accepted what he could pay."

"Mr. Bryce, this client of yours is going to the chair unless I can prove him innocent. I'm tackling a case which is cold. It is to your interest as well as my own that you help me. Who's the girl?"

Mr. Bryce met his gaze. "There is no girl," he stated too firmly.

Murphy rose. "O.K.," he said briskly. "Good morning."

HALF an hour later he was at the Fenway Arms studio in conference with the superintendent.

"Has the studio of Quentin Robbins been rented?" he demanded.

"It has," said the superintendent.

"What became of his furniture and paintings?"

"He didn't have anything but a cot bed and a couple of broken chairs," replied the superintendent. "I threw them out. A man came with an order for the pictures and I delivered them."

"Know him?"

"Yes. He's an expressman named Finch. Has an office on Massachusetts Avenue near Boylston."

"Who wrote the order?"

"Mr. Robbins himself."

Murphy thanked him and departed. Ten minutes later he entered the express office and found a stupid-looking man in shirtsleeves behind a battered and littered roll-top.

"Detective Murphy from headquarters," the reporter said importantly. "A few weeks ago, Mr. Finch, you collected paintings from the studio of Quentin Robbins."

"The murderer? Yeah, that's right."

"Robbins now claims he didn't write that order. How about it?"

Mr. Finch looked perturbed. "Do I know his writing?" he demanded. "It's up to the superintendent of the building. He took it and gave me the paintings."

"To whom did you deliver them?"

"Well," drawled Finch, "I wasn't supposed to say but I don't want to get into trouble. I got double pay for keeping my mouth shut and times are hard. I'll look up the address."

The tramp reporter's heart was singing. There was a mystery. His hunch was going to be justified. It wasn't a dead open-and-shut case.

As a matter of fact he had found more promising-looking crimes in the files, but he had chosen this because it appeared to be so obvious the police had the murderer that the newspapers had dropped the case after the usual flash. Any good reporter would have set to work as Murphy had done but the dying statement of the victim had killed the story from a newspaper angle.

Finch had found a certain page in his order book and his finger was running down the page. "I delivered them to Miss Phyllis May who lives in Brighton Place Road in Brookline," he said finally. "Don't tell her I told you."

"Rely on me," replied Murphy with a grin.

Brighton Place Road he knew to be one of the most exclusive streets in exclusive Brookline, the richest town in America. May was a Blue Book name. Already he had justified himself for wangling a fifty-dollar advance out of Tom Gorman.

THERE was a high green hedge at 57 Brighton Place Road, and a white flagged path leading up to a very large red brick residence in Colonial style which was set back a hundred and fifty feet from the street. Murphy pushed open the gate and walked up the path and rang the doorbell. When an authentic British butler opened it, the gray eyes of the investigator were gleaming.

"Is Miss Phyllis May at home?" he asked.

"Who is calling, please?" demanded the functionary.

"A man from the office of Mr. Bryce."

Murphy was certain that the guardian of the paintings was the paymaster of the lawyer. However he might be all wrong and he waited anxiously. But the butler was coming back. He looked benign.

"Please come in, sir," he invited. And coming down the stairs was a dryad in a blue crepe dress with eyes like purple patches of infinity, a mouth of sanguine curves, a dot of a nose, a skin of pink satin; a creature who was slight, slender, graceful and delectable.

While Mr. Murphy admired beautiful women, he was supremely conscious that he had no charm for them. During his checkered career, a few had made advances which anybody but a person as modest as the reporter might have considered encouraging, but he always suspected their motive. As he gazed now at this bright-haired, gracious wisp of femininity, he was thinking that her photographs would lift the tone of the front page of The Boston *Sphere*.

"How do you do," she said sweetly. "Come into this room, please." She led him into a morning room as charming as herself, closed the door, then turned to him eagerly, clasped her hands nervously and cried: "Oh, I hope you have good news!"

"I'm a newspaper reporter," he confessed with some embarrassment.

She turned white. "But you said—" she stammered.

"Bryce didn't tell me. I figured it out."

"Well, I have nothing to say," she declared with dignity. "It was wrong of you—"

"Listen, Miss May. Robbins is going to be electrocuted. For God's sake don't faint!" For the girl had staggered. "Bryce can't do a thing for him. I'm your only hope. I don't think he did it."

Miss May sank into a chair which happily was at hand and her eyes grew brighter. "Of course he didn't do it," she declared. "They can't convict an innocent man, can they?"

"It's been done. This lawyer is a fool and Robbins is another. The police have the victim's dying accusation and that's all they need to convict him. Why doesn't Robbins open up? Why does he refuse to see anybody? What's your connection with him and do you know why this girl accused him?"

"So many questions," she murmured. "Are you going to print what I say?"

"Maybe," he said truthfully. "I'm out to free Robbins. If you think more of keeping your name out of it—"

"I don't give a darn about keeping my name out of it. It's Quentin who won't let me see him or do anything for him."

"You're in love with him, aren't you?" he demanded.

"I am and I'm not ashamed of it," she said bravely.

MURPHY was pleased with her frankness. "Good girl," he said. "Now listen. My interest is getting a big story for my paper. If I can find the murderer, I've got it. And that sets Quentin free. I don't know him from Adam but I'll work just as hard as if he were my brother. Get me?"

She smiled. "I get you. I like you. What's your name?"

"Addison Francis Murphy."

"I thought you were Irish. How can I help you?"

"How long have you known Robbins?"

"I met him at a party about eight months ago."

"Know anything about his life in Paris?"

"Only that he studied there two years."

"I don't suppose he would tell you about any trouble he had had in the past—with women."

"I'm sure he never did anything dishonorable. I can't understand why he went to see that miserable woman."

"You hired Bryce?" he demanded.

"Yes. Quentin has no money."

"You might have hired a good one."

She looked distressed. "He was the fifth lawyer I asked to defend Quentin. They all said the case was hopeless."

"Did you try to see him at the jail?"

"He sent a message to me that he would never forgive me if I went there or mentioned that I was interested in him."

"You just feel he is innocent. You don't know anything about it."

"I know he is not a murderer."

"You ever see the Vanini girl?"

"No. I never had heard of her."

"You're going to be a great help," he said sadly. "I would like to look at his paintings. You have them."

"Is that how you found out about me?"

He nodded. "Bryce wouldn't tell me I anything. I took it for granted that you had hired him."

The girl came to him and grasped his right arm with both hands. "You are very clever," she declared. "You are my first ray of hope. I know you'll save Quentin."

"Sure. Where are the paintings?"

"In the attic. I had them sent in a packing case. My father doesn't know anything about Quentin and me. I had them delivered on the housekeeper's day out. Hawkins, the butler is my friend."

"Let's go to the attic."

Aided by the butler who produced a hammer and chisel, Murphy opened the packing case in a large, unfurnished, well-lighted attic and removed fifteen or sixteen unframed oil paintings from the case, stood them against the walls of the room. They were vivid, weirdly colored pictures, mostly landscapes. Murphy gazed upon contented cows and herds of sheep, rivers and groups of trees, and sunsets over land and sea. There was one nude, a dark, magnificently formed young woman whose black hair was veiling her shoulders and who had a red, almost transparent veil, around her loins. She was standing on a rock with a purple ocean behind her.

"Who's that?" he demanded.

"Some model he had in Paris. Artists have to paint nudes you know."

"Humph," remarked Murphy. He had seen pictures of Dolores Vanini in the files and this was Dolores Vanini. He kept his knowledge to himself.

"Let's put them away," he said after couple of minutes. "Nail up the box, Hawkins. I've got to be going."

Miss May accompanied him downstairs.

"Now, Miss May, please give me the names of some of his friends."

"I don't know any. You see our friendship was rather clandestine. My father abhors artists. We met in quiet cafés and a few times I had dinner with him in his studio."

"What would your father do if he learned about your engagement to this man accused of murder?"

"Send me to California to my aunt's. If it wasn't for that I wouldn't care if my friendship for Quentin were blazoned in all the newspapers."

"I'll keep it out as long as I can," he said sincerely. "I'll let you know how things are going. Good-by, Miss May."

"I'm going upstairs to pray for your success," she said fervently. "I—I've been very unhappy."

CHAPTER TWO

BRIDGE FOR A KILLER

ON THE sidewalk, Murphy looked at his dollar wrist watch. It was twelve-forty-five. In less than three hours he had accomplished plenty. Now he had a personal as well as a professional interest in the Vanini case. He liked that little girl and wanted to make her happy.

Of course he had turned up nothing which affected the state's case against Robbins. On the contrary the D.A. would consider that he had uncovered a motive for the crime. Dolores had been the artist's model and probably his sweetheart. He had met a rich girl and jilted the Italian model. When she threatened to go to the fiancée and tell all, he had killed her. The prosecution could have found this out, perhaps it had, but the dying woman's statement needed no corroboration.

While the papers would be glad to drag Phyllis May into the case, it still lacked every element of a mystery.

Murphy took a street car to the apartment house on Newbury Street in which Dolores Vanini had been living. He was not in the least discouraged. As Gorman had declared, he was a vanishing type of newshound but he was neither a drunkard, a dopester nor a wastrel. He was just a young man who got tired of being in one place, and when the mood came upon him he threw up his job and moved on. Frequently he departed for no reason from jobs in which he had made good, and found it difficult to secure an opening in the new community in which necessity forced him to apply for work. Often he was hungry, dirty and without a place to sleep, but he didn't mind. And, when he landed on a newspaper, finally, he worked hard and competently until the mood to move came upon him once more. Just now he was in high spirits and full of enthusiasm.

The apartment house was of a better class than he had anticipated. While not a *de luxe* establishment, it was not cheap. The superintendent told him that Miss Vanini had paid a hundred dollars a month for a three-room furnished apartment. He said that she had lived there for two months, paid her rent promptly and was a most desirable tenant. The man talked freely because Murphy claimed to be from the district attorney's office.

"Robbins was a frequent visitor, I suppose," Murphy observed. "Must have been since you identified him."

"Never saw him before that night," replied the superintendent. "We identified him when they brought him up here. It was easy because he is a handsome, striking fellow; looks like a movie actor."

"What work did Miss Vanini do?"

"None, so far as I know."

"How did she pay her rent?"

"That was none of my business."

Murphy grinned significantly. "Whose name was on the checks she gave you?"

"She paid cash on the first of every month."

"Well, well. Did she have many men visitors?"

"Not so far as I know."

"Well, who took her out in the evening?"

"She always went out alone."

"How about women friends? Chummy with any of the tenants?"

"None of them knew her. She was very exclusive."

"Have you rented the apartment?"

"No."

"I'd like to look at it."

"Say, your people were all over it weeks ago."

"I haven't been. New evidence has come up. Got to investigate all over again. By the way, how about her personal effects?"

"They're packed in her trunks in storage waiting for somebody to claim them."

"No relatives showed up?"

"Nobody. The city had to bury her. She had a couple of hundred in cash so she didn't go to Potter's Field. The body is in a vault in case her family wants to claim it."

MURPHY went up to Apartment G-4. It was neatly furnished and ready for occupancy. As he did not expect to find anything there he was not disappointed. Clues would hardly lie around for four weeks.

The apartment was on a corner of the building at the rear on the fourth floor. The living-room windows looked out upon an open space but the two bedroom windows revealed that there was a tall apartment building directly opposite, and that there was a terrace upon the fourth floor of that building whose parapet was not more than six or seven feet away.

This terrace contained potted plants and porch furniture, including a Gloucester hammock, and was protected by a huge red-and-white awning. French doors gave access to the apartment.

"Pretty nice, eh?" Murphy commented to the superintendent. "I bet whoever lives there pays a sweet rent."

"It's one of our group of buildings," replied the official. "The rent of an apartment with terrace is a hundred and seventy-five furnished."

"If these curtains were up the tenant over there could have looked in and watched the murder."

"As Miss Vanini was in bed when she was killed, her curtains, naturally, would be down."

"She had a night dress on and a kimona, didn't she?"

"That's the way she was found."

"For a lady who was so careful, wasn't that a queer way to receive Robbins?"

"Listen, I have troubles enough without worrying about what clothes the tenants wear when they receive company."

"I suppose so. Who lives in that terrace apartment?"

"His name is Smith."

"Illuminating. Married?"

"No. He's a traveling man. Away from home a lot."

"I see. Take me over and let me have a look at his apartment."

The superintendent, a red-faced, bull-necked man who had a short temper and was already bored by this superfluous inquiry, turned nasty.

"Why should I?" he demanded. "And how do I know you're from the district attorney's office? This woman told your people who killed her and you've got him in the jug. I've been polite to you but I'm a busy man."

"O.K., brother. If you doubt who I am, call up the D.A. and ask him if Mr. Jackson wasn't sent up here to look around."

"Oh, I'll take your word for it. Why do you want to enter that apartment?"

"Just a notion."

"Well, wait."

He phoned over to the other building. "Is Mr. Smith at home in F-Four?" he demanded. "No? Well, take the pass-key and go up with a man I'm going to send over there."

"Much obliged," said the Rambler.

A YOUNG woman was behind the desk in the lobby of the other building when he entered. She accompanied him up to the fourth floor and opened the door and Murphy strolled into Mr. Smith's apartment.

It was much more expensively furnished than the Vanini apartment and much larger. It was the living-room which opened upon the terrace.

The reporter walked through the rooms and opened a bedroom closet.

"Here," exclaimed the girl. "You can't do that."

"I want to know what closet room there is, don't I?"

"Oh, is Mr. Smith going to move?"

"Why do you suppose I'm looking the place over?"

Murphy had observed several articles of female apparel hanging in the closet.

He moved into the kitchen, shiny and spic-and-span and pulled open a door at the further end.

"That's a storeroom," the girl at his elbow told him.

It was a room about twelve feet long by four, without a window, and it contained only a broken chair and a long polished board of reddish wood which the Rambler recognized as koa wood, and which was nearly two feet wide and about ten feet in length.

"Ah-ah!" ejaculated the investigator. "Do you know what that is?"

"Sure," she replied. "It's a Hawaiian surfboard. Mr. Smith brought it from Honolulu."

"You don't say."

His agile mind had already fitted it to the wild notion which had caused him to demand an inspection of the apartment. Here was an artists' model who did no work, never went out except alone, had no visitors and lived in an expensive apartment. And the nude female painted by Quentin Robbins was a vivid, passionate person—a type which craved male society.

Murphy would have wagered that the garments in the closet had belonged to Dolores Vanini and that she visited Mr. Smith by means of the surfboard which he had brought so thoughtfully from Honolulu, and which would afford safe passage from her chamber window to the comfortable terrace.

He walked out on the terrace again. There were no windows looking down upon it from the sides of the buildings but there were windows above whose view was cut off by the awning. Dolores would have been visible only while she was crossing the bridge.

As he returned from the terrace, the apartment door opened and the superintendent entered accompanied by a man. This was a tall, heavily built person with penetrating black eyes and blue jowls. He was almost foppishly dressed. He had big features, jet-black hair, dark skin and spats. He did not look like an American.

"This is Mr. Smith," said the superintendent. "He just came in and I told him a man from the district attorney's office was inspecting his apartment. He called up the D.A. and was told that nobody named Jackson worked down there and that nobody had been sent to look at the girl's apartment because the case was all in the bag."

The big man strode toward Murphy, "Who in hell are you?" he demanded.

"Name of Murphy. Reporter from The *Sphere*," replied the Rambler brazenly.

"You are, are you? What's The *Sphere* wasting its time on the Vanini case for? They've got the murderer."

"We have reason to believe that they are holding an innocent man," declared Murphy. We've reopened the case."

"Oh, you have, have you? Well, what are you doing in my apartment? Eh?"

"I was thinking of renting one like it. I think the terrace idea is swell." replied Murphy insolently.

"I don't believe he is a reporter," asserted the superintendent. "I'll call a cop."

Murphy laughed. "Go to it," he invited. "Now, Mr. Smith, what were your relations with Dolores Vanini?"

The man's face turned purple. He ripped out an oath in a language unknown to Murphy, and plunged at him, his big right fist swinging.

Addison Francis Murphy, who was a first-class fighting man himself, deftly ducked the swing, and drove a straight right at the button.

Smith staggered back and his hand went to his hip pocket. The superintendent grasped his arm as a revolver came into view.

"For God's sake, Mr. Smith," he pleaded. "None of that. You get out of here, you—"

But Murphy, who was as discreet as he was audacious, was already at the door. He made the staircase in six strides and went down three steps at a time. He was jubilant.

PROGRESS. Lots of progress! Mystery coming up. Smith's insane rage was a dead give-away. He had had relations with Dolores Vanini. If he hadn't, he would have been astonished instead of furious at the insinuation. And he carried a gun and was capable of using it in a burst of passion. And his name was not Smith. He was some kind of foreigner.

The next thing was to get a line on Smith, find out who he really was. He must have lots of money for he was keeping the Vanini woman and maintaining an expensive hideaway himself. Which meant that he had excellent reason for not wishing his connection with Dolores known.

In the street the reporter's enthusiasm cooled a trifle. In the face of what he had learned, was the dead woman's statement in which she named Quentin Robbins as the man who had shot her. He had to get round that somehow.

AN HOUR later he was closeted with Gorman, who began by

jeering at him. "Hello, Rambler," the city editor remarked. "Made any progress?"

"What do you think of this? If I tell you something you know, stop me. Quentin Robbins is engaged to a beautiful society girl who has engaged Bryce to defend him. Know that?"

"No," confessed Gorman.

"Vanini was having an affair with a man named Smith who lived in an apartment directly behind hers, with a terrace which came within seven or eight feet of her bedroom windows. She used to crawl out to meet him on a Hawaiian surfboard. Comment on that."

"Interesting," said Gorman. "Give me the girl's name and write a story. We may have her picture in the 'morgue.'"

"Nix. I'm not writing anything till I have enough to carry you along for a week. Smith is an alias. The man is not an Anglo-Saxon, but a Latin. He has lots of money and some good reason for managing an intrigue by means of a Hawaiian surfboard."

The phone on Gorman's desk rang and he picked up the receiver. "Yes," he said. "Oh, hello, Mr. Rothstein… Yes, we have a man working on the Vanini case… Well, we're not so sure that Robbins killed her… Yes?… Well, I'll send the reporter down to see you. Name of Murphy… Tonight at eight."

He hung up, swung round in his chair and beamed upon Addison Francis. "You're stirring up something," he said. "Rambler, I know when I'm wrong. You've earned your fifty already. This Rothstein who called up is a big criminal lawyer here in town. He is in with the underworld and has a drag in politics. He wants to have a talk with you at his house at eight o'clock. Lives in Newton—Bellaire Street. I'll look the number up for you."

"How did he learn I was on the case?"

"Didn't say."

"Well, Bryce wasn't apt to tell him, so it must have been my friend Smith."

"Why not break the society-girl story tomorrow?"

"Whose mystery is this?"

Gorman grinned. "O.K.," he replied. "You want to follow up."

"I'm going to get something big," said Murphy confidently. "I told you the thing was too complete. The police took the confession, grabbed the boy, had him identified as visiting the dame and thought they had all they needed. I haven't told you half what I've picked up today. At this rate we can begin to shake up the town in a couple of days. Can I have twenty bucks for expenses?"

"I suppose so," sighed the city editor. "You tramps are all alike. I bet you haven't busted a thin dime."

"I'm expecting to blow in some dough tonight," replied Murphy untruthfully. From long experience on newspapers, the Rambler believed in getting advances whenever possible.

CHAPTER THREE

FIVE-GRAND ANTE

A LUMBERING trolley car with two flat wheels transported the inquiring reporter out to Newton and the conductor let him off at Crampton Street with the information that Bellaire opened on the right from Crampton two blocks down.

It was a region of fine red brick Colonial-type homes set in large gardens and protected from the street by fine shade trees. Mr. Rothstein, the lawyer, occupied Number 51, which was even larger and more substantial than its neighbors.

A manservant answered the doorbell and stated, upon learning the visitor's name, that Mr. Rothstein was expecting him in the library. This proved to be an imposing room, its walls lined with shelves filled with yellow, leather-bound law books, its furniture done in red leather.

A small, dark, keen-eyed man with a sharp, pointed chin and a hooked nose was standing before the open fire gazing reflectively into flames unnecessary upon a summer evening. He turned and gave the visitor a penetrating look.

"Mr. Murphy," he remarked. "Glad to see you. Sit down. Cigarette?"

"Thanks."

Rothstein pointed an arm and finger at him. "Now, let's get to the point," he declaimed. "You blew into town a couple of days ago looking for a newspaper job. You bunked Tom Gorman into giving you some cash and the promise of a berth in return for a big story."

"I don't deny it, Mr. Rothstein."

"You're what they call a tramp reporter, eh?"

"Well, I ramble."

"Boston doesn't look any better to you than any other town."

"Worse than most, to be frank."

"How would you like a job in San Francisco and the money to get there?"

Addison Murphy's bushy eyebrows went up. "You offering it to me?"

"Yes, I'm making you an offer."

He shook his head. "Sick of the West," he stated. "Boston will suit me for a few months."

"But you won't suit Boston. I'll give you five hundred dollars to get out of town."

Murphy grinned. "Now that's good of you, Mr. Rothstein. You don't look like a philanthropist, which makes it even nicer of you."

"I'm no philanthropist. I'm making a deal with you."

"In that case you'll have to raise the ante."

"A thousand bucks."

"Not interested."

"Five thousand?" he said without hesitation.

"Now you have awakened my curiosity. You called up Gorman to ask if he was opening up the Vanini murder case. He told you I was working on it. Why is it worth five thousand to get me to knock off work?"

ROTHSTEIN pulled up a chair and sat down opposite the reporter. "You're a shrewd fellow," he said. "I might as well be frank. Dolores Vanini was a nobody. So is Quentin Robbins. She named him as her murderer and her statement is supported by witnesses who prove that he had the opportunity. He will be tried, convicted and executed. The papers gave the yarn as big a play as it warranted and then dropped it. There is no doubt whatever of the man's guilt."

"I can't find any motive for it."

"It will be brought out in the trial. She was two-timing him and he discovered it. Jealousy—best motive in the world. That story is all washed up, Murphy. You can't get anything which will justify The *Sphere* in reopening it. So you won't land on the staff of the paper and in a few days you'll probably have to get out of town on a freight car the way you arrived."

"But you will make me a present of five thousand dollars so I can depart on a Pullman," remarked the reporter. "Damn sweet of you, I call it."

"I told you I was no philanthropist. A client of mine, a married man with a lovely wife and several fine children was mixed up with this Vanini woman. He will be ruined if his name is brought into it. Get me?"

"Yep. Robbins' lawyer will ruin him at the trial even if I accept your munificent offer."

"No. Robbins doesn't know the identity of the woman's lover."

"I see."

"Five thousand is a lot of money."

"I never had more than five hundred at one time in my life, I refuse your offer."

"You do? You intend to break up a happy home, to disgrace innocent children—"

No, Mr. Rothstein. I'm investigating a murder case. If I become convinced that Robbins killed this woman, I won't spring any kind of a story. My job is to unearth a mystery. If I find that Robbins did not kill her, why I'm going to run down the real murderer."

"Robbins is guilty as hell."

"Then your client doesn't have to worry about me."

"Why not take the five grand I've offered you now? Otherwise you won't even get a job."

"I'm an old-fashioned newspaperman, Mr. Rothstein," replied the other. "My kind of reporters have no use for money and can't be bribed. That all you have to say to me?"

"Only that you're a damn fool," said Rothstein angrily. "Good night."

Murphy rose and nodded and moved toward the door. The lawyer followed him.

"Won't change your mind?" he demanded. "Cash in hand."

"No, thanks."

"Well, sorry to have brought you all the way out here. It's a long walk to the street car. I'd send you down in my bus but my wife is using it."

"I've done a lot of walking in my time, Mr. Rothstein."

"Well, good night."

He slammed the door. Murphy moved down the path to the street. Passing the garage he observed—nothing escaped him—that the doors were only partly closed and two fine motor cars stood within. He grinned. Rothstein didn't care if he got sore feet. He walked down to the corner of Crampton Street and turned left toward Commonwealth Avenue and he observed, a hundred yards ahead, a motor car parked at the curb with its tail-light out. Newton requires parking lights on cars left in the street.

THERE was a wide field on this side of the street so the proprietor of the parked car could not be visiting. The Rambler's step slackened and his eye narrowed while his ears were alert. Very faintly he heard a low hum. The engine was running. Murphy glanced back. Across the field he could see Rothstein's residence on the cross street and, at that moment, a red light gleamed in one of the front windows. It went out, appeared again—and a third time.

That Rothstein was signaling to someone in the parked car the reporter was certain. Arrangements had been made that, if bribery failed, the reporter would be put on the spot. Tom Gorman had stated that the lawyer was in with the underworld.

Murphy drew forth a package of cigarettes, took one and lighted it, which permitted him a second's delay without awakening suspicion. Rothstein had made the appointment through the city editor of The *Sphere;* thus Murphy's visit was known and the lawyer was too astute to permit him to be shot down a short distance from his residence. The game must be to nab him as he walked past the car, drag him into the machine, ride him to some slum or to the waterfront of Boston or East Boston or Charlestown, put a few slugs into him and leave him in a place where a vagabond reporter might well have been rambling.

That meant that a machine gun was not at this instant trained on him from the back window of the machine. If it were, he was doomed.

He tossed away the match and, like a bounding gazelle, rushed across the street, leaped a two-foot hedge and tore across a big lawn. He raced past a stately Colonial house and over a five-foot stone wall at the rear into the yard of a residence of a street running parallel to Crampton. And, as he ran, he heard the roar of a motor suddenly given plenty of gas, and the sound of a car being rapidly driven down Crampton Street.

He had guessed right. Gunmen had been laying for him and watching Rothstein's for the signal to kill or let him pass. They had seen him approaching and had been baffled when he darted away.

However he was far from being safe. That car would patrol the neighborhood, swinging up one street and down another at top speed. They had had a look at him and they would recognize the pedestrian when he ventured to walk toward Commonwealth Avenue on any street leading to it.

In fact, as he passed the big home in the garden of which he had entered, a motor car was coming swiftly up the street and a spotlight was sweeping the sidewalk. Murphy ducked down behind a car which stood in the driveway and the death car tore past. But it would be back. It could cover the entire neighborhood in a few minutes and dash along Commonwealth Avenue while its occupants scrutinized persons waiting at white posts for a trolley car.

He rose, moved along the side of the car, a coupé, and thrust his hand through the open window. His fingers touched a bunch of keys in a leather case, and one of the keys was in a lock. Murphy jumped into the car, stepped on the starter, threw in the gears and rolled down the driveway into the street. He turned toward Commonwealth Avenue and, as he did so, he heard a door open and a man shouting—the car owner who hadn't thought it necessary to lock his motor.

Murphy chuckled and drove leisurely toward Commonwealth Avenue. As he reached the intersection, a big car with headlights and spotlight blazing, made a reckless left turn in front of him and sped up the side street. Again Murphy chuckled, turned his car in the direction of Auburndale and stepped hard on the gas. A couple of miles south he took a boulevard toward Waltham and drove along at sixty miles an hour through a wide-spreading residential section where traffic was slight.

From Waltham he drove to Cambridge, stopped his car in front of a drugstore. He took the registration card which he'd found in a pocket of the car into the store with him, and called up the owner from the pay station.

"Mr. Peter Yates?" he asked.

"Yes."

"Did you have a car stolen about half an hour ago?"

"You bet your life I did."

"You'll find it at the corner of Massachusetts Avenue and Holt Street, Cambridge. Much obliged."

He hung up on an owner who was incoherent with rage.

CHAPTER FOUR

THE MAN IN THE PEN

ON A trolley bound for Park Street Terminal, Boston, the Rambler considered the latest phase of the situation. It was evident that the Vanini case was dynamite. By a process of elimination only the man named Smith could be the client of Rothstein; therefore Smith and not Robbins was the slayer of Dolores Vanini.

He took no stock in Rothstein's statement that Smith only wished to keep out of the affair because of the effect of exposure upon his wife and children. A man with that motive might offer a bribe but he would not hire murderers. But the real killer of the Italian girl, who had the good fortune to have the crime fixed upon another in such a manner that conviction was certain, might be driven by self-preservation to take the most extreme steps to prevent further investigation.

Rothstein had been candid with the reporter up to a certain point, and had dared to be so because one of two things would happen; either Murphy would take the bribe and drop the investigation or he could be bumped off before he had a chance to report to his city editor. And Rothstein was sure that if Murphy were found dead in some dirty alley or in a waterfront dive, The *Sphere* would take no further interest in a murder case which had no news interest.

His visit of inspection to Smith's apartment had caused Smith to believe that the newspaperman had dangerous information in his possession. Not knowing that Murphy was groping blindly for a trail, he would assume that the reporter had a line on him before he dared intrude into the apartment.

Murphy saw clearly that Rothstein and Smith were now compelled to put him out of the way as quickly as possible. The escape of the reporter from the gunmen in the parked car was proof positive that he suspected a plot to murder him of which Rothstein was the instigator. He was pleasantly excited. Peril exhilarated this curious young man more than whisky; he was usually moved to sing when danger threatened. But now, being in a trolley car, he only hummed under his breath the refrain of that ribald ditty which begins: "*The old man came home just as drunk as he could be....*"

From Park Street he walked to the lodging house on Hancock where he had rented a room the previous night and paid a week in advance. He packed the suitcase which he had purchased in order to persuade a landlady that she could safely rent him a room—he had had no baggage when he dropped off the freight train in the Boston and Albany Yards—and left the place without giving notice.

A SUBWAY train took him to Charlestown and, in the shadow of the Bunker Hill Monument, he secured another room. After that he went into a pawnshop near the Navy Yard, purchased a thirty-eight caliber revolver and a supply of cartridges, then he did some telephoning.

He found the number of Phyllis May in the phone book, called it and asked for her. In a moment she was on the phone.

"Mr. Murphy," she exclaimed in low guarded tones, "have you news for me?"

"I'm positive your boy friend is innocent," he declared, "and I think I know the man who did it. You stop worrying, leave everything to me and get a good night's sleep."

"You—you're marvelous," she breathed. "Can't I see you and talk things over. I'm so excited!"

"Want to have lunch with me tomorrow?"

"I do. Of course I do."

He hesitated. "We can't be seen together. Come down to the Esmond on Hanover Street. It's a dump but the food's good and nobody will spot us there. Good-by."

His next call was the residence of attorney Bryce. The lawyer was not at home but could be reached at the Harvard Club. Mr. Bryce was inclined to be haughty when disturbed at his club so Murphy talked fast and to the point.

"I'm going to make you famous," he declared, "so snap out of it. Tomorrow morning I want you to see your client and tell him that he has to have a talk with me."

"I told you he would see nobody," replied the lawyer irascibly.

"Explain to him that I have found out about Miss May and that I'll publish in The *Sphere* that she is engaged to him, and accompany it with a four-column picture of her, if he doesn't agree to see me."

"You wouldn't do that," protested the horrified lawyer.

"In a minute I'd do it. That guy will fry if I don't save him, and you and he must play ball with me. Tell him I was offered five grand to drop this investigation today and refused it."

"Who offered you such a sum?"

"That's my business. You get taken into my confidence when you've shown you deserve it. Will you arrange that interview for me?"

"I'll try, Mr. Murphy," replied the lawyer in a very different tone. "Naturally I will cooperate with you. I wish to save my client."

"O.K. Make it in the afternoon. I'll call at your office at noon."

Murphy hung up, smiling with satisfaction, and found that he had time to witness the last show at a picture theater in Charlestown Square. It was a light comedy and very relaxing. After that he went to bed and slept soundly because he knew that nobody in Boston was apt to intrude upon his slumbers. It had been a very full day.

THE RAMBLER was sitting across from Phyllis May in the Hanover Street place. "You are a strange man, Mr. Murphy," declared the girl. "You admit being penniless but you refuse five thousand dollars and you don't seem concerned because these wretches are determined to kill you. And you are risking your life for a man you don't know. Why?"

"Answering your questions in order," he said with a broad smile, "I am a person of very simple tastes and owning more than fifty dollars at one time would bewilder me. I'm not worried about these thugs because I know how to take care of myself, and I'm staying on the job because I promised Tom Gorman a good murder story and because, if you like this egg, there must be something to him."

She reached across the table and touched his hand in an impulsive gesture. "You're like Don Quixote," she declared. "You're a most romantic person!"

"I'm a rambling wreck but I have a lot of fun. It was nice of you to meet me in this shoddy part of town. It was mostly for your sake. If this Rothstein finds you're interested, he is capable of blackmail."

"I have no money of my own," she said with a smile, "and I don't care who knows that I am in love with Quentin and want him set free."

"You're quite a girl. Just scribble a line to the boy friend that you have confidence in me and expect him to confide in me. I'm likely to need it."

"I'll do it now." She took a pencil from her purse, and wrote rapidly upon the back of an old envelope.

"I'm depending on Robbins to tip me to the identity of Smith," he told her. "I might spend a week trying to run him down and your fiancé might put me wise in a minute. I think he knows Smith. He might have caught Miss Vanini coming back from the other apartment on the surfboard."

"But you told me that the superintendent said he never went to see the woman. I so glad to hear that."

"We know he visited her one night and he might have called on her before—on some business, of course," he added because the girl looked distressed.

"Tell him not to think about me; that you're going to publish our engagement anyway. His life is at stake. Make him understand it."

"I'll try. I have a feeling that there are other reasons for his refusal to make any explanation. Don't look now—say something. In a minute I want you to size up a man three tables to your left. See if you know him."

SHE LAUGHED airily—a good actress, he thought—and presently glanced in the direction indicated. She saw a well-dressed blond man with a small blond mustache. He had a cup of coffee before him, a cigar between his fingers, and was gazing toward the opposite side of the café.

"I never saw him before," she said in a low tone.

"He came in directly behind you. He has been sitting where he could watch us, and he's been on the job every second once we began our lunch. Of course he may be interested in you as a beautiful girl but I can read faces pretty well and I think it is our meeting which interests him most."

"What can we do about it?"

"Nothing. I expect he will trail me when we leave. Did you tell anybody about me? Does anybody know you were coming down here to meet me?"

"No-o, well—yes."

"Who?"

"The girl who introduced me to Quentin. The only person who knows of our engagement. Her name is Gloria Knowlton. I was so excited I couldn't keep things entirely to myself."

"Who is she? School friend?"

"No. She's my manicure. She works for René in Copley Square. You see—well, Quentin was having his nails manicured one day and she introduced him to me. She only knew him as a customer, but naturally she was pleased that we fell in love and she hopes he won't be convicted."

"So it wasn't at a party that you met?"

"Well, I didn't know you as well yesterday as I do today," she answered shyly.

"Inasmuch as I haven't told anybody of our lunch date, if that is a spy over there, why you can thank Gloria for it. Will you promise me to supply her with no information whatever in the future?"

"I can't believe that Gloria—well, I promise," she said with heightened color.

"You leave now. I think he's going to trail me."

"But I haven't finished my coffee," she protested. "And I am enjoying our party."

"Finish your coffee. This is strictly business with me, Miss May."

She frowned and then laughed. "You are such an extraordinary young man," she remarked.

"I am middle-aged and battered," he said significantly.

"But not very middle-aged or much battered."

"Good afternoon, Miss May."

She made a moue and then beamed upon him. "You'll keep me informed?"

"And you'll keep your promise. Stay away from this manicure."

He rose and the girl shook hands and departed. The Rambler gazed after her admiringly. "Damn pretty kid," he said to himself. "Not very heavy up top. Now I wonder if she was trying to flirt with me. Guess not."

He ordered another pot of coffee, observing that the blond man made no effort to follow Miss May. After a cigarette, he paid his check, rose and, as he left the café, he noticed that the stranger was also departing. The restaurant was on the second floor of an old building and reached by a narrow staircase with a thick but musty carpet on it. As Murphy reached the foot of the stairs, the man was halfway down. When the reporter opened the front door and closed it behind him, he saw through the glass that the fellow was striding across the narrow hallway. He noted a taxi at the curb.

Murphy threw open the door, stepped back into the hall and almost collided with the blond man upon whose face was an expression of astonishment and consternation.

"You would, would you?" remarked the newspaperman and drove a wicked right at the point of the fellow's jaw. The victim had no chance to cover. The blow went home and the man went down and out. Murphy lit out of the building, leaped into the cab and ordered it to drive to Dock Square. At Dock Square he shifted to another cab which took him to the county jail.

ATTORNEY BRYCE was waiting for him in the sheriff's office and a deputy immediately departed to fetch the prisoner to a small private room which the sheriff had readily agreed to place at the disposal of the attorney.

"I was afraid we'd have to talk to him through the bars," remarked the reporter.

"He's only under indictment and the sheriff is a friend of mine. I expect to be present at this interview."

"Certainly. We've got to work together. Did he kick up a row about seeing me?"

"No. He said, if you had learned so much, he would like to have a talk with you."

"O.K.," called the deputy.

They found Quentin Robbins seated in a small bare room with handcuffs on his wrists. The deputy closed the door as he departed and locked it on the outside. The window was barred.

The prisoner was a young man of striking appearance. He had dark hair and eyes, a clear olive complexion, a straight nose and a mouth shaped like a Cupid's bow. His chin was negligible. The eyes were large but set too close together to please Murphy. He thought it was a weak, self-indulgent face.

"Glad to know you," the reporter said briskly. "I'm sure you didn't kill that woman so you don't have to protest your innocence."

Robbins smiled. His smile was waning; his teeth very white and so regular that they hardly seemed real.

"I'm very pleased to hear you say that," said the prisoner. His voice was very agreeable, finely modulated and musical. An artist, a handsome dog—no wonder the little May girl had fallen for him.

"We haven't much time," stated Murphy. "I've just come from Miss

May. She sent you this note."

Robbins glanced at it and handed it back. "Well?" he questioned.

"Why did Miss Vanini accuse you of shooting her?"

"I don't know."

"Why haven't you given your lawyer information which would help him. Do you want to fry?" demanded the Rambler.

"I don't want my fiancée dragged into this."

Murphy was watching him. He didn't believe him. "She's in," he said roughly. "I've seen a picture you painted of Vanini? When did you paint it?"

"A year ago in Paris."

"You were having an affair with her in Paris, weren't you?"

"We were friends," admitted Robbins.

"And the friendship continued when you came to Boston?"

"No? We split in Paris."

"She followed you to Boston though."

"She came here."

"And you resumed your friendship."

"No. I didn't know she was in Boston. I found out by accident a few days before the tragedy."

"You were afraid that she would break up your engagement with Miss May?"

"No," exclaimed the prisoner. "She didn't care anything about me. We were through, at least she was."

"So she jilted you. Is that it?"

Robbins nodded sullenly.

"As a matter of fact you were in love with her even after your engagement to this Brookline girl—"

"Look here. I fail to see what you are driving at," exclaimed Bryce. "We only have half an hour. Let me question him."

"You don't know anything about this case," retorted the reporter. "You were in love with her, Robbins?"

"No," said Robbins doggedly.

"Why did you go to see her that night?"

"Well I—wanted to know what she was doing."

"Did she ask you to call on her?"

"No-o."

"In fact she didn't know you were aware that she was in town. Is that right?"

"Well, I saw her dining at the Copley one night with a man. I followed them to her apartment house."

"And when did you call on her?"

"A few minutes after her escort went away."

"Did you have yourself announced?"

"No. I went up to the apartment. The elevator man told me which was her apartment."

"Well, what happened during your visit?"

"Nothing. She insisted she had no use for me. She ordered me out."

"As a matter of fact she was dressed for bed, wasn't she?"

"She came to the door with a kimona over her night dress."

"And when she ordered you out you departed at once."

"Well I—"

"You pleaded with her to take you on again, didn't you?"

THE MAN made an expressive gesture. "I lost my head. She always had an effect on me. I knew she hated me but—"

"Why did she hate you?"

"Well I—I can't answer that."

"What happened then?"

"She left me in the living room and went into the bedroom and closed the door. I followed her in."

"She had got into bed, hadn't she?"

"Yes, but she jumped out of the bed and pushed me toward the door. She said—well I saw it was no good and I left."

"Did you hear the shot fired?"

"No."

"Were you armed?"

"No."

"Ever carry a weapon?"

"No."

"And when you left the building what did you do?"

"I went to my studio."

"How did the police know that you were the visitor if you had never called on her before?"

"I don't know."

"You forget her dying statement," said the lawyer.

"That's right. What you've told us, Mr. Robbins, about clinches the case for the state. You had time to dispose of a weapon before you were arrested."

"You see? There was no use of my talking," Robbins replied sullenly. "I tell you I didn't kill her but if you publish my story, it will look as though I shot her because she wouldn't take me back."

"You would have jilted Miss May if she had taken you back, eh?"

"Damn it, I was out of my mind! The woman always made me lose my head. When I was arrested, I remembered that Phyllis would be involved and there didn't seem to be any use in making a defense. She said I shot her. Who would believe me?"

"Now we're getting somewhere. Why did she accuse you of shooting her?"

"I—I don't know," said the man slowly. He was staring at the ground.

"If she came here to break up your engagement, if you had jilted her, treated her abominably, she might have made the charge for revenge, especially as the wound in the breast was not supposed to be mortal."

"That must be your defense," declared Bryce. "In fact that's really the truth. "You have been lying to Mr. Murphy."

"I told him the truth," the man said doggedly.

"Why did she want to be revenged on you, then?" demanded Murphy.

"I tell you I don't know," said Robbins, whose distress was obvious.

"Look here—" began the lawyer.

"Later, Bryce," snapped the reporter. "This man who was dining with her the night before she was shot. Did you get a good look at him?"

"Yes. He was a big man. He looked like an Italian, heavy jaw, very dark, big chest. His dress shirt bulged."

"Did he go in with her that night?"

"No. He left her outside the building."

"Know anybody who answers to that description?" demanded Murphy of the lawyer.

"No. Sounds like a bootlegger. This is all beside the point."

"With whom did you study in Paris?" asked the reporter.

"Regnier on Montparnasse. What difference does it make?"

The door opened and the deputy entered. "Time's up, gentlemen," he said cheerfully. "Come along Robbins."

CHAPTER FIVE

SHANGHAI SET-UP

AS THE pair left the jail Bryce said: "Well, I may say I never listened to such an inconsequential line of questioning. I am tempted to throw up the case."

"Why? Because you don't think you'll win it?"

"Because my pledge as a lawyer is to so refuse to defend a guilty person and it is obvious, from his statement, that he is guilty as hell."

Murphy laughed. "Beg to differ," he answered. "Robbins didn't shoot the woman. Her confession was spite, revenge, see?"

"No. As an Italian she would be a devout Catholic. She wouldn't dare face the hereafter with a lie on her soul."

"Listen, brother, I've met as many atheists who were Italians as any other nationality, and furthermore she didn't think she was going to die."

"Well, you learned nothing helpful. He swears she had no reason to dislike him, to wish him punished for a crime he didn't commit."

"She had a reason and I've got to find out what it was. See you later." He leap into a cab and gave the driver Newbury Street as an address.

From a drugstore he phoned in to The *Sphere*.

"Tom," he said to the city editor, "send a cable to the Paris police and have them get a line on Quentin Robbins from Regnier, his teacher, who lived on Montparnasse?"

"Don't you know that cables are expensive?" replied the city editor.

"Also get the dope on Dolores Vanini, the model, from the same source," instructed the reporter. "I'll call up tomorrow for the reply. I'm on the lam, Tom. Have you heard from Rothstein?"

"Not a word?"

"Well, call him up and ask him if he knows my address. Say you haven't heard from me since last night."

"What happened at his house? Why in hell didn't you report?"

"Laugh this off. He offered me five grand to skip town, and, when I refused, tried to have me taken for a ride in a car parked a little way from his house. Don't mention that, please."

"I'll send the cable," cried Gorman enthusiastically. "Boy, go to it. You've got on to something big. Watch your step."

"Leave that to me."

"Now," said Murphy to himself as he hung up, "who in hell is Smith?"

After a moment's cogitation he produced a nickel, looked up the number of Jordan and Marsh, the largest department store in the city and put in a call.

"Connect me with the sporting-goods department," he requested.

"Hello, can I buy a Hawaiian surfboard in your store?" he demanded.

"Yes, certainly."

"I want a real one, made of koa wood."

"Oh," ejaculated the clerk. "Koa is rare and very expensive and we don't get boards of that material. We use hard pine in our factories."

"Any idea where I can get one of koa wood?"

"They might have a few at Pillow's. They specialize in sports stuff."

"Much obliged."

FIFTEEN minutes later the Rambler was talking to the manager of Pillow's exclusive sports shop.

"Hawaiian surfboards," the man informed him, "are too bulky to be exported much and koa wood is so expensive that it isn't used in their manufacture, any more—even in the islands. We have one in stock, though. Had it for years. It was brought here by a famous Hawaiian swimmer and surfboard rider who got hard up and sold it to us. It will cost you a hundred and fifty dollars. A lot of money for a plank, which is about all you can call the thing."

"I'd like to see it."

The manager walked with him to the Shore, Sand and Surf Department. "Jones," he said to the salesman, "dig out that koa-wood surfboard we have in stock. This gentleman would like to see it."

"It's sold, sir. Sold it a couple of months ago."

"I'm sorry," said the manager. "I didn't know it had finally been disposed of."

Murphy looked disappointed. "I had a special reason for wanting it," he stated. "I wonder if the fellow who bought it would sell. He's probably sick of it by now."

"Who bought it? Look it up, please," requested the manager.

"Don't have to. I sold it to John Moroni, the president of the Calabria-Sicilian Bank. He's rich as mud and about runs the Italian colony so I don't think he needs money. Wait—you couldn't get it from him because he hasn't got it. He bought it as a present for a friend—name of Smith. This fellow had come back from Hawaii and didn't bring any souvenirs to give to his friends. Moroni told me he wanted to shame him by sending him a Hawaiian souvenir."

"This Smith lives in Evans Street, doesn't he, back of Newbury?" put in the Rambler.

"I'll have to look that up." He referred to the books and returned in a moment. "That's right. Mr. Ralph Smith, at Eighty-five Evans. It's an apartment house, I believe."

"Well," said Murphy, laughing, "I'll have to give up the idea of the koa-wood surfboard."

"We have a number in hard pine and redwood. Redwood resembles koa-wood."

"No, thanks."

Murphy left the place jubilant. Moroni, of course, had sent the surfboard to himself. But why?

He was a banker, respected citizen, probably prominent in Italian church affairs, the sort of man who would have to conduct an intrigue with the greatest care. Not only bad for his reputation but bad for business if it were found that he was keeping an artists' model. And, falling in love with Dolores Vanini, he had worked out this elaborate method of carrying on the affair. Being a banker, he had Italian bootleggers on his books—and criminals. He could get service if he needed it.

A TAXI took Murphy to the Calabria-Sicilian Bank on Bowdoin Square. It was five minutes of three, almost closing time. Murphy walked boldly into the big ornate institution which was almost deserted. He glanced about keenly and saw what he was looking for. In a corner of the big banking room, at a post from which he had a clear view of the activities of the bank, behind a huge mahogany desk, sat Mr. Smith, the lover of Dolores Vanini.

A glimpse was all that the reporter needed and he turned on his heel and made for the exit. Thus he didn't see the bank president lift his head, half rise from his chair, and then beckon to a man in civilian clothes who was leaning against a marble table in the center of the big room.

The Rambler had not proceeded a block when a heavy hand descended on his shoulder.

"Hey, you," somebody said in a hoarse voice. "I want you."

The reporter swung about, shaking off the hand, and confronted a burly man with small mean eyes and a jutting jaw.

Instantly the man's left hand sought his throat and the always belligerent Murphy drove his right fist into the fellow's stomach.

"Resist an officer, would ye?" shouted the stranger. "Take that!"

His right hand came from behind him enforced by a nightstick drawn from a hip pocket. It descended on the forehead of the newspaper man with such violence that he went out like a light.

"Dip," the special officer explained to the passersby who began to crowd around. He flashed a police badge and beckoned to a taxi. "Here, you! Help me chuck him in," he commanded, whereupon two obliging citizens aided him to push Murphy into the cab where he fell upon the cushions like a sack of meal.

BY AND BY the Rambler came out of it. He was in total darkness. He was lying on a hard floor which was moving like a swing. And his nostrils were assailed by an odor which instantly affected his stomach. Stale fish smells horribly to a man who has been slugged and doped.

He sat up and groped about him. He felt for a match, found one and lighted it. Already he suspected where he was and the light confirmed his suspicion. He was in the hold of a wooden vessel which recently had been filled with haddock, cod and hake. She was rolling, this vessel, which meant that she was at sea. And the empty hold indicated that she was not coming back to port until she had a cargo of fresh fish. Shanghaied! Well, he was lucky he hadn't been taken for a ride in a motor car. Evidently Moroni had recognized the newspaperman as quickly as Murphy had identified him.

He rose. By standing on tiptoes his fingers touched the hatch above. He pushed against it... Fastened on the outside. It must be a small schooner since there was only a seven-foot depth of hold. He lighted another match and observed, either forward or aft, he couldn't tell which, a small door about two feet square and about four feet above the floor of the hold. He reached it as the match went out. It was a means of access to the hold when the sea was too rough to open the hatch. He pushed against it... Fastened, but it gave a little. He thrust his shoulder against it and it flew open revealing a cabin rimmed with bunks, a cold Franklin stove in the middle of the room... Empty. Murphy pulled himself through the opening and crossed the cabin to an exit reached by three steps. This he pushed open cautiously. He found himself in a two foot passage between deck house and stern. The wheel was located on the roof of the desk house and there was a man in rough garments who was steering the vessel.

It was night—no moon but many stars. Away off Murphy could see shore lights. His prison was a two-masted schooner of the rig known as knockabout. There was a fresh breeze and reefed sails were set. He heard voices amidships. He looked astern and saw a dory at the end of a towline.

Without hesitation he went over the stern, holding onto the towline. It had been taut but it slackened and he went up to his waist in cold water. He grasped the bow of the dory as it rushed at him and pulled himself aboard. The wind sweeping from bow to stern of the schooner prevented the slight noise of this proceeding from attracting the attention of the man at the wheel.

Having spent a few months during a dull period in the newspaper game as a deck hand on a lake schooner, Murphy knew about knots, and in a few minutes was able to cast loose the dory. And then he discovered that the boat contained no oars.

This was unfortunate but he had a notion he was safer afloat in the frail craft than on board the fishing vessel. In all probability its skipper had been cautioned against bringing him back to port.

The dory rode the waves like a cork and shipped almost no water. Murphy found the chill night air uncomfortable, being wet from the waist down, but there was nothing he could do about it so, eventually, he laid down in the bottom of the boat and went to sleep.

The following afternoon about three o'clock, the fishing schooner Alice K. landed him at the fish pier in South Boston. The stray dory had been sighted at dawn, apparently empty and, as fishing vessels always have use for a dory, the skipper of the Alice K. had picked this one up and found a man asleep in it.

TOM GORMAN met his reporter by request at Brock's waterfront café on Atlantic Avenue. "I want to see you," he had declared over the telephone. "Yes, I have replies to the cablegram. No, I'll tell you nothing. Yes, I can get down to Brock's. Be there in fifteen minutes."

His manner was hostile, the reporter noted as his chief was getting out of the cab. He glowered at the young man standing in the doorway of the café and pushed by him and went up the flight of stairs to the restaurant.

"Before you say anything," the city editor began nastily when they were seated at a table, "take a squint at this."

He handed the Rambler a copy of the rival morning paper.

"Motive for Vanini murder discovered," Murphy read aloud. "District attorney makes public new evidence which he says confirms dying accusation against artist, Quentin Robbins."

"District Attorney Daniel Powers, late last night, supplied a Journal reporter with details of the latest development in the Vanini murder case," the story began.

"Robbins while in Paris had a love affair with his model Dolores Vanini, abandoned her, and came to Boston where he opened a studio. In Boston he made the acquaintance of Miss Phyllis May, beautiful Brookline society girl, and became engaged to her. Miss May is the daughter of Ronald May, millionaire exporter. The engagement was kept a secret because the father was certain to object to a penniless artist as a son-in-law and the young couple were planning to elope.

"Dolores Vanini appeared upon the scene. Learning of the engagement, she threatened to go to Miss May and expose the past life of her fiancé. Robbins went to her apartment to plead with her and when she persisted in her determination, he killed her. As the public already knows, Miss Vanini was conscious when a doctor and police sergeant arrived and had just time to murmur that Quentin Robbins had shot her when she went into a coma and never recovered consciousness.

"The district attorney stated that her accusation made in the presence of witnesses was really all he required for a conviction, but Robbins' need to keep from his fiancée the knowledge that there had been another woman in his life supplied a logical motive for the crime."

"Well," said Murphy, after reading the screed, "they haven't got hold of the girl's picture, anyway."

"Scooped on our own story," commented Gorman bitterly. "We

reopen the case for the benefit of our competitors. You're a hell of a reporter."

"Did you bring the cablegram with you?"

Gorman drew an envelope from his pocket and flung it disgustedly across the table. It was a cable from The *Sphere's* Paris correspondent.

> Regnier had no pupil named Quentin Robbins. Dolores Vanini was the mistress of Alphonse Galtier, French thief, convicted and sent to Devil's Island ten months ago upon evidence of Joseph Mortimer, American artist. Mortimer left France after friends of Galtier had made an attempt on his life. Vanini was deported to Italy as an undesirable.

"Helpful?" asked Gorman ironically.

The Rambler grinned mirthlessly. "Not very. Listen, boss. The Journal is just attracting attention to the Vanini case again, which makes everything hotsy when we spring the real story in a couple of days. Now let me tell you what I've discovered."

"Well," said Gorman after the reporter had finished, "it looks as though Moroni was putting up for the girl, and it is obvious that he will go to any lengths to remain out of the limelight. If you can find people who saw him crossing that surfboard bridge, or who saw her going to his terrace by means of it, we can run a story though it doesn't help Robbins any. You think Moroni killed her but why didn't she accuse him instead of Robbins?"

"I've a notion but I can't tell you about it yet. Can I have the cablegram?"

"Sure. It cost us a hundred dollars, young feller. What are you going to do now?"

"Make a call on Moroni."

"Well," said Gorman grinning, "if he bumps you off we'll have a story though it won't be worth the money I've invested in you. As for Robbins, he'll get the juice as sure as my name is Tom Gorman."

"See you later, chief," replied Murphy. "Shake?"

Gorman laughed. "Oh, sure. You've done pretty well at that, Rambler. I wish you luck."

CHAPTER SIX

TIME TO RAMBLE

HALF AN hour later Murphy was in the Boston immigration office running down the passenger manifests. After an hour's work he found what he had hoped to find. Joseph Mortimer had arrived in Boston from Cherbourg upon the United States liner "America." Quentin Robbins then, was an assumed name. The Rambler congratulated himself on this quick confirmation of a theory based on the cablegram. He had thought it more likely that Mortimer would have landed in New York and come to Boston by train than that he would have arrived in the city on one of the infrequent passenger services. Most likely the fellow had had very little money, had taken passage upon a cabin ship and settled in Boston because it was his port of arrival, and for no other reason.

So Mortimer was in fear of his life. In Paris he had been in love with Vanini who had deceived him with this French criminal. Mortimer himself might have been a crook, a member of a criminal band, who had betrayed Galtier in revenge for stealing his sweetheart. Galtier's European criminal organization would be out to punish him.

That explained his change of name. And why he dared not supply his lawyer with a defense. If he revealed that he was wearing an alias, Phyllis May might turn against him. Of course he hoped that something would happen to save him from the electric chair. A fine husband he would make for a sweet, innocent, loyal girl like Phyllis.

Vanini, if she had loved this Alphonse Galtier might have followed Mortimer to Boston with murderous intent. Murphy swung about and addressed the immigration inspector in charge of the files.

"Has John Moroni, the banker, been to Europe recently?" he demanded.

"Sure. He went over to Italy to get a decoration from Rome. Came back about three months ago. I remember because the Wops in the North End gave him a big reception at the South Station. He landed in New York from one of the Italian liners."

Things were beginning to dovetail. Moroni had met Vanini in Italy. Probably he had brought her to America with him and then, back in his own bailiwick, where he had to watch appearances, he had established her in the ingenious manner which Murphy had discovered.

That meant that Vanini had not followed Mortimer. Most likely she hadn't known he was in Boston until he called on her.

No doubt he had told her the name he was using in Boston, when he had endeavored to resume their old relationship while the girl was seething with hate against him for his betrayal of her French lover.

So when a bullet plunged into her breast, she venomously had charged him with the crime.

On the other hand, if Mortimer were a bad character who had not hesitated to betray his French rival to the police, it was very likely that, infuriated by her refusal to resume their love affair, he had drawn a gun, aimed it at her and pulled the trigger.

Against this, was Murphy's boast that he would supply The *Sphere* with a fresh murder story, and the active hostility of John Moroni.

Moroni, of course, might be actuated solely by fear of scandal. This the Rambler doubted very much. He had sized up Mortimer as a rat and Moroni as a wolf.

"Much obliged," he said to the immigration official.

Murphy liked Phyllis May. She was a swell girl. It would be awful if he got Mortimer out of jail and Phyllis married him. However, the story in The Journal would probably settle that. Mr. May would take active measures.

He looked up Moroni's residence in the telephone book. The banker lived In North Cambridge. Now, how did The Journal get the Phyllis May story? That manicure girl might have sold it. No, in some way she was connected with Moroni or Rothstein, because a spy had followed Phyllis to her lunch engagement with the reporter. The story had been given to The Journal by Rothstein to clinch the already strong case against the accused.

It was the frantic effort of a guilty man to protect himself.

THE RAMBLER phoned Phyllis May, who answered in person. "How could you," she mourned. "I—I trusted you, Mr. Murphy—"

"Listen, kid," he said earnestly. "I work for The *Sphere*. I had nothing to do with that story. I told you yesterday that the fellow in the restaurant was trailing you, and I found out afterwards that it was true. I suppose you are in trouble."

"I'm leaving for California tomorrow afternoon," she said weeping. "My father's sister is going with me. My father is furious."

"Well, I've learned a lot more and I never quit a case until I've solved it. I may have your friend out before you start west." He hung up and walked slowly up State Street.

The shot was fired about ten-thirty. Mortimer had seen Moroni leave Dolores at her front door. He had called on her fifteen minutes later. He had been in her apartment only four or five minutes according to his story.

Now that would have given Moroni time to walk around to Evans Street and ascend to his apartment. Then what?

Why that was their system! He said good night at the door of the apartment house, went round to Evans Street and became Mr. Smith. He took the surfboard out of the storeroom and laid it from the terrace to her window ledge. Of course! Smith went into her chamber via the bridge. A girl would be afraid to crawl over the thing to the terrace. He should have thought of that before.

So Smith crawled across the surfboard and arrived at the window. And at that moment Mortimer was in the bedroom. He had the girl in his arms—probably kissing her. And she was pushing him toward the door. Smith thought the man was her lover. As Mortimer rushed out of the apartment, Smith came in through the window. He had the jealous Latin temperament and he carried a gun. Dolores had crawled back into bed, sat up, received a bullet in her breast and fell back. Smith, horrified at what he had done, scuttled back across the surfboard and escaped from the apartment.

The shot had been heard all through the house. A doctor rushed in and so did a police sergeant called in from the street. They found the girl conscious.

Doctor Wilkes had admitted at the inquest that he had examined the wound and told the girl that it was not very serious. The sergeant had demanded to know who had shot her.

Of course Vanini knew who had shot her but she knew that Moroni had fired from an impulse of insane jealousy. He was her protector and supporter. If she accused him, it meant the end of her luxurious life and his disgrace. If she covered him, she could have anything she liked for the rest of her life. And there was a scapegoat, the man she had driven out, the betrayer of her French lover Alphonse Galtier. Any woman of her type would have done what she had done—accused the man she hated.

Shock more than the bullet wound had killed the girl. She had not regained consciousness to right the wrong she had done. Why the case was perfect against Moroni only Rambler Murphy couldn't prove any part of his theory.

AN IMPOSING-LOOKING motor car turned between two stone posts into a driveway from Wilbraham Street, North Cambridge, and rolled up under the *porte-cochère* of a very large old-fashioned mansion with a mansard roof. It was eleven-thirty in the evening. From the car descended Banker John Moroni. He was in evening dress for he had entertained a party at the Pop Concert in Symphony Hall. Between his lips was a fragrant Havana cigar. Mr. Moroni, for the first time in a couple of days, felt at peace with the world.

He unlocked his front door, switched on the hall light and ascended with heavy step to the second floor. The servants were asleep. His wife and family were at the summer place on Cape Cod and he rather enjoyed being alone in the house. At the second floor he switched off the downstairs lights, and pushed open his chamber door. Entering he felt for the light switch, threw the room into illumination. Then he staggered back against the wall and ejaculated something in his native tongue.

There was a man seated in a chair with his back to one of the windows—a homely young man with a white face and staring blue eyes.

"Keep away, keep off," cried Mr. Moroni shrilly. "God protect me from the dead that walk!"

"Not dead yet," said the young man. "Don't shout. Shut the door. You and I are going to have a talk."

As he spoke a revolver appeared in his right hand. He held his left hand behind the back of his chair.

Moroni rallied instantly. He closed the door. "So you are not dead, spy," he gritted. "What are you doing in my house?"

He moved resolutely toward the Rambler who lifted his weapon.

"I'll shoot," Murphy exclaimed. The glitter in his eyes convinced the banker who stopped short.

"You thought I was feeding the fishes by this time, eh?" jeered Addison Francis Murphy.

The big man smiled nastily. This was a situation which might work to his advantage since the fool had broken into his home. Some trick to disarm him and he would give him the choice of getting out of town or going to jail for a long term as a burglar.

"You had your chance," he replied. "You refused five thousand dollars. What on earth do you expect to gain by obtaining access to my bedroom and menacing me with a revolver?"

"I have the goods on you, Moroni," declared Murphy. "You're a family man with a good reputation. I don't think you intended to shoot. Your jealous rage—"

"You're mad, I believe," exclaimed Moroni who paled a little.

"I'm giving you a chance. Confess and I'll let you get out of town before I break the story."

"You damned impudent rat of a reporter—"

"Keep back! You were seen going over that surfboard bridge, Moroni. You were seen crawling back to your terrace after firing at Dolores Vanini and wounding her in the breast—"

"You lie, you scum. How dare you—"

"And Robbins was seen leaving the apartment, by a person who heard the shot, immediately after Robbins had left. He will be released tomorrow—and the case against you is stronger than the case was against him."

THE BANKER looked shaken but quickly recovered. He picked up a chair and set it in the middle of the floor facing his inquisitor, sat down in it. He had inspected the room. They were alone without witnesses. Murphy would never leave the house alive. He had to catch his interest until he could spring, or get the gun from his own pocket.

"You seem to forget, my friend," he said with a scornful smile, "that Miss Vanini accused this Robbins on her deathbed."

"After being assured that the wound was not fatal. No, Moroni—Dolores was shrewd. She needed you and she had no use for Robbins, whose real name, by the way, is Mortimer. Whatever induced you to get mixed up with an international criminal like Dolores Vanini?"

"Damn you, will you traduce the dead?" shouted the banker, his face turning purple.

"She was the moll of a French crook named Alphonse Galtier, Moroni. The French government deported her to Italy. You're just a fat elderly sucker. She played you. She had no earthly use for you."

"That is not true," exclaimed the banker who jumped to his feet and waved his arms. "She loved me."

"You were a good thing and she didn't want to lose you. That's why she accused Robbins."

"I tell you she adored me," exclaimed the Italian whose vanity was being stabbed in a vital spot. "Even when she held my bullet in her breast she forgave me. That's love, you dirty crawling spy!"

"Bah, she was Robbins' mistress in Paris. She belonged to Galtier. Stand back, murderer."

Tears rolled down the banker's cheeks. "I didn't mean to shoot," he declared. "I saw her in his arms. He was kissing her. I pushed up the window and shot her, but she insisted it was nothing. She told me to go; that she would accuse him. She loved me as much as I loved her."

"Well," said Murphy coolly, "your confession is going to make a good newspaper story."

"It is not," replied the banker who recovered his composure as quickly as he had lost it. "I deny everything. You have no proof of any sort and it is your word against mine, a tramp against an eminent citizen. This is the desperate expedient of a man who has no evidence. Well, I'll give you five thousand dollars to leave town. If you refuse, you won't live the night out."

And then the banker plunged at him. Murphy could have shot him but Murphy was not a killer. The man had drawn close as he made his offer. For a second the muzzle of the weapon was against his big chest and the reporter hesitated. In the next second the gun was torn from his grasp and he went over backward, a huge right hand clutching his throat. And then he lay flat on the floor while the eminent citizen set about throttling him with all the power and savagery of desperation.

MURPHY battered at him with both fists; he brought up his knees against the man's stomach; he fought as he had never fought before, but he could not break the grip upon his throat, and a film was floating before his eyes and he was choking—choking.

As they threshed about something twisted around the right ankle of the banker. He pulled but it held fast. His fury abated a trifle and without relaxing his grasp he lifted himself and looked down. An insulated wire was wound around his ankle and lying upon the floor was a round metal object.

With an oath he jumped to his feet and dragged his victim with him. "What is this?" he demanded.

Although the death grip had been removed, Murphy was unable

to speak for second.

"What is it?" roared the banker although he knew well enough what it was.

"A microphone," the Rambler ejaculated thickly.

With an exclamation of horror, Moroni released the reporter, picked up the mike, twisted his leg out of the wire and saw that the strand came through the window before which the reporter had been seated.

Cursing hysterically Moroni rushed toward the window, whereupon Murphy swooped upon his revolver which lay neglected upon the floor, picked it up and covered the other.

"Stick 'em up," he commanded.

The banker turned. His face was ghastly.

"The wire crosses your grounds and goes over the wall at the rear. Behind the wall are the city editor and managing editor of The *Sphere* and a shorthand expert who took down your confession, Mr. Smith-Moroni," stated Murphy blandly. "As a public speaker, your voice is well known. Now get over to the far corner of the room, behind the bed. Quick! I'll shoot this time, having felt your gorilla grip."

He was almost sorry for the eminent citizen as he backed slowly across the room and took up the indicated position.

Murphy backed to the window, threw up the sash, slipped outside onto the roof of the side veranda, swung by his hands and dropped ten feet upon soft grass. Too late he realized that he hadn't frisked the banker, and he zigzagged as he ran through the night toward the rear wall, while he kept a weather eye on the lighted window.

Boom.

A revolver shot. It came from the banker's chamber and it was not fired out the window. Murphy went over the wall by means of a step ladder which he had left in place and dropped into the arms of three men.

"He fired after you!" exclaimed Gorman.

"Did you get the confession?" demanded the Rambler excitedly.

"Every word of it."

"Well," said Murphy, "he tried to murder me twice not counting just now but I'm sorry for the poor devil."

"Boy, oh, boy, what a story!" chortled the city editor. "Why are you sorry for him?"

"He loved the woman and he's just blown out his brains."

THEY were lunching at the Copley Plaza two days after the suicide of John Moroni.

"So of course," said Phyllis May. "I couldn't marry him when he was going round under an assumed name, and when he was in love with a bad woman even after he was engaged to me. And I told him last night that it was all a mistake. I'm afraid I was very indiscreet to fall in love with a man I didn't know anything about, don't you think so, Mr. Murphy?"

"You were," said the Rambler. "You dames go cuckoo over a handsome man. You had a lucky escape, I'll say."

"I'm very sorry for Mr. Robbins or Mr. Mortimer or whatever his right name is, and I'm glad that he is out of prison but I wouldn't dream of marrying such a man. So father says I don't have to go to California. Isn't this chocolate parfait lovely—you haven't told me your first name."

"Addison," he said laconically.

"I don't really like handsome men at all," said the girl whose eyes were very bright and very blue. "I like men who do things, who are fearless and who are literary."

"Oh, my God!" muttered Mr. Murphy.

"Such an experience as we have had together makes people friends very quickly, doesn't it, Addison?"

"Yep," he admitted.

"And father is so busy he doesn't want to go away for the summer and I've decided to stay home with him. So we'll see a lot of each other I hope. Were you ever in love, Addison?"

"No," replied the Rambler. "Listen. I've got to get out on an assignment, Miss May. We've been having lunch for two hours so you'll have to excuse me."

"Well, I suppose you have to go," she said sadly. "I'll call you up tomorrow and we'll have lunch. Father wants to meet you. He says you must be quite a man. When will you come to dinner?"

"Pretty soon," he said nervously. "I've paid the check. Good-by."

On the way to the office Mr. Murphy did some serious thinking. Phyllis was about the prettiest girl he had ever met and as sweet as honey, and she had been loyal to that scoundrel Robbins until his true character was exposed. She was hero-worshipping a tramp reporter just now and if one Addison Francis Murphy played his cards right— He shrugged his shoulders.

"Well, Murphy," said Tom Gorman jovially. "You're the white-haired boy around here. Your salary is going to be a hundred and a quarter. Did we put it over on this town? Did we put it over?"

"We did," replied the Rambler. "I'm sorry, Tom, but I'm fed up with Boston. I'm leaving now."

Gorman gazed at him in consternation. "You can't. We need you. Look, maybe the managing editor will raise the ante."

"No use," said Murphy quietly. "I thought I might stay here all summer but I can't. I'm rambling."

Gorman humped his big shoulders. "O.K., hobo," he said sullenly. "I'll get you a bonus for the Moroni story if I can. You'll go on like this and die in a flop house some day. You're set for life on this paper. Get sense, will you?"

"Some day maybe," replied Addison Francis Murphy with a far-away look in his eye. "Not yet. If anybody tries to get my address, you don't know what's become of me."

He shook hands with the editor and nodded pleasantly to the members of the staff who greeted him on his way out.

Gorman gazed after him until he had closed the door behind him, sighed, shook his head and then picked up a sheet of copy. "Ah, what the hell," he remarked and dismissed the Rambler from his mind.

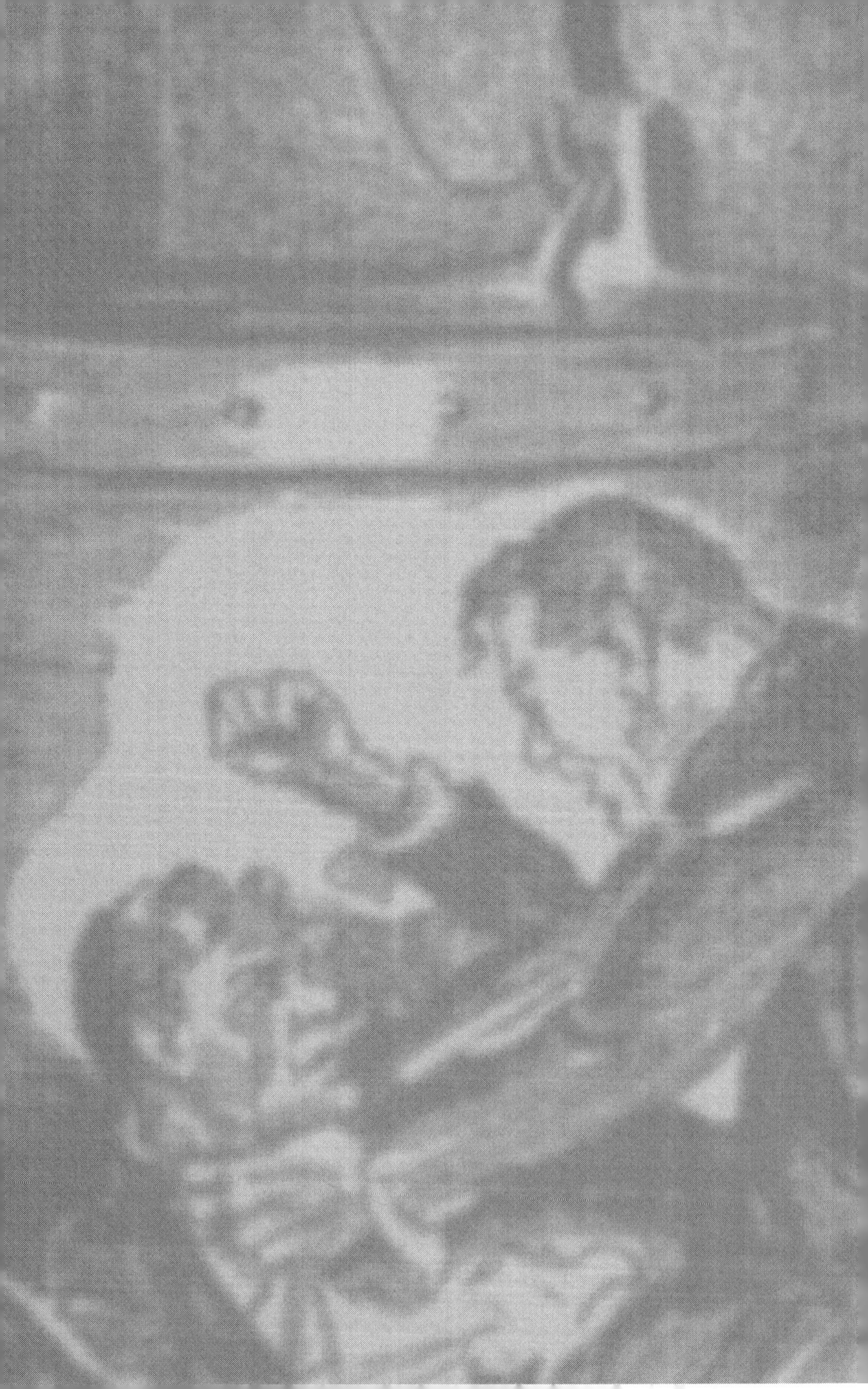

GHOST CITY SET-UP

THE MINUTE "RAMBLER" MURPHY SPOTTED THE MAN IN COMPARTMENT C ON THE RENO LIMITED HE SMELLED DANGER. FOR HE KNEW THE DIVORCE CAPITAL OFFERED SMALL PICKINGS FOR A BIG-CITY CRIME KING. HOW COULD HE GUESS THAT BOWERS WAS OUT TO DIG THIRTY MILLIONS IN LOOT FROM A WORKED-OUT GHOST MINE, AND TURN THE ABANDONED CONDADO SHAFT INTO A BLACK HOLE OF HORROR?

CHAPTER ONE

THE MYSTERY MAN IN C

ADDISON FRANCIS MURPHY—known widely in the newspaper profession as "The Rambler"—was in funds. In his pocket was exactly three hundred and forty-four dollars and several cents. For about two and a half days he had been riding on Pullman cars. It was Mr. Murphy's custom to travel either by Pullman or freight car. Being inflicted with an urge for travel, he sustained the luxury of the Pullman or the filth of a box car with perfect equanimity. His destination was San Francisco.

That Murphy had money was by no means his fault but due to the fact that he had spent an evening in a New York speakeasy with an honest author by the name of Walsingham. Made loquacious by two or three glasses of authentic beer, Murphy had told the story of an exploit at a private camp in the Adirondacks to which the writing man had listened intently.

A month later, to his intense astonishment, Mr. Walsingham presented Mr. Murphy with a large check which was fifty percent of the profits of the Adirondacks yarn. Walsingham who was the kind of author who goes abroad for ideas, had written the story and sold it to a magazine of large circulation.

Naturally Addison Francis had gone down to The New York Planet office, confided to the city editor his candid opinion of him, and was summarily discharged after which he had purchased a ticket to San Francisco. It was mid-summer and he had heard that they had cool summers in Frisco.

IN HIS car on the Overland Express were several women who were nervous, fussy and looked like character actresses, and whom he shrewdly suspected to be getting off at Reno, the Mecca of divorcées. There was also a young woman who would have been worthy of the ardent attention of a young man of normal propensities. Murphy was neither blind nor indifferent to the fair sex; merely wary of it.

In the first place he didn't care much for his own face and suspected the motives of girls who seemed to think he was attractive; and in the next place he couldn't use them in his scheme of things. In the opinion of the Rambler, all girls, no matter how beautiful were crazy on the subject of marriage. And, when they had married a fellow, they went house hunting and expected him to settle down with them in some suburb for the rest of his life and pay off the interest on mortgages, go to church and push baby carriages.

Lots of newspaper editors who thought the Rambler was crazy but admired his craft as a journalist, had suggested that he was in his thirties and ought to settle down. Murphy liked change.

But this girl up ahead was very beautiful. She had much jet-black hair and eyes like deep inky pools. Her profile was as perfect as if she had been able to order it herself; her olive skin was clear and like satin. Her figure left nothing whatever to be desired. She appeared to be about twenty-five, an age when a girl begins to have sense.

She lifted the slab high above her head.

During the first day Murphy had considered making her acquaintance. During the second day he was content to admire her respectfully from afar. That was because the conductor had told him who she was.

It appeared that this very lovely person was Mrs. Georgia Van Arden, wife of Reginald Van Arden, a leader of society in New York and a chaser if there ever was one. Having got sick of that stuff, Mrs. Van Arden was going to Reno to shuffle off the tie that bound her to the night-club hostess' friend and companion. Of course the conductor didn't tell him all this. It was the business of a good reporter to know everything that was going on and Murphy had read in a scandal column in New York that the Van Ardens were regretting their connection with each other.

There was class in every line of the young woman. There was sweetness mingled with her hauteur. Murphy thought she was a swell-looking girl and wished she were not so horribly wealthy and that he was good-looking and had no objections to settling down. With a girl like that, a fixed place of abode might not be intolerable.

Murphy had never worked in Reno and didn't want to. He liked big towns where things happened. He had no more notion of getting off at the Divorce Capital than he had of embarking for the moon until he happened to pass a compartment in a car up forward, while on his way to the club car at the head of the train. As he was approaching the entrance to this compartment, a porter carrying a tray with a couple of bottles of ginger ale on it, pushed open the door and Murphy caught a glimpse of a man who was sitting with his back to the engine.

The Rambler's blue eyes narrowed and his nostrils quivered.

The porter entered, closed the door behind him and presently came out without the ginger-ale. Murphy who had stopped in the vestibule forward, waited until the colored man had disappeared and then walked back and halted in front of the door of the compartment which the porter had just left. It was Compartment C.

He turned the knob, the door opened, and he stepped in. The man who sat facing the engine uttered an angry exclamation and leaped to his feet. The man on the other seat looked up sharply and shrewdly.

"Gosh," said Addison Francis, "I made a mistake. She said Compartment C.

"You will oblige me by getting out," snarled the man who was standing. He was a tall, elegant and striking person with a small brown mustache.

"Exit laughing, buddy," remarked the seated individual. "Wrong pew and give the dame my regards."

Murphy turned his sharp eyes from the angry individual to the other and inspected him carefully.

"Sorry," he said cheerfully. "She said Compartment C but it's the car ahead, I guess. Not the wrong pew, mister, the wrong church."

HE STEPPED out and closed the door and, changing his mind about a smoke in the club car, he returned to his own Pullman. He noticed that Mrs. Van Arden was no longer in her section but had retired to the drawing room directly ahead of it which she also had engaged.

The Rambler looked at his watch. One hour to Reno. Going to his seat he picked up his bag, placed therein a couple of books and magazines and rang for the porter.

"Stopping off in Reno," he stated. "Fix my ticket please."

"Yas, sir. Be there in an hour."

The Rambler leaned back with a half-smile upon his plain face. His eyes were snapping. He was putting two and two together, and there was nobody in the country who could make four out of two and two faster than the young man in question.

The haughty person in the compartment up above was Reginald Van Arden, husband of the beautiful lady who was getting off at Reno. It was curious that Mr. Van Arden was traveling on the same train with his estranged wife; and suspicious that he was keeping out of her sight. But that wasn't what made the Rambler think it might be worth while to stop off in Reno. The humorous party who had talked about the wrong pew was queer company for Reginald Van Arden. Murphy had identified him at a glance. He was unfavorably known to the police of New York City as "Soft" Simpson. He was a jackal for the underworld lion, "Big" Bill Bowers, and was completely out of focus away from New York City.

As a reporter Murphy knew a lot of people who didn't know him. And he had the newspaperman's gift for being up to the minute on current events. And one particular spot in his brain was solely for the purpose of storing away information about prominent people.

A few days before he had observed an item in a newspaper headed, "Fifty-story Van Arden Building in New York up at auction."

It appeared that that token of the wealth and power of the great family had been foreclosed by the bank which held the mortgage and, there being no bidders, the bank had been forced to bid it in and take over its operation.

That the Van Ardens were in straits he had known when he left New York. The two hundred and fifty million dollar fortune held in trust for about twenty members of the family had been entirely invested in the N.W. and R. railroad which had been paying twelve percent interest in Nineteen Twenty-nine and had been quoted at two hundred and fifty dollars per share. At present the stock was down to fifteen dollars a share, no dividends were being paid and the road was about to go into a receiver's hands.

Van Arden, naturally, was dependent upon his wife for support.

Georgia, daughter of the late John Gregory, the Alaska mining king, had fifty millions worth of gold-mine stock; she had no children or near relatives and her husband might expect to inherit. Losing a wife like that was going to be a severe blow to one of Broadway's liveliest playboys.

It occurred to Murphy that Mrs. Van Arden might find unexpected obstacles in the way of her divorce; that her stay in Reno was not apt to be dull and peaceful. If Soft Simpson left the train at the divorce capital, one Addison Francis Murphy had better make Reno a stop-over also.

WHEN the train pulled into the station at Reno, Murphy was standing in the vestibule and he was first to hop off. The hour was eleven at night. He stepped across the platform, waved away the red-cap, set down his bag and waited.

From his car emerged the four or five ladies who looked like character actresses. From the car ahead descended Mr. Soft Simpson. Van Arden was going on, apparently, for he did not leave the train.

Just as the conductor was shouting "All aboard," the beautiful lady descended followed by a small, plump blond person, evidently her maid.

Three or four flunkies jumped forward. A magnificent limousine was waiting across the platform, undoubtedly wired for in advance. She stepped in, followed by her maid, and rode away. Simpson hailed a taxi. Murphy heard him say "Hotel Golden," and he in turn rolled off.

Satisfied, Addison Francis picked up his bag and turned his face toward Reno.

There was a steel frame arch across the Main Street which stated in glaring letters and with no diffidence—"Reno, the Biggest Little City in the World."

For a quarter of a mile ahead the buildings on both sides were blazing with lights and beyond, abruptly was total darkness.

Murphy, after inquiring the way to the Riverside Hotel, struck boldly up the street. Temptation beset him as he made his promenade. Mr. Murphy's ever present sin was dice, and everywhere were establishments, the business of which was gambling. He had glimpses of crap tables and roulette tables, well patronized. He passed saloons with swinging doors and white-aproned barkeeps, and the bars were well lined.

Unlike many tramp journalists, Murphy was not a hard drinker and when he had a "hen" on he never drank at all. He continued to walk swiftly and was not tempted by the keno parlors where there were places at huge oval counters for a hundred players who battled for cash prizes.

Presently he came to ornate public buildings, crossed a bridge over a swiftly running stream and found himself at the portal of the Riverside which he knew to be the swanky hotel of the city.

With the assurance of a man with money in his pocket, he entered, secured a room and bath and followed the bellboy upstairs. Before opening his bag, he sat down at his desk and wrote a telegram which he addressed to a good friend on The New York Clarion. After that he rang for the boy, gave him the message and proceeded to take a bath. In another half hour Mr. Murphy was sleeping peacefully.

AT ABOUT eleven next morning the Rambler came down stairs and entered the breakfast room. Hardly was he seated when a boy brought him a telegram. He read it, nodded with satisfaction, and tore the yellow slip into minute pieces which he stuffed in his pocket. He was whistling under his breath, an indication that the hunting instinct was awake.

Murphy had just put away an ample portion of ham and eggs washed down by two or three cups of steaming coffee when a vision entered the breakfast room, till then tenanted only by the journalist. Murphy, by the way, would fiercely have resented the word journalist. He was a newspaperman.

Mrs. Van Arden had slept very well for a lady with a broken heart. Her black eyes were sparkling and there was authentic color in her smooth cheeks. She wore a green suit of some soft material which made her look like a young dryad. The head waiter came on the run and three or four waiters and bus-boys sprang to attention. Her eyes roamed over the room, took in the lanky young man, recognized him, and became opaque. She glided past him and was placed at a table by the window. She ordered coffee and rolls in a low but clear tone and then became absorbed in contemplation.

Murphy watched her stealthily while he fought a battle with himself. There would have been no battle if he had not been more or less fascinated by the lady. If he did not let events take their course, he would not have any reason for remaining in Reno. On the other hand—

Making his decision he paid his check, rose and walked over to the young society matron.

"I beg your pardon Mrs. Van Arden," he said respectfully. "May I have a minute of your time?"

She lifted her regal head, drew her ripe lips into a thin straight line and turned upon him the eyes of a basilisk.

"You were on the Overland," she said. "You were bound for San Francisco but you changed your mind and got off at Reno. No, you may not have a second of my time."

"I assure you it's important," he said earnestly.

The young woman cast upon him a withering look. "You have paid your check," she said coldly. "Kindly leave this room. If you annoy me further I shall inform the hotel authorities."

Murphy's face was flaming and he thrust forward his solid jaw. "O.K., lady," he said harshly. "And much obliged to you. Good morning."

Addison Francis was muttering to himself as he reached the lobby. Deliver him from a swell-headed dame! So she thought he was a masher, eh? She fancied herself, she did. She had seen him on the train. She had even found out that he was bound for San Francisco. She flattered herself that he had left the train at Reno on her account. Well, he had, but not for the reason she supposed. The hell with her.

He walked to the newsstand and purchased the two or three morning and afternoon newspapers of which Reno is proud. He didn't think much of them, he didn't. Small rags with press services and boiler plate. Probably the staff was a man and a boy and a pair of shears. With the depression, the prospect of getting a job was nil.

MURPHY had a trait in common with many newspapermen but one hard to understand by a person not connected with the profession. Personally he was shy. In his own interests he would not dare to demand a favor, to trespass on people's property, to ask a woman an impudent question. When arrayed in the panoply of a reporter, however, Murphy was transformed into a hard aggressive go-getter. There was no question he dared not ask, nobody's privacy upon which he dared not intrude.

While there was not a better investigator in the land, he was completely at a loss when he was not working for a paper. In the matter which now concerned him, he didn't know what he could do about it unless he had a job, so he started out to find one.

At the first two offices he met with short shrift. At the third he was turned away by a surly city editor and was leaving the city room when there entered a rolly-polly bald-headed man with a red face and the expression of an irritated pig.

"Look where you're going," this person snarled. He threw an irate glance upon the offender and suddenly his round face split into a broad beaming grin.

"I'll be blistered!" he exclaimed, "if it ain't Rambler Murphy."

"Hello, Wart-Hog," replied Addison Francis. "Do you work here?"

Wart Hog, so called, did not resent the appellation but he was affronted at the question.

"Work here," he exclaimed. "Why I own the joint."

"I knew you'd arrive at a bad end," remarked the Rambler. "You poor porker, how come?"

Chuckling with complacency the Wart Hog seized his arm and conducted him to an office marked "Publisher."

"I saved my money," he explained. "And my wife had a little dough when I married her. So, a couple of years ago, I bought this rag and I'm making a metropolitan journal out of it."

"Yeah? By its make-up I judged it to be The Bingville Bugle."

"And don't call me Wart Hog," commanded the publisher. "That name never followed me away out here. If you start it I'll murder you."

"O K., Mr. Peter Gamble. Now in the matter of hiring a reporter—"

Mr. Gamble lifted a pudgy hand and his amiable expression changed.

"We're in the red, Murph," he pleaded. "Honest, I couldn't put on anybody without firing a couple of married men that are working for office boy's wages."

Mr. Murphy grinned, thrust his hand in his pocket and produced a roll of bills.

"In that case," he stated, "I'll pay you ten dollars a week to put me on the staff."

"Are you cuckoo?" gasped the publisher who looked, at the moment, apoplectic.

"For one week. Then I have to go to Frisco. Honest, Pete, I need the job as a cloak."

"You got a story," accused the Wart Hog. "I know you. Something's up."

"I think there is going to be a story that will hit all the wires and I'll sell it to you, when it breaks, for a hundred bucks."

"But you're going to be working for us," protested the publisher.

"Not after I get this story," replied the Rambler with a grin.

"Well," commented Mr. Gamble, "it had better be good."

"Do you have such things as police badges in this jumping-off place."

"It's a bumping-off place for people that talk like that. This is a metropolitan city, young fellow. I can have you made a deputy sheriff if I want to—without pay, of course," he hastened to add.

"Do that little thing. Introduce me to the pinhead on your city desk and tell him I keep my own hours."

"O.K. I want you to come up to the house and meet the wife and see the kids."

"Sure—some time. I'm going to be busy," said Murphy evasively. He didn't think he would care to meet a woman who would marry the Wart Hog. Mr. Gamble was not popular in his days as a New York police reporter. He had a mean streak a yard wide and in the Rambler's opinion was well qualified to be a newspaper publisher.

However Gamble had mellowed. He refused the ten dollars which Murphy offered him. "Aw, heck," he exclaimed, "I'll let you work for us for nothing. That's the kind of guy I am."

CHAPTER TWO

THE GIRL OF THE PULLMAN

MRS. GEORGIA VAN ARDEN stood by the window of her hotel suite and looked down upon the ambitious city of Reno. As she was on the seventh floor she practically had a bird's-eye view of the metropolis—which looked to her as if it didn't cover more than a couple of square miles—and of the surrounding country which was flat bleak and most unprepossessing. In the distance she saw the

Rocky Mountains which, on the Nevada side, are gray, brown, grassless, treeless and displeasing.

Marooned in this place for six weeks—and she was bored already. Georgia knew that divorcées killed time during their probation by sneaking out of town, crossing the state line and visiting Lake Tahoe, only thirty miles distant but upon the Pacific slope of the Rockies and as lovely as the Garden of Eden. But her lawyer who had just left had warned her that she couldn't risk crossing the state line.

"You are a celebrated woman, a society leader," he explained, "and wherever you go, you are news. So, if you step off the soil of Nevada, you'll have to start your six-week's residence all over again."

"Isn't there a nicer place than this?" she had asked petulantly.

"Mrs. Van Arden, this is all there is to Nevada that is endurable."

"Darn it," remarked the young lady.

"Furthermore, bear in mind that you are the most important divorcée that Reno has had for a dog's age. You can't expect not to be seen if you go to night clubs and gambling palaces."

"They bore me but, if I feel like it, I certainly shall go where I like in Nevada."

"Don't forget your husband is contesting your suit. Undoubtedly he has detectives watching you. If you are the least indiscreet, the judge may not be able to grant your divorce."

"I am never indiscreet," declared the young woman, "that is—hardly ever."

She opened a jeweled cigarette case, offered a cigarette to the attorney and lighted one herself.

"What does one do for amusement?"

"Well we have picture shows, hotel dances, bridge—"

"Bah! I was told that you were very influential. I'm paying you a preposterous fee for your services. Can't you do something about these detectives who are watching me?"

"Maybe," replied the lawyer whose name was Phipps Rawson. "This is a wonderful state, Mrs. Van Arden. It is practically owned by a man who is a close personal friend of mine. He names the governor and the mayor, he controls the police, he has a finger in everything. Let me find out who is on your trail and I can have him run out of Nevada. Just the same, be careful. Every home in Reno is open to you, of course. Our society ladies would be flattered to entertain you. They will all call on you."

"And I won't be at home to them," she said rudely. "I'm not going to be bothered by small-town society women, thank you."

"Well, you have your car and chauffeur. We have good roads—"

"But they don't go anywhere," she complained.

Mr. Phipps Rawson, who was a native Nevadan, took his leave muttering. He privately hoped that Mrs. Van Arden would come near to perishing of ennui since she was too snooty to mingle with the best people.

After a while Mrs. Van Arden changed her dress, fixed her face and set forth to see what Reno had to offer. It was about four o'clock in the afternoon.

If she had known that things were going to be like this, she was thinking, she would not have bitten the head off of the young man who had had the effrontery to address her in the breakfast room. She had had plenty of time on the Overland Limited to inspect the passengers and this young man had interested her. While he was homely and loose-jointed and a careless dresser, he had nice eyes and, she had observed, an intriguing smile. He looked as though he had a good sense of humor. Before she had married and lived two years with Reginald, Georgia had owned a sense of humor.

Suppose the fellow had left the train at Reno because she had descended there? A man might admire a woman without offending her. If he hadn't been so crass in addressing her this morning, they might have become acquainted. She was going to need an escort for she intended to see whatever was to be seen in Reno, and he would have served better than local talent. She hadn't seen a sophisticated-looking man since she arrived in the place and this whimsical-looking individual suggested extreme sophistication.

SO THE heiress to fifty million dollars wandered alone, lonesome and blue, down the main street of Reno and finally stopped in an arcade to inspect cheap gew-gaws because she had nothing better to do.

And while she was looking in the window she observed the young man saunter past the entrance to the arcade, glance in and continue on his way.

Life didn't seem so bleak to Mrs. Van Arden. She smiled at her reflection in the window mirror and went on up the street turning left at the next corner and stepping into a drugstore. Presently the young man strolled slowly past the drugstore. He was following her.

Three times more during her tour of the little city she spied the fellow in the middle distance and, with a heightened color, she returned to the hotel and ensconced herself in the vacant lobby. Georgia was a well-bred young woman with the inhibitions of her class who, despite the aberrations of her worthless husband, had conducted herself with circumspection and decorum. But she was about to be free; she was naturally gay-minded and at present was not averse to adventure. Of course this idiot should have found somebody, if only the hotel clerk, to present him to her, but she was in the wild and woolly West and she might as well forget conventions.

In two or three minutes, Addison Francis Murphy entered the hotel. He looked a little startled because he had not expected to find a lady of her social position lolling in a big chair in a hotel lobby. Georgia gazed at him solemnly and crooked her finger.

"Young man," she called softly.

Murphy pulled off his hat. "Marm?" he answered.

"Why are you following me?" she demanded gravely.

If the Rambler had known anything about women he would have realized that the lady was not affronted but he was still hot from recollection of the way she had burned him up in the breakfast room.

"It's a small town," he answered stiffly. "People who are out walking are apt to encounter each other."

"What is your name, please?" she demanded sternly.

"Addison Francis Murphy, Mrs. Van Arden," he replied.

"What made you think you could speak to a well-bred woman without an introduction?"

"You looked as though you had good sense," he retorted. "I found out different."

People couldn't talk like that to Georgia. Her dark eyes flashed dangerously.

"You are uncouth," she said angrily. "Don't you dare address me again."

"Don't want to," he said indifferently. "Seems to me that it was you who addressed me this time."

"Oh," she cried. "Don't you follow me, either, or I'll call an officer."

Murphy grinned impudently. "And look out that you don't follow me, Mrs. Van Arden," he retorted and hastened into the elevator, the door of which had opened at that instant.

He left behind him a very furious young woman. She clenched her hands tight to keep from shouting something slaying at his back. But well-bred girls didn't do such things. After all it served her right for having spoken to him. She could see now that he wasn't a gentleman. How had it been possible for her not to have discovered that before? He was quite a common person—ah!

When the elevator came down again she went up in it and in her room she put in a call for Mr. Rawson. She tapped her foot impatiently on the carpet while waiting. She was smiling with satisfaction for she had solved the problem of the redheaded young man.

"Oh, Mr. Rawson," she said when the lawyer came on the line. "You boasted of having influence an hour ago."

"No boast, Mrs. Van Arden."

"Good. I have identified my husband's detective. His name is Addison Francis Murphy. He is tall, thin, not bad-looking and is living at this hotel."

"Great work," exclaimed the lawyer. "What do you want done?"

"I want him taken out of my sight. Do something about him."

"We'll run him out of town, Mrs. Van Arden. He must be a dumb cluck to let you spot him."

"He is unusually stupid, it seems to me," she said spitefully. "Of course you won't hurt him."

"We'll handle him with gloves," the attorney assured her.

She hung up the phone. "The beast!" she exclaimed, and she didn't mean Mr. Phipps Rawson.

RAMBLER MURPHY, having been able to establish a system of espionage upon the movements of Mrs. Van Arden, by means of subsidized bell-boys and garage men, because of his newspaper connection, was able to devote some attention to the gentleman who had left the train at Reno and put up at the Golden Hotel. This individual was registered there as William Hornung. The morning following his arrival he had called at the telegraph office and sent two wires. Rambler tried to establish friendly relations with the sour-visaged woman in the telegraph office with a view to getting a peek at the Hornung messages, but he made no progress whatever.

He dropped in on the chief of police whose name was Casey, introduced himself as a reporter on the Reno *Recorder* and was cordially received. The chief explained to him why Reno was the safest, most orderly city in the United States.

"Crime, young feller," said Casey, "comes from what they call vice. Vice is going in for gambling, loose women and liquor. Wine, women and cards, see. Governments abolish them by law, but that only aggravates the demand for them and makes them more profitable. Naturally people supply the demand and that makes them criminals. Robbery, murder and all that follows. For bootleggers, gamblers and prostitutes—being law violators anyway—don't see why they shouldn't go the whole route.

"About the only other crimes arise from unhappy marriage relations. A man gets sick of his wife but he can't get rid of her so he beats her up, knocks her round and sometimes murders her, especially if he is stuck on some other dame. Am I right?"

"There is much in what you say," the Rambler admitted with a broad smile.

"Well," said the chief complacently, "in the free state of Nevada we look at things in a broad way. This is a man's state, see. We never did pay much attention to women reformers and ministers. So we make gambling and prostitution legal, and we never did have any laws against liquor. And, in a state where the population is all against prohibition, naturally the federal government is wasting its time bothering about it. So the police don't have to bother about gamblers and wild women and bootleggers; they're not criminals in Nevada. And when a man and woman who are married can't get along, they just walk down to the courthouse and the judge sets them free without any trouble at all. So crimes 'passional', as the French say, don't happen in Nevada.

"What's the result? A decent woman can go anywhere in this town without being molested. You can gamble your head off without worrying about being raided. And I hear it isn't hard to get a drink of good liquor. It takes the kick out of these things to have them legal. When a man can go out and raise hell without violating the law, he don't crave to raise hell. You can play roulette in most places for a nickel a chip and know you're up against an honest man. And married couples know they got to treat each other right or they can walk down the street and get rid of each other.

"About ninety percent of police business in other states is law violations that ain't crimes at all in Nevada which leaves us free to devote all our attention to real crime and its elimination. We don't have hard characters hanging round Reno because there's no money in our games to draw hard characters. Ain't it a fact that your big criminals in New York are all mixed up with gambling, booze and dames?"

"Yes," admitted Murphy.

The chief chuckled. "About all our trouble is with traffic violations by people from other states. No sir, there ain't much excitement for reporters in Reno."

"Still you have some hard characters."

"Oh, a few cowmen get drunk and want to fight. We handle them easy. We haven't any gangsters to bother about. Personal liberty has reduced crime to a minimum."

"And a young woman who comes here to live for six weeks and secure a divorce runs no risks of any sort."

"Not if she behaves herself. Some of the men who are here for divorces are of bad moral character but we keep a sharp eye on them."

"The old bandits and badmen of Nevada don't exist any more, eh?"

"We've wiped them out," the chief assured him.

"Well, glad to get the low-down, Chief. Good afternoon."

FROM police headquarters Murphy went to the Golden Hotel, which, being cheaper than the Riverside, was the dwelling place of the professional gamblers and visiting ranchers. He amused himself putting coins in the gambling machines which decorated the lobby as he watched for his man.

He had to get a line on Soft Simpson. The presence of the New York crook in Reno boded ill for Mrs. Van Arden but what sort of peril threatened her the Rambler couldn't figure out.

There might be a bold scheme to compromise the girl so that the Court would refuse to give her a divorce. Murphy couldn't see how this could do Van Arden any good since Mrs. Van Arden could always refuse to give her husband money. It might be blackmail but any sum secured in that way would be small change to Reginald. Having had millions, he would want millions.

If the young lady died suddenly, Reginald would come into the whole Gregory fortune provided his wife hadn't willed her money away from him. As young women dread the thought of death and do not anticipate it, it was quite possible that she had not made a will.

Soft Simpson, alias Hornung, however, was not a gunman. If murder were on the docket, he would probably engage local talent. The Rambler wanted to find out what acquaintances Simpson would make in Reno.

He could get the dope upon any suspicious local character through the police, trail him and be on hand to prevent foul play. While his attitude toward Mrs. Van Arden was anything but friendly, an attempt upon her life was a big story. And to pin it upon her unworthy husband, as he might be in a position to do, would be a bigger one.

His meditations were interrupted by a heavy hand on his shoulder. A thick-set, solid citizen with big feet and a walrus mustache was standing beside him.

"Name of Murphy?" he asked in a whiskey tremulo.

"That's right."

"The chief wants to see you," stated the stranger.

"I left his office fifteen minutes ago," declared the reporter.

"Yeah? Well he wants to see you some more."

"O.K. brother," said Murphy cheerfully.

Chief Casey, who had been urbane and garrulous upon the Rambler's recent visit, was very professional in his manner when the reporter entered again.

He was a small sharp-featured Irishman with blue eyes which now had a glint in them.

"Sit down," he commanded. "That's all, Jones."

The other went out.

"I been looking you up, bo," the chief said with a portentous nod. "I talked with Gamble. He says you offered him ten bucks a week for a job on The *Recorder*. What's your game, eh?"

"I like to be a reporter," replied Murphy. "This being a free state, its no crime to pay for a job, is it?"

"You told him you had a big story up your sleeve."

"Mr. Gamble has been indiscreet," remarked the Rambler.

"You don't say. I forgot to tell you, Murphy, that Reno considers ladies who come a long distance to establish residence here as honored guests. We guard and shield them, we do. We don't want anything to interfere with their enjoyment while they are here. We don't want skunks spying on them, if you know what I mean."

Murphy grinned. "Oh, you have skunks in Reno?"

"They come in from outside sometimes and we chase 'em right out like we are going to do with you."

"Exactly what do you think I am, please."

"You're a dirty rat of a private detective sent to make trouble for a poor girl with a broken heart. You were hired by her husband to get evidence against her."

"If I were, I am within my legal rights. If the lady in question does nothing incriminating, no evidence against her can be procured."

"Would you like to go to Frisco or to New York. You get a free ticket on a Pullman to either place."

"I like it here. I think this is the finest big little city in the world. I admire its broad viewpoint. I don't want to leave town."

"That's all," said the chief crisply.

"May I ask where you secured your information?"

"You may ask nothing."

"But—"

"I have no authority to run you out of town. I asked you to go by yourself. What happens to you after this doesn't interest me."

"It's no use to tell you I'm not a detective and no woman's husband has hired me to watch his wife?"

"I'm busy," stated the chief.

Murphy walked quietly back to his hotel. When he asked for his key the clerk said: "Sorry you're leaving us, Mr. Murphy. Your bags are packed and waiting to be put in a taxi, just as you ordered over the telephone."

"Mistake," said Murphy curtly. "Whoever phoned you was talking about some other Murphy. Send my bags back to the room."

The clerk looked surprised. "Well, just as you say, sir," he answered.

CHAPTER THREE

RUN OUT OF RENO

THE RAMBLER dined well, and at length, about seven in the evening and did not fail to study the other patrons in the dining room. There were half a dozen young, rather good-looking women who ate alone or in couples; three or four traveling men and the usual number of dowagers to be found consuming large quantities of food in any hotel room. Mrs. Van Arden did not appear.

The Rambler's interest in the beautiful lady had been personal in the beginning but strictly professional since morning. At present his attitude toward her was distinctly lukewarm.

She had suspected him of being a detective and had asked the police to remove him. Because of her great name and social prestige the chief had attempted to oblige her but had no authority to do more than to request him to leave. Of course Casey had phoned the hotel to have his bags packed.

Murphy grinned sourly. The snooty Mrs. Van Arden was going to be punished for her treatment of a well-wisher. She was making it hard for Addison Francis Murphy. When whatever was going to happen to her had happened, Mr. Murphy was going to be seriously handicapped. He had acquired the badge of a reporter and had counted upon the influence of a newspaper and the usual cooperation between police and journalists. Now he would have to be a lone wolf, or to express it better, a lone bloodhound.

He smoked a cigarette, after drinking his coffee, and then decided to stroll around and see what sights there were to be seen.

The Riverside, it should be explained, is beyond the river which bisects the city, and is opposite various public buildings which are dark at night. To reach the brightly lighted business and gambling section one must walk about a hundred yards.

Murphy had reached the middle of the bridge when rapid footsteps behind him caused him to glance back. Two men were close behind him. He continued on his way but before he had proceeded a dozen feet they had overtaken him. One stepped to his right side and the other to his left.

The Rambler made a threatening gesture of hand to hip where he had nothing but a handkerchief but the pair acted quickly. The man on his right grasped his arm and the man on the left pushed a gun muzzle against his stomach.

"Stand still, you cheap dick," growled the gun operator. "No funny business."

A closed motor car which had been standing in front of the hotel and was approaching slowly glided up to the curb.

"Get in," commanded the fellow who had hold of his right arm.

"Am I being taken for a ride?" asked Murphy calmly. "You guys are going to get in trouble with the biggest detective agency in the United States."

"We love trouble," said the gunman with a chuckle.

The other opened the rear door and Murphy, prodded by the weapon, stepped in. They followed him and one sat on either side of him.

Murphy might have been gravely concerned had this happened to him in Chicago or New York but he suspected that the city authorities had instigated his capture, and while they might be disagreeable they were hardly likely to countenance murder. And, if the Rambler had life, he had hope.

The car turned around and, gathering speed, tore through the residential section. In about a minute they were out on a highroad. Addison Francis had a glimpse of a sign board beneath an electric light which said "Carson City," with an arrow pointing in the direction they were taking. And then suddenly they were out of the city limits and hitting it at sixty.

"You ever been in Nevada before?" asked one of the two men. Murphy had sized them up and decided they were not policemen. They looked more like cattlemen of the type he had seen in the Golden lobby or as he passed the entrance to the crap and roulette shops.

"No," he replied. "I suppose you know that you're violating the law."

"Give him a crack in the jaw?" suggested the man on his right.

"If he opens his trap again, I will," promised the man on his left.

MURPHY remained discreetly silent. They had not been traveling more than ten minutes when the car swung into a side road and stopped. The chauffeur alighted with a flash lamp and walked to a sign board. With natural interest, Murphy saw the light illuminate a sign—"Virginia City, 15 miles."

"O.K.," said the chauffeur, returning. "This is the road."

It was a road which was in bad shape and apparently not often used for the pace slowed to less than twenty miles an hour and was accompanied by sharp jolts and jars.

Virginia City, the newspaper man recalled, was the famous ghost city of Nevada. Back in the Seventies it had had fifty thousand population and was the richest town in the United States per capita. A billion and a half in hard money had passed through its banks in fifteen years. He had read that it was practically uninhabited nowadays.

For half an hour the car bumped its way across a plain and then began to climb a stiff grade. Steadily it went upward, twisting and turning upon a mountain road. Its motor expressed its dissatisfaction by snorts and consumptive coughs. It was a cheap car. For half an hour it climbed with steadily diminishing speed and then it came to a full stop.

The chauffeur looked back. "Got to stop and let it cool off," he declared.

"Can you turn it around?" asked one of the Rambler's captors.

"I can back down a few yards and turn there."

"That'll do," said the other man.

"We can drop him here," suggested the other. "No use bustin' the injine."

The first speaker pushed open the door. "Get out," he said laconically.

"Why? What for?"

"You're pizoning the air," replied the fellow. "We was going to take you up to Virginia where there ain't nobody but coyotes and where you'd be in good company, but, hell, you can walk the rest of the way. Don't come back to Reno. We gave you a break this time."

"What will happen to me if I do come back?"

"You won't live long. Get out." Murphy stepped out of the car, which immediately slid back a few yards to a wide place in the road, turned and headed down the hill.

There was a moon and the weather was not cold and Murphy was safe and sound but exceedingly annoyed. He had been run out of town all right. They had taken pains not to dump him on the highroad where he might get a lift from passing cars but had turned into a side road which climbed a mountain to a ghost city upon which there was no traffic at all.

He stood in the middle of the road gazing after the winking red tail-light of the descending motor car. He estimated that they had traveled at least twelve of the fifteen miles to Virginia City. While he could walk back to Reno, it was a gravel road and he wouldn't make very good time. Five or six hours. On the other hand, if he went on to Virginia, which wasn't completely abandoned, he believed, he might pick up some kind of conveyance which would land him in Reno in an hour or so with no damage to his shoes.

He turned and started up the hill. He was not aware that he was climbing the Gieger Grade, one of the steepest grades in America, and that he had been put out of the car at an elevation of six thousand feet. He started off briskly but in a few minutes he was panting from exertion in a rarified atmosphere. He heard dogs barking—at least he thought they were dogs until he remembered the country was uninhabited, so they must be coyotes.

AT THE end of the first hour he had climbed about a mile and he was very tired but he was heartened, as he rounded a bend in the grade, to observe the headlights of a car a hundred yards distant.

The Rambler chuckled with satisfaction. He would be back in Reno an hour after his captors had reported that they'd deposited him in a wilderness from which he wouldn't escape in a hurry.

The car ahead was stationary and he heard the sound of a hammer. Evidently its chauffeur was changing a tire. That was luck. They might have refused to stop for him on such a lonely road.

He approached the car unobserved by its proprietors who were trying to insert a jack under the rear wheel and having trouble on gravel and a steep grade.

They looked up startled as he spoke to them and one of the pair turned a flashlight on him.

"You don't look like a bum," said a voice from the dark. What you doing here?"

"Walking to Virginia City," answered Murphy.

"Get at the front wheels, will yer?" requested the unseen man less gruffly. "If we can get this cart sidewise we can jack her up."

"Will you give me a lift down to Reno?"

"You said you was going to Virginia."

"Can't I change my mind?" asked Murphy, laughing.

The two men went around to the front of the car without making a reply and Murphy joined them. In the light of the headlights he observed with much interest that one of them was Soft Simpson, on the register of the Golden Hotel as William Hornung. Hornung, apparently was too much preoccupied to recognize in the pedestrian the man who had blundered into the compartment on the Overland.

Murphy helped them to jack the car and change the tire, thankful for the darkness at the rear of the car. When the job was done, he made to enter the machine but was rudely repulsed. "You keep right on walking," suggested Hornung with a chuckle.

Having no desire to impress his personality on Simpson, Murphy experienced no disappointment at the fellow's refusal to give him a lift. If he did return to Reno, they would only run him out of town again, and, a second time, he might not escape rough treatment.

He continued his arduous climb up the grade, forgetting his fatigue in mental activity. Hornung, alias Simpson in New York, was not in the least likely to be interested in the ruins of Virginia City—it was probable that he never had heard of the place before arriving in Reno. But Van Arden, of course, knew the history of the town. The original Van Arden fortune had come out of the Comstock Lode upon which Virginia had been built.

It looked to Murphy as though those working for the protection of the peace of mind of gay divorcées had conferred a favor on him in marooning him halfway up the Gieger Grade, and fortune had given him a break in causing Hornung's rear tire to get a puncture in this particular place.

Decidedly it would be a good idea to continue on to Virginia City.

The wire which Murphy had sent from Reno to New York had been to inquire of his newspaper friend the financial condition of Reginald and his whereabouts. The reply had stated that Van Arden's tailor had just secured a judgment against him and that the society man had left for Murray Bay, near the Gulf of Saint Lawrence, a few days before.

To get to Murray Bay, it was necessary to go to Montreal and from Montreal he could have taken train for Chicago and booked on the same express which carried his wife Renowards. Why?

Because he wanted Soft Simpson to identify her. And because he intended, when circumstances were auspicious, to make her listen to reason.

He could have left the Overland at Truckee and made his way to Virginia City by motor car. It was a perfect hideaway. Probably he had just had a conference with Hornung.

THE RAMBLER, a good hiker, was in a condition of extreme fatigue when, about midnight, he reached the outskirts of Virginia City. He tramped for half a mile along a shack-lined avenue, completely deserted, and finally came into a region of three- and four-story brick buildings, the windows of most of which were broken or boarded up, and upon the ancient doors of which were big padlocks.

Nowhere could he discern a gleam of light. It was veritably a city of the dead.

No—there ahead and to the right was a faint glimmer. He quickened his step. The light came through a dirty show window and revealed a lunch counter inside. A waiter sat on a high stool behind the bar, his head pillowed on his arms, fast asleep.

The Rambler entered but he had to touch the man to wake him up. "Hot coffee and a sandwich, please," he requested.

"Tank's empty. I'll have to make some fresh."

"Which is a break for me."

In about ten minutes he was served a sandwich made of stale bread and a cup of fairly decent coffee.

"Didn't know there was enough business here for a restaurant," he remarked.

"Things are pickin' up," replied the waiter. "A bunch of the unemployed is up here poking round in the old mines. Not that it does 'em any good."

Murphy, having eaten, surveyed his surroundings. A kerosene lamp shed a faint illumination but revealed that the place was of vast extent.

"Used to be a dance hall and gambling joint," the waiter explained.

As he was speaking the door opened and there entered a man of unpleasant visage. He wore a leather jacket, puttees, corduroy trousers and four or five day's growth of beard. He was low-browed and ugly.

"Hello, Tim," he said in a rumbling basso. "Cook me a New York cut steak with onions and French fried and be quick about it."

"Like hell I will," replied the waiter. "You owe this joint too much now."

"How much?"

The waiter consulted a dirty note book. Five fifty-five," he stated.

To the café man's astonishment, the newcomer took from his pants pocket a roll of bills, and peeled off a twenty from the company of at least four other twenties.

"Step on it," he said hoarsely. "Here's your jack."

"I can't change twenty," confessed the waiter with a ludicrous change of manner. "How come, Luke? You been broke for weeks and I know it."

"Never mind how come. I got a job, now."

"I'll change it," suggested Murphy. He took the twenty, and gave the waiter a ten and two fives. Immediately the restaurant man hastened to the kitchen to fill the order while the man with a job thrust his change into his pocket and surveyed Murphy with interest.

"You come up with him, eh?" he demanded in a low tone.

"Sure," said Murphy at random.

"Yeh. What's his name, eh?"

The Rambler hesitated for a fraction of a second. "Hornung," he ventured.

Out came a dirty horny hand. "Put it there, pard," said Luke heartily. "How much are you getting out of this?"

"Same as you."

"Hundred bucks, eh? Say, it's so long since I seen big money, I still think it's counterfeit."

"You're wrong," Murphy said, smiling and assured. "Hornung is working for a big shot."

"Yeah. When is it coming off?"

"Pretty soon."

"Well, I'm standing by. Say, I'll buy you a drink."

"Isn't the town locked up?"

Luke laughed loudly. "Been locked for fifty years but I know how to open it. Wait till I throw in this chuck. I ain't had a feed like this for six months."

"I'll hang around," stated the Rambler with a cryptic smile.

CHAPTER FOUR

GHOST-TOWN SET-UP

A FEW miles outside of Reno is a very interesting establishment known as the Oaks. It was established, as Tom Hobbs, the loquacious proprietor, explained to Mrs. Georgia Van Arden, for no other purpose than to provide for ladies of refinement and good taste who were forced by certain circumstances to spend a few weeks in a small city. It was a place where they might feel free to come with the assurance that they would meet only high-class people and that no one would presume to suppose that, because a girl was divorcing her husband, she would stand for any rough stuff.

"Anybody coming here can be assured of perfect privacy," said Mr. Hobbs in conclusion.

"Really?" inquired Mrs. Van Arden with gentle irony. "In that case why are you sitting here with us and doing so much talking?"

Mr. Hobbs grew very red and rose hastily.

"But I was just telling you—"

"You've told us," she said curtly.

Without a word the proprietor turned away and hastened to the bar where he demanded a stiff drink from his own private stock.

"That Van Arden dame is a Tartar," he confided to the bar tender. "Good-looking but got a tongue like a side-winder. The hell with her."

Mr. Phipps Rawson, who had been dragged, not with reluctance, from his own fireside to escort the wealthy divorce seeker, who declared that she never went to bed before one or two in the morning and must be taken somewhere amusing, ventured to chide his client.

"Hobbs has a big drag in this town," he told her. "You didn't have to bite his head off."

"I can't abide speakeasy proprietors," she said scornfully. "They are an oily tribe."

"Hobbs isn't like the others."

"That's true. He is more objectionable. Incidentally, this is a very dismal establishment, and that orchestra is dreadful. Tell them to stop."

"But they have to play for the dancing," he protested.

She gazed contemptuously at three couples who were circling the room and were apparently about to melt into three individuals. "I doubt if they would notice if the music did stop," she said. "This champagne is very nasty. It's synthetic."

Mr. Phipps Rawson, who had supposed the Oaks was "the last word" and the liquor superb, privately opined that the lady was difficult. However a man could take a lot of punishment for ten thousand dollars which was twice as large as any fee he had ever received.

"Maybe you'd like to buck the Tiger," he suggested.

She pushed back her chair. "Let's," she agreed. Georgia, who was wearing a red-satin evening costume which made her look so beautiful that she would have caused the divorce lawyer's hard old heart to go pit-a-pat if she hadn't been treating him like a menial, electrified the few people at the tables as she crossed the ballroom and went into the gaming room. There were no players and the two croupiers were amusing themselves and keeping their hand in by rolling the marble and trying to make it go into the predestined cup with a remarkable measure of success.

Mrs. Van Arden handed them a thousand dollar note—something which hadn't been seen at Reno gambling tables very frequently of late—and bought a huge stack of chips.

Carelessly she began to play numbers. Here was a chicken ripe for plucking and these were the boys to do it. But something wasn't clicking. Both croupiers were too young to be exposed to the effulgence of Georgia Van Arden. Her name also had a hypnotic effect, and the fact that she was so wealthy that she was totally indifferent to profit or loss. Nimble fingers did their best. Surely, when the girl was only betting on a sixth of the numbers, experienced wheelmen should have been able to shoo the pill into one of their own thirty cups but they couldn't do it.

Not even when the horrified face of Proprietor Hobbs appeared over the lady's shoulder, could the boys make good. The pile of chips in front of the siren grew enormously. Rawson, who never gambled, had the impudence to place chips upon those numbers which his client was playing and he won also.

AN HOUR had passed and the lady's luck did not change. Hobbs sent in two middle-aged croupiers whose fingers proved to be all thumbs. She had twenty thousand dollars in chips in front of her and something had to be done. Hobbs disappeared and then an alarm bell clattered noisily.

The croupiers did something, the floor opened and the table bearing Mrs. Van Arden's chips vanished into a yawning hole.

"Everybody out," called Hobbs from the doorway. "A federal raid."

"How amusing," remarked Georgia who had begun to enjoy herself.

Rawson, who knew that the one federal prohibition man in Reno was asleep in his bed, turned to Mr. Hobbs.

"Pay the lady off and we'll go," he said sharply.

"What were her winnings?" asked Hobbs.

"About twenty thousand dollars," said a croupier mournfully.

Hobbs reluctantly opened a safe and counted out twenty thousand dollar notes. Not only had she almost ruined the place but she had forced it to close for the evening and it was only one in the morning.

"Well," said Rawson as they sat back in her hired car. "You had an exciting evening after all."

"Exciting?" she said witheringly. "I was bored to death. It was a fake raid, of course. Those swindlers hated to lose their money."

"Oh, no. They have a huge bank roll," he answered, deliberately mendacious, but he had to uphold the reputation of the town. "It was a real raid. They always get tipped off so there is no danger. You could go out there alone and be unmolested. In fact the state of Nevada is safer for a woman than any place in the country and—"

Mr. Rawson pitched suddenly forward and so did Georgia for the chauffeur had jammed on his brakes. Out of a side road, a car had darted and parked directly in the middle of the narrow dirt road.

As the driver brought the limousine to a stop, both of its rear doors were pulled open and a masked man appeared on each side of the car.

"Get out," they said simultaneously.

Without a whimper, Georgia descended at the left and Rawson, sputtering with fear and anger, at the right.

Crash.

A heavy club struck Rawson on top of the head and he dropped with a low moan into the dust.

Georgia was treated differently. A chloroform-soaked handkerchief was jammed against her nose and she didn't know what happened after that.

The unconscious body of the lawyer was tossed back into his car and then the four tires were shot full of holes. During the affair the chauffeur had sat frozen behind his wheel. He saw the girl placed in the other car; observed the two masked men jump in with her and noted that the machine went away at seventy miles an hour.

Fifteen minutes later, a party from the Oaks came by and took Rawson in to Reno. The chauffeur remained at his post to await a garage car carrying four new tires.

In twenty minutes the chief of police of Reno had been informed that the wealthiest divorcee in the United States, the richest girl who had established residence in Reno in many years, had been abducted by masked bandits.

The morning papers stopped their presses. The wires carried the news to every city in the United States. The big story which Rambler Murphy had anticipated had broken and he had not been on hand to get it. If Georgia hadn't used Mr. Rawson's influence to get the Rambler run out of town, Addison Francis Murphy would have been on the job, of course. Her misfortune was her own fault without doubt, but that didn't make things any easier for her.

The Governor of Nevada was waked out of his slumber and told how the fair fame of the state had received a punch in the eye. He ordered every state officer to the aid of the city police. He issued a statement, that he would hang the miscreants when and if— There was no sleep that night for Chief Casey and his reserves. Political big-wigs rumbled orders at him. No stone was to be left unturned.

Even the prohibition officer issued a statement. An enterprising New York newspaper despatched a reporter by plane to Murray Bay to ask Mr. Van Arden if his wife's misfortune might not be the means of bringing about a reconciliation. In fact there was hell to pay.

IT WAS luck had caused Murphy's encounter with Luke Grogan in the lunch room. Grogan had taken him to a shack in Gold City, a suburb of Virginia where he was introduced to two unpleasant characters called "Lefty" Smith and Tom Sanders who had come in the previous day from Carson City in the guise of tramp prospectors. These were city crooks, despite their high boots and gallon hats and flannel shirts. They had hired Grogan who knew the country and presented him to Soft Simpson for approval. They accepted the Rambler as Hornung's representative without question because—a break for Murphy—Hornung, having everything set, was leaving Reno by train next day and "the boss" as they called him would take charge next night.

They spent the remainder of that night in drinking bad whiskey of which they had an abundant supply and used most of the next day for slumber. Murphy dared not ask questions lest he betray himself and he waited in the hut with the sodden brutes with growing impatience.

From the very beginning the Rambler had assumed that pressure would be brought to bear upon Mrs. Van Arden to make some settlement upon her husband, in return for his not contesting her divorce. But now he realized that any such agreement could be annulled upon the grounds of duress. And her abduction would make it evident that her agreement had been obtained by force.

Since she had made no will and had no near relatives, Van Arden, in case of her death, would inherit her entire fortune. While Reginald wasn't capable of so gigantic a crime, Soft Simpson was. The husband had called criminals into conference. Simpson was small fry and he wouldn't have gone West with Reginald if he hadn't been instructed to do so by some big shot.

Murphy believed that it was on the cards to throw the girl down the shaft of some old mine.

But would they do it immediately? The Rambler thought not.

Because the husband, not the criminals would inherit. They had to make him a participant in the crime to compel him to give them the lion's share of the profits. And, in all probability, they would drop

Rambler Murphy to the bottom of some thousand-foot shaft too, if he lifted a finger to save her.

Murphy was nearly as much in the dark as Georgia must have been regarding what was going to happen next

About five o'clock, Luke was sent out to buy grub, each man contributing a dollar. On his return he fried ham and made sour-dough biscuits on a broken-down wood stove. About seven in the evening they set out for an unknown destination. They walked several miles in the dark and encountered nobody, and finally arrived in the ruins of Silver City where Luke conducted them to the shaft-house of the Condado Mine which he had selected because he had found a winch in the shaft house, and a hundred yards of steel cable, in good condition. Luke, the only one who knew anything about mining, spent several hours in repairing a donkey engine and finally pronounced it fit. A huge hoist bucket was found in an outhouse and dragged to the mouth of the shaft, and then Grogan demanded a volunteer to go down. There was no eagerness to volunteer but Murphy, who wanted to know what it was all about, decided to take the risk.

"He'll lower you," Lefty Smith informed the Rambler, "until you come to some level that you think will do. You take this flashlight and look around. I'll hold a rope and pay it out and you give it a yank when you want the bucket to stop and two yanks when you want to be hauled up."

With considerable trepidation, Murphy had stepped into the bucket and said that he was ready. The ancient engine grunted, groaned, sputtered and finally functioned. He descended into the black hole of the shaft. Murphy had never been in a mine; he didn't know what they meant by a "station" and he passed several levels without being aware of it. When finally the bucket arrived in what his flash revealed to resemble a room, he signaled to stop.

CONVINCED as he was that his companions were preparing for the reception of Georgia Van Arden, he hadn't dreamed that they planned to hide her in the depths of a mine, but he saw that this "station," so-called, was admirably suited to be a prison. He pulled twice on the rope and, to his relief, the bucket began to rise.

In the course of several interminable minutes he reached the surface and stepped out.

"O.K.?" asked Lefty Smith.

The Rambler nodded.

"Hundred-foot level," reported Luke Grogan. "So that's all right."

"Douse all lights," commanded Smith.

"Aw, they ain't nobody round here to see 'em," protested Saunders. "If there was they could have heard the old steam engine."

"You can see a light farther than you can hear a sound," Smith replied. "Blow out that lamp, Grogan."

Darkness descended.

After an hour, in response to Saunders' pleading, they covered the windows of the ancient shaft house, relighted the lamp, sat on the ground and played black jack, at a quarter a bet, for hours.

Not a word was said to enlighten the Rambler regarding what was on the docket until Saunders remarked: "Suppose they don't get her. Maybe she's stayin' in the hotel."

"Wherever she is, they'll get her," replied Smith. "That right, Jonesey?" Murphy, who had given his name as Jones, hastened to agree.

About two-thirty in the morning they heard the hum of a motor car and the game was abandoned. A moment later the car stopped outside the door of the shaft house. All present except Murphy, who didn't have one, drew weapons after which Smith opened the door.

Two men entered bearing a slight figure wrapped in a blanket.

"All set?" demanded one of the burden bearers.

"Everything oke. We're parking her at a station on the hundred-foot level. Jones has been down and looked it over."

Both newcomers looked sharply at Jones.

"Who in hell are you?" one of them demanded. There was a tense second.

"Hornung sent me up here," replied the Rambler with dry lips.

"Hornung. Who's Hornung?" snapped the man who was holding Georgia in his arms.

Murphy stepped close to him. "Ever hear of Soft Simpson?" he murmured.

"Sure," replied the fellow with a laugh. "Which of you guys is going down? Somebody has to take her and stay with her."

"I got to work the hoist," Grogan hastened to state.

"Jones better go down. He knows the layout," said Smith quickly.

"Take her," commanded the fellow who was carrying the young woman. He placed the girl in Murphy's arms. Not for years had the Rambler held a girl in his arms. He experienced a thrill.

"I'll go," he declared. "I was sent up to stick with her."

They helped him into the bucket. He held the girl with one arm and grasped the chains with another, and looked around the ring of grim faces to make sure he would never forget one of them.

"Lower away," he instructed.

CHAPTER FIVE

BLACK HOLE OF HORROR

WHEN GEORGIA VAN ARDEN again became aware of things, she was lying upon a musty old sofa with broken springs in a huge and curious room. It was fully forty feet square. Its walls were plasterless boards and there were no windows. It was low-ceilinged and the ceiling was rough rock as was the floor. There were two or three ancient wooden chairs, an old pine board table of the kitchen variety. Most puzzling of all was the fact that there was a hole eight feet square in ceiling and floor. A wooden handrail with a gate protected occupants of the room from falling into the hole in the floor.

She noted rude doors in two of the walls. The place was lighted by two kerosene lamps, one on the table and one set upon a chair. She stared for a moment in bewilderment replaced by alarm, then uttered a sharp cry, flung off a blanket which had been tucked around her and sat up.

"How do you do, Mrs. Van Arden," said a voice whose tones were not unfamiliar. A man who had been sitting in a chair tilted against the wall a few feet from the head of her couch rose and bowed to her ironically.

"You," she exclaimed. "You—you scoundrel!"

Addison Francis Murphy grinned exasperatingly. "You never did think much of me," he observed. "How do you feel?"

She flung away the blanket, rose unsteadily to her feet and faced him. "What does this mean?" she cried. "Where am I? Let me go at once, you villain!"

Murphy rose politely and confronted her. "It means that you have been abducted, Mrs. Van Arden," he said gravely. "I don't think your life is in danger but your pocketbook is going to get badly dented. I'd like to take you out of here but it isn't possible."

"Bandit, kidnaper, criminal," she cried wildly. "You'll be hanged for this. Oh, how can a man with a face as honest as yours be such a beast. Help me get away and I'll see that you're not punished."

"I'm none of those things, lady," said Murphy whose face was crimson. "Do you remember that I spoke to you in the hotel breakfast room yesterday morning? Well, I wanted to warn you that you were in danger."

"A likely story," she said scornfully.

Georgia, in her low-necked gown, with her marvelous eyes and naked arms and shoulders, was a perturbing sight even for a man like the Rambler. He felt moved to justify himself.

"I twigged something was up on the train," he said earnestly. "That's why I got off at Reno."

"Don't lie," she said contemptuously, "You're a miserable private detective set to spy on me by my husband. I'll buy you. I have twenty thousand dollars."

"You had," he corrected. "I suspect the boys who brought you here relieved you of your cash." She thrust her hand to her bosom where she had placed the bills given her by Rawson at the Oaks. They were gone.

"Are you sure you haven't taken my money?" she sneered.

"Positive. Sit down, Mrs. Van Arden, please. Believe it or not, I'm your friend."

"I don't believe it."

"You will. I'm a newspaperman. I was keeping an eye on you in Reno because it would be a good story if anything happened to you. You're a public personality you know. You thought I was a dick and had me run out of town. If you hadn't done that you wouldn't be here now."

GEORGIA was almost persuaded because the Rambler was a convincing individual but she couldn't overlook the circumstances.

"I'm here because I was abducted," she said tartly. "What are you doing here?"

He grinned. "I'm on guard to see that you don't do anything rash."

"My jailer! Then everything I said about you is true."

"It looks bad," he admitted. "I had to join the gang to be of use to you."

"I want nothing from you unless you take me away from this awful house at once."

He gazed at her fixedly. "It's not a house," he said slowly. "And there is no way I can get you out of here at present."

"Not a house? What is it?"

"It's what they call a 'station' in a mine," he astounded her by stating.

"A mine—how can it—why—that couch, those chairs—"

"That," he said pointing to the hole, "is a mine shaft. In olden times two elevators ran up and down. We're on the hundred foot level. We came down in a big bucket and that's the only way we can get up. This is a famous mine in a place called Silver City, a few miles out of Virginia City. It has been abandoned for thirty or forty years. For heaven's sake, missis, don't faint."

Georgia was very near to collapsing but she rallied. "It's not credible," she gasped. "I—I don't believe you."

"I can't help that," he said curtly.

"Well," she said, "tell your confederates that I will pay whatever they ask—fifty thousand, a hundred thousand."

"If this thing goes through, I figure it will cost you about half of what you've got," he said solemnly. "Do you know where your husband is, Mrs. Van Arden?"

"In Murray Bay, Canada, I believe. What of it?"

"He was on the Overland with you, in a compartment up forward. I expect he's going to show up some time today."

She sat staring at him. "Reginald responsible for this outrage?" she said after a few seconds. "You're mad. He is a weakling."

"He's flat broke, isn't he?"

"Why yes, I believe so."

"Well, he's a night-club boy and knows a lot of big shots. Probably he sobbed on the shoulder of one of them and was told how he could get your coin—for a consideration. I'm no financier so I don't know how he could work it. Do you?"

Georgia smiled for the first time. "I am inclined to trust you," she said. "There is something about you, but I don't understand. You're a member of this gang—you admit it. I knew you were a hireling of Reginald's, of course. He wanted to catch me doing something I shouldn't and prevent my divorce."

"No. If you paid enough you could get the divorce anyway. Let me tell you the whole thing from the beginning. I can't help you if you don't trust me."

He told her about his recognition of Van Arden and Soft Simpson in the compartment on the train.

"And you took no personal interest in me at all?" she asked rather vexedly. "You thought of nothing but a newspaper scandal?"

"I liked your looks," the Rambler admitted, "but I'm not much for running after girls. I had worked it out that they would run you over into California," he continued, "and if they had snatched you and got away I wouldn't have known where to look for you. When you had me chased out of Reno—"

"I'm sorry but what could I think?"

THE RAMBLER was magnanimous. "Well, that's all right," he said. "It put me in the running again. When I found Soft Simpson was coming down from Virginia City, a place where he would never go except on business, it struck me that this ghost country up here would be an ideal hiding place, if they really were going to carry you off and not bump you off."

"Won't they kill you if they find out that you're not one of this gang?" she demanded.

"I don't intend for them to find out."

She frowned in concentration. "There will be a search," she declared. "People will have seen the car coming here. They'll find this mine."

"Mrs. Van Arden, this is an uninhabited country. Nobody lives along the road up to Virginia City. Almost nobody lives in Virginia or any of these ghost towns and there are hundreds and hundreds of abandoned mines. You've vanished off the face of the earth and that's no figure of speech."

"But these men will be observed. They have no business here."

"There are a lot of amateur prospectors roaming around, trying to pick up gold and silver for grub money. That's what these birds are pretending to be. Can we figure out your husband's game? Does he hope to force you to take him back?"

"My money is in my own name and, as soon as I am free, I can leave him. It can't be that. Mr. Murphy, will you forgive me for thinking badly of you?"

"Oh, sure. What else?"

"I don't know," she said in a piteous tone. "I'm—I'm afraid. Can't you take me away somehow?"

"There may be a chance but not now. There is no way of getting out of the mine except by means of the shaft. The bucket is at the surface and we're a hundred feet down. That's why the air is so bad. You're safe here till they want to let you out and the only reason they put me down here is that you might go crazy and jump down the shaft."

"I shall," she declared, "before I give them a penny." She crossed to the opening and looked down but saw only a black hole.

"How deep is it?" she asked, shuddering.

"I believe these silver mines went down a thousand feet or more."

She turned very white and went back and sat down on the couch.

"I suppose you've made a will," he said casually.

"Eh? No. I was going to when I secured my divorce. I'm alone in the world. I was thinking of willing my property to the Red Cross. Why?"

"Nothing. We've got to talk about something."

The young woman suddenly lost her nerve. She began to weep, then to laugh wildly, to wave her arms, to shout.

"Shut up," he ordered.

"Down in a coal mine, underneath the ground," she sang shrilly.

Murphy grasped her by the shoulder with his left hand and slapped her savagely on the cheek with his right. "Stop it!" he roared.

The treatment, though rough, was efficacious. She stopped but turned on him in anger.

"You beast, you brute!" she cried. "Get out of my sight!"

"Call me what you like," he said coolly. "You were off your nut and you might have jumped down that hole."

She stared at him blankly for a second, then covered her face with her hands.

PRESENTLY, she looked up and smiled very sweetly. "Thank you," she said softly. "I'm not afraid now. I'm placing myself in your hands."

"You lie down and see if you can't sleep some more," he said gently. "Don't talk. Close your eyes."

Meekly she obeyed him, Murphy frowned at the opposite wall.

Georgia threw off the blanket and sat up unexpectedly. "How long must we wait?" she demanded.

"I have no idea," he replied.

"What are you going to do when they come?"

He laughed mirthlessly. "Look for an opportunity to be helpful," he said shortly.

Suddenly she extended both hands to him. "I'm glad you are with me," she declared. "It would be horrible to be alone and worse to be with one of those beasts who abducted me. I'm not afraid, now. I was thinking just now that you would know how to handle them."

"I hope you are not flattering me," he muttered.

The awful stillness of the mine was broken by the creaking of the winch. The girl grew white. "They're coming," she gasped.

"Abuse me to them," he said hastily. "Demand that they take me out of here when they come."

"But I don't want you to go."

"It's the best way to keep me as your jailer."

"Oh, I see."

Presently the bucket appeared in the opening above. It was empty. It stopped at the floor level, bumped against the shaft wall and Murphy grasped its edge and looked into it.

"Food," he stated. After removing four sandwiches and two bottles of beer, he pulled twice on the rope which was fastened to the rail of the bucket and it ascended.

While they ate, Georgia felt moved to confide in her companion some of her troubles with the gay Reginald. She was sure of him now and exceedingly friendly. No girl in America had more charm than this young woman when she wished to be agreeable, and the Rambler's rancor against her dissipated rapidly. He was amusing her by telling tales of newspaper life when the rattle of the winch warned them that the bucket was again descending. He glanced at his watch. It was eight P.M. by his reckoning.

"Buck up," he said sharply to the girl. "It's the zero hour, I think."

There were two men in the big tub when it dropped through the hole in the ceiling. Both were crouching and the lamp revealed white worried countenances.

Murphy exclaimed softly. He boasted that he was never surprised at anything but he was surprised now.

One of the two men was Reginald Van Arden but it was the presence here of the other which astounded him.

Big Bill Bowers, overlord of the Bronx, was the second occupant of the bucket. Twenty-five hundred miles from his accustomed haunts; pallid with fear as he rode in the swaying bucket in the shaft of an abandoned Nevada mine. Big Bill Bowers!

Murphy stooped over, rubbed his hands in the fifty years' accumulation of dust on the stone floor, and smeared it on his face. He had contacted Big Bill in the past and didn't relish the idea of being recognized.

He heard an angry exclamation from Georgia who had recognized her husband. Both men were staring at her, Bowers with admiration in his pig eyes.

CHAPTER SIX

MURDER MINE

THE BUCKET touched the side of the shaft, came level with the floor and Murphy stepped forward and gave a hand to big Bill. With a sigh of relief the criminal stepped out upon solid ground. His eyes were fixed on the beautiful woman.

"Cripes!" he exclaimed. "Some dame!"

Van Arden Stepped out in his turn. "Hello, Georgia," he said with obvious embarrassment. "Hey, look out!"

For Georgia was rushing at him with claws extended. Murphy stepped behind her and deftly pinioned her arms by her side. In her fury the girl kicked back at him with sharp French heels.

"Snappy work," commented Bowers in his deep basso. "Make 'em behave. Girlie, that ain't no way to greet your loving husband."

"You're in a tough spot, Georgia," said her husband. "And you'd better get wise to yourself."

"Kidnaper," she retorted. "Make this beast let me go. That's the least you can do."

"Let her go, bo," commanded Bowers. "I'll make her behave, myself."

She turned blazing eyes on Bowers. "Who are you?" she demanded.

"Me? I'm a friend of your husband. I want to see the boy get a square deal. Take her over to that couch, you. Your name's Jones, ain't it?"

"That's right," said Murphy.

Bowers, whose soubriquet "Big" was descriptive stepped in front of her.

"Now lady," Bowers stated, "We ain't goin' to waste time on you. My friend Reggie, here, is your lawful husband. You run out on him and left him flat broke. You got minions and he ain't got anything. Do you call that fair?"

Georgia looked him over contemptuously and did not speak.

Reginald came forward. "Georgia," he said, "I'm desperate. You're going to be kept a prisoner in this awful place till you listen to reason."

"What is reason?" she snapped scornfully.

He drew from his pocket a legal document. "This is a separation agreement dated ten days back and notarized," he said in a voice which was unsteady because Van Arden, though worthless and a wastrel, had not been a criminal very long. "You sign it and we'll let you go."

"And what am I to sign?" she asked in a bitter tone.

The man hesitated.

"Come on, get it over with," rumbled Bowers.

"It is an equal division of your property," said the miserable husband who dared not meet her eyes.

Georgia laughed shrilly. "You fool!" she declared. "It wouldn't hold. The false date won't deceive anybody. The whole world knows I have been abducted. There is no question whatever that you will go to jail for a long time."

"It's no crime for a man to carry off his wife," declared Van Arden. "You can't scare me, Georgia."

"If it isn't a crime, the fact that you forced me to sign over half my fortune would invalidate the document," she retorted.

During this discussion, Murphy stood, tense and anxious, six feet away. It was obvious to him that Bowers was not present to witness the signing of a document worthless on the face of it and Van Arden was weak-minded to think so.

"You're too damn smart, girlie," growled Bowers. "If Reggie had your brains, he wouldn't need your money."

"Damn you, what do you mean?" snarled Van Arden.

Bowers stepped back a few paces and suddenly pulled from under his left armpit, a large automatic.

"Jones, go stand alongside of Van Arden," he thundered. "Quick!"

"But Bill!" protested the husband.

"The hell with half her dough. We want it all," declared the gangster. "She's got fifty million, ain't she?"

Van Arden waved the document vaguely.

"If she croaks, you get it all, don't you? She ain't got no will, has she?"

GEORGIA stood up, very white, trembling; her eyes fixed imploringly upon the Rambler who had stepped to the side of Van Arden.

"There is no question of murdering my wife," protested Reginald who was shaking with terror. "For God's sake, Bill—"

"You two guys grab her and chuck her down the hole," commanded Bowers. "Quick, or I'll drill you."

"No, no, for God's sake—" Reginald's voice was falsetto with fright.

The automatic's cruel muzzle covered him. "Quick," roared Bowers.

Murphy stepped to Georgia's side, grasped her right arm and pressed it reassuringly.

Surprisingly, Van Arden rallied his forces. Into his fear-stricken eyes came a cunning look. "Shoot me and you don't get a penny of her money," he screamed. "You don't dare to shoot me."

Bowers scowled ferociously and Murphy spoke. "Chief," he cried, "if you fire a shot, the whole damn mine may cave in. The timbers are all rotten."

Slowly Big Bill lowered his gun. He hesitated. "Yeah?" he sneered. He thrust the weapon back into its holster, took a few steps forward and towered over the unhappy amateur criminal.

Wham.

His huge fist smashed into Reginald's face. The force of the blow sent Van Arden flying half a dozen feet and threw the big man off balance. And then Big Bill had the surprise of his life. A hard, bony fist driven with all the force of a hundred and fifty pounds slammed against the point of his jaw. Partly from the force of the blow, partly because he was unbalanced, he pitched ever and Murphy threw himself upon him, driving at his head with everything he had.

If Big Bill Bowers had not been a rough-and-tumble scrapper who had risen from pushing around packing boxes on a pile to dictating to Tammany Hall, the unexpected assault would have overpowered him. But it was impossible to knock Bill out and he could fight with fists and feet and teeth. For half a minute the Rambler smothered him and then superior weight and strength began to tell.

"You dirty double crosser!" he roared. "You rat, you trimmer, I'll tear you apart!"

Slowly he rose to his feet, dragging the wild-cat, Murphy, with him.

Meantime, Van Arden had recovered sufficiently to sit up and was gazing in bewilderment at the battle. Georgia was upon him instantly. She shook him violently. "Help him, help him," she commanded. "Don't you see he'll get killed?"

Her husband pushed her away. He was *hors de combat* and content with his position.

Bowers had Murphy at arm's length, his big left hand gripping his throat, his right fist battering his face. Georgia, who came of a fighting tribe, could restrain herself from interference no longer. She rushed at the giant gangster and grasped at his right arm. He disposed of her with a straight-arm, and the girl fell and went slithering across the floor toward the wall.

Taking advantage of the second's diversion, Murphy tore his throat free and drove his right into the big man's only vulnerable spot, his stomach. Bowers grunted and then rushed like a bull. The Rambler tried to sidestep, trod and slipped on the hand of Reginald Van Arden—he was still sitting on the floor—and measured his length.

"By God, I'll chuck you down the hole," roared Bowers. He grasped the Irishman, who was flat on his face, in his enormous hands, lifted him a few inches and suddenly pitched forward without a sound and fell across the Rambler's body. Murphy twisted out from under him.

"Glory be!" he exclaimed.

GEORGIA held in her two hands a lump of ore as big as a flagstone. She had brought up against it as she slid across the floor. In desperation at her champion's fall, she had lifted its thirty pounds above her head, darted forward, and dropped it on the back of the head of Big Bill Bowers as he stooped to grapple with Addison Francis Murphy.

"I—I've killed him," she whispered with stricken eyes.

"Small loss," muttered Murphy grimly. He stopped and whipped the automatic from its holster under Bowers' left arm and leveled it at Van Arden who was up and advancing.

"Get back," he snapped.

"I say, my man—by heavens, it's the fellow on the Overland!" exclaimed Georgia's husband.

"How are you?" remarked Murphy. "Keep your distance, skunk."

He stooped, caught Georgia above the knees, and lifted her into the bucket and jumped in after her.

"Here, take me with you," pleaded the woman's husband.

"To hell with you," snarled Murphy and gave two pulls to the signal line.

Their last glimpse of Reginald showed him standing at the rail with his arms lifted imploringly.

Then Georgia's arms were around his neck. "God bless you," she cried hysterically. "I'll be grateful all my life. What a man you are! They were going to kill me. You saved me!"

He gently removed her arms. "You had a lot to do with your own salvation, lady," he remarked. "And we're not safe yet by a long shot. Lie down in the bottom of this thing."

"But why?" she demanded.

"Because we're sailing right into a hornet's nest. Get down, I say, and keep your head down. I'll see for both of us."

The bucket rose steadily, the rattle and creak of the Winch soon became clearly audible.

Murphy, the gun clutched in his right hand, gazed upward anxiously. How numerous was the reception committee? What were his prospects of getting the girl away? It had been two to one below—it might be ten to one on the surface.

A faint illumination was penetrating down the shaft. Now the surface was only a dozen feet above. His head was at the floor level. Luke stood at the winch lever. Smith and Saunders were sitting on the floor smoking. A fourth man was standing near the exit and turned as the bucket appeared.

The Rambler's left hand was resting on the top of the girl's sleek black head and pushing it further down. His right, with its weapon, was concealed by the side of the bucket.

The fellow at the door was an Italian, well dressed but low-browed with sharp black eyes.

"Who's this?" he shouted. As if by magic a revolver appeared in his right hand.

"O.K." drawled Smith. "It's Jonesey. They sent him up."

But the other man took a step nearer and was able to look into the bucket.

Crack.

The automatic in the Rambler's hand spat fire while the gangster's eyes were conveying to his dull mind that a woman was in the bucket. He dropped.

"Stick 'em up!" bellowed Murphy turning the weapon on Smith and Saunders who had reached for their guns.

Luke Grogan, who had shut off the donkey engine, reached for the lever which would drop the bucket. Out of the corner of his eye, the Rambler saw his action, moved his weapon and sent a bullet into the chest of the ruffian.

Crack, Crack. The other two had taken advantage of the diversion to draw and fire but their speed affected their aim. Astonishment at the sudden shift of a companion into a murderous enemy put them at a disadvantage. Murphy dropped Lefty Smith. He winced as a shot from Saunders grazed his scalp, then sent three bullets into the body of the survivor of the quartet.

"All clear," he said cheerfully. "You can come out."

But Georgia did not move. She had fainted.

THE gunman who had accompanied Big Bill Bowers was dead. Grogan was dead. Smith was badly wounded and Saunders had four bullets in him and was unconscious. Murphy lifted the girl in his arms and ran with her from the shambles. Outside the shaft house stood a small sedan, vacant. He set Mrs. Van Arden in the front seat, shipped behind the wheel, found the key in the lock and started the car.

He drove at a dangerous speed over a poor road toward Virginia City, not that he feared pursuit but because he had things to do. Presently Georgia stirred, opened her eyes, sighed, and then broke into thick heavy sobs.

"Quit that," he snapped. "Everything's O.K. now."

"But the shooting, the killing, the blood—" she cried wildly.

"Can't make an omelet without—breaking eggs. We were in a tough spot, Mrs. Van Arden."

Georgia wiped her eyes with her fists, her very dirty little fists. "I can't express my gratitude," she murmured. "You were amazing."

"Lucky is the word," he said shortly.

She began to laugh. "Reginald," she exclaimed hysterically. "He's down in that hole!"

"Don't you go goofy on me," cried Murphy. "I've got nerves, myself, young woman. Sit still and shut up."

She was cowed and silent for a moment, then she reached up and touched his cheek. "Blood!" she exclaimed. "You're wounded."

"A scratch on the top of the head—nothing."

Georgia drew a deep breath. Her eyes were shining brightly.

"Nothing," she repeated. "You are the bravest man I ever met. That horrible creature would have murdered me. I owe you more than I can ever repay. If I live to be a hundred—why are you stopping? What place is this?"

"Virginia City. I think there's a telephone in the lunch room here."

"Never mind telephoning. I'm alone in the world. Nobody cares what has become of me."

Murphy chuckled. "About a hundred and thirty million people are probably all hopped up over your disappearance. I've got to send a doctor up to the mine and phone the story in to the *Recorder*."

"What Story?"

"What story? Your abduction, the plot to murder you. The death of Big Bill Bowers—and the fact that your husband is down there on the hundred-foot level."

"I forbid you to print anything," she said excitedly. "I won't have scandal, Mr. Murphy."

"Listen," exclaimed the ruffled Rambler, "all I get out of this is the big exclusive story. I'm phoning it, Mrs. Van Arden and that's that."

"I am very rich, Mr. Murphy," she said softly, "and very grateful. You can ask me for any reward you please. I like you. I want to be friends with you. I admire you more than any man in the world. Be sensible. Don't put this horrible story in the papers."

Murphy was getting out of the car—in his eyes the fanatic glare of a reporter with a scoop. "Be through in about ten minutes," he said coldly. "Make yourself comfortable."

AFTER the Rambler had phoned his yarn to The *Recorder* office he returned to the car and drove down the Gieger Grade toward Reno.

Georgia said nothing but occasionally gazed up at him with a shy worshipping smile.

Halfway to Reno, a procession of cars met them. They contained the mayor, the chief of police, the Wart Hog, owner of The *Recorder*, and other prominent persons. The mayor threw open the door of his big limousine. Georgia refused to enter. She rode into Reno with her rescuer's right biceps clasped possessively in both her small hands. Mr. Murphy liked the feel of it—and he didn't. The rapt smile upon her beautiful face perturbed him. If he didn't look out, he was likely to acquire a very rich and lovely wife.

Georgia had considered the Rambler not unattractive when she inspected him on the Overland. And she had been privileged to see a strong clever man in action. Most women have to take their lover's prowess on faith and, during a life time, never get a chance to test it. As she sat beside him during that memorable ride, she was making up her mind to keep him around until she was rid of the publicity incurred by her incarceration in the Condado Mine. After which she would marry Addison Francis Murphy and settle down with him on the Gregory estate on Long Island.

And the astute Mr. Murphy sensed his danger. Marriage with a beautiful but domineering grass widow of incredible wealth would be a calamity. She was a swell girl—she certainly had turned the tide of battle back there with her slab of ore but—

He stopped before the Riverside Hotel, opened the door, stepped out and helped her to the sidewalk.

"But you're coming in," she exclaimed as he jumped into the car.

"Got to go to The *Recorder* office and fill in details of the story," he said firmly.

"Oh, then I'll expect you at ten in the morning for breakfast."

He nodded.

"You promise—"

"Oh, sure," mumbled the Rambler. He drove away as the celebrities who were close behind them crowded around her.

At midnight the west-bound Limited rolled into the Reno station—an hour late. Out of the shadows came a young man with a suitcase who thrust a ticket at the porter of one of the Pullmans and climbed aboard.

The porter deposited his bag in his section and Addison Francis Murphy dropped into his seat, heaved a deep sigh and wiped his fevered brow. He had received a hundred dollars from the Wart Hog and that was all his recent achievement had profited him. However he was perfectly contented.

In a few seconds the lights of the biggest little city in the world had dropped behind.

"Gosh," murmured the Rambler. "That certainly was one swell girl."

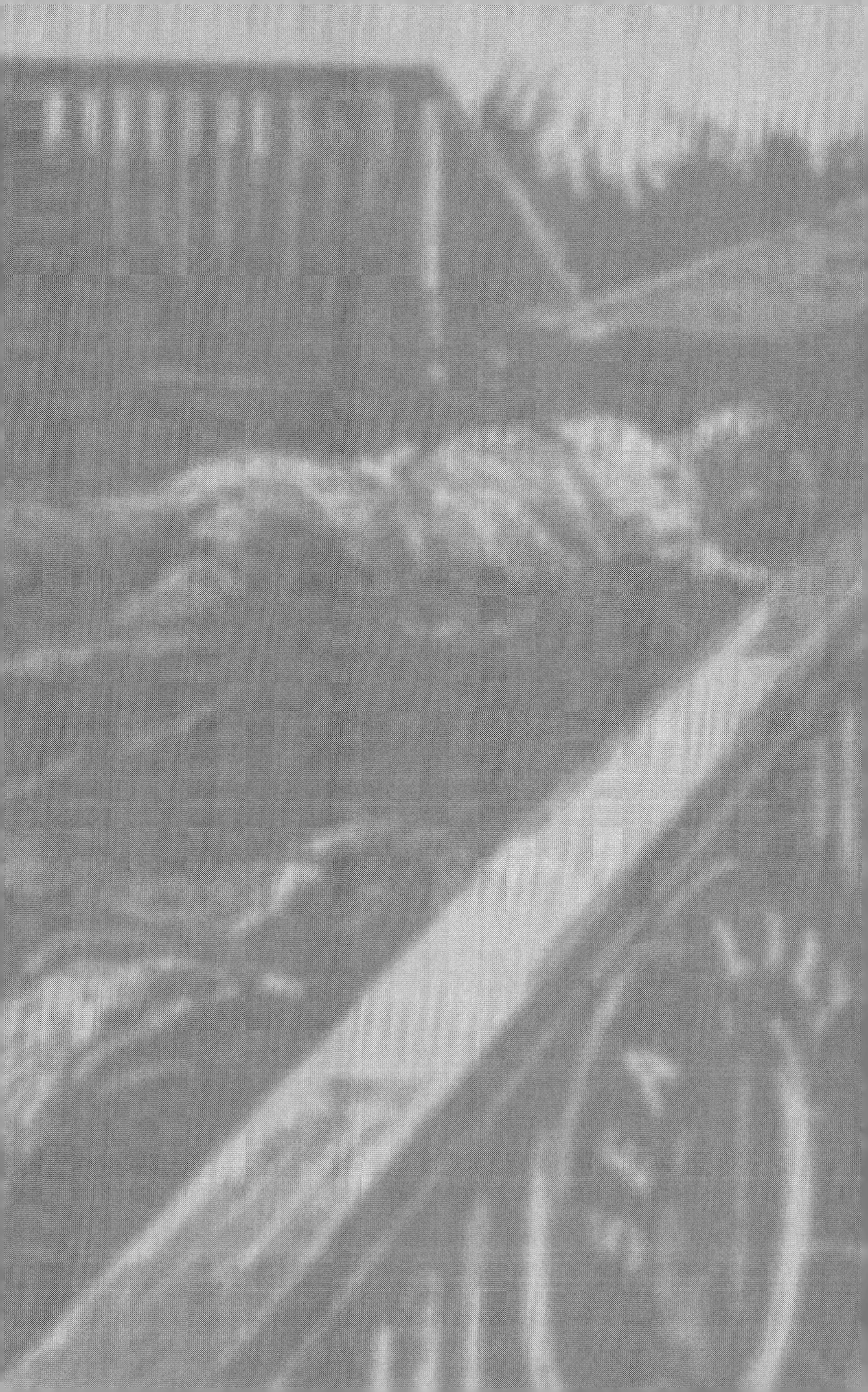

GO-BETWEEN

IT WAS BAD ENOUGH TO WAKE UP WITH THE KIND OF HANG-OVER THE RAMBLER HAD WITHOUT FINDING THAT HE'D DRUNK HIMSELF INTO THE MIDDLE OF A HUNDRED-GRAND ABDUCTION MYSTERY THE NIGHT BEFORE. BUT DRUNK OR SOBER, NEWS WAS NEWS TO THAT ROVING RED-HEAD—THE MORE DANGEROUS THE BETTER. EVEN WHEN IT MEANT TAKING HOT LEAD FROM BLUE STEEL BEFORE HE COULD BANG OUT HIS STORY.

CHAPTER ONE

THE MORNING AFTER

A**DDISON FRANCIS MURPHY** awoke with a very bad hangover. Sunlight was pouring through a window; brilliant sunlight which hurt his eyes. He closed them tightly.

Something was annoying his ears too. A peculiar swishing sound, which seemed to work according to some system because it had a rhythm to it. In the state of mind he was in, this noise puzzled him. It sounded like ocean waves. It was waves. Maybe Los Angeles had been engulfed by the ocean for its sins, in some cataclysm of nature, and the sea was now beating against the hills of Beverly. In which case he'd have to go somewhere else to get a newspaper job. All right. He didn't care much for Los Angeles.

He dozed off and awoke sometime later. The waves were still pounding against his eardrums, but his head didn't ache so much. He placed a foot, tentatively, upon the floor. Yes, there was a floor, all right, and he was in a bed. That was something to start on. Bed. Floor. Sunshine. Waves.

Mr. Murphy rose unsteadily and went to the window. He was in a room on the second floor of a house. He was looking down upon the Pacific Ocean.

He observed that there was a yard in front of the house with a fence on either side and the ocean at the bottom of it. There was a long array of fences to right and left. Furthermore these yards were inhabited by dead people, mostly women with golden hair who lay upon their stomachs motionless and more or less naked. There was one right under his window.

No. She wasn't dead. She rolled over, saw him at the window, lifted a sunburned arm and waved it at him.

"Bah!" exclaimed Addison Francis Murphy. He reached up and

He socked them—one by one—as
they came through the door.

pulled down the curtain. He heard a peal of silvery laughter.

Even now the room wasn't as dark as it ought to be to please a fellow who felt the way he did. Where was he? How did he get here? Who was the hussy? Where were his clothes?

It was the custom of Mr. Murphy, when retiring, to drop his garments where he happened to be standing when he removed them, but now there were no garments in the room. Gradually he became aware that he was wearing a pair of wine-colored satin pajamas which were too small for him. He caught a glimpse of his face in a mirror on a bureau and closed his eyes to shut out the awful spectacle. At best, Mr. Murphy's features were not beautiful, being of a remarkable ruggedness; but today there was upon them a mushroom growth of reddish hair, and the eyes were bloodshot.

Turning away, Murphy espied a closet door. With no hope in his heart, he opened the closet. There were his garments, placed neatly on hangers!

He had finished dressing and was rubbing his thumb and forefinger against his beard when there came a knock at the door.

"Use your own judgment about coming in," he said gruffly.

The door opened and there appeared in the doorway a girl in bathing suit. It was a very small bathing suit for a tall girl. It revealed yards of slim, shapely golden legs and astonishing quantities of golden bosom and golden arms. There was a pretty face set on a long, slender neck and, on top, a mass of golden hair like a halo. She smiled winningly.

"Hello," she said.

"How are you and aren't you ashamed of yourself?"

"This is the beach," she retorted.

"The question is, what beach?"

She laughed heartily. "Malibu, you goof," she replied.

"Malibu. I've heard of it. Motion picture paradise. Who are you?"

"Mary Monmouth."

"I never heard of you."

"Well," she said, smiling, "I don't even know your name. You claimed you were known as the Rambler."

"Lady, how did I get here?"

"You came with a party. I only knew one or two of them. We found you after they left. My maid and I undressed you and parked you in this room."

"Did you put my clothes in the closet?"

"Yes, of course."

He sighed with relief. "I knew I couldn't have done that. Who was I with?"

"Armand Pierre and George Nelson and a slew of girls."

"There must be some mistake. I don't know those guys and I hate women."

She sat down on the side of the bed and put her arms behind her head and laughed in his face.

"I hate men, so that's that. Would you like to have me open a can of tomato juice?"

"Just give me the can; I'll swallow it."

She laughed and left the room.

ADDISON FRANCIS MURPHY lay down on the bed again. "Let's see," he said. "I got here yesterday morning. I called on all the city editors and there were no jobs. I hadn't eaten since the night before. I sat on a bench in the Plaza Park and a fellow alongside of me gave me a drink of gin. Gin on an empty stomach started me off. That's why I don't drink gin. I went into the Biltmore and shook hands with a total stranger and made a quick touch. He gave me ten dollars. He introduced another guy and we went into a bar and had more gin. From then I was walking in my sleep,"

The girl came back at this point in his meditations, with a tray upon which stood a tall glass filled with a crimson liquid with ice in it. He pounced upon it and drained the glass. For the first time he smiled.

"Seems to me I've seen you somewhere," he stated.

She nodded. "Last night you saw a lot of me."

"I wouldn't remember that."

She laughed gaily. "You asked me to marry you. I have witnesses."

He yelled in terror, and made a leap for the door.

"Hold on," she cried. Tears of mirth ran down her cheeks. "I turned you down."

He stopped in his flight. "I thank you," he said gravely. "I wouldn't care to marry anyone. But I've seen you somewhere."

"Do you go to motion pictures?"

"Not if I can help it."

"Well, I'm considered a very successful film actress."

"That's it. Thanks for the night's lodgings. I'll be going now."

"But you have no money."

"I can walk to town."

"From Malibu?"

"Sure. How far is it?"

"Thirty-five miles."

"Oh," said Murphy. "The city of magnificent distances. I forgot. How did you know I had no money?"

"Looked in your pockets. When people pass out here, we always look in their pockets. Sometimes they have articles of great value which we lock in the safe."

"Very considerate of you. Well, I'll be on my way."

The girl smiled at him bewitchingly.

"Don't be in a hurry. You're a quaint character. I'll invite you to have lunch and dinner."

"Good-bye," said Murphy firmly.

"You're the first man I ever met who turned down one of my invitations," she said resentfully. "What sort of a person are you, anyhow?"

"Addison Francis Murphy and I don't like girls," he told her. "I particularly don't like girls who go round with no clothes on."

"I'll put on a dress if you're going to be like that. Look here. It's Sunday. You told me last night you were out of a job and had to land one on a newspaper. You can't find an editor on Sunday; and I'll send you into town tomorrow morning in my Rolls."

"I'm walking."

"You're an imbecile," she said tartly.

"O.K.," said Murphy coldly.

"Look here. Why do they call you the Rambler?"

He grinned, having achieved his end, which was to get out of the influence of this houri. "Because I ramble," he said. "I'm what's known as a tramp newspaper man. I don't like any place very long. I don't think I'm going to like Los Angeles at all. Too many girls with long legs."

"Suppose you get out of my house," she said, thoroughly incensed at last. "And if you're a tramp, you won't mind walking thirty or forty miles. You give me a supreme pain. Amskray."

"I'm going," he said with a broad grin. "You're all right, kid. You ought to have thrown me out last night."

"This way," she said curtly.

He followed her downstairs into a large and richly furnished living-room, through a most attractive dining-room and through an exit at the rear. A colored man was coming up the walk from the road.

"I'm all over my mad," said the girl then, laying a friendly hand on Murphy's shoulder. "Jones… Get out the car and take this gentleman into town. What are you going to use for money, Rambler?"

"I'll get along, thanks. And, if you insist, I'll accept the ride in the bus."

A COUPLE of minutes later, Addison Francis Murphy lolled in the back seat of a fifteen-thousand-dollar motor car as it passed through the gate which separates the estates of Malibu from the highroad. He tightened his belt, being hungry, and watched with lack-luster eyes the unending vista of sea and rock and sand as the car sped towards town.

In five minutes the car passed a small, white-painted cottage located on a slight eminence at the left of the road, its rear-seat occupant unaware that, within, a conference was going on which was going to have a remarkable effect upon his immediate future….

"There it goes," said a man at the window of the little house, as the car passed. "She's sending the bum back to L.A. Jones will be away at least two hours. The maid will leave in fifteen minutes to spend the afternoon with her sister at the north end of Malibu. Mary will be alone in the house. Eli Grant's house next door is closed. We'll run Mary in there and keep her until night and then we'll swim her out to the motor-boat. It's a cinch."

He was a tall, dark fellow with a handsome face. In the silent screen days he had been a famous heavy. Talking pictures had ruined him and, though Armand Pierre was still seen about Hollywood and was still welcomed in many homes, nobody knew how he earned a living.

"I'm taking your word for it that we can collect," said the second of four men in the room.

This one was a short, squat individual with a broad, flat nose and a huge mouth and small, evil eyes. His name was Nelson and, by profession, he was a gambler. The other two persons present were of a type more familiar in Chicago than in Los Angeles. They were aliens, dark, sleek, not bad looking and exceptionally well dressed—almost too carefully dressed.

Pierre approached the table around which the other three were seated.

"I'll tell you again," he said. "Mary is starring in 'Honor Above All.' It's the most expensive film that Sublime Pictures have ever shot. It's three-quarters finished and they're in a million and three-quarters. Delay will cost them thirty thousand dollars a day. They can't lose Mary without retaking the whole picture, which would bankrupt them. They're in a spot. We'll have the dough within twenty-four hours after we notify them that she's in our hands."

The two gunmen nodded.

"I'm taking the chance," the gambler said.

"Why not wait until night and snatch her?" suggested one of the gangsters.

"Because," said Pierre, with patience, "by four or five o'clock, her house will be full of people. We may not get another chance to catch her alone."

"Yeh, but they'll look us over at the gate. You're a prominent guy. When the word goes out, they'll have our descriptions."

Pierre laughed, crossed to a closet and opened it. "Giolitto and Jerome—you wear girl's clothes," he said. "I put on a make-up. It's my business. We put a black wig on your bald head, Nelson, build up your nose and you'll look like a motion picture producer—even worse. We go in with the stolen car out back, which we abandon. They'll have descriptions but they'll do nobody any good."

"Yeh, but these fellows at the gate ask questions...."

"Not if they see girls. We tell them we're calling on somebody and are expected and we'll go right through. Are you telling me how they run Malibu?"

"Say, boss, suppose these folks that show up go round asking questions?"

"The house will be empty. We're hidden next door and that place is boarded up. I have a key to the back door. Mary is gagged. There's no moon tonight. The motor-boat will signal as soon as she's off the house. We're all good swimmers."

"It's a cinch," decided Nelson. "Let's get dressed up. Make me up for some big producer, Armand."

CHAPTER TWO

MASQUERADE

HALF AN hour later, a small sedan turned out of the highroad and stopped at the gateway to the private beach of Malibu. There was an attractive brunette beside Pierre in the front seat. Pierre himself had become a blond man with fat cheeks. Nelson bore a striking resemblance to a certain famous Jewish producer and the girl beside him was a sinuous brunette.

"House 29," said Pierre to the attendant. "Expected."

The man nodded and the car rolled on.

Malibu Beach, it should be stated here, is a curious summer colony located on the Pacific Ocean about one-third the distance from Los Angeles toward Santa Barbara. It is a part of the Malibu Estates, a vast ranch as large as several Eastern counties. The shore front is leased, not sold, to the occupants and according to the terms of the lease, the houses erected upon it revert to the land-owner after a comparatively short term of years.

Because of these conditions, the most extravagant of film stars have been deterred from constructing here the type of dwellings familiar to visitors to Hollywood and Beverly Hills. Each lot is narrow, and despite the fact that there is an almost perfect beach from San Francisco down to the Mexican line, the beach houses here are so close together that their side-walls are only a dozen feet apart. Residences rarely exceed fifteen or twenty thousand dollars in cost and are built of wood or stucco, with one or two exceptions.

Being guaranteed as to the character of their neighbors and protected from intrusion by the guards of the estate, beautiful young women live here alone without fear. The fact that she was alone in the house on this day did not, therefore, concern Mary Monmouth in the slightest degree.

After the departure of the rather boorish young man named Addison Francis Murphy, Mary had returned to her sand garden in front, lain down on the sand, a pillow under her face, pulled down the straps on her bathing suit, and, naked to the waist, absorbed the health-giving rays of the sun.

The tranquillity of the resort, despite the number of its inhabitants, was remarkable. It was the hour of the siesta or sun bath. In every yard people were lying, very much *deshabille*. In another hour or two the colonists would go from house to house demanding and getting cocktails. Later hordes, with or without invitation, would barge in from the city.

Now, as Mary lay there in the sun, a voice greeted her from the interior of her house.

"Oh, Mary," it said. "Come on in."

"Darn it," said Mary to herself. "They're coming already."

She didn't know the voice, but that didn't matter. She couldn't remember half the people who intruded on slight acquaintance. She rose, brushed the sand from her bathing suit, pulled up the shoulder straps, waved her hand gaily and ran into the house.

As she stepped through the door she was grasped rudely from behind. Before she could cry out a handkerchief saturated with chloroform was pressed against her nose.

"Nelson, keep watch out back," snapped Pierre, a moment later. He was now holding the already unconscious girl in his arms. "Jerome, go out on the porch and warn me if anybody is in sight."

A minute passed.

"All clear this way," Jerome said then.

"Come ahead," called Nelson from the walk between the two houses.

PIERRE slipped out the back door, ran around to the end of the party fence, pulled open the door, already unlocked, of the house which was closed and boarded up, carried Mary into a bedroom and laid her on the bed.

He was immediately joined by his fellow kidnapers. From beneath his skirt, Jerome produced several lengths of rope. In a moment the unfortunate film star was bound. She was already coming out of the influence of the drug but, before she had quite recovered consciousness, they had gagged and blindfolded her.

"Now," said Pierre. "No talking. We have seven or eight hours to wait."

"How about these damn clothes?" inquired Jerome.

"Take them off. Did you bring the bag with the bathing suits?"

"Yep."

"Well, it's hot in here. We'll get into bathing suits and put the costumes in the bag."

Outside, the colony already was coming to life. People in bathing suits were moving along the beach, laughing and talking. The cocktail moochers were busy. Some of them entered the Monmouth house, calling for the hostess. Not finding her, they assumed that she was visiting and coolly made free of her liquor supply, knowing she would not object.

Late in the afternoon, a car disgorged half a dozen laughing people who entered Mary's house, waited for her an hour, drinking in the meantime, and then departed in search of other friends in the colony.

Before dark, at least thirty visitors from town had been disappointed, but not made suspicious, by not finding Mary. They simply had a drink, then moved on to other houses. By eight o'clock, there was nobody in the film star's house except the maid, who was in the kitchen. And at eight, a motor-boat with a winking light appeared off the beach.

The ticklish part of the job undertaken by Pierre and Nelson now began. They opened the beach-side door of the vacant house, carried the girl out on the porch and waited a moment. The moon was not yet up and it was black as pitch. There were people dining in the house on the other side, but nobody was on the porch. Mary's house, of course, was deserted. They carried her down the steps and across the yard over a sand mound and, in a few seconds, were moving down the steep beach.

Here Pierre unbound the girl and removed the gag.

"You're swimming," he whispered. "Make an outcry and you get a knife in your back."

She shuddered. "I won't," she promised.

Pierre and Nelson rushed with her into the breakers, and Giolotti and Jerome brought up the rear. In a few moments, they were outside the surf line.

Pierre, who carried in his left hand a flashlight, now raised his arm and turned it on, briefly. The motor-boat had already drifted some distance down the beach, but watchful eyes saw the flash and the boat got under way. It was necessary to use the flash twice more before the boat reached the swimmers.

Then strong arms drew them from the water. In a few moments the boat was churning its way southward. Mary Monmouth, sobbing her heart out, was locked in the cabin, and the conspirators, outside, were congratulating themselves and having drinks out of a bottle.

IT was nine-thirty of that night.

"Miss Monmouth calling, Mr. Solomon," Mr. Solomon's butler announced.

Mr. Solomon was sitting in the living-room in his huge house in Beverly Hills. He was having a soiree. A dozen stars of Sublime Pictures were present, and a number of writers, directors and heterogeneous "Yes" men.

"Maybe she decided to come, after all," said Mr. Solomon hopefully. "I'll take the phone here, Addison."

This, as it happened was a grave error of judgment on his part....

"Speaking for Mary, Mr. Solomon," spoke a voice unknown to the producer.

"Well, what you want?" he asked angrily.

"I thought you might like to know," said the unknown. "Miss Monmouth was kidnaped from her Malibu Beach house an hour or two ago. You can have her back for one hundred thousand dollars."

Mr. Solomon emitted a roar like a stricken bull. "Mary's been kidnaped!" he cried. "You bring her right back, you dirty—"

"The price will go up fifty thousand for every twenty-four hours delay. You know what your overhead costs you. Inform the police and the ransom will be doubled."

The man hung up. Instants later the wildly chattering party was massed around Mr. Solomon, the while he wrung his hands. "Listen, folks," he said pitifully then. "We got to keep this from the police. I want everyone here to give his word not to tell the police. I got to get these kidnapers a hundred thousand by tomorrow and twice as much if the police know about it."

"How? When? What are the arrangements?" people demanded.

"He didn't say. He hung up on me."

Male voices rumbled; female shrieked and chattered. In the noise and confusion Miss Marybell Stevens, film reporter for the *Daily Tabloid,* slipped unnoticed from the room and out of the house. In five minutes she was in a drug store pay-station phoning in the story of the kidnaping of Mary Monmouth. In three-quarters of an hour the quiet of Sunday night in downtown Los Angeles was disturbed by newsboys shrieking an extra.

Rambler Murphy, sitting on a bench in the Plaza, heard the cries. He had no money to buy an extra, but he called to a newsboy who ran squawking through the park.

He took the paper from the boy's hands, perused the headline and the red fudge on the front page which contained all that Miss Stevens had been able to gather.

"I don't believe it," he stated, and handed the paper back to the newsboy.

"Why you—" The newsboy, whose father was a longshoreman, emitted a string of expletives which would have done credit to his parent. But Rambler Murphy was far away by the time he had finished.

Murphy made a bee-line for the office of the leading morning paper, the *Recorder.* He brushed the office boy aside and bore down upon the city editor, who was perusing the Tab extra with the angry expression of a scooped editor.

"Mr. Browning," said Murphy.

Mr. Browning scowled at him savagely. Here was an outlet for the passion which was surging in him.

"I told you there were no jobs, you damn—"

"I'm the last person who saw Miss Monmouth before she was kidnaped," said the Rambler swiftly.

"You were!" exploded the editor. "Why the hell didn't you say so! When did you see her? Where—"

"I have to have ten dollars," said the Rambler. "In advance."

"O.K."

"And a job. I'll find Miss Monmouth and round up the kidnapers."

Browning leaned back in his chair and inspected Murphy intently.

"I heard about you over at the Press Club," he said. "You're known as one of the best reporters in America but you're a born bum. Our staff is full up—"

"I'm getting a job out of this somewhere," interrupted Murphy firmly.

"Wilson of the New York *Inquirer* was telling us at the club how you dug up that Adirondack Camp story," said the city editor thoughtfully, "and somebody else remembered that you had caught a murderer in Boston who turned out to be president of a bank.... So you're not a panhandler, anyway. I'll give you ten bucks and put you on this case; but if you fall down you go out on your ear."

"Swell. Fine."

"Let's hear what you've got."

Murphy told him how he had waked up at Miss Monmouth's, of her hospitality and his determination to return to town.

"Your yarn isn't worth ten bucks. Oh, I'll give it to you...."

"I know it isn't. I can make a good little story out of it, though—and I figured it would give me an entré here. I've got an idea how this job was pulled off, but I'm keeping it to myself until I test it."

"Grab a typewriter and knock out a description of the house and a report of your experience. It's good human interest. Shows what a swell gal she is."

CHAPTER THREE

THE RAMBLER'S REFERENCES

THE RAMBLER tightened his belt another notch, and was busy for half an hour. He wrote a smooth, vivid and colorful story which Browning read with approval.

"You know how to make something out of nothing," he said. "You're probably starving to death or you wouldn't be asking for cash. Go out now and eat and shave and come back. By that time we'll have more facts to go on, maybe."

"You're a pretty good guy," said the Rambler from the heart.

Browning grinned. "I'd like the open road myself only I've got a wife and two children to support. Never marry, Murphy."

"Who? Me? Don't be silly."

The *Morning Recorder's* first edition containing the news of Mary Monmouth's kidnaping, interviews with her producer, Mr. Moses Solomon, and with the Chief of Police of Los Angeles, and a signed article by Addison Francis Murphy describing the film star as last seen and her last words to anybody previous to her disappearance, was on the street at eleven P.M.

At eleven-thirty the Rambler, escorted by two detectives, was ushered into the office of the chief of police. Chief Watkins, who had risen through all the ranks to his present position, was a gray-haired, red-faced and solidly built man who called a spade a spade.

"Listen you," he commanded. "You're a suspicious character. Suppose you give me reasons why you shouldn't be locked up as one of the kidnapers."

Murphy, who had faced many chiefs of police in his time, grinned cheerfully.

"I'll give you," he said, "the names of ten prominent persons in various parts of the country who are under obligations to me, and will testify that while I am a damn fool, I am a worthy citizen."

"Yeh. Name one."

"Mr. Henry W. Johnson, who owns the *Recorder* and several newspapers in the East. I understand that he is now at his home in California, and I happen to know he never goes to bed until two in the morning. Phone him."

"I'll do that little thing," said the chief grimly. He put in the call. "In the meantime, give an account of yourself."

"With pleasure. I was drunk last night. I hadn't eaten for quite a while. I took a drink of bad gin and it went to my head. I met a guy in the Biltmore lobby, got talking to him and he bought me more gin. I don't make a practice of drinking. Apparently I got in with people and we went places. I don't remember a damn thing. I woke up in Miss Monmouth's cottage this morning. You read my story in the *Recorder*, so that's all there is—there isn't any more."

Chief Watkin's phone jingled

"Is this Mr. Johnson?" he asked most respectfully.

"Yes," said a brittle voice over long distance. "What can I do for you, Chief?"

"A suspicious character, a tramp newspaper man named Addison Francis Murphy, has just had the unqualified nerve to give you as a character reference."

The publisher chuckled. "So he's in California, eh? A very good man, Chief. Last of a vanishing type of newspaperman. I know him well. I've authorized the editor of the *Recorder* to put him on the staff. If anybody can find Mary Monmouth, he can."

"Shake, bo," said the chief as he hung up. He related what Johnson had told him. "You must be quite a guy to have that old crocodile recommend you," he added. "Will you work with us?"

"Always glad to cooperate, Chief. How do you figure the job was done?"

"We have descriptions of the kidnapers," Watkins said. "Two men and two women. They went into Malibu about noon. They had a small black sedan which we have located. It was stolen, so that's no help. They were not seen to leave and no persons answering to their description have been found there."

"I only had a glimpse of the place," said Murphy, "but I know they wouldn't have to pass through the gates unless they went out in a motor car. They could have walked across the marshes."

The chief nodded grimly, fingered papers on his desk. "Here's a copy of the descriptions; not much to go on, but they may help. Glad to have met you, Murphy." He shook hands warmly. "Good night."

THE RAMBLER walked smiling into the pleasant summer night. He was shaved and well fed. He had a job. He had taken a long chance that Johnson would remember his name, and he was highly pleased that the great publisher had endorsed him.

One of Murphy's troubles was excessive modesty. In a dozen cities he had a record of excellent journalistic achievement, but the wanderlust always carried him away before he could cash in on his reputation.

When he said that he didn't drink very much, he spoke the truth. His vice was gambling. There had been no need for him to arrive in Los Angeles penniless. He had thrown up a job in San Francisco and had intended to go south with a couple of hundred dollars; but a crap game on the Barbary Coast had taken the two hundred and he had stowed away on a coasting steamer bound for Los Angeles.

It was nice that Johnson had remembered him. It was news that

Browning had consulted the publisher regarding taking him on the *Recorder*, and it was up to him to find Mary Monmouth to justify Johnson's faith in him.

In addition to that, he wanted to find Mary for her own sake. His words to Mary Monmouth to the contrary, the Rambler was by no means insensible to female beauty and female charm. Ill as he had been this morning, the blood had flowed faster through his veins when he gazed upon her practically undraped loveliness.

If he had hung around there for lunch and dinner he might have fallen in love with Mary Monmouth—and love was something that Murphy couldn't afford to fall into. Love meant marriage. Marriage meant staying in one place. So he had been gruff, even rude to the very sweet young woman—and his cowardice, he assured himself, had been in part responsible for her present predicament.

It angered him that he couldn't remember the events of last night. Apparently he had been walking in a dream and couldn't recall the dream. He would know the fellow he had met in the Biltmore. He remembered certain faces in a speakeasy. After that, it was all a blank. In his entire career he had never had such an experience.

In the search for the kidnapers, he realized he was horribly handicapped by being a stranger in Los Angeles. He had no friends here, so far as he knew. The geography of the place was unknown to him. However crooks are alike wherever you find them, and the Rambler's knowledge of human nature would stand him in good stead. He wasn't discouraged. The kidnaping had taken place in Malibu and in Malibu he would be, first thing in the morning. Just now he had better get the information supplied by the chief of police into the night editor's hands….

AT EIGHT o'clock the following morning, Addison Francis Murphy passed through the gates at Malibu Beach. He found a policeman on duty at Mary Monmouth's house. Along the whole shore, there was no other sign of life.

Maloney, the cop, inspected his credentials and greeted him cordially.

"Been on duty since midnight and just got word to stay here until noon," he said. "The servant girl beat it when she heard her mistress had been snatched, and it's damn lonesome."

"I notice that the house next door is closed," said Murphy. As a matter of fact he had observed that the day before, and it had suggested something to him.

"Yep. It belongs to a motion picture man named Eli Grant. He's in Europe."

"Any ideas about how the job was pulled?"

"Lieutenant Hope was here until four this morning. He can't figure it at all. The kidnapers came through at noon and vanished into thin air along with the girl. I been looking at her pictures. She's a swell dish."

"I met her. Very pretty."

"How about you holding the fort while I go over to the road-house outside the gates and get me some breakfast?"

"Sure. Glad to oblige."

Murphy, who was anxious to get rid of the policeman and hadn't yet figured how to manage it, had assented eagerly.

Hardly was the policeman out of the house before the reporter had slipped through the fence to the house next door. He pulled off the boards on a basement window, kicked the window in, and crawled through.

From the basement he ascended to the first floor. He walked from darkened room to another. There was a large bedroom on the ground floor at the rear. All other rooms were in order, but here the bed-clothes had been pulled back. Obviously somebody had been lying in it, recently. A glance around the room showed him an ashtray full of cigarette butts. On a table were four glasses. He could smell whisky in one of them.

He found nothing else of interest and he was out of the house within five minutes after he had entered. He replaced the boards over the broken basement window. When the officer returned from his breakfast, Murphy was sitting on the Monmouth porch, quietly smoking a cigarette.

Mr. Maloney was a county officer, Malibu being outside the wide-flung frontiers of the City of Los Angeles. He was not a particularly bright policeman but a sociable one. He talked on now at great length, while Murphy, occupied with his own thoughts, made but laconic answers.

This was a motion picture city, film capital of the world. Miss Monmouth was a film actress whose disappearance was holding up a tremendously expensive picture.

Obviously, the prime spirit in the kidnaping must be a person familiar with motion picture conditions. An actor, perhaps.

Now the kidnapers had entered in a stolen car and had run the gauntlet of the guards at the gate. Naturally, a description of them would be sent far and wide, which would be very bad business for them. So, they must have taken into account the fact that they would be inspected and their descriptions learned.

Women kidnapers were unusual. It was eerie likely that the women were female impersonators. And why not stage make-up to disguise the men? In that case their descriptions would be worthless.

They had whisked Mary into the vacant house next door and kept her there for some time, judging by the cigarette butts and the indentation in the middle of the bed.

The Rambler's thoughts were at this juncture interrupted by the shuffling sound of approaching footsteps. A moment later, a colored woman came around the corner of the house and mounted the porch. She stared, open-mouthed, at the Rambler.

"Say!" she exclaimed. "Yo' was the gen'man that passed out night before last. Poor Miss Mary and me, we put you to bed."

Murphy smiled genially, and the maid smiled with him. "I left in such a hurry I wasn't able to thank you," he explained.

"I jus' come back to tidy up," the maid said. "I wouldn't stay here alone foh worlds."

"By the way," the Rambler asked abruptly, "what dress was Miss Mary wearing when she was carried off?"

"I dunno, suh. I wasn't here."

"You know her wardrobe. Have a look."

"And that's an idea," put in Officer Maloney. "The lieutenant never thought of that."

"And see if you can find her bathing suit," Murphy added.

WHILE Maloney accompanied the maid into Miss Monmouth's bedroom, the Rambler sat staring at the beach.

During the winter season at Malibu, the sea has a way of ripping up the beach and piling the sand in high mounds in front of the cottages. When the residents open up their houses, they usually have to shovel away a ridge of sand four or five feet high in order to get a view of the ocean. As Mr. Grant, Mary's next door neighbor, was in Europe, there was a high sand wall at the bottom of his yard, while the beach level had been restored in front of the inhabited houses.

Maloney came out of the house much excited.

"Murphy!" he declared. "The dinge says she ain't taken any of her dresses. And she can't find the lady's bathing suit."

"Looks as if she went away in her bathing suit, doesn't it? See if you can find such a thing as a shovel, old man. We need exercise, you and me."

"Speak for yourself," said the cop. "What you want with a shovel?"

"I thought I'd tackle that sand mound next door."

Maloney grasped his arm.

"You don't think they murdered her and buried her there?"

"They couldn't collect ransom for her that way."

"Well, I'm not doing any digging today," stated Maloney flatly.

Murphy shrugged his shoulders. "Suit yourself," he said. "I am." He went inside and returned a moment later with a large sand shovel, which the maid had produced from the basement.

The cop's eyes followed him uncomprehendingly as he walked over and inspected the mound for footprints. The wind had been blowing and the sand was dry; footprints, if there had been any, were eradicated. Next Murphy, with the shovel tackled the mound near the bottom. After removing a few shovelfuls at one place, he tried another spot.

He dug desultorily for half an hour before the shovel struck a solid substance. Breathing rapidly, Murphy set to work to uncover it. In a moment he drew forth a small suitcase, old, battered and made of straw.

It was most unfortunate, he realized, that the county police officer still had his eyes glued upon him. He wouldn't be able to keep his find to himself. In fact, Maloney already was coming at a run.

"What you got?" he demanded.

"I'm making a guess," said Murphy as he handed it over, "that we shall find inside that, two female dresses, and several wigs and false noses. Open up, Maloney, and see if I'm right."

The suitcase being unlocked, the officer had it open immediately. He lifted up a print dress and a black satin dress. Beneath it were four theatrical wigs, and two suits of men's clothing, with linen.

"What do you figure these things are for?" demanded the cop.

The Rambler laughed. "These are the costumes worn by the kidnapers. They were four men and they don't resemble in any respect the descriptions supplied by the gateman."

"By golly, feller!" burst out the admiring policeman. "You ought to be a detective!"

"I'm a reporter. That's even better."

"How come you figured out they'd bury these things here?"

"Because if they threw the bag into the ocean it would be washed up on the beach. They couldn't carry it through the surf that runs on this coast, and they couldn't leave it in Eli Grant's house. They took a chance that nobody would dig into this mound."

Murphy turned back toward the house. Once inside, he called the *Recorder*.

"Rewrite man," he demanded. "Big developments in the Monmouth case."

"Give me the facts," answered the day city editor.

"Four men, two of them disguised as women, kidnaped Mary Monmouth. They took her into the vacant house next door, kept her there until night, and wearing bathing suits, swam with her out to a waiting motor-boat."

"How do you know?"

"I've found evidence of recent occupation of the Eli Grant house next door. I found a suitcase containing two suits of male apparel, and two female costumes, two black female wigs, one blond man's wig and one black male wig. It was buried in a sand mound in front of Grant's house. As Mary Monmouth was carried off in her bathing suit, and as these kidnapers left their clothing behind them, it's obvious that they took to the surf. Which means a boat was waiting for them."

"Great work, Murphy."

"Any developments in town?"

"Solomon has been told that he must pay $200,000 because he let the police in."

"I'll be seeing you," said the Rambler. "The suitcase has been nabbed by the county officers. No doubt the costumer who sold or rented the costumes will be located and may be able to help. Here's a description of the women's costumes. No markings on them and no marks on the wigs."

"Hold it. I'll give you a rewrite man."

Ten minutes later the Rambler had shaken hands with Officer Maloney and was starting back from Malibu.

He had a feeling now that it was no coincidence that he had passed out in the home of a celebrated actress who was scheduled to be kidnaped the following day. He had been planted there for some reason. And it was curious that he couldn't recall any but the earlier incidents of the previous night. Liquor had never before had such an effect on him. He suspected now that he had been drugged.

Anyhow, he'd let the paper hunt for the costumer, and try to find out what motor-boats had been rented the previous night, and what could be learned about the people who had stolen the car. He hoped also to locate the hospitable gent who had met him in the Biltmore....

CHAPTER FOUR

THE SEA LILY

ABOUT FORTY miles from Los Angeles and some seventy miles south of Malibu is a popular and attractive resort called Balboa. Balboa is built upon a long, narrow sandspit chopped up by inlets and canals, and seen from the hills of the mainland, it offers a suggestion of Venice.

The Pacific beats eternally upon the beach of Balboa, but between the peninsula and the mainland is a stretch of quiet water several miles in length, containing an island more or less appropriately named Lido.

At the present time Lido is a popular headquarters for yachts, speedboats and houseboats, some of which can be rented by the week. Armand Pierre had used money supplied by George Nelson, the gambler, to rent a houseboat called the *Sea Lily* for a month. About nine o'clock in the evening following the capture of Mary Monmouth, he boarded the *Lily,* carrying a briefcase in which were copies of all the evening papers.

The *Lily* was moored at the mouth of a sluggish creek, and by the side of a marsh so vile smelling that no other houseboat was tied up within half a mile of it. Its windows were curtained and revealed not a trace of light; this Mr. Pierre noted with approval. As he came over the rail, a rough-looking person, wearing a sailor's white uniform, bobbed up to greet him.

"Who's this?" the sailor demanded.

"Pierre. Make the rowboat fast."

"O.K., boss."

Armand crossed the deck and pushed open the door of the deckhouse. He entered a brilliantly lighted room and interrupted a poker game, being carried on by five shirtsleeved players who included Nelson, Jerome and Giolotti, as well as two others named Travis and Rosenbaum. Travis was a tall, thin Englishman with deep-set eyes, high cheekbones and a habit of breathing exclusively through his mouth. He was by profession an air pilot. Rosenbaum was New York East Side Jewish. Each man of the five had a stack of chips, but Nelson had the largest stack.

"Well?" demanded the gambler.

"Not well," said Pierre. "The police have ordered Moe Solomon not to pay the ransom. And this bum that you picked up, Nelson, is a newspaper reporter."

"Yeh?" said Nelson. "I slipped him ten bucks on account of his nerve in asking for it and his smartness in knowing I was the only guy in Los Angeles who would slip him ten bucks; but it was your cute idea to take him out to Mary's."

"She always parks the stiffs and sends them back to L.A. on Sunday morning," retorted Pierre. "It was a sure way to get her chauffeur out of the place."

"Yeh, but we could have got somebody else to pass out. Or one of the regular guests might've done it."

"Anybody else would have known us. This fellow was a stranger and he was in a trance when we met him."

Nelson shrugged his shoulders. "Well, he don't know us, and so what."

"How do we know he wasn't shamming? I tell you he's a reporter on the *Recorder*. Here, read this…. Name of Addison Francis Murphy. Full account of how he woke up in one of Mary's bedrooms and how she looked and what they said to each other and how she sent him to town in the Rolls."

Nelson perused the article.

"And how's this hurt us?"

"He can put two and two together. And if he ever gets a look at your mug—"

"I'm sitting right here until the cash comes in."

"How's Mary?"

"O.K. Got her locked in the provision hold. I threw a mattress down there and one of the boys dropped her grub and water. I guess she'll keep, all right."

PIERRE sat down and fanned himself with a newspaper.

"Hot in town. There's hell to pay."

"You said we'd get the dough in twenty-four hours. They're up."

"I thought, in his own interests, Moe would keep it dark. He told me on the phone it wasn't his fault. There were people in the room with him when he got the message and one of them was a newspaper woman. She broke her word. He says he'll turn a hundred thousand over anyway we say."

"You just said the police wouldn't let him."

"That's right. But Moe wants Mary back at work. He'll come through if we can work out a way of getting the money. The cops are tailing him and all his agents. Things are so hot I think we better hold off a few days."

"And let the cops or the damn newspapers locate us."

"We're safe here. They figure she's either in Los Angeles or Frisco or across the line in Mexico."

"Well…" said Nelson resignedly. "Want to buy a stack of chips?"

"I'm too nervous. I'm sorry for that poor kid down in the hold on a night like this."

Nelson gazed at him balefully.

"She can take off her bathing suit," he sneered. "Listen, you ham actor… Don't you go soft on us. This was your bright idea. Now get hard."

"Give me a stack," said Pierre. "I may as well play, dammit. I'm nervous as hell."

The words had hardly passed his lips before the quiet of the cabin was abruptly shattered by the roar of a gun! The electric light globe above the table, the only illumination in the cabin, broke into a thousand pieces and darkness descended upon the players.

They leaped to their feet as one. Every man had a gun in his hand, peering into the dark. The door to the deck was slightly ajar, and a thin slit of darkness, less opaque than in the cabin, showed through.

"Got you," said a harsh, loud voice. "Come out, one by one, with your hands over your heads."

Nelson, beside Pierre, lifted his gun arm. Pierre pulled it down. "No shooting," he whispered. "That one shot was bad enough."

"You're trapped. You can't get away," said the voice. "First man out or I'll shoot into you. I don't care if the shots are heard."

"Get going, boys," said Nelson. "Here you, Giolotti. You go first."

"Hurry," commanded the unknown.

The Italian stumbled across the cabin. He pushed the door open and stepped out. They heard the sound of a heavy fall.

"Next," commanded the master of the situation.

There were no volunteers. Nelson pushed the man at his right. "Go on," he snarled. "Where the hell—" He had suddenly missed Pierre, who had been close to him on the other side.

Pierre was gliding through the passage to one of the bedrooms. He opened the window, pushed up the screen and squirmed his way through. He managed to stand on the window-sill, reached the top of the deck-house with outstretched arms and pulled himself up. He heard another body land on the deck with a heavy thud. He crept like a cat along the deck until he came to the railing.

Three of his companions now lay flat on the deck below. Behind the door stood a man with a revolver grasped by the muzzle. Pierre drew his gun from his pocket, then pushed it back again. More shots from the houseboat would cause investigation.

"Come on, you rats," growled the man below. Pierre had both legs over the rail. He sprang then, and his shoes struck the fellow on the shoulder blades. The man pitched forward and Pierre fell beyond him. Pierre got up. The other man lay still.

This solitary police straggler had supposed he could capture six men single-handed, thought Armand Pierre with a disdainful smile. He grasped the unconscious hero under the armpits. "Got him, boys," he called triumphantly, and dragged the man into the living-room of the houseboat.

"He was alone," he exclaimed. "Get another light bulb and put on your masks. We'll see how badly he's hurt."

"You're not yellow," remarked George Nelson to Pierre. "I hand it to you, boy."

"One of you go out and wake up those fellows on the deck," Pierre directed. "He knocked them out with his gun-butt."

"Can you beat that for nerve," commented Travis. He was on a chair and fumbling for the light bracket. In a few seconds the juice went on and the room was again lighted.

"The bum!" exclaimed Nelson.

"He's coming to," Pierre said. "Careful…"

ADDISON FRANCIS MURPHY was endeavoring to sit up. He was a little dazed, for he had struck his forehead on the hard deck, but he was recovering.

He saw above him three men wearing black cloth masks which dropped below their chins. He grinned.

"Looks like I came to the right shop," he observed.

"Say, fellow," demanded Nelson, "what made you think you was good enough to take on a crowd, eh?"

Murphy laughed shortly. "Don't rub it in," he said. "I thought a mob mean enough to carry off a pretty kid like Mary Monmouth, would be yellow as hell."

"Insolent bloke," commented the Englishman. "I say, let's dash his brains out."

"Your name is Murphy and you're a reporter on the *Recorder*," said Pierre. "What brought you away down here?"

"Oh," said Murphy coolly, "I was just rambling round."

The trio who had been flattened by the newspaper man came into the room.

"Is that the guy that slugged me?" demanded Giolotti. "Say you—" He drew back his right foot and then drove the toe of his boot brutally into the ribs of the man sitting on the floor. Murphy winced with pain, but suppressed a groan.

"Quit that," growled Nelson. "You have to talk fast to save your skin, fellow. How'd you find us?"

"Why," said Murphy, "I figured it out that a houseboat was the ideal place to hide a kidnaped girl. And on this coast there aren't many safe locations for a houseboat. So I thought the Lido was a good spot to start hunting. I've been on board half a dozen but this was the only one where there were men enough to make a poker game."

Jerome, who had gone out on deck again for a reconnaissance, now returned. "Got a knife?" he inquired. "I found Joe bound and gagged and tucked away at the stern."

"He's lying like the devil, anyhow," said Nelson. "Let's knock him on the head and go on with the game. If there was anyone with him, he wouldn't have tackled us alone."

"And being a reporter, he wouldn't spill his story until he had it," Pierre declared. "I know these newspaper dopes. But we won't knock him on the head yet. We'll put him on ice."

There was a mutter of indignation and protest, especially from the three who had felt the weight of the Rambler's clubbed revolver.

"You fools!" exclaimed Pierre. "We're lucky that that one shot didn't bring a mob down on us. And we don't want a dead body on the boat and if we throw him over into this lake he'll be found. Besides, he's going to be useful. Watch him a minute, men…."

He took Nelson by the arm and led him into a bedroom.

"He's our line of communication," he said. "I'll work it out. We'll hold him until tomorrow—"

"There's only one safe place to put him," put in Nelson, grinning beneath his mask. "That's down in the hold with the girl. No windows, no doors, nothing but the hatch, bolted on the outside."

They went back to the living-room. "The little woman is probably lonesome, boys," Nelson said. "We're fixing her up with company. Get up there, fellow, and trot along with us."

Murphy rose. He was in a very low frame of mind. He had been a fool to tackle the houseboat single-handed, but he had to be sure. And he hadn't been sure that it was Mary's hiding-place until he caught snatches of conversation from the poker players, which floated through the thin walls of the deck-house. Then he had acted on impulse.

"Frisk him boys," commanded Nelson.

They fell upon him with a will, but they were disappointed to find only five dollars and a package of cigarettes in his possession. Murphy was then pushed through a corridor between two bedrooms, past a kitchen and into a pantry. There was a trap-door in the floor, the bolts of which were drawn.

"Look out below," called Nelson. "A present for you, girlie."

Murphy looked into a dark hole. He saw a ladder leading down and began to descend. The trap door was slammed down before his head was below the floor level, but he dropped from the ladder and avoided a fractured skull.

CHAPTER FIVE

A JOB FOR THE RAMBLER

THE RAMBLER dropped three feet and landed with a jarring thud. As he landed, he heard a terrified gasp from just beyond him.

"A friend, Miss Monmouth," he said.

"I have no friends," came from the darkness. "Who are you? Why have they put you down here?"

"I'm the sap who passed out at your party Saturday night," he said. He tried to peer into the darkness. "I'm a newspaper reporter named Addison Francis Murphy."

"I remember you," Mary said, and despite her predicament, she laughed aloud.

Murphy was feeling about in his pockets. He found a paper of matches which the searchers had overlooked or didn't care to take. He lighted one. He was in a compartment about twelve feet long and fifteen feet wide, which was partly filled with packing cases, kegs and soap boxes. Sitting on a box, six feet away, was a young woman in a bathing suit.

"I was looking for you," he said lamely.

She laughed again, "You seem to have found me."

"Yes," he said ruefully. "I'm afraid I can't help you. I made an ass of myself. Schoolboy stuff."

"I feel you're a friend," she replied. "Oh!" The match had gone out. "Light another one, please."

"No. They may come in handy."

"Well, come over and sit close to me. I've been horribly frightened, Mr. Murphy. These men are savages."

"Tough crowd, all right." He felt his way toward her and dropped on the floor of the hold at her feet. "Your disappearance has created a sensation," he said, smiling to himself. "You're on the front page of every newspaper in America. Big publicity, Miss Monmouth. Excellent in your business. No doubt about that."

"Yes, if I live to enjoy it."

"Oh, you're safe. You're worth a hundred thousand to these crooks."

Suddenly she broke into sobs. "I've been thinking of the Lindbergh baby," she said brokenly.

He reached out and patted that part of her which happened to be nearest. It was a naked thigh. She pulled away.

"Excuse me," he said. "I mean they'll pay the ransom and the publicity will be worth it to the film company." He happened to know that the police were determined to capture the kidnapers at any cost to their victim, but there was no need to frighten her.

"We may not be left here together," he said. "Tell me. Do you know the name of a man who was at your party night before last? A tall, dark man with a rather large nose, very large black eyes and exceptionally fine teeth. He wears sort of extreme clothes, slim-waisted.

"That's Armand Pierre. Of course I know him. But what has that to do with—"

He told her the story of his meeting with Nelson and Pierre, and what followed up to the time of his passing out. Then he added: "I got a job on the *Recorder* on the strength of your kidnaping and went down to Malibu. I found the costumes these four birds wore, buried in the sand outside the house next to yours.

"I decided that my being at your house the night before you were snatched was no coincidence, and I had a hunch these two men who were so good to me had their reasons. Well, tonight I saw this Pierre get out of a roadster in front of a drug store on Olive Street. I remembered him. He went to the telephone booth. When he came out I was tucked away in his cargo hatch. It was a long, rough ride. Fully an hour.

"When he stopped, I waited a few seconds before I lifted the cover of my hiding place. He had parked the car on a dark street and he was halfway down the street. A sign at the corner said 'City of Balboa.' I trailed him. He took a rowboat at a boat landing. I stole one and rowed after him, a long way back. I would have lost him except that this was the only vessel in this part of the bay. I ran the boat into the marsh, waded through the mud, came aboard from the land side, knocked over a man on guard and tied him up with one of his own ropes. I gagged him with my handkerchief and listened at the deckhouse door.

"If I'd had any sense I'd have gone after the cops; but little Willie wanted to fight Injuns. I tackled them. Now look at me. And that's my story...."

"**I THINK** you're the bravest man I ever heard of," she cried. "Why, I never heard of anything so daring. And such amazing deduction!"

"And here we are in the bottom of a houseboat. I'm going to light a match and look around."

"I'm not afraid, now that you're here. You inspire confidence. Really you do."

"I wish I could inspire myself with some. I had it knocked out of me."

He explained to her, then, just how he had been vanquished.

"But it was such a mad method," she cried. "Why didn't you fling open the door and order them to throw up their hands—"

"As in the movies." He chuckled. "Because you can't cover six armed men with one gun. One of them would have potted me. The other way was also risky; but I knew Pierre was an actor and I supposed the others were rats—"

"Please, Mr. Murphy. I am an actress."

"What I mean is, that I didn't suppose they were professional killers. I was wrong. Three or four of them are gangsters, by the look of them."

He lighted a match and started an inspection of the place.

"This," he announced, "is an old barge with everything above-deck removed and a house built on it. Its sides are too thick to kick through." The match went out.

"I wish I could see you, Mr. Murphy."

"I wouldn't do it, lady. I'm just as glad I can't see you."

"Why?"

"You're too darned good looking."

"I think that's the sweetest compliment ever paid me."

"Plain statement of fact."

Murphy lighted a match again and began to move boxes and barrels, which moved the more easily because they were empty. He had hoped to find something he could use for a weapon... a forgotten axe or a heavy stick which might serve as a club.

Despite the absence of port-holes or doors, there was air of a sort in the place. Ventilation had been provided because it was a provision storeroom.

Finally, having used all but two of his paper matches, Murphy felt his way back to the girl. She was quiet, but when his shoulder touched her shoulder he knew that she was shaking with silent sobs.

"Listen, kid," he said. "Get this in your head. You're safe. You'll be turned loose in a day or two. This is uncomfortable but you're not in pain, so stop crying."

"I shall," she said in a very low tone. "Are you safe?"

"Oh, sure." He was far from sure, but there was no sense in confiding his fears to her.

Half an hour passed. Mary's hand crept into his and he squeezed it encouragingly. Her hand was soft and very small for a tall girl. There was something about holding her hand that bothered him. Women had no business using electricity on a fellow.

Footsteps sounded overhead. Bolts were pushed back and the trap-door lifted.

"Come up here, Murphy," called one of the bandits.

Mary threw both arms about him in a paroxysm of fear.

"No, don't go. Don't leave me," she implored.

"No choice, kid. You'll be all right."

"But maybe they'll k-k-kill you."

"Nothing like that. I'm all right. Keep a stiff upper lip."

"Let go that dame and come up here," commanded the voice on the deck above.

He turned the flashlight upon the lover-like spectacle below.

Murphy patted her upon the bare shoulder and went up the ladder.

TWO MASKED men, guns in hand, were waiting for him. One of them he knew to be Pierre. The other, by his figure, he judged to be the gambler who had loaned him ten dollars.

They conducted him into one of the bedrooms. In the living-room the others could be heard talking in a good poker game.

"Here's the situation," said Pierre. "You can sit down, Murphy. I presume you remembered me and that you trailed me down here from town. I don't give a damn. You've been chinning for an hour with Mary and you're probably sorry for her. So are we. That kid is going to die unless you deliver the goods for her."

"In that case, she isn't going to die," said the Rambler gravely.

"You know what happened to a couple of kidnapers up in San Jose," said Nelson. "They were lynched. They're putting a bill through the legislature that the governor will sign in a few days, making kidnaping a capital offense. We get ours whether we kill her or not. In short, we're desperate."

"I hope you get yours, boys. Got a cigarette?"

"Sure," said Nelson. He passed over a package of cigarettes and a paper of matches. Murphy lighted one and thrust the pack into his pocket.

"Moe Solomon, president of Sublime Films," said Pierre, "has agreed to turn over a hundred thousand in unmarked bills. Trouble is that the cops are all around him. Anybody who leaves his house for any purpose is trailed. The police want to catch us and they don't give a hoot what happens to Mary. We're stumped and so is Solomon. It costs him thirty thousand for every day the girl isn't at the studio."

"You're just breaking my heart," Murphy informed the speaker.

"So you're going to help us."

"Yes, yes."

"As a reporter on the *Recorder*, you can call on Solomon at his house for an interview. You'll give him a password which he already knows. He will slip you the money. You'll bring it to us tonight and you can take the girl ashore."

"I'm unworthy of such a great trust," the Rambler said mockingly. "Suppose I bring the police down on you…."

"Did you notice a seaplane moored in the bay as you came on board?"

"Yes. I saw it."

"We'll be aboard it. In an hour we'll be in Mexico. You'll find Mary, but she'll be dead."

"And suppose I give you the money and you hold out for another ransom."

"Do you think we'd take any further risk?" demanded Pierre.

"No. You're petrified as things are," said Murphy, and laughed. "Of course I'll get jugged for aiding and abetting kidnapers."

"If you do, you'll be the first person who paid a ransom who's been jailed."

"We're on a spot, fellow," said Nelson. "We know we take a big chance. You can go to L.A., spill everything to your damned paper and get a lot of cheap glory. If you do you're responsible for murdering that little lady down below. I've sized you up. Of course if you think we'll scram and leave her here safe and sound after you've double-crossed us, why you'll go ahead and double-cross us."

"No," said Murphy thoughtfully. "You're filthy enough to murder an innocent girl out of spite."

"We don't want to hurt a hair of her head," Pierre said eagerly. "We're forced to take a chance on you and, as you can get away from us, the girl's life has to be the stake. I'll kill her with my own hand and, I don't mind telling you, I've been in love with her. Make up your mind."

"If I refuse, I'll get my throat cut."

"And if you fall down on the job, she gets her throat cut," said Nelson hoarsely.

MURPHY was making smoke rings, thoughtfully.

"This money comes from a film company," he said slowly. "It's not rung from the blood of relatives. Any film company would gladly spend a hundred thousand to get the publicity this job is getting Mary Monmouth. I hate to enrich a mob of cutthroats. I think there's a fifty-fifty chance you wouldn't have the guts to kill her if you were forced to get away in a hurry, but I don't want to put her in any risk of her life.

"Of course, I'm not at all sure the cops won't put a trailer on me if I call on Moe Solomon. I'm a new man in town. I was the last person to talk with her before she was snatched. I give you my word I'll get the money from Solomon, if he gives it to me, and I'll bring it here without tipping the cops, but what happens if they are on my tail?"

"We put a couple of bullets in Mary and take off in the plane," said Nelson grimly. "It's up to you to make sure they don't get wise to you."

"And what happens to me when I turn over the cash?"

Nelson laughed queerly. "Want a cut of it?"

"Just release Miss Monmouth."

"She goes free when we have a hundred grand in our hands," said Pierre. "Maybe your paper will give you a bonus. Anyway, you'll have a scoop."

"O.K. Let me get started."

"You'll come back alone and unarmed," Pierre warned him. "We're nervous. If we notice anything suspicious before you return, we'll clear out."

"We'll consider you double-crossed us and you'll find a female corpse down in that provision hold," said Nelson. "So watch your step."

"If that should happen," Murphy replied, "I'll chase you murderers all the way to hell. I'll never let up; so bear that in mind."

"We understand each other, Murphy," said Pierre. "I'll row you over to Balboa."

The Rambler hesitated. "Can I speak to her? I'd like to tell her that I'm going to get her ransom."

"No. And you'll never get to see her again unless you bring back the money and no bloodhounds," the gambler assured him.

"What do I say to Solomon? Suppose he refuses to come across?"

"The password is Malibu," said Pierre. "Come on."

The prisoner passed through the living-room of the houseboat, jumped into the rowboat tied up at the accommodation ladder. Pierre followed and picked up the oars.

Halfway across the stretch of water, they passed close to the moored seaplane, dimly visible in the darkness because of her mooring light. The Rambler inspected it. It was a small plane, seating at the most two passengers with the pilot. The precious pair intended to double-cross their followers and escape in the plane with as much of the ransom as they could get away from the rank and file!

Pierre had removed his mask when they left the houseboat and pulled toward the Balboa shore. He rowed nervously.

"Solomon lives in Beverly Hills," he said. "Where's your car?"

"Oh," said Murphy, "I came down in your cargo hatch. Recognized you when you went into a drug store."

Pierre swore under his breath. "I'm washed up in L.A.," he said. "I expected to be identified, but with this money and what I know about make-up they'll never catch me. You can take my car. I'll show you where it is. You'll find Solomon's house watched; you'd better phone up from your office that you're coming for an interview. Make him talk with you in private. Malibu's the password, remember.

"And when you leave his house, go to your office and write something to disarm suspicion. Then get down here as fast as you can. If you're followed, do something about it. Here's your gun. But come aboard the houseboat unarmed."

They reached the boat landing.

"If the police come with you," said Pierre, "we'll get signals from the shore. Time enough to dispose of Mary and make our getaway. Bear that in mind."

He led Murphy to a touring car, old but of a good make. "Good luck," he said, but did not offer to shake hands. "You can't miss the road to L.A."

CHAPTER SIX

FOLLOWED

AS THE RAMBLER bowled swiftly along through the night, he was forced to conclude that the kidnapers had displayed good judgment in pressing him into service. No decent man would risk the murder of a young girl for a newspaper exclusive.

While his attempt to take the houseboat single-handed seemed rash, and was certainly futile, he had been forced into it by circumstances. Having boarded the boat, knowing only that one of his Saturday night companions had rowed out to her, he had been at once attacked by the deck hand, whom he had knocked out and bound and gagged.

If he had gone for help then, the eventual discovery of the gagged man would have warned Pierre that the houseboat was suspected, and the criminals would have departed in haste, either taking their victim with them or putting a bullet into her.

It wasn't a case of capturing the kidnapers now. Mary was a hostage for his return with the ransom. Her life, perhaps, was in his hands. And in his hands also, was one of the biggest newspaper stories in years; but he couldn't spring it.

He was the go-between of the bandits.

He could use the phone and have the mob captured inside an hour, and there was a chance that Mary would be found alive; but he dare not take the chance.

The Eastern type of gangster kidnaper might refuse to release the girl after receiving the money. But these were one-shot brigands. A hundred grand would satisfy them. He had to go through.

At eleven o'clock he was in front of the *Recorder* office. He went inside, told the city editor he had no developments to report, and then phoned Solomon's residence.

"Tell Mr. Solomon, please," he said, "that Mr. Murphy of the *Recorder* is on his way out for an interview. Mr. Johnson, the publisher, especially wishes details upon cost of daily delay upon Miss Monmouth's film."

"Just a minute, sir," requested the servant. After a moment he returned. "Mr. Solomon says, 'Come ahead out.'"

In thirty-five minutes Murphy was in Beverly Hills. Five minutes later he arrived at a great gate with huge posts which looked like stone, but were stucco. Two policemen were on duty. They questioned him but permitted him to pass when they saw his newspaper card.

Parked in front of the house were half a dozen automobiles, two of which were newspaper cars. Three or four reporters and a pair of police detectives were sitting on the front steps. When Murphy told the officers he had an appointment for an interview, the reporters at once demanded to know what was up.

"If you go in, we go in," one of them declared.

"I don't care if he doesn't," Murphy answered with assumed nonchalance. "This interview was arranged by phone between Mr. Solomon and Mr. Johnson, the publisher."

They insisted upon accompanying him to the front door; but there they were stopped by the servant, who told them that only Mr. Murphy could enter.

The Rambler was conducted into an ornate study, where a pudgy fat man with a huge nose and very bald head was sitting behind a desk too big for him. Murphy observed with satisfaction that the curtains were down.

"Are the windows closed?" he asked.

"What a question," commented the producer. "Sure they are. I hate drafts. Say, young feller, I'd never give you this interview if my friend Johnson hadn't asked it. I'm tired giving interviews. What good do they do? What right have the cops got to interfere with my business? My God, I'll loose this hundred thousand in one week—and if they kill her, it costs me a million dollars, so help me."

"Malibu," said Murphy softly.

"Eh. What's that?"

"Malibu."

SOLOMON'S eyes popped wide.

"You come from them? Ain't you a reporter?"

"I'm a reporter and I come from them," said Murphy rapidly. "I located them but they captured me. I had to agree to be the go-between to save Miss Monmouth's life. If I'm not back with the ransom money in a few hours, they'll kill her and scatter."

"I got the money," said Solomon. "Yesterday I would have given it but the police won't let me. My house, they got surrounded. My employees, they search." He pulled open a drawer and slapped on the table a thick pad of banknotes. Their bulk dismayed the reporter. He couldn't leave the house carrying such a package.

"Inside your pants," said Solomon eagerly. "Look. They think you got a pot belly."

Aided by the producer, he padded his abdomen with big bills. They gave him an appearance of being ten pounds heavier below the belt, but might not be noticed when he buttoned his coat.

"Now give me some facts regarding your studio costs on this picture."

"What's that?" screamed the producer. "Go, man, go! I want that Mary reports to work tomorrow. Tell her how much it costs me. Ask her to come for just a few scenes if she can."

"I've got to talk to you at least ten minutes, or the boys outside will be suspicious."

Reluctantly the producer seated himself and gave figures enough to make the reporter's head dizzy. Finally he had enough.

"Control yourself, Mr. Solomon," pleaded Murphy as he turned to go. "Anybody who looked at you now would know something important has happened. If word gets out, and the cops trail me, you'll lose your money and be responsible for Miss Monmouth's death."

Solomon wiped his bald head with a big handkerchief.

"That's right. I must be calm," he agreed. "Look. I sit here after you go, then sneak up to my room without saying anything to my guests. You sure you'll get her home safe?"

"You bet," said Murphy. He wouldn't have bet on it himself, but his assurance was necessary to keep Mr. Solomon from having hysterics.

He had made notes on some sheets of copy paper, which he showed when the newsmen surrounded him at the door.

"Hell," said one disgustedly. "We've all got that stuff."

"I know it, but Johnson phoned down and said to send out and get it, so what could I do?"

One of the detectives stepped close to him and tapped his breast and side pockets as well as his hips. He felt the reporter's gun but that didn't interest him. In California all sorts of people carry weapons of defense.

"O.K.," he said. "You can go along."

Uncertain whether or not he was being pursued, the Rambler drove down to Los Angeles at a reasonable pace, parked his car in the rear of the *Recorder* building, went up to the city room and sat down at a typewriter. He did not use his notes, however. He wrote the story of his experience at Balboa, the fact that he was forced to be the go-between, the treatment of Mary Monmouth on the houseboat and the identity of the chief kidnaper, Armand Pierre. He left nothing unsaid which might be helpful in running down the kidnapers and, when he had finished, he put the story in an envelope, addressed it to the managing editor, and put it in the managing editor's letterbox. He knew that the managing editor did not arrive before ten-thirty A.M. and that his secretary did not come in until ten. By that time he would have concluded his business at Balboa and Mary Monmouth might be back home at Malibu.

AFTER that the go-between went downstairs, found his car and headed south. There was considerable traffic and he was hopeful but not assured that he was unshadowed.

It is about twenty miles from Los Angeles to Long Beach, which is the best route to Balboa but also the most traveled. Murphy turned off while still in thickly settled Los Angeles and followed a sign which said, "Balboa via Santa Fe Springs."

This road led him through a district where oil derricks were as thick as trees and where the air was tainted by oil.

Far back, a pair of headlights gleamed like cat's eyes. Out through the country he sped and became uneasily aware that the car behind did not gain nor could he drop it.

So he hadn't escaped suspicion. He had been picked up at the *Recorder* office and they hadn't lost sight of him.

It was a lonely road and, for some miles, straight as an arrow. Murphy fretted and cursed. The fool police were going to murder Mary Monmouth.

Maybe one of Solomon's servants was a police spy who had listened at the door. After having accomplished his mission successfully so far, he couldn't come to grief now.

It was only ten or twelve miles more to Balboa. The road curved ahead. At the right, he espied a side road. He swung into it and turned off his lights. In a few seconds the other car, rounding the curve, flashed by the turn-off. The Rambler backed into the ditch, swung his car about, and waited. A minute passed and he heard the sound of a motor coming back. The car was coming slowly.

A policeman's business was to take chances. He thought of the poor girl in the bathing suit, crouching in the musty hold of the houseboat.

The headlights fell across the road. Murphy grasped his wheel and stepped on the gas. There was a horrified shout from the car on the main road.

Crash! Murphy's car plunged into the side of the other car.

It turned the other car over on its side with a sickening rending of wood and metal. A man emitted a piercing howl. Murphy saw a body hurtle out of the opposite side of the open touring car and heard its thud as it landed in the road. He backed. Both his fenders were telescoped and one of the headlights was smashed. The other car lay on its side. There was one policeman in it. Badly hurt, perhaps. And if the wrecked car caught fire, he would be burned to death.

He stopped his car twenty feet down the road and came back. The fellow lying in the road stirred and moaned. Murphy stopped over him and struck a match. It wasn't a policeman. It was an Italian of a type familiar to the Rambler. He rolled him over and touched his hip. Nothing. He pulled the man's coat open. There was a gun in a shoulder holster.

Thrusting the weapon into his pocket, he looked into the overturned car. The chauffeur had been caught behind his wheel. He was unconscious and was pulled out into the road with difficulty. He, also, was an Italian who carried his revolver under his left arm. Murphy unfastened the leather strap and removed gun and holster.

Both men were alive but badly hurt. There was no car in sight now upon this stretch of road through practically uninhabited country. Yet he had to go on. In a few minutes, no doubt, a car would approach, discover the wreck and lend aid.

The Rambler ran to Pierre's somewhat battered automobile, jumped in and sped down the road. His bumper and fenders had prevented injury to the motor, while his one headlight gave sufficient illumination.

Addison Francis Murphy, who had assumed that he was attacking a police radio car, was immensely relieved to find that its occupants had been gunmen. He suspected they were members of Pierre's gang who had been sent to Los Angeles to pick him up at the *Recorder* office.

Pierre, who had warned him that the girl's life depended upon his shaking off pursuit, hadn't calculated that his own followers might be mistaken for police. He knew there had been seven in the gang; now two of them had been disposed of.

IT WAS the Rambler's intention to turn over the stack of banknotes and secure the release of Mary Monmouth, but he was not going to let the bandits escape if there was any way to prevent it. He had no plan. He would take advantage of opportunities which might present themselves.

After a couple of miles the road made another turn and far ahead he saw a brightly lighted boulevard across which cars were speeding. During the trip to town with Pierre, he had kept his eyes open and he knew this was the main road from Long Beach to Balboa. He stopped his car, removed his coat, and adjusted the gun straps over his left shoulder. There was a chance that Pierre would be content with tapping his pockets, since only professional gunmen carried their weapons tucked under the left arm.

A few miles down the highroad he saw a sign, on a road opening to the left, to the effect that Newport and Balboa were in that direction. He turned. The zero hour was approaching.

Murphy's conviction was that, after he had turned over the ransom, he would have to battle for his own life.

Pierre and the fat man, for the sake of the money, had risked his broadcasting their description. Before the police could lay hands on them their plane would land them in Lower California, Mexico, a thousand mile long peninsula which is lawless except for a strip close to the American frontier. It was quite unlikely that they would leave Addison Francis Murphy behind to direct the pursuit. When he went on board that houseboat, he was going to his death and he knew it.

He flashed through Newport and ahead lay Balboa. He found a street leading along the bay shore and finally picked out the boat landing where Pierre had put him ashore. He parked his car and walked toward the float.

As he stepped upon the platform two men who had been lying in a rowboat, jumped up and stepped ashore.

"Murphy?" one asked softly. It was Pierre.

"That's right."

"Got the money?" demanded Nelson.

"You bet."

He glanced around. It was very dark. It was so late that the whole town had gone to bed. Pierre thrust the muzzle of a gun against his stomach.

"Hand it over."

"Nothing doing. Where's the girl?"

"We'll send her ashore as soon as we reach the houseboat."

"She comes ashore with me."

Pierre prodded him with the weapon. "Do as you're told," he snarled.

"Go ahead. Fire that gun. Wake the town. See how far you'll get with the cash," said Murphy.

The fat man pulled at Pierre's arm.

"He's right," he declared. "No shooting. We're on the level, Murphy. If you've got the cash, Mary's no use to us."

"Frisk him, then."

CHAPTER SEVEN

THE DOUBLE CROSS

NELSON TAPPED his pockets and to Murphy's disgust, pressed his hands against the left breast of the reporter.

"Ah-hah," he exclaimed. "Trying to put something over."

He opened the man's coat and found the holster. He drew out the weapon.

"I ought to put a bullet in you, you rat," Pierre growled.

Murphy shrugged his shoulders. "Fire away," he said with more indifference in his voice than his heart.

"Where's the money?"

"Inside the front of my pants."

Nelson touched the bulging abdomen and chuckled.

"Sure that's money?" he demanded.

"Look here, boys. I've taken this chance to get the girl. I've got one hundred thousand in five hundred and one hundred dollar bills. Now you keep your part of the agreement."

"Fair enough," said Nelson.

"Stand right where you are," Pierre commanded. "Come here, George."

He led his companion away and Murphy heard them whispering.

They returned. "O.K.," said Nelson. "We'll row out to the houseboat. You'll turn the money over and we'll count it and then we'll bring you and the girl ashore, if you give your word to drive straight with her to Los Angeles. We have to have an hour in which to make our getaway."

"I'll give you my word we won't stop between here and Los Angeles."

"Get in the boat," said Pierre harshly. "Sit at the stern where we can both watch you. No funny business."

Murphy stepped into the boat and sat down at the stern. Pierre took the oars. Nelson sat directly in front of Murphy, a revolver in his right hand. The little boat moved out on the black surface of the bay.

No word was spoken. The oars were muffled and made little sound. Just how much good had he done Mary Monmouth, the Rambler wondered. They would take the money and then bump him off. Maybe they would carry off the girl with them. Minutes passed. Pierre rested on his oars and flashed a flashlight four times.

Over at the right were four answering flashes. Pierre resumed rowing and presently, very dimly outlined, Murphy saw the seaplane a hundred yards ahead.

And now he understood their plan. They were not going to the houseboat. In a couple of minutes they would run alongside the plane. Its motor would start. They would put a bullet in the head of the bearer of the ransom, secure the money and board the plane. Its pilot was waiting and ready. Two men would be left on the houseboat with Mary Monmouth. In their fury at being abandoned, they would probably kill her and get away as best they could. Whether Mary lived or died, Addison Francis Murphy would have come to the end of his earthly adventures.

The idea did not appeal to him. He drew up his knees, leaning back on the seat. Suddenly he drove both feet with every ounce of strength available at the fat stomach of the gambler two feet away from him.

The shock received by Nelson was terrific. His breath went out of him like air from a blown-out tire. His arms spread wide and his gun went flying out of the boat. He toppled over backwards.

Murphy was up, tearing loose the board on which Nelson had been sitting. He lifted it above his head. Pierre dropped the oars and reached behind him for his gun. Nelson had fallen partly against the port side of the boat.

Unable to reach the oarsman before the weapon would spit fire, Murphy stepped on the port rail of the boat and his weight, with the two hundred pounds of the gambler, caused it to tip over.

The occupants went into the water, but Murphy was holding the heavy three foot plank.

The whole thing happened so suddenly that neither of the bandits made an outcry. All three men sank silently beneath the black water.

BUOYED by the board, Murphy came to the surface almost at once. Suddenly a head appeared, three or four feet distant. He launched himself toward it. Kicking hard with his legs, he lifted himself partly out of the bay, raising high his piece of planking. A hand came out of the water holding a revolver. Pierre had continued to clutch his weapon as he went head first into the sea. Its muzzle was less than a foot from Murphy's breast. With an oath, he pulled the trigger.

Nothing happened. A moment's immersion had wet the cartridges in Pierre's magazine—cartridges guaranteed, no doubt, to be waterproof.

And then, down came the boat seat with vicious force upon the top of the head of the bandit leader!

Pierre disappeared. Murphy peered into the murk for a sight of Nelson. He heard a stifled cry and swam toward the right with no intent to rescue. Nelson was gone, however. At least Murphy couldn't find him. And Pierre was gone—for good, he hoped.

His own plight would have been serious save for the piece of planking, for he wore heavy shoes and his clothes were horribly heavy.

Holding onto the plank with one hand, he struggled until he succeeded in getting off his shoes. Then he managed with great difficulty to swing out of his coat. He tried to get his bearings. The plane was no longer visible but as he strained his eyes, the pilot again made use of his flashlight. It was enough. Murphy knew, now, the direction of the marsh at the side of which the houseboat was moored.

Four of the seven men had been disposed of. One was on the plane. That left two on the houseboat. Odds of two to one did not worry Rambler Murphy.

The water was not cold but he was thoroughly chilled before his feet struck the mud of the marsh, and he fell exhausted on the shore. The fate of the pair who had been in the boat did not trouble him—they had intended to break faith, rob him and slay him, and he had struck first.

Blessing the absence of a moon, he crept along the shore, narrowly escaping a quicksand at one spot. Ahead loomed the bulk of the houseboat, blacker than the night itself. For the second time that evening he crept up upon the land side and lifted himself over the rail. His eyes, somewhat accustomed to the darkness, could distinguish no one on deck. But presently he heard a man cough. The cough came from the other side of the craft and forward.

Shoeless, his feet made no sound. The fellow was leaning over the rail, waiting for the return of the boat. Murphy was behind him. Murphy, who had not abandoned his bit of planking, brought it down on the fellow's head as he had crashed it down on the head of Armand Pierre. He caught the man as he crumpled. It was the white-clad seaman, overpowered for the second time that night. This time, he needed no gag or bonds....

There was a revolver in his pocket which the Rambler secured. Six bandits out of the way.

He approached the deck-house, and pulled open the door. The seventh man, an Italian, sat at the table with rows of cards in front of him. He laid down a card as the door opened, glanced up. As if by magic, a revolver appeared in his hand.

Two shots rang out simultaneously, but Murphy had had a chance to aim. A bullet hit the Italian in the chest and he fell forward on the table. The Rambler heard a leaden slug hum past his right ear.

"Seven," he exclaimed. He ran at top speed along the corridor and into the pantry. He pulled the bolts of the trapdoor to the hold.

"Miss Monmouth," he called.

NO ANSWER. His heart sank. Had they already disposed of her?

"Miss Monmouth!" he roared. "Mary!"

"Yes," said a shaking voice.

"Thank God! It's Murphy. Come up."

"I must have been asleep," she said in a puzzled tone. "Maybe I'm still asleep. Where have you been, Mr. Murphy?"

"Come on, kid," he pleaded, "Everything's all right They've gone. You're safe."

"Oooh," she moaned.

Murphy slid down into the hole and stumbled over the girl. She lay stretched on a mattress. She had fainted.

When she came to, she was lying on a bed in one of the chambers. Murphy was rubbing her hands and staring down at her anxiously.

"What became of them?" she asked.

"Some of them are dead, I expect. There's a wounded man in the room out there and another on the deck."

"Where are the police?"

"Well, it didn't seem necessary to call the police. I handled the situation in my own way."

The girl sat up, stared intently at him and astounded him by throwing her arms around his neck and pressing her lips to his. Being human, Addison Francis Murphy responded properly. When she released him, his head was going round and round.

"You cuddle down here," he said nervously. "It's about time the police did come into the picture."

He went into the living room, inspected the Italian who was alive but unconscious, and went out to look at his handiwork on the deck. This man was unconscious.

Murphy drew his revolver and fired five shots into the air. Reflecting that he was now without ammunition, he secured the weapon of the wounded man in the living room. When he returned to the deck, he heard the roar of an aeroplane engine and saw a searchlight laying a white beam the length of the bay. The airplane had cast off her moorings and was moving rapidly. In a moment she had attained sufficient speed and rose into the air.

A few minutes later a lighted motor boat with a siren blasting the silence of the night came into view.

FOR THE FIRST time in his life, Addison Francis Murphy thought that he really was in love. Mary Monmouth was beautiful. Mary had magnetism plus. Mary was infatuated with him. In fact Los Angeles for several days had been more or less crazy about Reporter Addison Francis Murphy. The Chamber of Commerce had made resolutions about him. The Mayor had given him the keys of the city. Mr. Solomon made a magnificent gesture and turned over to him five thousand dollars.

The Rambler and Mary had been guests of honor at a great banquet at the Ambassador. He had been on the set at Sublime to see her act. They hadn't had much time together but they understood each other. Publisher Holt had agreed to pay Murphy a hundred fifty dollars a week. He had had so much glory he was sick of it.

But the hip hurrah was over and Murphy was going out to Malibu to have dinner with Mary. There would be no other guests. Addison assumed he would be an engaged man when he left and he didn't think he minded. Mary was wonderful.

The dinner was wonderful too. Mary had thrown herself into his arms and held hands with him during the caviar and soup. Then she wanted to hear the story of his life but before he could open his mouth she was telling him the story of her life. Murphy could only listen....

From that she switched to her work in the studio and told in detail the parts that she had played and how successful they had been. She sent for her folios of press clippings. She revealed to him the art of being a great actress. It seemed to the Rambler that he had never heard the pronoun "I" used so often in the course of a couple of hours.

And while she talked Murphy was thinking. She was a wonderful girl but she was entirely self centered. She loved him, maybe, but he was going to be part of her entourage, one of her possessions. And when they were together she would discuss her art and her achievements. Night after night. Year after year. And she would tell him what they were going to do, not ask him. She was a great girl but she needed a special kind of husband.

Murphy glanced at his watch. It was nine P.M.

For some reason he had been reading steamship ads lately. Places to go on a honeymoon. There was a steamer sailing tonight for Tahiti. At midnight. He could make it in three hours. Only Mary wouldn't let him go.

"Excuse me, Mary," he said abruptly. "Now, sit still. Sure, I'll be back."

A moment later, Miss Monmouth heard a motor car starting and departing at great speed.

Her maid entered. "Mr. Murphy said to tell you he had to go," she said. "And he don't know when he'll be back."

"Oh," exclaimed Mary Monmouth.

And at midnight, a young man with no baggage and no hat but with five thousand honest dollars in his pocket, bought a ticket at the pier and went on board the 20,000 ton South Sea Liner *Malola*.

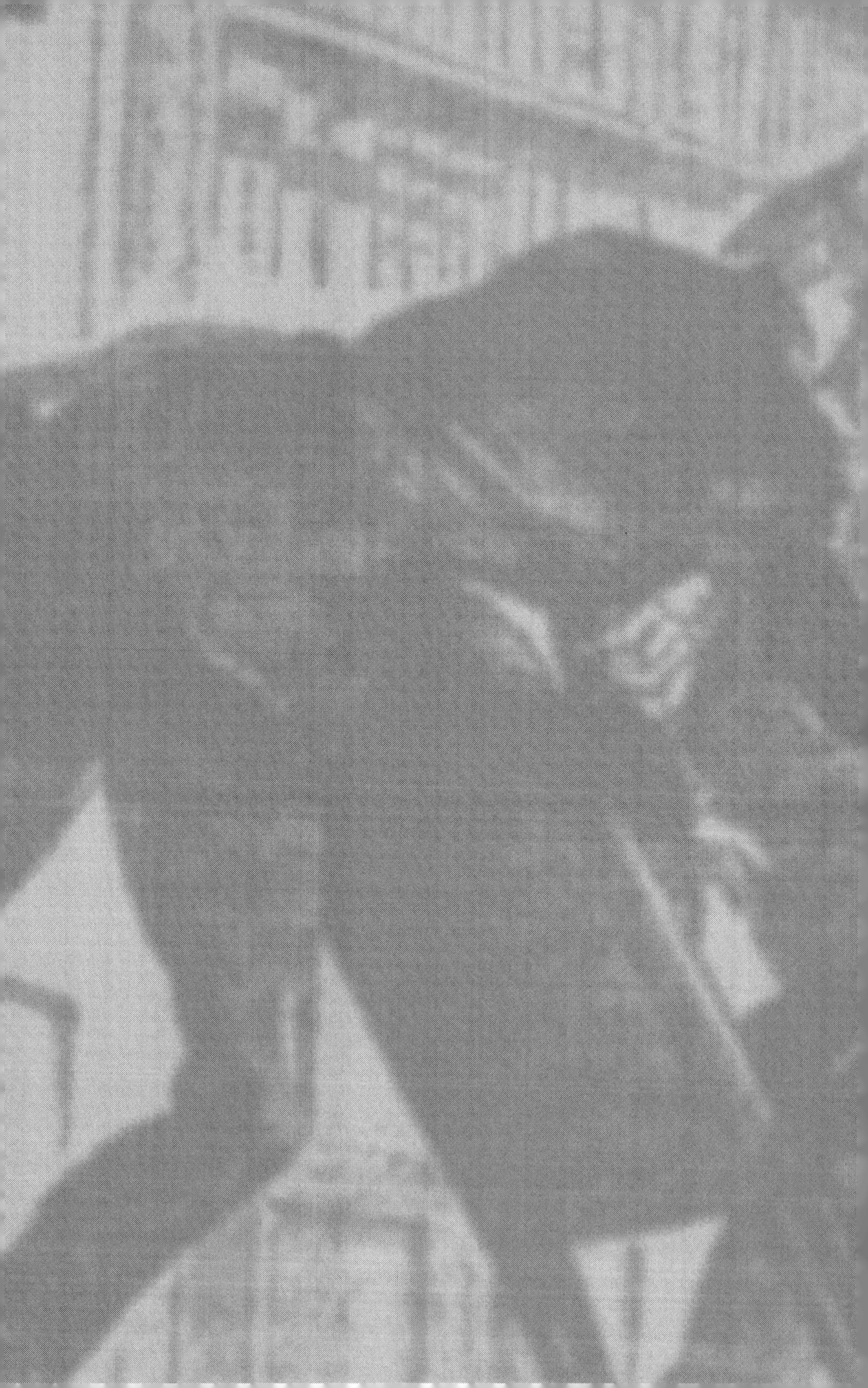

MURDER REEL

She'd checked in at the Crescent—apparently from nowhere—and two days later lay dead—a knife in her breast. Who was she? Where had she come from? Why was she killed? That was all Murphy had to answer when he began to buck a two-weeks-cold murder set-up.

CHAPTER ONE

BATTLE ROYAL

AMONG THE passengers listed as arriving from Tahiti on the *Cannonmoor* of the Green Star Line was Addison Francis Murphy, journalist.

Hard-bitten editors on San Francisco papers read his name and profession on the list sent round by the steamship publicity department and grinned. Mr. Murphy was well known to most San Francisco editors.

Jack Halligan, city editor of the *Post,* brought the list into Peters, the managing editor and pointed out the name with a stubby forefinger. "The Rambler's in town," he remarked. "Seems he's become a journalist."

"Run his name in the morning edition with 'journalist' after it," said Peters. "That'll make him sore. Red rag to a bull, eh?"

Halligan sat down, reached forward and deftly abstracted a cigar from the vest pocket of his boss, who brought up a protecting hand too late.

"Oh, well, you can have it," agreed Peters. "Maybe Murph has gone high hat. He made a bundle of dough on that kidnaping case in Los Angeles."

Halligan laughed. "I've worked with the nut in half a dozen towns. I'll bet you ten to one he's broke. Boss, I want to grab him and put him on the Foster case."

"What's the matter with your high-powered staff?" sneered the managing editor.

"Stopped cold. Somebody will nab the Rambler if we don't."

"We're running over our budget. The chief's talking about another salary cut. We can't take on a high-priced man."

"He'll work cheap if he's broke and he'll blow town in a month anyway. If anybody can find out who killed Jane Foster, it's Murphy. And boy, what a story that will be!"

"O.K. Go get him," said, the managing editor. "Maybe he's started back to L.A. to marry that motion-picture star he ran out on."

Halligan laughed. "He's probably touring San Francisco, tonight, studying post-Prohibition conditions."

"Never heard that he was a stew."

"Oh, the Rambler doesn't drink much but he likes to be where there's action. I'm going to put my assistant in charge and go after him."

"Willing to sacrifice yourself on the altar of duty, eh? If you get drunk I'll fire you."

"Not a chance, boss," said Halligan not too firmly.

THE CITY EDITOR of the *Post* was correct in his surmise regarding the outlook of Addison Francis Murphy. The Rambler had no intention of going back to Los Angeles where he was highly regarded and where a beautiful young film star was pining for him, assuming that picture stars ever pine. He was always the earnest student of sociology and he was fascinated by the aspect assumed by San Francisco since the repeal of Prohibition.

At the moment when the executives of a great newspaper were discussing him. Mr. Murphy was sitting in a place on Commercial Street which was not supposed to be an open saloon but which resembled one to a startling degree.

He had landed from the steamer at five P.M. He had taken a cocktail in a café in Geary Street. He had worked down through Chinatown and he was now seated at a wall table in what had been a popular resort in the days of the Barbary Coast. There was a half-consumed glass of beer in front of him, a cigarette between his lips, and an evening newspaper spread out on the table. He was reading that the murder of Jane Foster was unsolved after three weeks but that the police were leaving no stone unturned.

The din in Jerry's Joint was deafening. A radio was going full blast which didn't deter people from dropping nickels in a mechanical piano or bursting into song themselves. There were gobs from naval ships; oilers, wipers, deck hands and engineers from the commercial fleet. There were ships' officers getting drunk out of uniform. There were girls galore.

He went over backward as the chair drove into his stomach.

A blonde with a wide-brimmed hat and a low-necked dress was ogling Murphy from a neighboring table. A brunette twitched his back hair playfully as she passed. He ignored her.

The Rambler didn't care about lights-'o-love personally but he was glad they were present. They gave color to a spirited scene. This was better than Tahiti where it was represented by deported Parisiennes and lewd half castes and houris of pure chocolate hue.

Three months in the Islands and five thousand dollars gone to the bow-wows. He never regretted spent money. The future had no terrors for him. He still had ten dollars and, when that was gone, he would crash some newspaper.

Those Islanders could shoot craps, he mused, a half-smile upon his tanned face. Most of his money had gone the dice route. Broke again. Better than being a film star's husband listening to her relate nauseous details of the day at the studio. That had been the most narrow squeak of his career.

A plump girl with a doll face and bleached hair suddenly plopped on his lap. "Sweetheart," she cooed. "Buy baby a drink."

Murphy rose and spilled Baby on the floor, helped her up and heard some new wrinkles in profanity. He waved to the waiter, paid for his beer and departed. There were at least twenty more joints on Commercial Street which he ought to investigate. Of course they would all be like this but maybe one of them would be different.

At eleven he arrived in a spot known as McGurk's. It was different. In the middle of the floor there was an elegant fight going on, a free-for-all, a veritable battle royal. Murphy's blood tingled and his Irish blue eyes sparkled and his Irish fists clenched. He had learned discretion, however, so for a while he watched the fight.

It was a small saloon and there were at least twenty people, including half a dozen women, in the merry whirl. There was not an upright table and the floor was strewn with broken glass. He saw two or three men who were down and being stepped on, and he could see the rise and fall of a bung starter indicating that the bartender was in the fray.

ALL THE participants were yelling as well as laying about them and, in Murphy's opinion, the affair was delectable. Too bad that the police would be along in a few minutes to stop it.

There is always a cause for a bar-room fight and the Rambler endeavored to discover the cause of this one. When there was a rift in the mass he found it. There was a very large man in the geometrical center of the brawl who was working both arms like pistons. On his face was a seraphic smile, despite a cut over the left eye, a bleeding lip and a blood-clotted scalp. Every now and then he opened his mouth and uttered an ear-splitting war whoop.

Murphy's eyes danced and his smile broadened. Why he knew the fool! Drunk as a lord and belligerent, as always when drunk. Big Jack Halligan who had worked with the Rambler on the New York *World* and elsewhere. Dear old Jack.

"Atta boy, Jack! Wow!" Murphy catapulted into the mob, hurling men and women to right and left. "Give 'em hell, Jack," he howled. "Take that, damn you."

"Sock 'em Rambler," replied Halligan. "Oh, you would, would yah?"

And now the battle waged more fiercely than ever, and through the door came sailors in uniform who waded in regardless. Halligan was down, slugged from behind. Murphy straddled him, raging like a Viking—there's plenty of Viking blood in the Irish. Oh, it was a beautiful brawl!

As all good things must come to an end, the riot squad intruded, wielding night-sticks vigorously. Quickly the warriors scattered and heavy hands descended upon the collar of Mr. Murphy. A club put out his lights and he and Halligan and three men and one woman were tossed into a patrol wagon.

Halligan sat up and grinned at Mr. Murphy who was just recovering consciousness. "You big fathead," he said. "I was looking for you."

Murphy rubbed his sore head ruefully. "You always did get me into trouble, you lug," he charged.

"All out," called the cop on the steps of the wagon.

In a moment the battered sextet was lined up before the desk lieutenant at the station.

"Ten days in the cooler, we'll get," said Murphy sourly. "And it's your fault, you baboon."

"Oh, yeah?" countered Mr. Halligan.

"Hello, Jack," exclaimed the police lieutenant cordially. "Drunk again, eh?"

"Sober as a judge, Lieutenant."

"Well, get the hell out of here. Lock up the rest of them."

Halligan jerked his thumb at Murphy. "This bum is my pal," he stated.

"Outside, both of you," growled the lieutenant.

"Seem to know you in this man's town," commented Murphy as they went down the station steps.

"Why not? I'm city editor of the *Post*."

"You are, are you? Well, I want a job."

"You've got one," stated Halligan. "Why you moron, I was out looking for you."

"Did you suppose I'd be hanging out in a joint like that?"

"Oh, no. You weren't there at all, were you?"

"I just happened in," said Murphy.

CHAPTER TWO

THE FOSTER KILL

MANAGING EDITOR PETERS said: "Now listen, Rambler. You're on trial. I'll give you two weeks to land the murderer of Jane Foster. Come through and you're set here, though I don't suppose that will interest you."

"It does," said Murphy gravely. "I'm all washed up with rambling. Any way I've been 'most everywhere."

"This Foster Case is buttoned up. Unbutton it. I expect there's politics behind it and the rackets. The police act suspiciously as though they were tipped to lay off. Our boys can't get their teeth in anything. We've men on our staff smarter than you ever were, but you're an outsider. You're not spotted as a reporter wherever you go. You've a chance."

"O.K. Tell me the story."

"All right. Jane Foster is a beautiful woman who came to the Crescent Hotel about a month ago. She engaged an expensive suite. She saw nobody during her three days at the hotel but she put in one telephone call. She called Barney Upton's house. Barney Upton is a big politician—he has a finger in every pie. He says he didn't get the call and he doesn't know the woman. On her third night at the hotel, a stiletto was stuck into her heart.

"Her pictures were telegraphed all over the country and to London and Paris. Nobody knows her. She registered as from New York but we don't know how she got here. Nobody on any of the through trains on the day she arrived remembers her and she was not hard on the eyes. She might have come by motor. She didn't arrive on a steamer so far as we know. There is no clue regarding the murder."

"First-class mystery."

"It would be better if we could identify her. It's dropped out of the papers for lack of ammunition. Upton is probably lying when he says he knows nothing about her but we can't get back of his denial."

"I want a hundred and fifty a week," said Murphy.

"That's more than we pay anybody just now, old man."

"And expenses," said Murphy ruthlessly. "This story is worth ten thousand to you, you skinflint."

Peters shrugged. "Five hundred bonus if you break the story."

Murphy rose. "For some reason I'm kind of tired," he said smiling. "Soft easy life in the Islands and no exercise on the steamer. I'll be in tomorrow morning and read the clippings on this woman. Give me an order on the cashier for fifty bucks advance and warn that inebriate Halligan to keep away from me."

"Where will you put up?"

"At the Crescent, naturally."

Peters coughed. "Murphy," he said, "we fellows who knew you when, are dying off fast. The new breed of editor hates tramp reporters. Get wise. Make good here and you're fixed for life. Oh, hell, what's the use talking to you."

WITH a clean shave, a neatly painted left eye and some scratches that hardly showed, Addison Francis Murphy arrived early next morning at the office of the *Post* which, being a morning paper, was almost deserted at that hour. He got the files of all the San Francisco papers and for two hours was absorbed in them. He read everything which had been published about the murder of Jane Foster, made copious notes, and then went into the "morgue" and secured photographs of the dead woman. There were several photographs which had been found in her room, but none of them bore the photographer's mark, which was curious.

He knew that prints must have been made up and sent to every listed photographer in the country by the police, and assumed from Peters' statements that no results had been achieved by this form of investigation. There were also pictures of the woman taken after her death which bore little resemblance to the others.

She appeared to be a woman in her late twenties. She had chestnut hair, brown eyes and regular features. There was an air of refinement about her. According to the police reports she had a brown mole between her shoulder blades, a corn on the little toe of her left foot, a scar on her right little finger about half an inch wide, and an appendicitis scar.

No papers had been found in her room or on her person. No pocketbook, jewels or money had been found so the presumption was that she had been robbed.

By the time Murphy had finished his research work Jack Halligan had come in and was at his desk in his private office. The Rambler pushed open the door and entered. A very pretty blond girl who was taking dictation looked up and eyed the visitor with interest.

"Miss Jewett," said the city editor gravely, "this repulsive specimen answers to the name of Addison Francis Murphy. By profession he is a bum, by avocation, a reporter. My advice to you is to shun him. Women, on the beauty-and-the-beast principle, throw themselves at his head and sup sorrow."

"Really, Mr. Halligan," exclaimed the girl, her eyes dancing with mirth. "Are you trying to interest me in Mr. Murphy?"

"Scram," replied the city editor. "I'm warning you for your own good."

Murphy grinned at the girl shyly. "I reckon you know this fellow if you've been working here any length of time," he said. "He never uttered a coherent word since he was born."

"Pleased to have met you," replied Miss Jewett, and exited laughing.

"My wife jawed all night," said Halligan. "I explained that it was all your fault so she wants you to dine with us tonight and try some of her ground glass."

"Got another date," replied the Rambler taking the chair vacated by the pretty secretary. "Any theory of the Foster case you might have would be cockeyed, but let's hear what you think about it."

"No doubt that Barney Upton had her bumped off," said Halligan. "This dame bobbed up out of his dark past. Object, blackmail. No doubt about it at all, so all you have to do is prove it."

"Just like that, eh?"

"It's the general theory. She got hers between eleven P.M. and two A.M. according to the medical examiner. Between eleven and two that night, Barney, the chief of police, the mayor and their wives were playing poker at the mayor's house. Suspicious, eh?"

"Makes it difficult. According to your obituary envelope on Upton, he is a quiet, mild-mannered citizen who is president of the Ballard Bank, director in a lot of corporations and chairman of the Bigger and Better City Committee, who is known for his philanthropies and was a candidate last year for United States Senator."

"And in addition to that he is a so-and-so. Ask anybody who has run up against him."

"All you have on him is the fact that she called his residence on the day of her arrival,"

"Well, he's the only person she called."

"It was a neat murder. No fingerprints, no clues of any sort. Nobody seen entering or leaving her suite. No identification beyond the hotel registry."

"Right. No photographer admits making those photographs we found in her room. No maker's mark on her luggage. No report yet on her lingerie and handkerchiefs, except that the underwear is a nationally distributed brand which might be bought in any department store. Listen, you only got this job because we're stumped."

"A word from Upton to the chief of police would make them go slow?"

"He's the boss of this village, though he doesn't parade the fact."

"You're a lot of help." Murphy rose. "I'll drop in now and then," he said.

"Look here, Rambler. I sold you to old Peters. Did you get any ideas about the thing from the files or what I've told you?"

"Between you and me," said the Rambler, grinning, "it looks like a clear case of suicide."

"Get out of my office, you louse."

MURPHY went back to the office which contained the obituary envelopes, thousands of them, and asked the attendant to hand him the one on Barney Upton—he had already inspected it once—sat down with it and began to go over the clippings.

They dealt with Upton since he had begun to figure in the news. He came finally upon a laudatory sketch of his career, the occasion for which was his election to the presidency of the Ballard Bank. According to this clipping, Mr. Upton had arrived in San Francisco in 1913 from Columbus, Ohio, and had secured work as a bookkeeper in the Mathewson Ship Building Corporation. At the end of four years he had gone to the Ballard Bank as assistant cashier. About that time he had begun to dabble in politics. He had been defeated for the state legislature in 1918. From that date he figured pretty steadily in the news.

Although he had scoffed at the city editor's theory that the woman had come out of Upton's past, it had been the Rambler's own. Since she had called no one but Upton, the only thing to build upon was a previous acquaintance with the boss. Murphy thought she might have known him in whatever part of the country he had left to settle in

San Francisco—that there might be a dark secret to uncover back East somewhere. But Upton had been in San Francisco for more than twenty years—the woman was in her twenties so her connection with him, if any, must have been here.

Thus the hope that by finding a part of Upton's life in another community he could find people there who knew the murdered woman vanished. And it was strange, if she were a San Francisco girl, that nobody had come forward to identify her.

The Rambler left the office, walked across Market and up Geary, and sat in the park in front of the St. Francis Hotel. Murphy could sit in city parks by the hour.

Absorbed in his reflections he was not aware that it had come to be noon; nor did he observe the trim, blond young woman who had recognized him, approached him and stopped before him as she spoke.

"It's hard to believe all the dreadful things Mr. Halligan said about you."

He started, looked up and grinned. His South Sea tan made his white teeth seem more white. "Hello, Miss Jewett," he said. "Don't believe anything he says. Have a seat."

"I've only an hour. Would you buy a nice girl some lunch?"

He stood up. "Which is a thought," he declared. "I'm in funds. How about the St. Francis?"

"Did I say no?" she asked impishly.

In two or three minutes they were sitting at a table in the ornate dining room of the famous hotel.

"I've heard all sorts of things about you," she told him. "They say you broke the heart of that screen actress in Los Angeles, and that a certain very wealthy New York divorcee wanted to marry you and that there were others. Just what is your power, Mr. Murphy?"

"It's applesauce," he assured her. "I'm a vagabond. I never saved a nickel in my life. I'm not interested in girls—at all."

"That's probably your power," she said shrewdly. "They've given you the Jane Foster case I hear."

"Yep."

"You won't solve that mystery," she assured him. "Certain people don't want it solved."

"Who?"

"Mr. Barney Upton for one."

"That's Jack's theory. She might have been killed by a hotel robber. Or anybody else."

MISS JEWETT looked at her plate. "I'll tell you something. I haven't mentioned it at the paper. I don't happen to like Tom Ferris who has been working on the case."

"No? Why?"

"He has disease of the hands. I mean he paws one."

"You're a temptation, you know."

"Am I?" She laughed. "Well, a girl who lived in the lodging house where I live has a sister who was the night phone operator at the Crescent. She has just left the Crescent and she's working in the office of Brown and Bowers who are the lawyers for the Ballard Bank. She got a ten-dollar-a-week raise."

"What's her name?"

"Francesca Montcalm."

"You think she didn't tell all she knew about the night Jane Foster was murdered?"

"I don't think anything, I know that Brown and Bowers fired a friend of mine who had the phone job in their office and who got twenty a week. Francesca Montcalm is getting thirty."

"You're entitled to a free lunch at any place you name, any time you want it," he said enthusiastically.

"You won't say where you got this information?" she asked anxiously.

"I'm an oyster."

She laughed and regarded him through half-closed eyes. "You're rather a homely man," she told him, "and I don't care for the exact shade of red in your hair. Just the same I won't lunch with you every day. You may have some hidden charm."

"Suits me. You're too darn good looking. I'm likely to slip."

"You'll have to some time. Every man gets married. He can't avoid it. Probably you'd like it."

He shook his head. "I couldn't stand the monotony. I go crazy after I've lived in the same place and done the same things any length of time. How about a piece of pie?"

"I'm looking after my figure, thanks. And I must be getting back to the office." She offered her hand frankly and departed. He gazed after her thoughtfully. "Now that's a nice girl," he remarked.

OUT IN the street he walked a couple of blocks in a brown study. "Upton's in it," he said finally. "The Montcalm girl was bribed to keep her mouth shut. No leads available. Well, let's draw his fire."

Calling a taxi, he gave the chauffeur the Ballard Bank as an address and was delivered before its ornate portal in a very few minutes. He was informed by the policeman on duty that Mr. Upton's office was on the second floor of the building. He went up to the second floor and entered the office of the president of the bank. There was a young woman at a desk there who gazed at him rather dubiously.

"I'm a reporter on the *Post*," he said. "Name of Addison Francis Murphy. Want to see Mr. Upton."

"You'll have to state your business."

"Sure. Fresh development in the Jane Foster case."

The young woman went into an inner office. She returned in a minute. "You may go in," she said.

The Rambler found himself in a large room equipped more like a library than a business office. There was a Persian rug on the floor, mahogany-paneled walls, rows of bookcases and a large mahogany desk with a glass top which was clear of papers. Behind the desk sat a small man, thin, dark with iron-gray hair and sharp black eyes who smoked a cigarette in an ivory holder. He fingered a small black mustache and eyed the newspaperman sharply, but when he spoke his manner was cordial.

"Thought I knew all the newspaper boys," he said. "You're a new one to me."

"I was brought to San Francisco by the *Post* to solve the Jane Foster murder," said Murphy bumptiously.

Mr. Upton laughed in what seemed to the Rambler to be a hollow manner. "They must think a lot of your detective abilities. We believe we have the best police force in America and our local reporters are pretty sharp."

"I'm considered the best newspaper investigator in America," said Murphy with even more pomposity.

Mr. Upton's eyes narrowed and his smile was not pleasant. "You don't look it," he retorted. "You look like a bar-room battler. Are you drunk by any chance?"

"Only a few months ago I cleaned up, single-handed, a mob of kidnapers in Los Angeles. The Mary Monmouth case. You may have heard of it," stated Murphy. "And I don't drink—much."

Upton's eyebrows went up and his manner changed. "I make you. You're this Murphy to whom Los Angeles gave the keys of the city. Sit down, Mr. Murphy. Have a chair. Have a cigar."

The Rambler concealed a smile and seated himself. "A cigarette if you like," he said. Upton passed him a box of cigarettes and Murphy lighted one.

"I enjoy meeting prominent people," said Upton dryly. "However I'm a busy man, Mr. Murphy. And I'm not interested in the Foster case except that, like every good citizen, I trust that the murderer will be apprehended speedily. May I ask why you did me the honor of calling? If you have fresh evidence you should inform the police, not a bank official."

"I happen to know that you held a long conversation over the phone with the woman," said the Rambler coolly.

Upton's face grew black and his eyes smoked. He clenched his fist and banged it upon the top of his desk. "You're a damned liar," he shouted.

"Then you deny this fact?"

"Deny it? Why you impudent rascal, of course I deny it. I never saw or heard of the woman and, if she called my house, I didn't get the call."

Murphy rose. "You'll hear from me later," he stated and strode out.

There were three telephones upon the desk of Barney Upton, one of them a private wire. For a moment after the departure of the insolent newspaperman, the banker's rage was so great that he was unable to control it, and he swore loud picturesquely and at length. Finally he reached for the private line. He was answered immediately.

"Stephano," he said hoarsely, "get hold of Brown. You and he meet me in half an hour upstairs at Jake's. That's all."

He hung up. "If it was any paper but the *Post*," he muttered. "I'd have him kicked out into the street."

The publisher of the *Post* was Barney Upton's political enemy.

CHAPTER THREE

THE GIRL IN THE NEWS REEL

MURPHY WAS humming contentedly as he walked along the street. In his opinion his visit had been a tremendous success. It wasn't a theory now, that Upton was concerned in the murder of Jane Foster; it was a fact. The Rambler was a pretty good psychologist. If Upton had been in the clear, he would not have admitted to his office a reporter with fresh developments in the case. Obviously he had been curious about them.

When the Rambler had blown his own horn, he had read concern in the man's face. And there was the fury of guilt in Upton's outburst when Murphy had accused him of having talked over the phone with Jane Foster. For all Murphy knew at the time, he had been a liar, as accused, but he was confident now that he had spoken the truth.

It's a ruse of war, when one does not know the location of an enemy, to draw his fire, and a criminal enemy is always apprehensive lest he has overlooked something, forgotten something, slipped up somewhere. And, when frightened, he hits out blindly. Now the Rambler, not for the first time in his career, had blandly offered himself as a target. Mr. Upton would take the offensive. It wasn't unlikely that he would call in the same tools he had used to eliminate Jane Foster, to dispose of the distinguished criminal investigator who had been imported by the *Post* to solve this killing. There was an excellent chance that Mr. Murphy would turn up a corpse as a result of his brashness.

He went into a drug store and looked up the address of Brown and Bowers. At five o'clock he would be waiting for Miss Montcalm. He had to see her very soon because probably she would be leaving the city shortly.

After that he strolled down to Market Street and began to inspect the posters of the various motion-picture theaters along the famous thoroughfare.

The Rambler liked, occasionally, to view motion pictures but his taste was curious. What he liked were Wild Western pictures and film serials and detective films, of the type turned out in Poverty Row in Hollywood, and sold to houses which continue to charge only ten or fifteen cents admission. The more incoherent they were the more they amused him.

The bill at a ten-cent house called the De Luxe looked attractive. It consisted of a thriller entitled *The Crawling Death* and a Western, featuring Tim McCoy, called *Good Bad Indian*.

The house was small and dirty, the audience frowsy. The films were old and beginning to crack and the sound tracks were worn, but the plot of the Indian picture was sufficiently lurid to tickle the Rambler, who leaned back in his chair absorbed.

By and by the film was succeeded by a news reel. In such establishments, news reels are practically ancient history being anywhere from a month to three months old and given to the theater free, or sold for a dollar or two a week. This one dated itself as at least three months old by a Roosevelt radio address which Murphy had read in the newspapers long ago.

After flashes from London, New York, New Orleans and Paris the reel showed a Chinese festival procession on the Bund at Shanghai. The camera caught a section of the throng of spectators which was largely European and American, switched to the vanguard of the procession, and then picked up a rickshaw which was stalled in the mob of spectators. There were a man and a woman in the rickshaw. Murphy's casual gaze changed to an astounded interest but, in a fraction of a second, the rickshaw and its occupant vanished. He sucked in his breath. The woman was Jane Foster. Oh, it might have been a chance resemblance but she had turned her head as he gazed. The profile was like one of the death pictures, the full face like the studio photograph.

He gripped the arms of his chair, waiting impatiently until the reel had been run off and the trade mark of the company shown. It was a Pathé news reel.

MURPHY went into the lobby and to the box office. "Want to see the manager," he said to the girl.

"Go up the flight of stairs just inside the entrance to the theater. His office is at the top."

The manager was a small, seedy person who looked up apprehensively as though fearing a creditor was upon him.

"Reporter from the *Post*," stated Murphy. "Can you tell me the date and number of the news reel you've just shown?"

"What do you want to know for?"

The Rambler grinned. "I should tell you," he retorted. "You don't object to giving me this information, do you?"

"Certainly not," said the man. "What do I care what you want it for?" He looked in a book, wrote down a date and identification number on a slip of paper and handed it to Murphy. "Give us a boost some time will you," he requested. "We advertise with you but we never get a break."

"I'll speak to the dramatic editor. Thanks."

A taxi took him to the news-reel exchange. Murphy secured admittance to the sales manager, stated his name and occupation and produced the slip of paper given him by the theater manager. "Happen to have one of those reels in stock?" he demanded.

"That's an old one. We got a dozen in the shop."

"I want to take one to the *Post*."

"What for?"

"To check up on a divorce case," Murphy said with a grin. "Married man caught with a jane by your camera."

"You can have one. Deposit of twenty-five bucks."

With the reel in a zinc disc a couple of inches thick, Murphy was transported by a taxi to the Crescent Hotel. He went into the drug store and bought a reading glass, went up to his room, pulled forth the reel and began to unwind it. The thing was a thousand feet long and he had the room half full of celluloid before he found what he wanted. Under the reading glass he studied the woman in the rickshaw intently, then ruthlessly clipped the foot of film out of the reel, rolled it up, thrust it in his waistcoat pocket and hastened to the newspaper office.

There he secured the photographs of the murdered girl, unwound his film and compared them. There was no doubt in his mind that it was Jane Foster.

The murder had occurred on the night of May Fourteenth, Nineteen Thirty-four. On April First, the same year, she had been sitting in a rickshaw on the Bund in Shanghai watching a Chinese festival procession with a male companion.

Murphy studied the man. He was a broad-shouldered, heavy-jawed, weather-beaten individual in middle age. Murphy tried to fix his features in his mind. He purloined one of the photographs, put the others back in their envelope and, avoiding an encounter with Halligan or Peters, left the office.

This explained why no photographer had been found to admit having made the pictures. They had been made in Shanghai. Also why nobody had been able to identify the girl. She had arrived in San Francisco from China by steamship and the ship had sailed before the murder had been committed. The news reel had been shown in all up-to-date theaters weeks before Jane Foster was murdered.

The Rambler looked at his watch. It was only three o'clock. Next step was to find the steamer which had landed her in San Francisco about May Eleventh. Re-entering the *Post* Building he consulted the files of the paper of that date and found what he was looking for in a very short space of time. The Japanese steamer *Osaga Maru* had arrived with sixty passengers, first-class, and twenty tourist-class on May Eleventh and had sailed May Twelfth for Seattle. Jane Foster's name was not among them but she must have used another name.

One would think that some of the passengers would have recognized Jane Foster's picture even if the crew had departed at the time the murder was committed. Thing to do was to get their addresses and show them the photograph of the girl—jog their memory.

A visit to the steamship office procured that information and, with a long list of names and addresses, Murphy started to go places. On a trail the Rambler was indefatigable. In an hour he found three persons who had come from the Orient on the *Osaga Maru*, and none of them remembered the original of the photograph as having been on board.

"There were some American women in the tourist cabin," said a silk dealer named Samuels who had been aboard. "I only saw them from a distance. She might have been one of those."

"Thanks." He had a list of tourist passengers and every intention of questioning them, but it was going to take a lot of time. Might as well get some assistance. He glanced at his watch. It was four P.M. He had to catch the Montcalm girl at five. Anyway he had something to show Jack Halligan.

AFTER Halligan had inspected the bit of film and compared it with the photograph he declared excitedly: "You are the luckiest stiff out of jail, Rambler. Loafing in a movie theater on office time and you stumble onto this."

"Maybe I had a hunch," said Murphy, grinning.

"Bah, you were resting your dogs."

Murphy handed him the list of passengers. "Send a good man out with pictures of Foster to see these people. I've another lead I want to follow."

The city editor leaned back and put his thumbs in the arm holes of his vest. "She was in Shanghai," he said. "No doubt of that. We have to find the guy who was with her. I'll cable our Shanghai correspondent to get busy. As for the *Osaga Maru,* every person who landed from her was questioned by the police and reporters and shown her picture. They didn't recognize her. Of course she might have come by an earlier boat. We'll check up. Boy, we'll be well on our way when we find out from Shanghai who she really was, what she did for a living and with whom she was joyriding in that rickshaw. You're not a bad news hound, Rambler."

"I get by. Go after the *Osaga's* passengers a second time."

"Oh, sure. Say, my wife's still sore at me. Gone to her mother's. What say we have dinner at seven, eh?"

"No roughhouse tonight."

"I'm a reformed character," said Halligan virtuously. "Besides my bruises still hurt."

"O.K."

AT TEN minutes to five, Rambler Murphy entered the law offices of Brown and Bowers, which were located across the street from the Ballard Bank. He stepped into the outer office. There was an information clerk behind the rail at the right and a telephone operator behind the rail at the left.

"I'd like to see Mr. Malcolm K. Mandelbaum," said Murphy to the information clerk.

She shook her head. "No such person in these offices."

"I'm sorry. Do you know if he has offices in this building?"

The girl giggled. "Never heard of anybody named Malcolm K. Mandelbaum," she replied. "There can't be any such person."

Looking huffy, the Rambler retreated. He had managed, while talking with the clerk, to get an eyeful of the phone operator who was a pretty, dark girl in her late twenties, wearing a blue crepe dress. When she came out of the elevator in the building lobby at two minutes after five, Mr. Murphy stepped up beside her and touched her arm.

"Miss Montcalm?" he demanded.

She looked at him with recognition. "Why you're the man who was asking for Malcolm K. Mandelbaum."

"There isn't any such person," he said solemnly. "I'm a police inspector and I want to have a talk with you."

He saw fright in her eyes and the color fade from her cheeks. He took her arm and led her out of the building without resistance. She was trembling.

"Nothing is going to happen to you," he said, "if you tell the truth."

"About what? You have no right to arrest me."

He was helping her into a taxi. "Police headquarters," he told the driver and jumped in beside her. "Hey, wait. Drive through Golden Gate Park first."

"I don't believe I'll have to take you down to headquarters and give a nice kid like you the third degree," he said. "You'll talk."

The girl began to weep loudly. Murphy looked distressed. He hated to bully a young woman but he had a notion that he must work fast. Upton would take a hand in proceedings almost at once.

"What did Upton say to Jane Foster the night she called him on the phone," he said harshly.

"I don't know," she sobbed. "I didn't listen in."

"How long did they talk?"

"I don't know. Two or three minutes maybe."

"How did you know it was Upton who was talking."

She wiped her eyes. "I know his voice very well. He often has calls from the Crescent."

"How many other times did he call her?"

"He didn't."

"You know they met the night she was murdered."

"I don't know anything of the kind," she wailed. "How can you be so cruel."

"But the night after she died he called on you, eh?"

"He did not. I tell you he didn't."

"Then where did you meet him?"

"At Jake's restaurant."

"In the public restaurant?"

"In a private dining room on the second floor."

"How much did he give you to forget that he had answered Miss Foster's call?"

"A h-h-hundred dollars."

"And promised, as soon as no attention would be attracted by your leaving the hotel, to get you a better job."

"Y-es."

"What reason did he give you for suppressing the fact that he talked with the woman?"

"He said it would distress Mrs. Upton."

"You know Upton pretty well don't you? You've been on parties with him?"

"Once or twice," she confessed. "Everything was proper though,"

"So when you were questioned you just said Miss Foster had called Mr. Upton and that's all you knew about it. You had to admit that, because it was on your record."

"Yes."

"You positively didn't listen to their conversation?"

"Honest, mister, there were a lot of calls at the time. I couldn't."

Addison Francis pulled some copy paper from his breast pocket and began to write rapidly with a fountain pen. He filled two sheets of paper. "Sign each of these or go down to headquarters," he commanded. She signed with a trembling hand. The cab was rolling slowly through Golden Gate Park at the time.

"Stop the cab," shouted Murphy. "Can you write your name, driver?"

"Better than you, maybe," replied the chauffeur belligerently.

"Stick your John Hancock here, under witness. Here's five bucks for you."

"Well, what's it about?"

"About five bucks."

With a grin, the cabby signed his name on each page. Murphy signed below him, folded the papers carefully and replaced them in his pocket.

"You better not be seen with me, Miss Montcalm," he said. "I'll send you home in this taxi and get out and take a street car as soon as we leave the park. For heaven's sake don't cry. You were guilty of being an accessory in a murder and this puts you in the clear."

"But Mr. Upton will be angry."

"You keep your mouth shut and pretty soon it won't matter how angry he gets."

HE LEFT the cab after a few minutes and phoned the *Post* from a drug store. "Halligan," he said. "Know a café called Jake's?"

"Don't be silly. I help support it."

"That's where we're having dinner."

"Say, Murph, the liquor's prime but the food isn't so good."

"What do you care about food?"

Jack Halligan laughed. "That's right," he replied. "See you at seven."

Murphy returned to the hotel, asked for a deposit envelope and placed therein the statement from Francesca Montcalm. While he didn't think that the girl would dare call Upton and confess that she had betrayed him, he felt reasonably certain that Upton was about to take measures in regard to himself. After that, Murphy went down to Market Street and bought himself a neat thirty-eight caliber revolver which felt good in his hip pocket.

About six o'clock he went up to his room to wash and change his shirt. He was in the best of spirits and was whistling as he unlocked his door and stepped inside. The whistle died in his throat. Two men were occupying his room. They had an open quart of whiskey and two glasses. On the table in front of them was a tangled mass of celluloid, the news reel, which they had been inspecting.

"Name of Murphy?" demanded one of them belligerently.

"You fellows have a hell of a lot of gall," he replied indignantly. To a man with his experience, it was evident that his uninvited guests were a couple of police detectives.

"How would you like to go up for vagrancy?" demanded the fellow with his hat on the back of his head.

"You couldn't make it stick," Murphy retorted. "Want to give a guy a drink?"

The bald-headed man whose hat lay on the floor grinned and poured a stiff drink of Scotch into a glass. "We can make anything stick," he stated.

Murphy took the glass, raised it toward them politely and sipped. "You cops always have good liquor," he said approvingly. "I'm living in a first-class hotel. I earn a hundred an' fifty dollars a week as a reporter on the *Post* so I'm a hell of a vagrant."

The first detective wagged his head. "You're in wrong in this town, kid," he said. "Certain party don't like you. People he don't like leave San Francisco in a hurry. If they stick around they get jugged. It's surprising how many things a guy can get jugged for."

"But the *Post* is a big paper," said the Rambler in the same vein. "It takes care of its boys the way a hen does chicks."

"Surprising," said the bald-headed cop, "how many chicks get on the broiler. What you doing with this old news reel?"

"Just playing with it."

"Yeah?" The hatted cop coughed and frowned portentously. "We know about you," he said. "Fresh guy. The *Post* don't need you. The town doesn't want you. Give you twenty-four hours to scram."

"And if I stick around?"

The bald cop looked mournful. "This used to be the toughest town in the world," he said. "Since liquor came back it's getting tough again. Every day you read about terrible things in the papers. We ain't got anything against you personal, buddy. We'd hate to have anything happen to you. Get wise. Get wise."

"I hope you're not going to take that bottle of Scotch with you when you leave," replied Murphy.

"You hope wrong," said the man with his hat on. He corked the bottle and pushed it into a capacious back pocket.

Murphy wasn't smiling when the door closed upon his visitors. He had drawn the enemy's fire all right and it was heavy artillery. Upton had the police force working for him. Did Upton expect to scare Rambler Murphy off a job? If he did he was a fool, and he didn't look like a fool.

With the *Post* behind him, Murphy didn't think a frame-up would be tried. Something more drastic would follow the police demonstration. The gun in his pocket felt good.

He was whistling again as he washed—something about a dream walking—though Murphy had no particular dream in mind even if he did think that Halligan's secretary was a very swell little girl.

CHAPTER FOUR

SHANGHAI SET-UP

AT ABOUT five after seven, the Rambler descended from a taxi in front of Jake's Café. Jake's had evidently been a speakeasy. It was a detached wooden house on Sutter Street with a parking lot on either side. A dozen cars were already parked. There was a big grilled gate at the entrance which stood open. One walked up three steps and was confronted by a heavy oak door, with the peep hole still there. However, the door was opened at his approach and in the hallway within stood Halligan and, to Murphy's surprise, Miss Jewett beside him.

"You need refining influence," said Halligan. "So I brought some refining influence along."

Her eyes were bright and her smile was eager. "I hope you don't mind," she said to Murphy. "You interest me strangely."

"Casanova was like that," muttered Halligan. The Rambler blushed and tried to slay his friend with a glare. "Let's eat and quit kidding," he said gruffly. "Captain, get us a table for three."

Jake's lower floor was a long narrow room with a bar at the far end, lined with booths on either side. The place was about half full. Halligan ordered cocktails and the regular dinner.

"You had some reason for picking out this joint, I suppose," he said to Murphy, "but don't discuss business here. It's a pol's hang out."

"Let's discuss me," suggested Miss Jewett, "unless Mr. Murphy would like to tell us about his sex life."

"You're a brazen brat," Halligan said reprovingly. "We are going to feed you and dismiss you and go places."

"Jack," said Murphy who drew an envelope from his pocket, "here's an order for you to get a deposit envelope out of the Crescent safe in case I don't show for a couple of days."

Halligan's smile faded. "In trouble already?"

"I sort of expect it. I've been stirring up the animals."

"Anything doing here?"

"Guess not. I want to see the proprietor. What does he look like?"

"Curly black hair and hook nose." Halligan peered out of the booth. "He's standing at the bar talking to Alderman Smith."

"I see him. A certain party is a patron of the place, I believe."

"Holds conferences here," said Halligan.

"Oh, well," sighed Miss Jewett. "I might as well eat and go home."

"Blessed if I know why I brought you," said Halligan frankly. "My wife wouldn't like it."

"Oh, I'm with Mr. Murphy," she declared, smiling quizzically at the Rambler.

"If he doesn't want you, I want you," replied Murphy, playing up.

As a matter of fact he was sorry the girl was along. He had things to do in this place.

"If I could believe you," she said mockingly. "Suppose you move, Jack, and let me go to the little girl's room."

WHEN they were alone Murphy leaned forward. "I called on Upton," he whispered. "Told him I could prove he talked to the woman. He ordered me out."

"You showed your hand, you damned fool."

"Had to get action. Not a darn thing to go on. Well, I found a couple of plain-clothesmen in my room. Gave me twenty-four hours to get out of town."

"You better watch your step," said Halligan gloomily. "You think, now, he had Foster put out of the way?"

"Reasonably sure of it. He's lying when he says he didn't talk to her. Oh—" He rose. Miss Jewett had returned; her face was white.

"I'm terribly sorry," she said, "but I'm sick. Please take me out of here at once. Quickly."

Both men rose; Halligan summoned the waiter. "Cancel the dinners. Here, take this five dollars. That'll pay for everything. Come on, kid."

They rushed the girl out into the open air, signaled a taxi, and Halligan lifted her in and jumped in after her.

"You take her home," said the Rambler. "Meet you in the Palace bar, Jack. I've business here." He slammed the door.

"Oh, make him come with us," she wailed.

"You can't make that idiot do anything," replied Halligan. The taxi started and he flung an address to the chauffeur.

She clutched his arm. "I'm not sick, you fool," she cried. "I wanted to get us out of the place."

"That's a fine thing to do to a couple of guys. What for?" he demanded testily.

"Make the taxi go back, please," she pleaded.

"Say are you struck on this egg?"

"Certainly not. He's in danger."

Halligan laughed. "Sure he is—most of the time. He loves it. How do you know—"

"Tell the driver to go back!"

He looked stubborn. "You're going home and I'll go back after

Murph. What's the matter with you anyway?"

"I was in the ladies' room," she said tensely. "There's only a thin partition between it and the men's room. I heard two men talking. One said, 'That's Murphy who came in with Halligan. Phone Stephano to get right over here.' The other man laughed and said, 'You mean to say that the sap walked right in here?' And the answer was, 'Yeah, but we can't do anything with Halligan around!'"

Halligan leaned forward and shouted to the chauffeur, "Drive like hell to that address." Then, "Kid, you're smart."

"Get out and take another cab. I'll go home alone."

"The Rambler is a broth of a boy in a brawl," Halligan assured her. "And I'll be back inside of ten minutes anyway."

"Oh, all right," she said resignedly. "You're pig-headed, of course."

IN TEN minutes Jack Halligan jumped out of the taxi back at Jake's and went inside. "Where's my friend, Louis?" he demanded of the head waiter. Louis looked surprised. "He went right out after you did, Mr. Halligan."

"Yes, but he came back again."

"Sure. He went down to the bar, had a drink and then he went out. I saw him go through that door." He pointed to the dining-room door which led into the hallway.

"I'm seeing for myself," said Halligan who pushed past him. He went the length of the room and spoke to the bartender.

"Big red-headed guy, tanned chocolate. See him?"

Tom, the bartender, nodded. "He had one and went away."

Jack Halligan left the dining room and stood in the hallway. After a second's hesitation he ran up the flight of stairs, pushed open the door of a private dining room and saw a girl sitting on a man's lap. "Excuse me," he said. He tried another door. Four men dining together looked at him indignantly. He apologized, slammed the door, and was confronted by Jake.

"I don't care who you are," declared the proprietor. "You can't do that."

"Watch me," retorted Halligan. He opened four more doors and saw a couple of other love scenes. Jake followed on his heels protesting.

"What you want, anyway?"

"A friend of mine, the fellow I was having dinner with downstairs."

"He ain't up here," declared Jake. "You can't bust in on my guests, Mr. Halligan, even if you are a newspaperman."

But Jack was gazing at the staircase to the third floor. "You live up there, don't you?"

"Sure I do."

"Well, show me your flat, Jake," he laid menacingly.

Jake spread out his arms. "Why not?"

He conducted Halligan through a four-room apartment on the third floor. It was richly furnished and absolutely empty of people, even to the closets.

"You don't want to come here any more, Mr. Halligan," declared Jake. "I don't have to stand for this, I don't. I've got friends in this town with a bigger pull than you got."

Halligan forced a smile. "I don't doubt it," he said. "It looks as though my friend did leave just as Louis and Tom told me. I'm sorry, Jake. To hell with you."

He left the place with many misgivings and drove to the Palace bar where he waited two hours for Murphy. During that interval he phoned the Crescent Hotel half a dozen times. After that he went down to police headquarters, not to report his friend's disappearance but to ask the night *Post* man on duty there if he knew of an individual whose first or last name was Stephano.

MURPHY returned to the restaurant after the taxi had carried off Halligan and the Jewett girl and walked straight to the bar. Jake was there talking earnestly to the bartender.

"You know a girl named Francesca Montcalm?" he demanded.

Jake smiled and shook his head but his eyes didn't smile. "So many ladies come to my place."

"She came here with Barney Upton," said Murphy bluntly. "You know him, I suppose."

"Everybody knows Mr. Upton," said Jake, "but he never brings ladies here."

"What can I get you, mister?" asked Tom the bartender.

"Scotch highball," he answered absently. "I thought you might know her phone number," he said. "My friends just ran out on me. Barney introduced me to her and she said she stepped out occasionally, but I didn't get her address."

He tossed off the drink which the bartender set in front of him and turned a propitiating smile on Jake. "A feller needs a dame when he wants to start on a binge," he remarked.

Jake grinned and rubbed his hands together. "I can get her here," he said. "I never seen her with Barney but she's on the call list. Come upstairs. I'll give you a private dining room and send her in."

"Why—er—all right," said Murphy indistinctly. Jake took his arm and led him through a door at the side of the bar which opened into the hallway. He conducted him upstairs. The Rambler's feet seemed heavy to him and his mental processes were not very clear. Seemed to be a good idea to find out if Jake actually could produce the Montcalm girl.

Jake pushed open the door of a private room. "Meet a couple of friends of mine," he said genially and then caught Murphy under the arms as he toppled.

"Got him," he said. "Watch him until Stephano gets here, boys."

If the Rambler had known what Miss Jewett had learned in the ladies' room he would have departed with her and Halligan. He was indiscreet but not so much so as to walk deliberately into a trap. He needed to get an admission from Jake that he had seen Francesca Montcalm with Barney Upton and, not being aware that he was already spotted, he had no suspicion that the drink he had ordered would be drugged.

They laid him on the floor of the private dining room and awaited the arrival of the person called Stephano.

WHEN the Rambler came to he was lying in a dirty bunk in a dirty forecastle, in a vessel which was at sea. Daylight was trying to force its way through very dirty portholes. A dozen disheveled men were snoring lustily in other bunks. The room was rising and falling unpleasantly. He felt sick; his head ached horribly. He became aware of an odor of sweat and the fumes of liquor from the mouths of his companions.

He put out his hand and touched the side of the vessel. It was iron or steel which meant that he was on a steamer, not a sailing vessel. Before he investigated, he knew that he had been robbed. His watch was gone; he had had little left of the fifty dollars advanced by Managing Editor Peters so its loss was of no consequence.

He tried to sit up and fell back nauseated. He knew what had happened to him. They had given him a Mickey Finn of potent quality and he had passed out on the second floor of Jake's. The stuff was beginning to affect him at the bar or he wouldn't have gone upstairs.

He had been turned over to a crimp and shanghaied on some filthy tramp headed for the South Seas or China or Australia. He had drawn Upton's fire all right. Oh, sure. And it had pulverized him.

He was licked. No use in fighting fate. The ship's officers would pay no attention to him. They had to have a crew and didn't care how they got it. He knew what was in store for him. This would be a coal-burning steamer on a long voyage, and such vessels find it almost impossible to get stokers nowadays; hence the recrudescence of the crimp profession. He was doomed to toil in the bowels of a foul ship deep in the tropics. Men went crazy and jumped overboard after a few days and weeks of such labor. He was strong but he wasn't built for a stoker. He wouldn't be able to stand it.

A man in the berth opposite woke up and began to curse viciously. He woke somebody else up who also swore fluently. After five minutes of that an engineer officer, wearing a torn, faded uniform coat of blue and no shirt, pulled open the door.

"Get up, you blasted scum!" he bellowed.

The fellow who had first awakened rolled out of his berth. "You dirty heel!" he roared. "You can't shanghai me." He was unsteady on his pins and went over backward from a blow of the engineer's fist.

"Fireroom watch," bellowed the officer. "Get up, you rats, or I'll bust your skulls."

Murphy climbed out of his berth which was in the second tier. "What ship's this, mister?" he inquired.

"What the hell do you care?"

The Rambler grinned. "I don't much. I'm not kicking. I had it coming to me."

"That's the spirit," said the engineer less belligerently. "Listen to him, you skunks. You're in for it. Make the best of it."

A FEW minutes later, eight men dressed in overalls and wearing nothing underneath them staggered out into the bright sunlight. They were marshalled toward the stoke-hole ladder up which was coming a procession of similarly clad stokers who, presumably, hadn't been brought aboard drunk or drugged, and therefore had been able to take the first shift below.

The day was cool but a hot blast came up the ladder as the Rambler climbed down to the bottom of the ship. She was a short, squat old hooker with a small deck house amidships. She had an old-fashioned triple-expansion engine and a single screw. She was a British ship for her ensign still hung at her taffrail. The stoke hole was narrow and the hot air was full of coal dust. The boss stoker thrust shovels into unwilling hands and, with kicks from heavy boots, taught the wretches their jobs.

Murphy, whose hands were soft though his muscles were strong, suffered tortures in a temperature of a hundred and twenty degrees. His eyebrows were quickly singed and blisters were raised on his hands in no time. During four awful hours he hurled coal into the furnace.

When the watch was over he was so weak that he was hardly able to climb the series of ladders which led to the deck and the open air. One or two of his companions had to be carried up by the relief stokers, and were dropped like sacks on the iron deck. Murphy lay flat on his back on a hatch cover, utterly exhausted.

He had learned below that he was on board the steamer *Bristol Brother* bound for Valparaiso, Chili—a voyage of at least six weeks and a journey across the broad sea of torridness. The stoke hole was horrible now, in the cool weather prevailing off the California coast. He could imagine it at the equator. Upton would have been more merciful if he had had the reporter bumped off in San Francisco.

He lay with closed eyes for half an hour thinking bitter thoughts. Halligan would get the Montcalm girl's statement from the hotel safe, but he wouldn't dare go after Upton without more evidence than that. Most likely he would identify the Foster girl, on the strength of the news-reel picture, but he would be far from discovering the murderer and motive for the crime. Three months would pass before Murphy could return to San Francisco, and by that time the Foster case would be buried so deep that it couldn't be resurrected. Assuming, that is, that Addison Francis survived the stoke hole.

He became aware of voices and opened his eyes. "Scrubby lot," said a heavy British voice. "The red-headed one looks husky, the rest are scum."

Murphy sat up grinning. "Why thanks, mister," he said. "Thanks for so much."

"What's the matter with the swab?" shouted the Britisher. "Blast you, why do you look at me like that?"

Murphy was staring incredulously at a middle-aged man wearing four stripes on his sleeve. "Say!" shouted the Rambler. "I want to talk to you."

He leaped off the hatch cover. The captain of the ship stepped back and the chief engineer, a dour, dark, Orkney Island Scotchman, stepped forward.

Crash! Smash! He had swung with his right against the side of Murphy's head, caught him with his left as Murphy swayed to the right and knocked him to the left. Then he drove one to the stomach which sent the stoker to the deck.

"Avast that!" ordered the captain. "The poor devil's out of his mind."

"I'll teach the insolent rapscallion!" cried the engineer.

"Put him in irons, if he's going to be like that," said the skipper. "But it's the first four hours below, no doubt." He swung about and walked aft.

"Pick this hog up and dump him in a bunk," commanded the engineer, and a couple of stokers carried the Rambler forward.

It was fortunate for Murphy that he had been too weak to offer resistance or he would have learned what discipline was on a British tramp steamer. He lay in his bunk battered and bruised but no longer hopelessly despondent. Shanghaied, doomed to hard labor feeding coal into furnaces, eliminated completely from the investigation of the Foster murder case—and now Upton himself had made a breach in the blank wall.

The captain of the *Bristol Brother* was Jane Foster's companion in the rickshaw in the news-reel picture.

CHAPTER FIVE

HOLD EVERYTHING!

ON THE third morning after the dinner at Jake's which hadn't been eaten, Hattie Jewett greeted Halligan with the query, "Any word?"

"No," said Jack Halligan sullenly. She turned away. He heard a suspicious sound. "You went and got a case on the fellow," he growled. "I warned you, didn't I?"

"I haven't got a case on him," cried the secretary. "Oh, why don't you do something."

"I didn't sleep last night," he said gravely. "The guy gets under your skin. He deliberately prodded Barney Upton to bring trouble down on himself, on the off chance he'd pick up a trifle of evidence. That statement from Francesca Montcalm is no good. She's disappeared. The taxi driver turned in his cab and vamoosed and Murphy's gone. And all it proves is that Upton had speech with Jane Foster. You can't hang him on that. No response to Peters' cables to Shanghai. And nobody knows who the devil Stephano is."

"He has such nice eyes and you have an irresistible desire to comb that red hair for him," said the girl softly.

"You have it bad, kid. Listen, he'll turn up. He's been in worse messes than this. If I could get hold of this wop Stephano! He's a criminal, of course. No doubt the police know him but they won't give us any help. And no newspaperman in town seems to have run across him."

Miss Jewett had dried her tears and was opening the city editor's mail.

Drawing each letter from its envelope, she flattened such missives as required Halligan's attention, placed in another pile those which she could take care of and tossed what needed no attention in her waste basket.

"Upton wants to see you," she exclaimed. "Listen. *Mr. Barney Upton would like the pleasure of your company at luncheon today if possible. Kindly phone me if it will be convenient for you to lunch with him at the Booster's Club at one. Stephen Fanov, Secretary.*"

"Wants me to lunch with him, eh? Handing me the old bull. He knows we have the Montcalm statement and knows it's no good. So he'll tell me in confidence that he did exchange words with Miss Foster, who turned out to be a stranger asking money, or something like that. He'll ask me not to embarrass him by dragging him into a case with which he has no connection, and let me feel the iron hand beneath the velvet glove. Well, call up this secretary and tell him I accept. Get a good lunch anyway."

"O.K.," she said dutifully. "Maybe he'll betray himself in some way. What was that secretary's name—Stephen Fanov. Funny name."

"Yeah. He's half Russian, half Korean. Upton picked him up when he went over to Vladivostok a couple of years ago on business for the bank. Crumbly looking egg but efficient as hell, I guess."

"Jack!" she cried. "Jack, I've got it! Stephano—see. Steve Fanov. Stephano for short."

Halligan brought his fist down with a thump on his desk. "By God!" he exclaimed. "Hattie, you get a raise! Stephano. Why it's clear as day! He does the dirty work. He killed Jane Foster. He k— I mean, he carried off Rambler Murphy. Don't you see? This half-caste is in Barney's confidence. He wouldn't hire a gangster to kill the girl. He'd send his secretary. Will I go to that lunch? Will I!"

The door opened and the managing editor entered. "Cablegram from Shanghai, Jack," he said joyfully. "Murphy made good all right. *Woman in rickshaw in news-reel flash of festival parade April First, identified as Mrs. Sophia Bundy, nationality English. Address London Hotel. Checked out April Seventh, destination unknown but passport viséd for United States April Fifth. Arrived in Shanghai June First, Nineteen Thirty-three, from Tokio. Occupation not given.* I've ordered an extra. Boy, we're getting somewhere! Any word from the Rambler?"

"None. How about the man in the rickshaw?"

"The cable doesn't mention him. Probably couldn't identify him. Most likely she was on the loose and picked him up. I've assigned the story to Hastings."

"O.K. I'm invited to lunch with Upton."

Peters chuckled. "You'll be able to take our extra along with you. Clean beat. Where's the rickshaw shot?"

"Murphy had it in his possession."

"Well, wire Los Angeles to send up the negative of the news reel. We'll use the prints tomorrow. Still think Upton had her bumped off?"

"I know it. Murphy's disappearance proved it, also Francesca Montcalm's vanishing act."

"You're right, of course, but we're a long way from pinning it on him."

"He's scared. That's why I'm invited to lunch."

"I wish I knew what had become of the Rambler," said Peters sadly.

UPTON, who had met the city editor of the *Post* upon numerous occasions, greeted him cordially and seated him at a corner table in the club café. His manner was bland and apparently he hadn't a care in the world. During lunch he discussed politics and business generally, but at the coffee he got right down to brass tacks.

"Halligan," he said sharply, "I understand you have a statement from a girl named Montcalm, who was night phone operator at the Crescent, which states that I talked to Jane Foster."

"That's right. Signed by two witnesses."

"Neither of whom can be found. Miss Montcalm appears to have left town."

"Wonder how you got the information."

"She called me up and told me. She said that Murphy claimed to be a police detective, that he frightened her, bulldozed her, and caused her to admit things which were not true by misleading questions. Now I didn't know the Foster woman, never heard of her, did not talk to her and I won't let your scurrilous rag drag me into the case. I am a man with a family."

"How do you explain getting Montcalm the job with Brown and Bowers?" asked Halligan bluntly.

"If you must know, I'd had an affair with the girl and promised her a good job. I've had her in private dining rooms in various cafés, Jake's for one. You see I'm frank. If you print what I've said, I'll sue you for libel."

"And you shipped her off somewhere when you heard about the statement."

Upton smiled and nodded.

"What did you do to Murphy?" demanded Halligan.

"Murphy? Nothing. What do I care about Murphy?"

"He vanished out of Jake's the other night in a most suspicious manner."

Upton shrugged his shoulders. "Perhaps Jake can explain. I've been candid with you, Halligan. Your paper will be in a bad spot if it makes insinuations about me."

"Here's something which will interest you, Mr Upton," said Halligan. He drew from his hip pocket a folded copy of the *Post* extra and handed it to the banker and politician.

As he spoke he was watching Upton like a hawk and he caught a look of apprehension on the man's face. It vanished in a fraction of a second.

"Interesting," Upton said dryly. "Englishwoman named Bundy, eh?"

"Ever encounter her when you were in the Orient?" asked Halligan.

"I did not." He passed back the paper. "I think I have made myself plain, Mr. Halligan. I'll hit back if my name appears in your sheet in any connection with the Foster affair."

"We've already printed that she called your house."

"And that I did not get the call. Good afternoon, Mr. Halligan."

Halligan hastened back to his office. As he opened the door he heard a soprano whose voice was lifted in song. The song stopped abruptly but Hattie Jewett turned a shining face upon her chief.

"What the deuce are you so hopped up about?" he demanded.

"Look," she exclaimed. "Look!"

She held up a yellow telegraph blank. Its date line was Los Angeles; its message was brief—two words, *Hold Everything,* and the signature was *Addison Francis Murphy.*

"He's all right. He's all right!" she exclaimed.

"He's all wrong!" shouted Halligan. "Just as crazy as ever. Hold everything! Where's he been? What's he doing down there? Doesn't he know we're worried to death about him? Hold everything!"

"I think he means he has big news for us," she ventured.

"Then why don't he tell us what it is?" cried the indignant newspaperman. "No address; no way of reaching him. I'd like to sock him in the nose!"

BARNEY UPTON resided in a large brick house on Nob Hill. It had been built in the late Nineties and was now shut in by tall apartment houses and hotels but it had been the home of one of the great captains of industry of the West and Upton was pleased to be able to occupy this seat of the mighty.

As it was the month of June Mrs. Upton was occupying their cottage on the Monterey Peninsula with her two young daughters, and the banker was occupying the house alone with his secretary, a manservant, a housemaid and a cook.

He had dined alone and, after dinner, went into the library. It was a huge room at the back of the house overlooking his rose garden and, beyond, the myriad lights of the City of San Francisco, hundreds of feet below. Fanov sat with him for a few minutes and received certain instructions after which he poured Mr. Upton a highball and departed as softly as a cat. He was a thin, sinister-looking man of thirty or thirty-five with the slightly slant eyes of a Mongolian but the light hair of the Russian.

Upton thoughtfully smoked a fifty-cent cigar. He had been a bit perturbed by the extra, but he had gotten over it. He had handled the situation well and there was nothing to worry about.

About nine o'clock the manservant entered. "A gentleman is at the door, sir, and wishes to see you. His name is Addison Francis Murphy."

Upton uttered a startled exclamation. He leaped to his feet—he was absolutely gray—and then he rallied and slowly sat down. "Tell him I'll see him in a few minutes," he said. "Get Stephano. Have him come in here through the rear hall." He clenched his hands so hard that his nails cut the palms of his hands. "Damn him! Damn him!" he muttered.

He pulled open a drawer in the library table, lifted out an automatic pistol and thrust it in his pocket. Stephano entered silently. "You damned fool!" cried the banker. "Murphy's back. You claimed he was safe on a tramp bound for Valparaiso."

"So," said the secretary. "It seems impossible. It is not so."

"He's in the front hall. He wants to see me."

"Well, Mr. Upton?"

"I'll let him in. Get in that closet. Leave the door ajar so you can hear." He glanced at the table and touched a book. "I'll drop this book if I need you."

"Yes, Mr. Upton." Fanov glided to the closet and vanished within it.

Upton walked to the open window and breathed deep of the balmy rose-scented air from the garden. After a minute, perfectly composed, he returned to his chair and touched the bell beside him on the table. The manservant entered.

"Admit Mr. Murphy," he instructed.

A moment later the Rambler strode into the room. Addison Francis' garments looked rather the worse for wear. There was a black bruise on his right cheek and his fingers were blistered and swollen, but his smile was ironic and his eyes had an amused light in them.

"I'll say it for you, Mr. Upton," he said. "This is a surprise."

Upton eyed him angrily. "What the devil do you want?" he demanded.

Murphy helped himself to a chair. "I want to tell you about myself, Mr. Upton," he said. "I'm a fellow who has reached a mature age and never made any money. It's about time I feathered my nest."

"What do I care what sort of fellow you are? What do you want?"

"What I'm trying to put over," said Murphy, "is that I'm willing to listen to reason. For about fifty thousand dollars, now, I'd leave San Francisco."

"Young man," exclaimed Upton, "if you think you can blackmail me—You've nothing on me, nothing whatever."

THE RAMBLER chuckled. "I didn't have a darn thing when they fed me a Mickey Finn at Jake's," he admitted. "It's funny how things are. This is going to amuse you terribly, Mr. Upton. You had me shanghaied on a ship commanded by Jane Foster's step-father."

"What?" roared Upton. "I told you I never heard of Jane Foster. What do I care about her step-father? And I didn't have you shanghaied."

"I mean Sophia Bundy's step-father. The Englishwoman you married in Vladivostok two years ago. Ain't that a laugh?"

Upton was again pale. "You're mad," he muttered.

"Before the Soviet Commissioner in Vladivostok," continued Murphy. "Your secretary was one witness and Captain Hope was the other. He was in command of the *Capricon* then. He has the *Bristol Brother* now. If you'd known that, you'd have picked out some other ship to have me shanghaied on, eh?"

Upton swallowed hard. "If this were true what of it?"

"You used a fake name to keep the marriage from getting on the cables. It doesn't matter what name you use in Russia to make marriage legal. And, at the time this country didn't recognize the existence of Russia so you figured it was no marriage at all. Just indulging a girl in her whim."

"You said something about money," said Upton. "I had been drinking vodka—I wasn't responsible."

"But such marriages are legal since we recognized Russia. You are a bigamist, Mr. Upton. That's why Sophia decided to drop in on you. You must have seen by the papers that Jane Foster has been identified as Sophia Bundy."

"If you are insinuating that I had anything to do with Jane Foster's death—"

"Murder," corrected Murphy. "She came from Shanghai on the *Bristol Brother*. She registered under an assumed name at the Crescent and called you up. The steamer sailed for Seattle next day. Captain Hope doesn't read newspapers so he didn't hear about the murder and she made up the name Jane Foster on the spur of the minute. He was at sea again when her pictures were published, and when he was back in San Francisco the case had dropped out of the papers. First he knew about the murder was when I told him."

"How much do you want?" asked Upton hoarsely.

"Plenty. You figured that Jane Foster was unknown in America. If you could get the papers establishing her identity and you as a bigamist, you'd be in the clear. But you didn't get the papers. I've got them."

"I—I don't believe you."

"You searched her room, or your agent did. He took her pocketbook and whatever he could find but the papers were not in her possession. She left them at the office of the agent of her step-father's steamer to be called for by Sophia Bundy. Want to look at them, Mr. Upton?"

"Yes," said Upton faintly. He stretched out his hand. Murphy drew from his breast pocket a fat envelope and handed it to him. Upton pulled from the envelope several documents, glanced at them hastily and laid them on the table.

"Fifty thousand, you said?" he asked shakily. As he spoke his elbow knocked a book from the table to the floor. The door of the closet opened and Stephano stepped into the room. He made no sound as he crept up behind Addison Francis Murphy. His right arm lifted and it held a long narrow-bladed knife of polished steel. He was behind the Rambler's chair and the arm descended—but Murphy had plunged forward. Directly in front of him on the library table was the glass holding Barney Upton's highball and the sharp eyes of the reporter had seen the assassin mirrored in the glass.

Stephano grunted as he made his stroke and he went over backward as Murphy's chair was driven into his stomach. As he fell, the Rambler pounced upon him, Stephano thrust with his knife, Murphy blocked the thrust and closed upon the thin wrist of the half-caste an iron hand. Stephano, however, was wiry and knew the tricks of Eastern wrestlers. The pair rolled over and over. Barney Upton, his automatic in his hand, stood ready to put a bullet into the Irishman, but there was a kaleidoscope of entwined bodies, legs, arms and fists upon the Persian rug.

A heavy blow on the temple of the Eurasian from the big fist of Rambler Murphy stiffened Stephano at last. Murphy, breathing heavily, got upon his knees. Up went the pistol arm of Barney Upton, whose eyes were spitting hate and death. His finger touched the trigger but the bullet went wide because the arm was grasped by two brawny hands.

"Tut, tut, Upton," chided Jack Halligan. He had catapulted from the top of a ladder beneath the library window. Now a second and third newspaperman piled into the room.

Upton tore himself loose and stood facing them, ghostlike and trembling.

"Nice work, Rambler," said the city editor of the *Post*. "Reckon you'll hang for the murder of Jane Foster along with your Korean pal, Barney."

Upton drew a deep breath. "I think not," he said softly. And before he could be restrained he placed the muzzle of the automatic in his mouth and sent a bullet up into his brain. He was dead as they caught him in their arms.

CHAPTER SIX

TIME TO RAMBLE

MANAGING EDITOR PETERS, Murphy and Halligan were talking together later in the evening. "Only way in the world we could have pinned it on him," Peters said. "Of course you could have proved motive—your documents did that—but he had an alibi that was steel-riveted and there were no witnesses to the entrance or departure of Stephano at the hotel. We'll probably dig up people who saw him that night; now that Barney is dead and the ban is off. Fanov will hang all right. The attempt to assassinate you will persuade any jury that he killed the woman. Probably used the same knife."

"It's a lucky thing you had that bit of film in your clothes," said Halligan. "You couldn't have done business with Captain Hope any other way."

"I had trouble enough as it was," confessed the Rambler. "I had to work two days in the stoke hole before I could get a word with him. He's a good scout if he does get his crews from crimps. He faked engine trouble and put into Los Angeles, and came up to San Francisco with me and got his step-daughter's steel box from the agent's office. He was ready to risk his job and hang round to identify Upton as the man who married his step-daughter."

"It's astounding that a man in Barney's position would have dared to contract a marriage," said Peters.

"He knew that her certificate wasn't worth the paper it was written on because the marriage had been contracted in a country which didn't officially exist. He told her afterwards, and left her with a few hundred dollars when he returned to America. He was hard-boiled plenty. Recognition of Russia made things different."

"Just the same you took an awful chance taking those papers into Upton's house," said the managing editor.

"I don't mind taking a chance. He would have denied things until the cows came home if I hadn't flashed the papers on him. And when Jack told me that Stephano was the Korean secretary, I rather expected to be knifed which is why I never relaxed."

"Well," said the managing editor, "it's a big job you've done, old man. You're with us permanently, I hope."

"I sort of think I'm going to like working on the *Post*," said the Rambler. "I think a man is a sap to go wandering round the world. Get established. Settle down and grow rich. I like the idea."

"Oh, yeah," remarked Jack Halligan. "Kind of like Hattie Jewett, too."

"Say, I've only met her a couple of times," protested Murphy, turning scarlet.

A FEW days later having dinner with Hattie in a sung little nook up near the Beach, the Rambler explained to Miss Jewett how his views had changed. He had been seeing a lot of Hattie. There had been lunches, dinners, evenings at the movies, and suppers,

"Of course the real reason I like San Francisco, is you," he said at length. "You're a swell girl, Hattie. I feel very comfy with you. Why I bet you and I could get along wonderfully together."

"Is this a proposal, Addison Francis Murphy?" she demanded.

"Darned if it ain't," he said as though surprised. "Well, I stand by it."

She patted his hand. "You're awful nice," she said softly. Then she said: "You've been engaged before."

"Once or twice but those were different. How about it?"

"Nothing doing," she said harshly. "Oh, don't look like that. I mean it."

"But you've been going round with me," he protested.

"I fell for you hook, line and sinker the day I met you," the girl confessed. "I like you tremendously but I'm onto you, Rambler. Friendship, yes. Matrimony, no."

He looked so much like a disappointed baby that tears came into her eyes when he said: "You mean you don't love me?"

"I mean I've been in a newspaper shop long enough to use the old bean. You wouldn't last as a husband. I can't see you trundling a baby carriage."

He looked startled. "Would we have to—"

"We would. Babies are what women are for. And children like to know where their father is. And your wife is likely to be a widow, a young widow. Somebody's going to murder you, sooner or later."

"You're pretty hard-boiled," he said sullenly.

She nodded. "That's why you like me. I knew you'd ask me to marry you. I laid awake most of last night wondering whether I shouldn't take a chance. Well, I'm not going to."

The Rambler gazed at her solemnly and then a slow smile crept upon his countenance.

"You certainly do use your bean," he said. "You've got me going but it would be your funeral. I've been thinking that this West Coast climate is too monotonous. No spring, no fall, practically no difference between Christmas and Fourth of July. But I figured I could stand it if you married me."

"You see," she said, smiling dismally. "Take me home, please."

MISS JEWETT soaked her pillow with tears that night and along toward morning she came to a decision. A year or two with Rambler Murphy was worth having. And she was a stronger character than Addison Francis. She could make him behave. She had been a fool. She'd tell him so.

Her eyes were like stars when she came into the office of the city editor. She arrived early though she knew that the Rambler wouldn't show for hours. The big wild goose! She'd turn him into a barnyard gander and make him like it.

Halligan arrived almost on her heels. His eyes were bloodshot and his face haggard.

"Stewed again last night?" she said severely.

"I had an excuse. Dragged out of my bed by that damned Murphy at midnight, lugged from joint to joint and then out to the flying field at six this morning—"

"You mean he's gone?" she cried excited. "Where? What for?"

"For no reason—well he wants to see buds on the trees. Next stop New York."

"Ooooh," moaned Hattie Jewett.

"You were right to give him the aim the red-headed jackass… Say!"

For his faithful secretary had sprung at him, slapped him resoundingly across the cheek and rushed, sobbing, from the office.

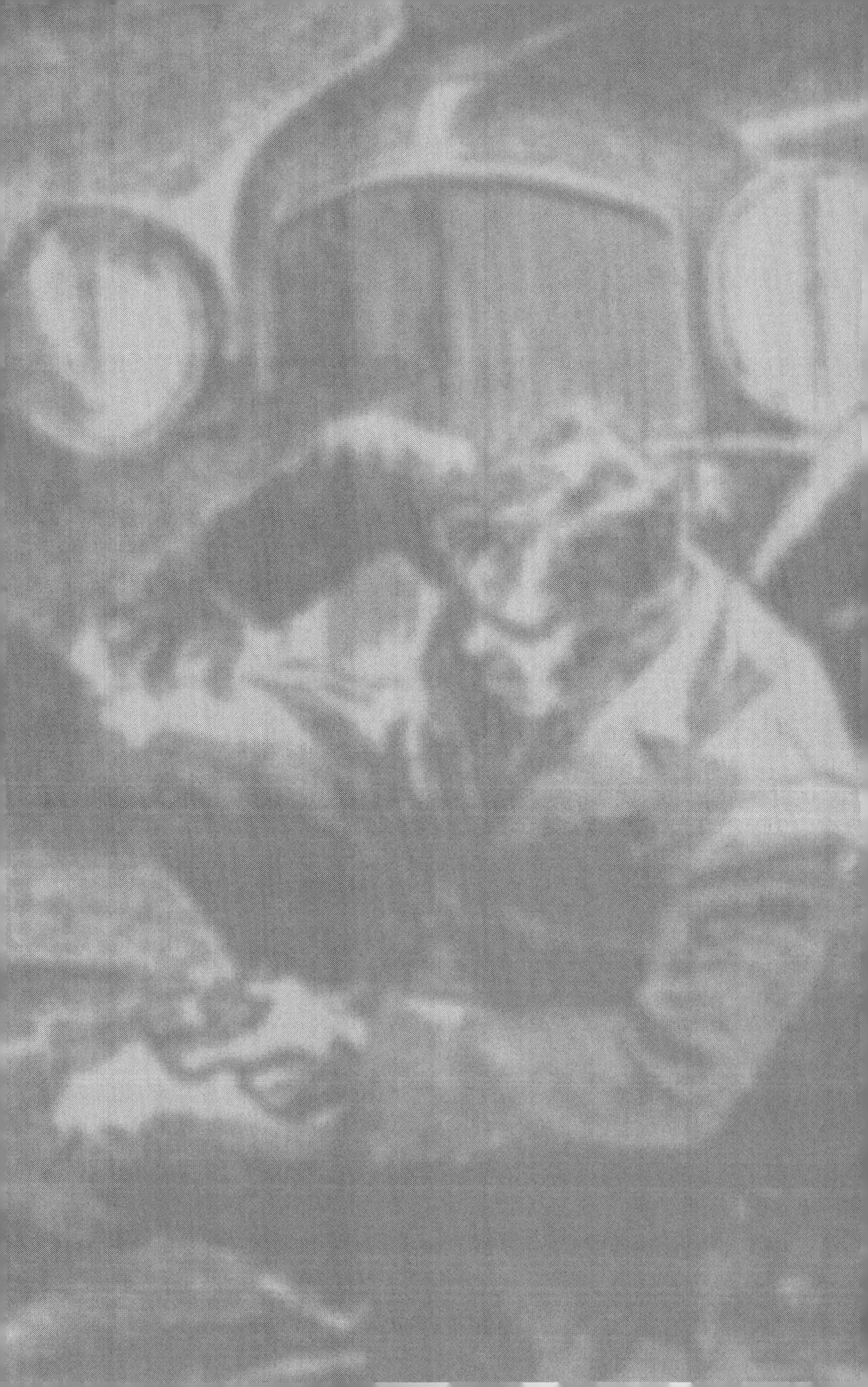

HEIR-COOLED

IT WAS A MURDER INHERITANCE THAT THE THOMPSON GIRL HAD ACQUIRED, BUT SHE COULDN'T EVEN COLLECT ON THAT UNTIL THE RAMBLER, THAT ROVING, RED-HEADED NEWS HOUND, STEPPED INTO THE BREECH AND FLAVORED THE LEGACY WITH A LITTLE HOT LEAD.

CHAPTER ONE

BLUE BOOK BABIES

ADDISON FRANCIS MURPHY had begun to ramble a few years back when he had been promoted from the street to the copy desk of the old *World.* Those jobs usually go to good men whose legs are getting weak or whose fingers, at the re-write desk, are not so nimble as they used to be. Being convinced that he was neither old nor decrepit, Murphy took to the road.

He liked the feel of a city room, though—it was the only home he had ever known. And, he thought, city rooms were all alike. For that matter, the newspaper business was standardized. He could walk into any newspaper office in any American city and instantly fit into the scheme of things—getting and publishing news are accomplished in the same manner everywhere. What bothered the Rambler was that they wouldn't take him on in a New York shop.

This day, Harry Desborough, the city editor of the *Bulletin,* waved a friendly hand to him. It was three in the afternoon and an edition had just departed. The tension was relaxed. Murphy went over, sat on the editor's desk, and mooched a cigarette.

"Nothing doing, Murphy," said Desborough, giving him a match. "Economy is the slogan."

"Just want to look in your morgue."

Mr. Desborough, who was a slender dapper man with a small brown mustache and spectacles, glanced at him sharply.

"What you got?" he demanded.

Murphy grinned. "I may have a tiger by the tail and it may turn out to be an alley cat. I'm not tipping you. You'd shoot out a staff man on my story."

"Oh, I wouldn't do that."

Murphy eyed him quizzically. "Wouldn't you?"

"Sure I would," confessed the city editor with a chuckle. "But I'll give you a break. Tell Smith I said to let you look at any envelopes you like."

"Thanks. It won't do you any good to check up on what I look at."

MURPHY went through a narrow, dirty passageway and arrived at a small room with stacks of shelves like a library. Instead of books, however, the shelves were choked with large manila envelopes. These were clippings regarding people whose goings-on seemed worthy of filing.

There was a fat, bald man, with a florid face and spectacles with thick lenses, who was busy with scissors and paste. This was Smith, keeper of the morgue. He glanced up and smiled jovially.

"Rambler! How the hell are you? Working for us?"

"How long have you been running a morgue, Hank?"

Mr. Smith shrugged his big shoulders. "Couple of years. A man has to live."

There was a roar as the car bore down with accelerating speed.

"I'm not on the *Bulletin*. Free lancing. Want to know if you have an envelope on Mrs. Martha Houghton."

"I'll find out." Smith inspected a card-catalogue. Five years back, Smith had been city editor of the *Planet*.

"Seems to me I filed something about her the other day," said Smith. "Yeah, Cabinet Four, Envelope Nine Forty-one. Just a minute. Made a new envelope. Here it is!"

He pulled out the contents of the envelope and handed Murphy a half-page from the Miami *Gazette*.

NEW YORK SOCIALITE WINS SOCIETY BATHING BEAUTY CONTEST, was the eight-line streamer.

There was a big picture with a graceful young woman in the foreground clad in a skimpy bathing suit. She was blond—at least her hair photographed light, and very pretty; appeared to be in her late twenties. There were only a few lines of reading matter. Mrs. Houghton was mentioned as a Park Avenue society matron. There was a short description of the contest and a list of entries. Murphy's eye wandered back to the picture.

There was a circle of men in the background and he stared at the man on the right. "Isn't this Franklyn Thompson, the big promoter?" he demanded.

Smith picked up the clipping and gazed at the picture.

"Sure is," he declared. "Looks pretty good don't he? What's the date on this? February Twenty-eighth, eh? He wouldn't have that grin on his face if he'd known he was going to be dead in two weeks."

"Dead? You mean to say that Thompson's dead?"

"Sure. He died—when did he die? Wait a minute." He reached for an envelope. "He died on March Fifteenth."

Murphy's long face grew longer. "March Fifteenth," he repeated. "Sure you haven't anything else on Mrs. Houghton?"

"Probably the first and the last time that dame will figure in the news."

"Let's see that Thompson envelope, will you?"

This file was thick, Thompson having been a gentleman of large affairs; including a couple of breach-of-promise cases and a scandal connected with the construction of a New York courthouse. However, Murphy was only interested in the final clipping. Thompson had died at his apartment in Murray Hill of heart failure. The body had been cremated. The estate, believed to be large, had been left to his cousin,

J. Robbins Thompson, yachtsman and polo player. His age had been fifty-three.

"Much obliged, Smithie," said the Rambler.

Five minutes after Murphy's departure the city editor barged in. "What did Murphy want?" he asked Hank Smith.

"Clippings on a society dame named Martha Houghton of Park Avenue. All we had was a squib about her winning a beauty contest in Miami a few weeks ago."

"What other clippings did he ask to see?" demanded the shrewd city editor.

"Franklyn Thompson, the promoter that died recently."

"Thompson died at home of heart failure. Never heard of the Houghton woman. Well, if he gets anything I'll hear from him."

A city editor can't be expected to remember everything. A few lines had drifted in only a week ago about a Mrs. Martha Houghton who had been robbed of her jewels. The yarn had no follow-up, so the incident had left no impression on Desborough.

BUT A FEW hours before, Murphy, loafing in a café had been interested in a remark by a discharged elevator man, formerly of the Hotel Princess, who had been standing near him at the bar.

"They gimme the gate for taking the crooks up to the dame's apartment," he growled in response to an inquiry from the bartender. "That's what they said, but I know why they gimme the gate."

"Why did they?" asked the bartender.

The fellow shrugged his shoulders and departed. Murphy questioned the barkeep, learned that a woman at the Princess had been robbed of a lot of jewels a week before—and nothing more. It didn't sound like much of anything; but, being unemployed, he went to the police station and made inquiries.

A Mrs. Martha Houghton, widow, had been robbed of gems worth a hundred and ten thousand dollars—uninsured. The robbers had entered at nine A.M.; tied up the maid and the elevator man; threatened the woman, who was in bed; and departed with the jewels. The robbery had been reported at five minutes past ten.

There were two things that made Murphy curious. One was the lack of insurance on the jewels—that indicated a certain kind of widow. The other was that an hour had elapsed before she notified the police. He considered that suspicious.

Too, he was very much interested in the fact that Franklyn Thompson showed in the Miami newspaper picture. A coincidence, perhaps, that they were both in Miami at the same time.

Being a beautiful woman, it was natural that Mrs. Houghton should enter the society bathing-beauty contest. And when there was a chance to look at a crowd of pretty girls who were practically nude, it was a sure thing that Thompson, whom Murphy knew to have been a chaser, would show up.

Therefore, it seemed an ordinary coincidence that the promoter, who had been caught on a corner of the plate when the photographer took Mrs. Houghton's picture, had died on the day when Mrs. Houghton was robbed. It was also interesting that his body had been cremated. He hadn't died of pneumonia, typhoid or smallpox. Heart failure. A man can be the picture of health one minute, and die of heart failure the next.

Very thoughtfully, Murphy left the *Bulletin* Building and took the subway. During various periods of employment in New York, he had acquired a large acquaintance. Murphy was an engaging young man and a good mixer with men. Being shy, he didn't get along so well with women.

He rode uptown and went into an office building near Forty-second Street at Broadway and climbed to the quarters of Mike Minovitch, theatrical producer.

Mr. Minovitch was short, and fat. He was at leisure on account of not being able to find money to produce a sure-fire hit that was lying on his desk. In fact, money was so hard to get that he had fired his secretary and was holding the fort unaided—not that anybody was likely to storm the fort except bill collectors.

"If it ain't Rambler Murphy," said Minovitch, grinning cordially. "Heard you was engaged to one of them fillum stars out in Los Angeles."

"Idle rumor. Got a cigarette?"

"Moodier Murphy you ought to be called," grumbled the producer.

"The tide is kind of low, Mike. Listen. You know all the good-looking dolls in New York."

"Do I? You bet I do," said Mike complacently.

"Know that baby who won the bathing-beauty contest in Miami—the society show—name of Martha Houghton?"

"Oh, that one! You mean *Martha* Houghton?"

"Yeah."

"Never heard of her. Was she ever on Broadway?"

"Supposed to be a widow. Lives on Park Avenue."

Mike grinned. "I ain't invited over there much, but the Broadway frails—why I know them all."

RAMBLER leaned back in his chair, puffed on his cigarette and let his eyes roam around the office. The walls of the office were covered with large photographs of beautiful stage ladies, some of them wearing scanty garments and some—art photographs—wearing nothing at all. The pictures, one and all, bore highly complimentary dedications to the Buddha-like person behind the big desk.

Murphy inspected them, set his chair firmly on the ground, walked behind the desk and pointed to an "art photograph" of an extremely pretty blonde.

"Like her looks," Murphy remarked. "Name of Mary Dean, eh?"

Mike twisted around. "Oh, her! Old timer. She was in my Frolics of 'Thirty."

"What became of her?"

"Got ritzy. Heard she married some rich guy. Three years is as long as they stay in a Broadway chorus. After that, they go to Hollywood, get married, or something."

"Ever see her since?"

"Yeah, she give me the ice one night 'bout a year ago, maybe two, at the Colony. She was with some real-estater—let's see—say, I remember it was this Franklyn Thompson. You know the fellow that Betty Bell got fifty grand from, for breach of promise, five years ago?"

"Got to go," said Murphy. "Be seeing you."

"So she won a beauty contest in Miami," mused Mike. "Maybe she'd like to go into my new show—if I get a show. She's probably back in circulation."

Murphy departed. He whistled as he walked down the single flight of stairs. Mary Dean was Martha Houghton and Martha Houghton had been seen about with Thompson. Perhaps Thompson was paying her expenses in Miami. The demi-mondes turn into socialites on the train going south.

And that made it very queer that Thompson had elected to die on the day Mrs. Houghton was robbed. Murphy was not a scandal monger and it would serve no purpose to reveal that a man, decently dead, had an illicit connection with the woman at the Princess. Yet, a sixth sense told him that there was a mystery here which would be well worth unraveling.

Half an hour later he was calling upon a realtor named Manning. Manning gave him a cigarette and greeted him cordially. Once, the Rambler had done a favor for Mr. Manning.

"Find me the owner of the Princess Hotel on Park Avenue. I mean the boss, not a holding company, nor a mortgage company," Murphy said.

"Easy. It's owned by the Eureka Land and Building Company and it's likely to be sold. The largest stockholder in the Eureka recently died," Manning said.

"Name of Franklyn Thompson?"

"That's right. Why ask me?"

"Why sell it? Profitable, isn't it?" Murphy's questioning was insistent.

"All these swank apartment buildings are in the red. Thompson's heir needs coin and I hear he's going to liquidate all the Thompson holdings."

"Know him?"

"Nope. Understand he's a Blue Book baby."

The Rambler took his leave without ceremony.

CHAPTER TWO

INSIDE STORY

THE RAMBLER said to the operator at the Princess Hotel: "Kindly tell Mrs. Houghton, that Mr. Addison Francis Murphy is calling, representing the Thompson estate."

"Just a minute," the maid upstairs answered, "Mrs. Houghton will see him."

A few moments later, Murphy was ushered into a luxuriously furnished and well lighted living room on the third floor. He selected a comfortable chair, helped himself to a cigarette from a Sèvres china cigarette box and rudely lit it before the arrival of the hostess. Murphy didn't think Mary Dean would be aware of the breach of etiquette.

He heard a murmur of voices in an inside room and a striking woman entered—tall, graceful, yellow-haired. With a lightning glance, he was aware that Mary Dean had hardened and become sophisticated since she had escaped from the kindly management of Mike Minovitch. He decided that she was as smart as a steel trap.

She smiled politely. Her mouth was large but her teeth were flawless; so when she smiled, the effect was dazzling.

"I have no notion why a person concerned with the Thompson estate should call on me," she observed as she seated herself. "But I'm curious, like everybody else—which is why I let you in."

"Miss Dean, Mike Minovitch sends his regards," said Murphy, smiling broadly.

The woman leaped to her feet, her hands clenched; two red spots appeared in her cheeks and her blue eyes flamed.

"Get the hell out of here!" she cried furiously.

"I merely mentioned it to show I know all about you," he said blandly. "So sit down and take it big."

Slowly she sat down and gazed at him defiantly.

"Well," she challenged. "I don't deny I was a chorus girl. Why should I?"

"No reason at all. Mike says that he heard about your winning the beauty contest in Miami. He wanted me to tell you that you can always get a job with him when, and if, he has a production."

"What are you, a reporter?"

"I represent the Thompson estate."

"Humph. What do you want to know?"

"What steps are you taking to recover your jewels?"

"I reported the loss to the police. What else can I do?" she asked sullenly. "And what does the estate care?"

Murphy smiled. "Have you the bills-of-sale for those gems?"

The woman looked alarmed. "Say, is this cousin of his so low, so dirty, that he would try to rob me—"

"We just want to be sure that they really were stolen," said the Rambler.

She sighed with relief. "They were stolen all right."

"Please tell me the circumstances."

"Well, they're very queer. I was in Florida for six weeks. About a week before I returned, the office downstairs phoned my maid that there were two men there with a package. They said it was a present for me. She told them to come up. I'd kept the maid and left the apartment open because I allowed a girl-friend to stay here while I was south. That night she opened the package and it was a case of Scotch. She put it in a closet and forgot it.

"Well, I returned from Florida about a week ago and the next morning the office notified the maid that the same two men, who had brought a package before, had another package. Naturally, she said to bring it up."

SHE WENT on, tonelessly, as if she had learned the story by rote. "They are very strict in this building about admitting tradesmen or delivery men and always inquire whether such people can go up to an apartment. And the instructions are, that the elevator which brings them up will wait for them. Oh, I forgot to tell you that one night before I came back, my friend opened one of the bottles of Scotch and it contained water. When the maid opened the door, she recognized these men and began to bawl them out for playing a joke. One of them pulled a rod and stuck it in her face.

"'Get back into the dining room,' he said, 'And keep your mouth shut.' Of course she was horribly frightened and did as she was told. He took rope from his pocket and tied her to a chair and pasted tape over her mouth. The other man went back to the elevator, drew a rod on the boy, made him come into the dining room and tied him up with the maid. After that, they came into my bedroom and woke me up; it was only nine o'clock but I was sound asleep.

"One of them jammed a gun against my chest and held his other hand over my mouth.

"'If you scream, I'll shoot,' he said. 'Point where you keep your jewels.' I pointed to the bureau where the casket was. I was going to put them in the vault that day, because I usually didn't keep them here on account of not insuring them.

"While one of them took the stuff out of the casket, the other pulled down the bedclothes and made me take the rings off my fingers and looked to see if I had any articles hidden in the bed with me. When they had all my property, they told me they would come back and kill me if I didn't wait an hour before giving the alarm. Of course, I was horribly frightened."

"You would be," said Murphy sympathetically.

She nodded. "I told all this to the detectives from police headquarters," she said resentfully. "It stirs me all up to tell it again. Well, I went looking for the maid. I released her and the elevator boy and he ran downstairs. It seems they had run the elevator down themselves and the people in the lobby thought, of course, that the boy had brought them down."

"You'd know the men again if you saw them?" Murphy inquired.

"Oh, yes."

"I'd like to talk to the maid."

"This is a different one. Ella left, without notice, the night of the robbery."

"You and Mr. Thompson have a nice time in Miami?"

"I wasn't there with him," she said angrily.

"Did he come home with you on the train?"

"No!" she shouted.

"And the last time you saw him was in Miami?"

"Yes."

"Must have been a shock when you heard he was dead."

"It was," she said curtly.

"Are you mentioned in his will?"

"Why should I be?"

"You and he were great friends, weren't you?"

"At one time, maybe."

"Know J. Robbins Thompson?"

"Very slightly—what is it Jane?"

"Mr. Smith calling," said the maid.

"Ask him to wait. No, bring him in," Miss Dean amended.

It looked like Murphy had learned all he could from her, as he rose to depart. Her story was straightforward and sounded truthful; in which case, he had been wasting his time. It had been an ingeniously planned robbery, but it was an old story—no paper would reward him with ten dollars for it.

A LOW-BROWED man in seedy tweeds entered the room. He had a blue felt hat in his hand, a cigar in his mouth and a grin on his face—which faded instantly when he saw the Rambler.

"By all that's holy, Rambler Murphy!" he exclaimed.

"Hello, Jake," said Murphy uncomfortably. This newcomer was a cheap racketeer of his acquaintance, a tout, a trimmer, and one not above sticking up a man if he thought it safe.

"You know this fellow, Jake?" demanded Mrs. Houghton.

"Sure. I know the Rambler. What paper you working on, bo?"

"A reporter!" screamed Mrs. Houghton. "How dare you come here, sticking your ugly nose in other people's business? Get out! Get out this minute! It's lucky you came, Jake. He was asking too many questions."

Murphy's spirits rose as he glimpsed this chance for escape. He bowed satirically and then Jake took command of the situation.

"Don't mind her," he said. "She's always noivous like that but a great feller. This is a good guy, Martha. Who you woiking for, Murph?"

"*Bulletin,*" said Addison Francis untruthfully.

"Have a seegar?" asked Jake, cordially, producing one from a vest pocket bulging with the weeds.

"No, thanks. Don't like cigars."

"How come you're bothering with the robbery? It was in all the papers. No developments—"

"Are you going to kick this bum out?" asked the elegant Mrs. Houghton irascibly.

Jake made a placating gesture. "She's a good kid but kind of excitable," he explained to the newspaperman.

"The dirty rat has dug up that I used to be in the chorus and insinuates that Thompson was keeping me," cried the "good kid."

"So what?" inquired Jake. "Neither of them things is a crime."

"But he'll make a scandal. He gets in here claiming he's from the Thompson estate—"

"Huh?" ejaculated Jake. "I heard he didn't leave a bean. That was a gag, eh, Murph?"

The Rambler nodded. "Sort of."

"The idea, Murph," said Jake with apparent candor, "is that Martha met a sap in Florida—multi-millionaire that wants to marry her. You spill any dirt and you ruin the kid's chances."

"Just what's your status in this establishment?" inquired the reporter.

"Who, me? I'm just a pal. I knew Martha when she was a nail-scraper in a barber shop—"

"You big-mouthed stooge," screamed Mrs. Houghton, "what's the idea of telling that to this cockroach?"

Murphy was again on his feet. "Don't worry, Mrs. Houghton," he said. "I appreciate Jake's frankness and I'm not retailing dirt."

"Then what did you come here for?" she demanded belligerently.

"Yeah," drawled Jake. "What was the idea, feller?"

The Rambler grinned at the eager pair. "Checking up," he said. "There's a rumor, Jake, that Franklyn Thompson didn't die a natural death."

Mrs. Houghton—who had been on her feet glowering at him, her cheeks flushed with anger—grew deadly pale. Jake bit through his cigar and that part of it which wasn't in his mouth fell to the floor.

"But I can see that Mrs. Houghton wouldn't know anything about that," he finished. "So I'll be on my way."

Leaving them standing like two statues, Addison Francis Murphy walked swiftly from the living room and slammed the door behind him. Having invented the rumor, he didn't care to expand on it—it was a shot in the dark which seemed to have been amazingly effective.

When the door slammed, the woman flopped into a chair. "What is he, a detective?" she gasped.

"Naw, a reporter. At least he used to be. I'll get a line on him."

He picked up the phone. "Look up the number of the *Bulletin*," he demanded. As soon as he got it, he dialed.

"Gimme the editorial department. This it? I want to talk to Mr. Murphy, the guy they call the Rambler."

"Nobody named Murphy on the staff," replied the person who answered the telephone. Jake hung up.

"He's a liar," he muttered. "He don't work there. Well, I got to do something about this red-headed mick. Lucky I come in, Martha. Don't you open your trap to anybody, see? Don't you let no strangers in here, no matter who they say they are. What did he ask you about?"

"The robbery, and he asked me if I came back from Florida with Frank."

"I'm getting busy," said Jake grimly.

ADDISON FRANCIS MURPHY spent the next two hours entering and leaving drinking establishments on Lexington Avenue, and side streets, within a radius of a few blocks of the Houghton residence. He had a photographic memory, and, if he saw the elevator boy again, he would know him. Mr. Murphy had the patience of a cat and the persistence of a bloodhound, when he was working on a story. And he was now convinced that he had a story on which to work.

The effect of his closing remarks to Mrs. Houghton and her disreputable friend, Jake, had convinced him that there was something peculiar about the sudden death of Franklyn Thompson. It was obvious that the pair had information, regarding it, which was not shared by the general public. Whether it was guilty knowledge, he didn't know, but it certainly looked as though his parting shot-in-the-dark had frightened them.

The intimacy of the "socialite" with the tout and racketeer was, in itself, peculiar. Women of her type can't continue friendship with men who knew them when they worked in barber shops. Of course Mrs. Houghton's elegance was a very thin veneer—she had talked like a gun moll when she became excited.

Murphy called up the county recorder but the will of Franklyn Thompson hadn't yet been recorded. If it contained a request for cremation, as often happens, the speedy burning of the body would not be a suspicious incident. He went downtown and inspected the death certificate. It was signed by a Dr. D. Burvis Clark, whose address was given as Princess Apartments. He didn't have enough to go on to tackle the doctor. That would come later.

If, as Jake had insinuated, there was practically no Thompson estate, it seemed to remove the obvious motive for murder. The dead man's heir, J. Robbins Thompson, wouldn't be interested in the removal of his cousin if there wasn't a fortune to be inherited. Thompson, however, was reputed to be very wealthy—he had been in Florida, spending wildly, up to within a few days of his death.

It must have been a terrible blow to J. Robbins, the Blue Book baby. And if he was bitter, he might talk.

Murphy phoned his real-estate acquaintance, Manning. "Know who are attorneys for the Eureka Company?" he asked.

"Sure, Ekans and Ekans at Five Twenty-one Fifth Avenue. Thinking of buying the concern, Rambler—"

Addison Francis laughed. "I never invest in losing propositions. I hear that Thompson died broke."

"News to me. Possible though. A lot of these big guns could use five dollars, in cash, the way business is."

ABOUT twenty minutes later the Rambler entered an elaborate apartment building in the East Sixties and asked to be announced to J. Robbins Thompson.

"Mr. Thompson is away," said the operator. "Miss Thompson is at home. Would you like to see her?"

"I didn't know that there was a Miss Thompson."

"His daughter."

"Well, say Mr. Murphy is here from Ekans and Ekans, attorneys for the late Franklyn Thompson."

"She will see you," said the operator, "Apartment Four Seventy-two."

A pale, but exceptionally pretty young woman opened the door of the apartment and smiled at him eagerly. "How do you do, Mr. Murphy," she said. "Please come in. I'm Miss Thompson."

Murphy as always, when suddenly confronted with beauty, blushed to the roots of his hair and grew diffident. The girl removed his hat from his nervous fingers, hung it in a closet and then preceded him into a large and beautifully furnished living room.

She dropped into a chair and sighed. "Ah," she said. "I'm so glad you came. I've been so worried."

"I came to see your father," he said, much embarrassed.

"But you know he's not here and that I'm without funds! Did you bring me a check?"

Murphy stared at her, vocally paralyzed. The girl had great, appealing brown eyes and thick, chestnut hair and small exquisite features; but there were dark circles under her eyes and her mouth was twitching nervously.

"Why should you be without funds?" he asked hesitatingly.

"Have I got to go all over it again?" she demanded. "I wrote your people all the circumstances. I don't understand—excuse me—"

The phone was ringing. She stepped to the instrument which was on a table beside the chair in which the Rambler had seated himself, and picked up the receiver

"Yes, yes," she said impatiently. "Put them on."

Murphy observed that it was growing dark outside. A few hours ago he had overheard a casual remark in a saloon. Then, he had never heard of Martha Houghton or J. Robbins Thompson. Now, he had his teeth in a whale of a story.

"Ekans and Ekans?" she exclaimed. "Yes, this is Miss Thompson. Yes, Mr. Ekans."

Murphy measured the distance to the door. It looked as if he would have to run for it.

"Oh," said the girl. It was more like a moan. "A-all r-right."

The phone fell from her feeble grip. Her knees crumpled. Murphy caught her as she fell. He carried her to a couch and placed her on it. He then did what unnerved people do in such a situation—he went over and picked up the telephone receiver and replaced it on its stand. He gazed down in alarm upon the white, set face of the young woman.

HE TOUCHED her forehead. She had only fainted—she wasn't dead. The thing to do was to sprinkle water on her. He found the bathroom, filled a tumbler with water and dribbled some on her forehead. In a couple of minutes, she opened her eyes and smiled up at him wanly.

"I'm so sorry," she said. "Such an exhibition. I'll be all right. Please get me a towel. My face is all wet."

When he came back, she was sitting up. She wiped her face dry.

"Bad news?" he asked. He forgot he was the representative of Ekans and Ekans.

She nodded. "I fainted from weakness, I guess, as well as shock."

"Weakness?"

"I—I haven't had anything to eat since yesterday morning."

He glanced around the expensive apartment—her dress was plain but not cheap.

"Why didn't you eat?" he asked stupidly.

"Because there is nothing to eat and no money!" she answered sharply. "Why did you come here, anyway?"

"To take you to dinner," he said grimly. "Put on your hat and coat."

"I won't accept charity from Ekans and Ekans," she said defiantly.

Murphy lifted her off the couch. "You're getting fed by a guy named Addison Francis Murphy and stop your nonsense."

"All right," she said meekly. "I'll be ready in a moment."

She came out of one of the bedrooms wearing a gray cloth coat and a little black hat. He took her arm and led her quickly to the elevator. "There's a fair restaurant around the corner," she suggested. "It's the nearest."

"You poor kid," he murmured with ready sympathy.

"It's the worry as much as not eating," she explained.

"You're going to be all right," he assured her. He felt in his pocket. Enough money for the best a "fair" restaurant'd offer. In a couple of minutes, the girl was drinking soup. Her eyes were brighter already. She was a small, slender, wistful sort of girl—not at all the type he expected would be the daughter of J. Robbins Thompson.

She munched a roll. She consumed two rolls and sighed with satisfaction.

"I don't understand how a young woman can be living in a two-hundred-a-month apartment and have no money for food," Murph observed.

She flashed him a smile. "It's being done, nowadays," she said. "Of course, your firm didn't believe my story. Mr. Ekans was positively brutal."

"I'll go down there and knock his block off. Not knowing which of them was rude to you, I'll knock both their blocks off," he promised.

"Not knowing—but you work for them!"

He eyed her apprehensively. "That was a stall to get in to see you," he said. "I'm a newspaperman. Sit down. You're eating a steak."

"But this is dreadful," she murmured. "Why—what for—"

"I'm not going to publish anything about you. Think of me as a friend," he pleaded.

"I don't know you."

"Murphy's the name. You'd feed the hungry, wouldn't you?"

"But it's so humiliating."

"I wanted to get some information regarding the Thompson estate," he said, "and I knew you wouldn't see a reporter."

SHE SMILED bitterly. "I'll give it to you. There is no Thompson estate. Not a penny. I haven't heard from my father for two weeks. I spent my last cent a week ago. I wrote Ekans and Ekans explaining my situation and asking them to advance me a few hundred dollars pending the settlement of the estate, which is customary, I believe. Mr. Ekans told me, over the phone, that what cash my cousin had in the bank was impounded—that all his business enterprises were insolvent, that he owed them several thousand for legal services and they could do nothing for me."

"But you have friends—"

"Do you suppose I'd tell my friends? I've even pawned my rings—they went some time ago, with my bracelets."

"You've a grand piano—"

"It's a furnished apartment. Nothing in it belongs to me," she said bitterly.

"You mean to say your father left you without funds?"

"He left me a few dollars. He was going to Florida to have it out with Frank Thompson and promised to wire me money as soon as he received some. I—I haven't heard from him."

"I understood your father was rich—a yachtsman and a polo player."

"Up until a year ago, we had plenty of money. Father's fortune was invested with his cousin, Frank—it has paid us no interest for a year. My cousin advanced cash on account of future dividends—barely enough for us to live on. He said things were only temporarily depressed. He gave father five hundred dollars when he went south, six or eight weeks ago, but sent us nothing after that. That's why father decided to have a showdown with him."

The steak arrived and she attacked it voraciously. Murphy ate with less heartiness. He had a lot to think about. His sympathies were already ardently enlisted on the side of the girl.

"How much money did your father invest with your cousin?" he asked.

"I don't know, exactly. I know we had an income of about thirty thousand a year and my cousin promised it would be fifty thousand."

"You've the securities?"

"Yes. They're in my vault. I asked the lawyers if they would advance money on them but they said they are worthless."

So Franklyn Thompson the crook had swindled his cousin? Here was a motive—revenge. The disappearance of the polo player was suspicious, but Murphy wasn't going to pin murder on this girl's father if he could help it. If he was the sort of man she described, credulous and confiding, he wasn't the type.

Suppose Frank Thompson had committed suicide? Why cover it up? If much money were involved, the heirs might smother the thing; but the heir was missing and it was to nobody's profit to make Thompson's death appear due to heart failure. If murder had been committed and the doctor certified it as heart failure, he had committed a felony for which he must have been highly paid.

No, if it wasn't for the consternation of the Houghton woman and Jake, he'd take it for granted that nothing had been covered up and that there was no story.

"I can't eat any more," the girl said with a sigh. "I think I want to go back to the apartment."

He conducted her to the door. "I want to talk to you some more," he said, "but I have something to do—"

"Not the newspapers, please—"

"I'm printing nothing about you, Miss Thompson. I'll be back in ten or fifteen minutes."

She gave him her hand. "There is something about you which inspires confidence," she declared. "You're nice. And I don't feel nearly so depressed."

In twenty minutes he entered the apartment heavily laden.

"What on earth—" she cried.

"Canned goods," he said. "Enough to feed you for a week. Inside of a week, I'm betting you're going to have all the money you want."

Her eyes filled with tears. "I oughtn't to permit it," she said, "but—but—"

"But nothing. Where's your kitchenette?"

He placed his array of canned provender on the shelf. "This is for lunch and breakfast," he said. "We're dining together tomorrow night—unless you have an engagement—"

"We've dropped all our friends because we couldn't reciprocate their hospitality," she confessed. "Father is very proud—but I can't go on living on your charity."

"I have a hunch you're going to be in the money. There is something very funny about this business. What's your first name?"

"Geraldine."

"Mine's Addison Francis," he confided. "We're friends, see."

She nodded and laughed. "All right, only—"

"Only nothing. I've got to go now. I'll be round at six tomorrow night—if you don't hear from me sooner."

"I'll be ready—for dinner," she said with a rather pitiful smile. "And I'll try to be good company."

CHAPTER THREE

BLACKJACKS AND BRASS KNUCKLES

RAMBLER MURPHY hailed a taxi—a necessary extravagance. He had emptied his pockets to buy the canned goods and they demand a nickel, cash in advance, to ride on the subway.

When he reached the *Bulletin* office, he told the taxi-driver to wait, in a manner so imperious, that the driver had no suspicion that his passenger was penniless.

As Murphy had anticipated, the city editor had dined and was back at his desk.

"Hello, Rambler," Desborough said. "I suppose your tootsies are cold."

The Rambler pulled up a chair and grinned at him. "Send somebody down to pay off my taxi," he demanded, "and write me an order on the cashier for a hundred bucks."

Mr. Desborough's eyes grew sharp but his answer was sardonic. "So you've turned confidence man, eh?"

"When I turn in this story, I get fourteen hundred more—take it or leave it."

"Buy a pig in a poke, eh?"

"Oh, I'll give you a hint."

"If I like the hint, you go on salary at hundred and twenty-five, which is all we'd pay Frank Ward O'Malley if he were alive and wanted a job. Things are tight, Rambler."

"O.K. Suits me. This story will blow the town wide open."

"Yeah?"

"Franklyn Thompson, the promoter, was murdered! How do you like that for a beginning?"

Mr. Desborough swallowed hard. "Can you prove it?"

"Wire Miami tonight, regarding the murder of an unidentified man, from fourteen days to a week ago. I wouldn't be surprised if they had a stiff in the morgue who turned out to be J. Robbins Thompson, cousin of Franklyn, polo player, yachtsman and Blue Book baby."

"Frank Thompson is supposed to have died of heart failure and his body was cremated. What proof have you that he was murdered?"

"None, yet, but I expect to get it. I'm only giving you a hint—I've a few things up my sleeve that I'm not telling you."

Desborough pulled an order blank from his desk and began to scribble. "This comes out of your first week's salary. It's all you get if you don't break the story before your week is up."

Murphy laughed. "The taxi-meter is ticking. That's expensive. I expect to have a nifty expense account, chief."

He picked up the cashier's slip and put it in his pocket. The city editor leaned back in his chair, took off his glasses and polished them.

"You're no better than a tramp," he asserted. "You're going to get bumped off, some day, and be buried in a pauper's grave. You are a bad example to modern newspapermen—you are an evil influence on any staff. But, it's my private opinion, that you are the best gol darned reporter in America and the only man who could get dough out of me in advance for a story you haven't got. Now get the devil out of here and deliver!"

Murphy's eyes were misty. "Thanks, old man," he said huskily. "I'm going to cut out rambling. I'm going to keep this job."

"Oh, yeah?" jeered Mr. Desborough, who was not unmoved himself.

Nor was his confidence in Rambler Murphy jarred much when, shortly after midnight, a wire came from the Miami police that there were no unidentified homicide cases in the Miami morgue.

"Maybe they haven't found him yet," he said with a shrug. In the past, he had seen Addison Francis Murphy pull big stories out of nothing—as a conjuror pulls rabbits from a hat.

WHEN he had cashed his check, Mr. Murphy went uptown to Eighth Avenue and purchased a serviceable overcoat in a second-hand store. The Rambler had arrived from the south minus an overcoat, and short of funds. His blood was thin, due to sojourns in the South Seas, in California, and in Louisiana. He had merely put on an extra vest and hadn't bought an overcoat until he had landed a job.

It was characteristic of the man, that he took it for granted that his job was safe. It depended upon his accomplishing the task he had promised Desborough he would accomplish; but that didn't worry Addison Francis Murphy. The possibility of failure never even occurred to him.

After the new coat had been tested in the chill March wind by a three-block walk, he turned into a small unclean-looking Eighth Avenue movie house which displayed the lurid posters of Poverty Row productions. But there was nothing that Murphy liked so much as films of violent action with galloping horses—they amused him heartily and he could think without bothering about following the alleged plots.

He had a notion that Geraldine's father had been put out of the way in Miami—perhaps by his scoundrel of a cousin, perhaps by those who wanted Franklyn Thompson put out of the way. He must believe that, or accept the theory that J. Robbins had returned to New York when his relative did and had something to do with the sudden finish of Franklyn. He didn't care to tolerate that theory because Geraldine was a very nice girl. Besides, if the impoverished polo player had killed his cousin, he didn't have enough cash to persuade a fashionable doctor to sign a fraudulent death certificate.

However, he wasn't sold on the idea that Geraldine's father was either dead or a murderer. It needed something sensational to get the hundred dollars out of Desborough. If it turned out that J. Robbins was not dead in Miami, he expected to prove that Franklyn Robbins had been foully dealt with in New York. That, alone would be big enough news to cinch his job.

ABOUT eleven thirty, after he had seen one western picture twice and a lurid South Seas drama once and a half, times, he left the film house and wended his way to Mundy's. It is on Broadway above Times Square, and is a hangout for jockeys, horse players and touts. He rather expected to see Jake Smith there and he wanted Jake to see him.

Jake was there, at a table with three men, none of whom Murphy knew. But their heavy faces and loud clothing indicated that they were members of the racing fraternity.

Without appearing to be watching, he scrutinized Jake and his companions. Jake recognized him almost immediately, rose, and came over to Murphy's table without more ado.

"How are yer, Murph?" he asked with a beaming smile. "How's tricks?"

"Fine."

"Have a drink?"

"I've ordered a beer."

"Got a good job on the *Bulletin?*"

"Sure."

"You're a liar," declared Jake with a sudden change of manner. "You don't work on the *Bulletin*."

"I was a bit previous in my statement. I now work on the *Bulletin*. I brought in a good story and landed a job."

He watched Jake digest this.

"Look here," said Jake, again being friendly. "I like you, Rambler. You're a good guy. This Houghton doll is a friend of mine. She's got a lot of friends. Get me?"

"I get you."

"A man's health is worth more than a job! Lay off, see?"

The Rambler grinned. "I've a hunch there's a big story in your girl-friend and my hunches come through."

"O.K.," said Jake sullenly. "O.K., for you, bozo."

He left the table, but, instead of returning to his own, walked to the rear of the big café. Murphy ordered another glass of beer. He remained for twenty minutes longer, then paid his check and departed. He slowly walked north on Broadway and three blocks up, turned into a dark side street running toward Eighth Avenue.

He cast a glance over his shoulder after he had walked a hundred feet. Two men had turned the corner and were hurrying in his wake. The Rambler began to whistle. He walked faster. They increased their pace. The street was deserted, save for a taxi which turned in from Broadway and drove past him. Halfway down the block, the taxi drew up to the curb, two men got out and went into a basement café up ahead. Murphy was interested only in the pair behind, who seemed in no hurry to overtake him. He slowed his pace. They walked slower. So they were after him, eh? Jake had no doubt put them on the job.

He continued to whistle contentedly. His purpose in going into Mundy's had been to encounter Jake. If what Jake and Martha Houghton were covering up was not very important, Jake would not take advantage of the opportunity put in his way. If his guess, that there was something queer about the death of Franklyn Thompson, was correct, Jake would do what he obviously had done. Called in some of the boys to take care of him. Now, the men behind were overhauling him. He walked more rapidly but they almost ran to keep up with him. He unbuttoned the new overcoat so that he could slip out of it easily.

While Murphy had no fear in his make-up, he was not without discretion. In this section of New York, in a block between two roaring avenues, he was confident that firearms would not be used. The boys would come at him with blackjacks or brass knuckles. However, to secure complete vindication of his theory regarding the Thompson demise and the Houghton jewel robbery, he could afford to absorb a beating. That was why he had obliged them by walking down a dark street.

APPARENTLY oblivious of pursuit, the Rambler continued until he had almost reached the basement café. His pursuers were only eight or ten feet behind him. He swung out of his overcoat, whirled—and the pair charged like a varsity guard and tackle.

One of them pulled a blackjack from his pocket. Before he could strike, Murph kicked him in the groin and he doubled over, in pain. The other fellow swung a ball of lead at the end of a six-inch strap. It didn't hit Murphy's head because he moved it out of the way and drove a staggering right hook at the man's jaw.

Taking advantage of the effect of this blow, he swung on the first hood, crashed his left against the side of the man's head and floored him. As the blow landed, the Rambler heard heavy footsteps behind him and caught a glimpse of new adversaries—the pair who had descended from the taxi had lurked in the basement area-way instead of entering the café. They had planned to take him, front and rear. Mr. Murphy had underestimated Jake's ingenuity. He was really in for it now.

He slipped a blow from a short club and took it on his left shoulder. It carried force enough to have broken a bone if it hadn't struck the shoulder pad. It dropped him to the sidewalk. A heavy boot drove against his side but he grabbed the boot, shoved, and the fellow sprawled on his back.

Whang! The fourth adversary had slammed him on the side of the head with brass knuckles. Murphy went flat again, half stunned. But Irish heads are hard and Irish fighters can fight even when they're practically unconscious. He staggered to his feet and, in his hand, was the blackjack dropped by the first thug whom he had laid low.

One assailant caught him around the waist. Another aimed a blow at his head. Murphy pulled back and the wrestler's head took the full power of the wallop. The man's arms loosened their hold. He sagged. Murphy drove his blackjack into the right biceps of the fellow who had hit him and was ready to face the rush of the man he had originally felled and the fellow whom he had dropped by grabbing his right foot.

Murphy was dizzy, sick, weak and cursing his folly in inviting this Donnybrook jamboree. There were two good men coming for him and the others would be in active service in a few seconds. He awaited their rush grimly, but hopelessly.

"Come on ye spalpeens," he gritted through clenched teeth, reverting to the speech of one of his dauntless ancestors, no doubt.

To his astonishment, the pair took to their heels, and, while he stood there, swaying and bewildered, the other two got up and ran for it.

Murphy became aware that the dark street was no longer dark. Half a dozen taxis and motor cars had stopped and their lights brightened things up. Windows were open and people were looking out and shouting and behind him were more heavy footsteps. He turned. Two cops with guns in their hands were coming as fast as their heft would permit.

"Now what do you think of that?" inquired Rambler Murphy and sort of sank down and went out, cold, on the sidewalk.

A FEW minutes later he woke up in a police ambulance. A uniformed officer was bending over him—a cop whose broad face had the map of Ireland on it. "You can't beat the Irish," said Murphy with a grin.

"I kind of thought you was a mick," said the officer. "Who was your boyfriends?"

"Some playful gorillas from Mundy's," said Murphy, sitting up and feeling of his head ruefully. "Get any of them?"

"They got into Eighth Avenue. We stopped to see if you was dead. Know 'em again?" the cop asked him.

"Those mugs all look alike. I see you salvaged my overcoat. It's new."

"Don't look new."

"It's new to me," said Murphy with a grin. "I'm a reporter on the *Bulletin* by the name of Addison Francis Murphy, if you want to know."

"Oh, we've been through your pockets. Butting in where you wasn't wanted, eh?"

"Something like that."

"Well you got a crack on the skull that would kill anybody but a thick-headed mick," said the other mick. "They figgered on dropping you quick and getting away. A taximan said the fight lasted a couple of minutes and it was better than Madison Square Garden. Can you walk into the station?"

"And out again," replied Rambler Murphy.

CHAPTER FOUR

SHYSTER SET-UP

THE NEXT morning, the Rambler glanced at his dollar-and-a-quarter watch when he awoke. It was 9:20 A.M. He had a big day ahead of him. He found a phone booth and dialed a number.

"Hello Miss Thompson?"

"Yes. Good morning, Mr. Murphy."

"Sleep well?"

"Wonderfully. I feel so much more cheerful."

"Can I come up and see you for ten minutes, right away? Business."

"Why, ye-es. I'll hurry and dress."

"Be there in a quarter of an hour."

Geraldine Thompson looked very pretty when she admitted him. She wore a white Chinese coat over black pajamas. She had put rouge on her cheeks and some color on her lips and fixed her hair. Her brown eyes were sparkling with pleasure.

"Say," he said enthusiastically, "you look swell!"

"Thanks to you, I'm not despondent any more."

She led the way into the living room and curled up on a big chair.

"I'll get right to it," said the reporter. "I've been thinking over your treatment by Ekans and Ekans and it's unnecessarily rough. Looks sort of queer to me. You sure your father is his cousin's heir?"

"Absolutely. Ekans and Ekans told me that, when they called to notify dad of Cousin Frank's death."

"Oh, they called up? Hadn't found out there was nothing in it for them, I guess. Quickly changed their attitude. I want you to go with me to a notary and appoint me your legal agent. How old are you?"

"Nearly twenty-two."

"Then you're of age. You have a right to do it. Trust me enough to take chance on me?" He grinned at her engagingly.

She laughed. "You're the only friend I can trust, apparently. Excuse me while I put on street clothes?"

"Wait a minute. I expect to get you considerable money and I'm going to loan you fifty dollars—"

"Oh, I couldn't—"

"Strictly business. Maybe you'll be able to pay me a commission by the time I get through with Ekans and Ekans. What are they—father and son?"

She nodded and laughed. "Considering that you got in here yesterday as their representative—"

"Well, I fessed up, didn't I?"

"If you're certain I'll be able to repay you—"

"Sure. Positive!"

"Then—in that case—" She accepted the loan.

HALF an hour later, with a document authorizing him to represent the Thompson heirs, Mr. Murphy entered, not the office of Ekans and Ekans, but the establishment of Carteret and Co.—the swankiest jewelers on Fifth Avenue.

Everything in this establishment was French. It had the atmosphere of a salon instead of a store—the absence of showcases—the frock-coated and waxed-mustached French clerks—the private rooms into which clients were taken to be shown trays of gems on small French tables.

He asked for the manager, met the usual opposition and beat it down by announcing that he represented the heirs of Franklyn Thompson.

Presently, Murphy sat in the private office of Monsieur Duchamil, gray-haired, black-eyed, dignified—and shrewd.

"How much does Franklyn Thompson owe you?" he demanded after displaying his power-of-attorney.

Being aware of the type of women to whom the late playboy had made presents, Murphy was certain that they preferred jewelry from Carteret's in preference to the equally reliable and much more numerous American establishments where other rich men bought gifts for their wives.

"Nothing," said Monsieur Duchamil. "Not a *centime*."

"Didn't he charge his latest gifts?"

The manager lifted his shoulders expressively. "We are forced to know very much about our patrons," he said. "We have our own system of inquiry. More than a year ago, we ceased to permit Mr. Thompson to charge his purchases."

"When was the last purchase he made from you?"

The manager consulted his book. "He bought a wristwatch with veritable rubies on March Fourteenth. Three thousand dollars."

"For Mrs. Houghton, of course."

"Monsieur has been well informed, I perceive. No doubt he intends, should the gems stolen from Mrs. Houghton be recovered, to impound them, no?"

"Unless he made them over to her, yes."

Monsieur Duchamil smiled. "It is not the custom among gentlemen of his type. They do not give such ladies certificates of ownership. When there is a rupture, they often demand their presents back—send lawyers and detectives to terrify the women. And Mr. Thompson was a hard man, if you will not be offended by my saying so."

"Not at all," replied the Rambler with a grin. "I'd like a list of gifts you know were purchased for Mrs. Houghton—if you know which are which."

"We have a record of several presents, sent to her by our messengers; and, upon a number of occasions, she came here with him and personally selected what she wanted—as in the case of the pearl necklace three years ago."

"I appreciate the way you are cooperating, sir."

The Frenchman smiled craftily. "While Miss Geraldine Thompson may not inherit much from Franklyn Thompson, she is a most beautiful young lady of high social standing, who, undoubtedly will marry a millionaire and become a valued client. And Mrs. Houghton will bear no malice—since we are forced to show our books to persons with authority."

Murphy gazed at him in admiration. "You certainly figure far ahead," he observed.

"In such a business as ours, foresight is most essential. I'll have a list of all purchases made by Mr. Thompson for Mrs. Houghton. Give me ten minutes and excuse me. My assistant will give you the list. A most important client is waiting."

IN TEN minutes, Murphy was gazing at a list of bracelets, rings, wrist-watches and necklaces of pearls and diamonds. His eyes were popping at their valuation—a hundred and ten thousand dollars. The woman had supplied the police with the true value of her lost gems. And this was a duplicate of the police list.

Whistling contentedly, the Rambler left the place. The robbery, in his opinion, was a fake. Mrs. Houghton, aware that Thompson was insolvent and that her jewels might be seized as assets by the creditors, had made her arrangements. That explained why the gems were not insured. Insurance companies deal harshly with perpetrators of fake robberies. It would be a good idea to locate that elevator man and get his version of the affair.

From the jeweler's, the Rambler went directly to the Princess Apartments on Park Avenue and demanded to see the manager. He was a fat, red-faced man, named Cronin.

He looked over the power-of-attorney and said: "Well?"

"Very well," replied Murphy importantly. "You're working for me, now. Franklyn Thompson is dead."

"I'm employed by the Eureka Company and in a few days, I'll be working for a bankruptcy receiver, I hear," replied Mr. Cronin insolently.

Murphy scowled at him. "No, you won't. Because, as the legal representative of the Thompson estate—the will was probated this morning—I'll chuck you out on your ear, this minute, unless you change your tone!"

Mr. Cronin changed his tone. "I don't want to offend you, Mr. Murphy," he said hastily.

"I've already dismissed Ekans and Ekans," lied the Rambler, "so they won't be able to protect you. You're my employee. If you don't like it, put on your hat and coat!"

"I've a family, Mr. Murphy. I'm contented here. What can I do for you?"

"You've been covering for Franklyn Thompson. I don't blame you. He was your boss. He's dead. Why did you fire that elevator boy?"

"Why—he was grossly negligent! He had no business letting the men, who robbed Mrs. Houghton, get away! I suspected him of complicity but had no proof—so I just fired him."

"So you'll get the idea of things, I'm telling you that that was a phony robbery. Thompson had been keeping the Houghton woman.

Her jewels belong to the Thompson estate. She pulled a robbery to swindle J. Robbins Thompson and his daughter."

Cronin was no longer red-faced. He was pale. "I swear I don't know anything about that!"

"But you knew he had been keeping the woman in this building."

"Well, I suspected it—though she always paid her rent with her own checks. She was pretty cagey."

"How long has she been living here?"

"Two and a half years."

"I see. What time did Mr. Thompson leave her apartment the night before he died?"

"About two A.M."

"Much drinking up there that night?"

"I don't know. They both drank heavily—I know that."

"O.K. You're the only person I've informed that the robbery was faked. If it gets to her ears that we are aware of it, you'll get fired on general principles. What other reason did you have for discharging the elevator man?"

"That's all."

Murphy knew, by instinct, when somebody was lying. He had a hunch now. "Give me his name and address, please."

"Why I don't know—"

"You heard what I said!"

Sullenly, Mr. Cronin went to a filing cabinet and copied down a name and address which he handed to his visitor.

It was Dominic Letora, 510 East 49th Street.

"Much obliged, Mr. Cronin. Play square and your job is safe. I'll recommend you to the receiver—if and when." The Rambler departed, well satisfied. He was like a scientist who could take a tooth or a shin bone of a prehistoric animal and, upon it, construct the entire skeleton of the extinct creature. But, unlike the scientist whose notion of the appearance of the animal could not be controverted, Murphy occasionally built theories that had been proved unsound. This one only demonstrated that Thompson had bought jewelry for Martha Houghton, and had been in her apartment the night before he died, but shed no light on his death.

SHORTLY before noon, the Rambler entered the suite of offices occupied by Ekans and Ekans. There was a large waiting room and a phone operator stationed behind a railing. There was one visitor, sitting on a bench at the rail, exchanging persiflage with the pretty phone girl.

This visitor emitted an astonished grunt when Addison Francis Murphy entered briskly.

The Rambler smiled at him gaily. "Hello, Jake," he said.

"How are yer?" inquired Jake with obvious indifference to the state of the newspaperman's health. "Wot you doin' here, eh?"

"Representing the Thompson estate," said Murphy, sitting down beside Jake Smith and beaming upon him genially.

"Still pullin' that, eh?"

"Not a gag, pal. Fact."

"Then what did you let us think you was a reporter for?"

"I told the lady who I was. I didn't give a damn what you thought."

"I ain't seeing nothin' in the paper about the rumor you spoke of," sneered Jake.

"Oh, you will," said Murphy in a cheerful manner. "The rumor is solidifying, Jake. In a day or two, I expect the papers will break with it—in a big way."

Jake leaped to his feet. "Got to go," he exclaimed. "I can't wait, Lulu. Be in again—soon," he said to the operator.

"But Mr. Ekans, Junior, said he'd see you in five minutes," she protested.

"Got to go," repeated Jake who moved hastily toward the exit.

Murphy smiled at the girl. "Which makes it nice for me," he said. "Tell Mr. Ekans, Junior, that Mr. Murphy, acting for the Thompson heirs, wishes to see him."

"I'll tell him," said the girl who left her switchboard, walked down a corridor and entered an office. Murphy lighted a cigarette.

This *looked* like the establishment of some very high-class lawyers; but if they represented a crooked promoter like Franklyn Thompson they were shady; and their heartless treatment of Geraldine Thompson was an index to their character. And, if Mr. Smith were waiting to see Mr. Ekans, Junior, it was most illuminating. It connected Mr. Ekans, Junior, with Martha Houghton—since Jake was a professional go-between, a journeyman crook, and not a master mind. Murphy knew Jake was no boy-friend of that hard-boiled baby, Martha. He had called on her with a message.

The girl returned. "Mr. Ekans will see you now," she said.

Murphy's sharp blue eyes encountered a pair of hard, gray ones as he entered the private office. The owner of the gray eyes was a man in the neighborhood of forty. He was dressed in loose gray tweeds. He had white piping on the edges of his vest and he wore white spats. He had big, bold features and a predatory air. He was handsome in way, despite a chin which was too solid and a mouth which was too big.

"You claim to represent the Thompsons?" he asked sharply. "I told the girl yesterday that we're washing our hands of the Thompson business. Frank Thompson owes us money—there's no estate. When the creditors get through with the Thompson enterprises, there will be a deficit and his personal effects will have to be sold at auction."

Murphy helped himself to a chair. "Most interesting," he remarked.

"If you've any notion of getting money out of us, nothing doing!" snapped Mr. Ekans, Junior.

"I understand J. Robbins Thompson is among the creditors?"

"Not at all. He's a stockholder in several Thompson enterprises. The stock isn't worth a dime. The creditors are persons who hold notes and other forms of obligations, in case you don't know what I mean."

"Oh, I get you," said the Rambler, thoughtfully. "If he was flat-broke, I'm hanged if I can see the object in murdering Franklyn Thompson."

MR. EKANS half rose from his chair but sat down again. His face had not changed expression. "Who says he was murdered?" he asked in a very mild manner.

Murphy shrugged his shoulders. "Very convenient that he had heart failure just when there wasn't any more use in living, eh?"

"I've heard him complain of a weak heart. The doctor says he warned Frank several times. Anyway he died a natural death. If he didn't, it's no concern of ours. We were simply his legal representatives."

"You going to grab the Houghton woman's jewels if they're recovered?"

"I've heard about you," said Ekans sharply. "You forced your way into the poor girl's apartment, pretending to represent the estate. You're a reporter and I'm about to kick you out of here."

"Lamp this, before you do anything rash."

He displayed the power-of-attorney. Ekans became less belligerent. "If you've any notion it will profit the Thompsons to blacken the reputation of a dead man—" he began.

"It was pretty black, wasn't it?"

"That's beside the point."

"Well, I've a notion that, when we find the murderer of Franklyn Thompson, we'll find that there was a lot of money in it for the killer and that the money should belong to J. Robbins Thompson."

"Thompson is dead. He died of heart failure and the body was cremated. Cremation was specified in the will. If he were killed, or committed suicide, there is no possible way of proving it and no object since he died broke."

"You'd be surprised how many people have been hanged for murder after heart failure was certified and the body was cremated," remarked Murphy, rising. "Well, I'll be seeing you, Mr. Ekans."

"Don't come back here," advised the lawyer. "You won't be admitted."

AFTER the Rambler had departed, the lawyer began to pace the floor of his office. Finally, he called a number and was told that it did not answer. He sat down at his desk. His face was very grave and he drummed nervously on the top of his desk with his fingers.

At the end of ten minutes the phone operator announced Mr. Smith. "Send him right in," Ekans said, eagerly.

Jake entered and slumped in a chair. "This Murphy came in while I was waiting for you," he said. "I faded and waited until he left the building. What did he want?"

"He has a power-of-attorney from the Thompson girl. He's a very sharp fellow and very suspicious. I think he came in chiefly to size me up. Of course, he can't possibly build up a murder case, but he can be damn troublesome. Jake, I want you to do something about him!"

"I came in to tell you," said Jake. "He's a proposition, that guy. Last night he was in Mundy's, see? When he left, I sent four good boys after him. He slugged it out with all four of them—till the cops came."

"Which means that he suspected you would sent thugs after him."

"Oh, sure. He's wise. I'd rather have the whole New York police force after me than that bird. He turned up a couple of jobs that were supposed to be safe and sound, when he worked on a paper here a couple of years ago."

"Well, he looks seedy. How about slipping him a few grand to blow the town."

"The damn fool won't take a cent. He's like that!"

"Well, he's a menace. Know anybody who will remove him?"
"For five grand, Birdy Bernstein would take an interest."

CHAPTER FIVE

FOUR DEAD MEN

THE RAMBLER'S afternoon was unprofitable. Dominic Letora had moved away without leaving an address. Cronin was not to be found at the Princess Apartments—Murphy hoped to choke out of him the fact that Ralph Ekans, Junior, was a visitor at the Houghton apartment. A phone call to the *Bulletin* informed him that J. Robbins Thompson had not been found in the Miami morgue. Murphy had suggested that Desborough wire to make the story sound more exciting and because he had to get money for the Thompson girl. About four o'clock the newspaperman selected a disreputable-looking movie theater where he stayed until six o'clock. He then presented himself at Miss Thompson's residence.

The Rambler was nonplussed when the girl welcomed him wearing an evening dress—he hadn't thought of dressing himself, and his dress suit was in a pawn shop in New Orleans, anyway.

"It doesn't matter," she assured him, after observing his expression. "Women dress for dinner and men often don't. I sort of hoped you'd take me where there is music. I'm low."

"If you don't mind my appearance," he said, "we'll go where there's an orchestra, but I'm not much of a dancer."

"I'm sure you're very good." She declared. It was nice to feel her little hand on his arm as they went out to a taxi. At her suggestion, they chose the Aladdin Restaurant which she said was chic and reasonable in price—an item of greater importance to the Rambler than she imagined.

This was a very swell girl, Murphy was thinking, and a fellow that didn't have prejudices against matrimony would probably go crazy over her. Murphy wasn't the marrying kind nor was he the type to take unfair advantage of a young lady in distress. He had an uncertain earning capacity and a deadly fear of being tied down. He had fled from a number of places and jumped good jobs because there had been girls who wanted to marry him; or girls he was tempted to marry. He probably would have succumbed if he had hung around.

A small Italian youth, in livery, helped him off with his overcoat. Murphy glanced at him, his eyes sharpened, and then he looked away. He escorted Geraldine to the table designated by the head waiter, excused himself, and sought the manager.

"What's the name of that cloakroom attendant?" he demanded. "I'm from headquarters." Mr. Murphy never had any scruples about misrepresenting himself.

"Letora. I only hired him today. Got anything against him, officer?"

"No, I think he's all right but he's a friend of a man I'm looking for. Send him into your office and leave us alone, please."

"Sure, sure, officer," agreed the worried café manager.

About twenty minutes later Murphy returned to his table smiling contentedly.

Geraldine gazed at him severely. "You've been gone a long time," she complained. "I've eaten my soup and sent yours back to be heated up."

"If there's anything I like, it's warmed-up soup," he declared. "You'll have to forgive me, Geraldine, because I've been working in the interests of the Thompson estate."

"In a place like this?" she scoffed. "Think of another one."

"It's a funny thing about the Thompson estate, but you can work on it any old place."

"That's a wonderful dance tune," she insinuated. "And I haven't danced for weeks."

Murphy rose. "Be careful," he warned. "If there's anything I hate, it's having girls riding on my feet."

"Of all the nerve," she exclaimed a moment later. "Why you're a dreadful dancer—you don't keep step to the music."

A hand touched the Rambler's shoulder. "May I cut in?" asked a young man. Murphy closed his right fist but Geraldine gave a delighted squeal. "Why Tom Meadows," she cried. "Imagine meeting you."

SHE SWUNG right into the arms of the youth in tail-coat, and, slightly bewildered, Murphy moved off the floor. Cutting in was a custom not practiced in the sort of places where he usually danced. This was a good-looking, slender, long-legged blond boy.

"Meadows," he muttered. "Swell name. That's what they call butlers in the movies."

There were a lot of encores to that dance and then Geraldine brought Mr. Meadows over and introduced him. Murphy rather ungraciously invited him to sit with them. He was an old friend. He had been abroad. He had tried to locate Geraldine since his return, two days before, but none of her friends had seen her. When the music started up again, he rose to depart. But Geraldine smiled pleadingly at Murphy and asked if he minded if they had another dance. The Rambler was forced to admit that they were a very fine dancing couple.

At midnight, Geraldine having danced steadily with Meadows, the Rambler stated that he had a big day ahead of him and suggested departure. Geraldine agreed meekly, if reluctantly. She gave Meadows her address.

In the taxi she was most apologetic. "He's a dear boy and we grew up together," she explained. "But I'm afraid I've treated you shabbily."

"Its O.K. Has he any money?"

"Lots."

"Well, I haven't. You'd better grab him."

She grasped his hand and looked into his eyes. "Please don't be jealous, Addison. I like you lots, but he's such a wonderful dancer."

"Who's jealous?" he asked indignantly. "I'm working for you, see? I expect to make money out of you—that's why—"

But Geraldine began to cry and he weakened and put his arm around her and he kissed her goodnight at the elevator.

THE TAXI returned him to his hotel, the Emerald, which was located on Forty-third Street, west of Broadway; a seedy thoroughfare, ill-lighted and made more gloomy by the elevated.

He paid off his taxi, oblivious of a pedestrian passing him on the sidewalk to his rear. He turned, as the taxi moved off, to face a man who held a revolver in his right hand, close to his chest.

"Take a walk, fella," said the stranger indicating Eighth Avenue with a nod. "A guy wants to see you."

The speaker had shoe-button eyes, a tight mouth, nostrils which expanded with excitement. His skin was gray and his finger moved nervously against the trigger. He was a hophead who would sooner shoot than not. Murphy, cursing himself for being so careless, obeyed instructions.

There was no sign of a cop—not a pedestrian on that side of the street. Murphy moved along about forty feet before a car slid up to the curb, a cheap black sedan.

"Inside, bo," said the man with the gun. The rear door opened, obligingly, and Murphy stepped in. There was a man in the rear seat who moved over politely. As the Rambler sat down, the fellow who had captured him, squeezed in beside him.

The newspaperman didn't ask any questions. In his adventurous career he had had similar experiences—had been within an inch of death a score of times. Nevertheless, he was surprised at this.

True, he had expected that Jake Smith would try to have him knocked on the head and placed in a hospital last night—but he didn't think he had nerve enough to try murder.

He had misjudged Ekans, it seemed. Ekans was a lawyer and had arranged things in the Thompson case so that he must think he was safe from exposure. He might be annoyed that a newspaperman smelled a rat, but, to have that newspaperman assassinated seemed beyond comprehension.

He felt the muzzle of a revolver against his kidney. A move, and, regardless of consequences, the hood would shoot.

The fellow on the Rambler's left, thrust his hand behind the prisoner and tapped his hip pockets. His friend, on the right, thrust his hand inside Murphy's coat and felt for a gun in a shoulder holster.

There was a man in front beside the chauffeur. A ray from an arc lamp illuminated him as the car turned into Eighth Avenue.

"How are you, Jake?" inquired Murphy genially.

Jake turned around. "See what you get?" he inquired.

"I'm thinking what you'll get," replied the Rambler.

Without warning, his companion on the left threw a left hook against the jaw of the prisoner.

"Where we goin'?" asked the fellow who had made the capture.

"Bronx Parkway," replied Jake.

"Aw, what's the use? Run over to the waterfront, plug him and pitch him out."

Jake looked back. "This mug ain't getting shot, see," he stated. "He's too well known. He's goin' to meet with a accident."

Murphy's eyes flickered with interest but Jake vouchsafed no further information.

THE CAR steadily worked its way uptown, occasionally stalled in traffic, often traveling at a forty-mile clip. Though the sooner they arrived at their destination, the sooner everything would end for Rambler Murphy, he fretted at the delay. After a long time, they were approaching Yonkers and were in thinly settled suburbs. And, suddenly, the car swung into the Park.

They traveled swiftly along upon a boulevard and then turned off upon an unlighted, but well paved, road.

"This'll do," said Jake Smith. The car came to a stop and he got out.

"Bring him out," he commanded. The man at Murphy's right opened the door and backed out, keeping him covered. The other followed, an automatic in his hand.

"This is an accident, see?" explained Smith. He reached into the car, fumbled and produced a coil of rope.

"You boys tie him up," he commanded, "and lay him down in the road. We're goin' to run over him."

"For God's sake, shoot me!" cried Murphy, panic-stricken.

"You're too well known," said Jake with a grin. "It ain't my idea, Murphy. I don't like it but I got my orders. Make him lay down, boys. You can tie him easier."

He climbed back into the car which immediately backed off a few rods.

"Lay down or I'll knock you down," said the fellow who had been sitting on Murphy's right in the car.

Murphy promptly lay down on the macadam. The gunman thrust his gun in his pocket. "Keep him covered," he said. He knelt at the victim's knees and proceeded to make a slip-noose around the feet of the Rambler, who would ramble no more. He was not accustomed to roping, evidently, for he had trouble with his knots.

"Catch this and wind it round his arms," he commanded, tossing the rope's end to the other man. This fellow caught it in his left hand and got on his knees at Murphy's shoulder.

"Lift up, damn you!" he commanded. He turned his head, said to Jake: "What's the good of roping him if we're running over him? That won't look like no accident—"

"We take the ropes off of him afterwards, nit-wit— Ah!"

Murphy, obeying instructions, reared suddenly. He came up swiftly, violently, and slammed the top of his head viciously against the chin of the gunman whose weapon was in his left hand and who had momentarily relaxed.

The blow hurt Murphy but it knocked out his enemy. With an oath, the man at his feet sprang up, and his hand went into his pocket.

BUT the Rambler had torn a gun from the nerveless fingers of the other's left hand. The Rambler fired one shot before the second thug could draw. The man got it in the middle of his chest, and fell. Murphy rolled into the ditch, tried to rise, but the rope around his feet prevented it.

There was a roar and rattle as the car bore down with accelerating speed. Jake Smith was leaning out of the car door, firing wildly. Murphy, from the ground, fired five shots through the windshield. The car, which had swung to the right to avoid the recumbent gunmen, yawed to the left. Murphy had a glimpse of the driver, who had fallen over on the wheel, and then the zig-zagging sedan passed over the body of the man whom Murphy had knocked out. It lurched to the left, plunged into the ditch and crashed into a stone wall beyond. There was a sickening rending of metal and a roar of escaping steam from the radiator.

Addison Francis Murphy was sick. However, he succeeded in unloosening the rope which bound his feet, gave a horrified glance at the grisly spectacle and fled as though demons were after him back toward the Parkway Boulevard.

He had had a glimpse of the body of Jake Smith lying in a twisted position close to the ditch where he had been hurled. The mashed form of the hood who had met the fate decreed for himself lay nearby.

A quarter of a mile took the Rambler to the main road. He made frantic signals to an approaching car and was ignored. He tried to stop a dozen cars before one obeyed his signals and this, to his joy, was a police car.

"Four dead men and a smashed car up this road a bit," he said to a sergeant.

"Collision? Accident?"

"Not exactly. I'm a reporter on the *Bulletin*. A crook named Jake Smith and three gunmen took me for a ride."

"How come?" demanded the sergeant sternly.

"I don't like auto riding—much. I took this gun off one of them. I haven't a permit to carry one, myself."

"Get in," said the sergeant. "Let's go, boys!"

CHAPTER SIX

BLOOD ON THE BLUE BOOK

AFTER A very satisfactory interview with Cronin, manager of the Princess Apartments, Addison Francis Murphy, without being announced, ascended to the floor upon which Mrs. Houghton's quarters were located. He rang her bell. When the maid opened the door, he pushed into the hallway despite her protests.

"Wake up your mistress," he said harshly. "Tell her an officer is here with a warrant for her arrest."

With a horrified howl, the maid rushed away and Murphy sauntered into the living room where he seated himself and helped himself to one of the lady's cigarettes.

He heard excited voices in the bedroom. In a moment, Martha Houghton, her yellow hair disheveled, a trailing dressing gown over her nightgown, rushed into the living room. She stopped, she stared, she opened her mouth and a rousing oath came forth.

"You!" she cried. "Why you lousy, damn—"

"Tie it, baby," he said coolly. "I know you learned it from the stage hands, when you were in the chorus. Ekans is pinched; Jake Smith died, after confessing; Cronin has told all and it's up to me whether you go to the chair as an accessory—"

She sank, half fainting, into a chair.

"Now listen, sweetheart," said Rambler Murphy. "You're responsible on account of the two-timing, but I'm giving you a break. You had Ekans in this joint on the night of March Fourteenth. Frank Thompson opened the door with his key. You hid Ekans in a closet in your bedroom. Thompson saw a cigar-butt and got suspicious. He opened the closet and Ekans came out, swinging his fists. He hit Thompson in the chest and his weak heart failed him. So, you two love birds had a corpse on your hands."

She was ruthlessly biting at her long, polished fingernails.

"You and Ekans went into conference. You had to get the body home but you needed help. So Ekans called in Cronin and the night elevator boy, one Dominic Letora.

"Ekans and Cronin took him to that nice first-floor apartment of his in the old Wentworth Mansion on Murray Hill, laid him on the floor and left him there. As he was all dressed when Ekans hit him, there was only a slight black and blue mark on the body. The doctor—he owes four-months' rent—took a piece of change and certified death from heart disease. After all, Ekans didn't intend to kill him."

"He didn't—I'll swear he didn't!" cried the woman eagerly.

MURPHY sighed. "So Ekans came back here, after leaving the body in Thompson's apartment, and you and he had another conference. The creditors would grab your jewels—you have no proof of ownership and Thompson bought them all at Carteret's and the bills-of-sale are among his papers. Ekans decided you'd better be robbed, so you were robbed the first thing in the morning."

"And then the elevator boy tried polite blackmail on Cronin and got sacked."

"Do you mean to insinuate I wasn't robbed?" she cried furiously.

Murphy laughed. "I'm telling you, lady. Those jewels are in your safety-deposit vault, along with the cash and bonds you were keeping for Thompson until after he took the 'poor debtor's' oath."

The woman scowled at him venomously. "It's a lie," she snarled. "I never—"

"Now the situation is this. I represent the Thompson estate but I haven't called in the police—yet. But when I do, Ekans will get twenty years for manslaughter, and they'll give you ten—as accessory before and after the fact—"

That unnerved her. She was weeping hysterically.

"But after all," the Rambler went on, "you didn't kill him. And it was Ekans' idea not to turn in the stuff you were holding for Thompson. All you were going to get out of it was the jewels. Put on your old gray bonnet, and a few clothes, and take me to your safety-deposit box—"

"You mean you'll give me a break?" she demanded, breathlessly.

"You turn over the contents of the safety-deposit box to me and I'll give you a running start," he declared. "You'll turn state's evidence—that's what I mean. I'll tell the district attorney we can't convict without you; but I've got evidence up my sleeve that would send away the pair of you."

She only hesitated for a second. "O.K.," she said firmly. "Ekans'd trim me in a second. I got to look out for myself."

"Which of your names did you use at the bank?"

"My real name," she said. "It's Martha Swartzman."

"How much dough were you hiding for Thompson?"

"About nine hundred thousand dollars," she admitted.

"Well, step on it before the police come."

IN TEN minutes, the Rambler set forth with the thoroughly cowed woman. They rode uptown to a branch of one of the great banks of New York City. In the privacy of a booth, Murphy counted Liberty Bonds until he was dizzy. The greenbacks were in stacks of five-hundred-dollar bills, total marked on each package; so counting that was comparatively easy. Ruthlessly, he sealed up, in an envelope, the hundred and ten thousand dollars' worth of jewelry, and forced her to write a statement to the effect that the contents of the box was the property of the late Franklyn Thompson. He then rented another box in the name of the estate of the late Franklyn Thompson and deposited a fortune therein.

"I don't want to testify against Ralph," she pleaded. "Let me scram, will you?"

Murphy hesitated and shook his head. "No," he said firmly. "We'll take a ride down to headquarters and you'll make your statement—after I've made them agree to hold you as state's witness instead of prosecuting you. And that's a better break than you deserve, Mrs. Houghton."

At headquarters, Murphy had a session with Inspector Gleason, after which, Mrs. Houghton was called in. Murphy had dictated a statement for her—read it and commanded her to sign it. She did so, meekly. She was locked up as a material witness.

Fifteen minutes later, the Rambler was writing upon a battered typewriter at high speed with the forefinger of each hand. The city editor of the *Bulletin* grabbed each finished sheet and rushed it to the composing room.

"Some story," Desborough kept muttering. "Jumping Jiminy, what a beat!"

When the job was done Murphy called Miss Thompson. "I've good news for you," he declared.

"And I for you," she said jubilantly. "Father is in Bermuda and sails for home tomorrow."

"Bermuda? How come?"

"He was broke in Miami and shipped for New York as a deckhand on a tramp steamer. He didn't know it was going to stop at Nassau and Bermuda. In Bermuda he met a friend who gave him money for his passage home and to send me a cablegram. Isn't that wonderful?"

"I'm coming right up."

THE RAMBLER told her that there was going to be a lot of money for her father and herself after the Thompson debts were paid. After he had shocked her by his yarn of robbery and murder, she said: "I think you were too kind to that awful woman. She seems to have had no redeeming qualities. Being a man, you were probably influenced by her beauty."

Murphy chuckled. "I needed her in my business," he explained. "Without her statement, all I had was a high-class theory. I couldn't pin the attempt to murder me on Ekans—Jake Smith died without confessing. All I had was what I squeezed out of Letora, the ex-elevator man—that Ekans had been in Mrs. Houghton's apartment and that Thompson had arrived, cockeyed drunk, at one A.M. Ekans and Cronin, the apartment manager, carried Thompson out, apparently unconscious from hooch, at two A.M.

"I then forced a confession from Cronin that Thompson had died in the woman's apartment and Ekans had induced him to save his employer's reputation by getting the body to Thompson's own apartment. I then called on the doctor, learned from him that Mr. Ekans had called at Thompson's apartment on business, March Fifteenth, and found Thompson lying dead on his bedroom floor.

"I had figured it out that Ekans had had a fight, probably with fists, and if Thompson had a weak heart, a blow in that vicinity might have caused it to stop. I scared the doctor into admitting there was a slight bruise in the vicinity of the heart, though he insisted he thought it might have been caused when Thompson fell on the floor. When I had the whole yarn constructed, I broke in on Mrs. Houghton, told her she was a murder accessory and would go up with her boyfriend, Ekans. She wilted, and grabbed the chance to save her own skin by turning state's evidence—"

"But—that was contemptible!"

"Sure, but she thought we had the goods! She didn't know that her statement as a direct witness was essential to conviction. We couldn't get a conviction if we prosecuted both of them, so we had to hold her as a witness and promise immunity."

"What I don't understand," said Geraldine, "is how you knew that my cousin had a secret hoard and that the jewel robbery was a fake."

"It's a funny thing about these middle-aged birds who get stuck on a dame," said the reporter. "They are crooks, themselves, but they believe their women love them so much they can be trusted. Thompson knew he was insolvent—a long time ago. Probably, when he persuaded your father to let him invest the money. He stayed in Florida for six weeks to avoid process-servers. But crooks, like him, always hold out on their creditors and tuck away a tidy sum to live on when they take the 'poor debtor's' oath.

"I wasn't sure that Thompson had fixed himself up until I learned, from Carteret, that the day he came back from Florida, he had paid three thousand, cash, for a wristwatch for Mrs. Houghton. If he was worrying about the future he wouldn't have done that. And, as there would be a search made for his assets, it was likely that Mrs. Houghton had them in a safety-deposit vault. He was her meal-ticket and while he lived she wouldn't dare double-cross him.

"When Franklyn died, Ekans got in *his* work. He persuaded her that they should keep Thompson's money; and they cooked up the fake robbery so that the estate couldn't grab the jewels—which they would be sure to learn he had given his sweetie."

"But that was all surmise?" she asked.

"Sure, and I didn't know under what name the woman had the stuff concealed. I doubted if she would have turned it over to Ekans so soon. Dames like that are pretty shrewd. I made her think that her only chance of not going up the river with Thompson was to take me to her safe-deposit box. Probably we could have squeezed the truth out of her anyway; but, if she held out, she and Ekans would have had a million to spend."

Geraldine's eyes were shining. "I think you're the most amazing man that ever lived and the best friend a girl ever had. Why, you've made us rich, Addison!" she said.

"Just getting your own money for you," he said with embarrassment.

The Rambler went back to work, an engaged man. Well, a fellow had to marry sometime, and he had wasted valuable years. He ought to settle down. He had a good job and he could get big money as soon as editors learned he was a reformed character. He and Geraldine could live on what he earned.

THE FOLLOWING night, when Murphy arrived at Geraldine's apartment, he was received by J. Robbins Thompson. Thompson was a big blond man, stalwart, powerful and athletic. He told the Rambler that his daughter had gone out on an errand for him but would be back very shortly. He was profuse in his thanks to the newspaperman, but there was something about him which the Rambler didn't like.

This Blue Book baby, who had left his daughter to starve and who would have had to hunt a job if Addison Francis Murphy hadn't found him a million dollars, was patronizing in his manner.

"That's all right," Murphy said stiffly. "Forget it."

"My daughter tells me that you and she are engaged," said Thompson, finally.

"That's right."

"Well, now, young man, Geraldine is young and impetuous. You came to her assistance when she was in dire distress. Naturally she is enormously appreciative, grateful—"

"Just what are you driving at?"

"We come of a very old family, Mr. Murphy—"

"So did that crook, Franklyn Thompson."

Mr. Thompson waved his hand airily. "A black sheep—all families have one. You are a newspaper reporter—an unusually clever one—but you are hardly—er—

"Listen, Thompson," said Murphy sharply, "I see you're not in favor of the engagement. Never mind! Don't answer! Well, I can support a wife. I'm marrying Geraldine, if she wants me. So what?"

"That's it—if she wants you. The reason she is not here, Mr. Murphy, is that she is having tea with a young man, Mr. Meadows. They were engaged, once, and she broke the engagement because I had lost my fortune. She feels obligated to you—"

"O.K. Let *her* tell me."

"*Ahem*. You must understand that I fully appreciate what you have done for us. I intend, when I come into my money, to give you a very sizable check."

Murphy jumped up. His eyes were blazing, his face was as red as his hair.

"You're a bigger man than I am and a trained athlete, but I'll bet—"

Geraldine walked into the room. "What has happened?" she cried. "Oh, father, what have you said to Mr. Murphy?"

Thompson looked confused and sat down.

"Are you in love with this Meadows?" the Rambler demanded.

Geraldine was very white and her eyes filled with tears. "I—I had tea with him—just to say goodby," she faltered.

The Rambler crossed to her and laid his big arm over her shoulder. "That's all right, kid," he said. "You don't have to marry me."

Geraldine buried her face in the Rambler's coat lapels. "But, I shall—I must!"

"Forget it. This Meadows is a swell dancer."

Half an hour later, in a corner of a café, Rambler Murphy sat with his first drink. With all his faults, he didn't care very much for hard liquor. However, he was feeling very much better.

"Imagine me married to Geraldine," he said to himself, "with a father-in-law like that. Besides, we would probably have had to live in Flatbush. The next thing, I'd be trundling a baby carriage."

MEET MR. MacISAAC

In response to numerous requests for more information about himself and to put straight several readers who seem to visualize him as a writing corporation or syndicate, Fred MacIsaac takes the floor to tell us who he is and how he does it. Mr. MacIsaac:

ALTHOUGH MY stories range over a wide extent of territory, it is not true as charged by one of your readers that I am four or five different people. I am a middle-aged person who has been engaged for more than twenty years in picturesque professions and who has a flealike propensity for travel. In twenty years it is astonishing how far one can roam and how many interesting people one can meet.

When I graduated from prep school I went to work on a Boston newspaper, and with my first five hundred dollars presented myself with a trip to Europe. In those vanished days one could travel first cabin from New York to Liverpool for seventy dollars and get a room at a good European hotel for about fifty cents a day. I lasted abroad four months on my five hundred.

For several years I worked as a ship news reporter in Boston, and during this time attended Harvard. Thus I met a lot of sea captains, college professors, literary lights and deep-sea fishermen while doubling in brass, as it were.

Music has always attracted me, and eventually I sold my services to a Boston paper as music critic, and during five interesting years consorted with opera singers and concert artists. It was a step from that to managing artists and putting on concerts and spectacles. Then I became a dramatic critic and became chummy with the big stars of the theater, most of whom are in the movies now.

My purpose in working was to get money to go places and see

things, and for years I went roving during the dull months in the show business. I wandered over five continents and got into trouble in most of the ports of the Seven Seas.

About eight years ago I drifted to New York and worked as a newspaper man, dramatic critic, press agent and such, until I met Bob Davis, the celebrated editor of the Munsey publications, who told me I was an author. He is the son of guy who won't take no for an answer, so I began to draw upon my experiences for fiction purposes. While I am not an expert in any trade nor an authority upon any race or nation, I am a fairly sharp observer, and a few months in a strange land makes me reasonably familiar with its people and customs. I learn languages rapidly and forget them more rapidly. At various times I have been able to make myself understood in Italian, Spanish, Greek, French, and even knew a few words of Russian. Please don't check me up on this statement because I have just come from Central America and my Spanish wasn't so torrid.

Probably I would be a better writer if I concentrated upon one type of story and set my yarns in the same locale, but I wouldn't have so much fun. Besides I love to excuse myself for spending a lot of money going to some remote place by telling myself that I need the local color for a story. I don't write about places I don't know pretty well because I don't want to be shown up by your smart readers. As soon as transit is rapid and safe to the moon and the planets you may look for some swell stuff about them from me.

Made in United States
Orlando, FL
09 February 2023